Praise for Portia MacIntosh

'Smart, funny and always brilliantly entertaining, every book from Portia becomes my new favourite rom com'
Shari Low

'I laughed, I cried – I loved it'
Holly Martin

'The queen of rom com!'
Rebecca Raisin

'This book made me laugh and kept me turning the pages'
Mandy Baggot

'A fun, fabulous 5-star rom com!'
Sandy Barker

'Loved the book, it's everything you expect from the force that is Portia! A must read'
Rachel Dove

'Fun and witty. Pure escapism!'
Laura Carter

'A heartwarming, fun story, perfect for several hours of pure escapism'
Jessica Redland

PORTIA MACINTOSH is the bestselling author of over 30 romantic comedy novels.

From disastrous dates to destination weddings, Portia's romcoms are the perfect way to escape from day-to-day life, visiting sunny beaches in the summer and snowy villages at Christmas time. Whether it's southern Italy or the Yorkshire coast, Portia's stories are the holiday you're craving, conveniently packed in between the pages.

Formerly a journalist, Portia has left the city, swapping the music biz for the moors, to live the (not so) quiet life with her husband and her dog in Yorkshire.

Website: portiamacintosh.com
Instagram: @portiamacintoshauthor

Also by Portia MacIntosh:

Off The Record
Always The Bridesmaid
Drive Me Crazy
Truth or Date
It's Not You, It's Them
The Accidental Honeymoon
Never The Bride
Here Comes the Ex

Marram Bay series:
Falling For You
Snow Love Lost
Met Your Match

Honeymoon For One
My Great Ex-Scape
The Plus One Pact
Stuck On You
One Night Only
Faking it
Life's a Beach
Will They, Won't They?
No Ex Before Marriage
The Meet Cute Method
Single All The Way
Just Date and See
Your Place or Mine?
Better Off Wed
Long Time No Sea
Fake It or Leave It

Trouble in Paradise
One Wild Night
Ex in the City
The Suite Life
It's All Sun and Games
One of the Boys
You Had Me at Château
Wish You Weren't Here
Too Hot to Handle

Love On Tour

PORTIA MACINTOSH

ONE PLACE. MANY STORIES

HQ
An imprint of HarperCollins*Publishers* Ltd
1 London Bridge Street
London SE1 9GF

www.harpercollins.co.uk

HarperCollins*Publishers*
Macken House, 39/40 Mayor Street Upper,
Dublin 1 D01 C9W8

This paperback edition 2025

1

First published in Great Britain as *If We Ever Meet Again* by HQ,
an imprint of HarperCollinsPublishers Ltd 2014

Copyright © Portia MacIntosh 2014

Portia MacIntosh asserts the moral right to be
identified as the author of this work.

A catalogue record for this book is
available from the British Library.

ISBN: 9780008761967

This novel is entirely a work of fiction. The names, characters and incidents
portrayed in it are the work of the author's imagination. Any resemblance to
actual persons, living or dead, events or localities is entirely coincidental.

All rights reserved. No part of this publication may be reproduced, stored
in a retrieval system, or transmitted, in any form or by any means,
electronic, mechanical, photocopying, recording or otherwise,
without the prior permission of the publishers.

Without limiting the author's and publisher's exclusive rights, any unauthorized
use of this publication to train generative artificial intelligence (AI) technologies
is expressly prohibited. HarperCollins also exercise their rights under Article
4(3) of the Digital Single Market Directive 2019/790 and expressly reserve this
publication from the text and data mining exception.

Printed and bound in the UK using 100% Renewable
Electricity by CPI Group (UK) Ltd

For more information visit: www.harpercollins.co.uk/green

For everyone I met on the road

Chapter 1

I wonder who started the bloody ridiculous rumour that women can multi-task effortlessly. I'd love to know so that I can send them a photograph of me right now (obviously someone else would have to take it for me) epic-failing my way to the office.

It's 11 a.m. on an exceptionally cold Monday morning and I'm late for work. Again, and as always. Currently dodging my way through the busy streets of Leeds, I'm desperately trying not to drop anything. In my right hand I have four take-away cups of coffee – in a holder obviously, I'm good but I'm not *that* good – my massive Mary Poppins-style handbag hooked on my left arm and my phone in my left hand. It's still in my hand because, as I was leaving Starbucks, I got a call from work and without a free hand to put my phone back in my bag, that's where it's going to have to stay.

Thankfully work is just around the corner from my flat, although I was supposed to be at the office by 10 a.m. Stopping at Starbucks has only made me even later but I'm hoping the coffees will score me some brownie points with the staff. If you can't be on time, the least you can do is suck up to people.

Just one more road to cross and I'll be there. Balancing on the edge of the curb in my silly yet beautiful shoes, I feel like the slightest breeze could knock me off my feet. As the green man appears, I step off the pavement with everyone else. Eyeballing the window of my office for angry faces, I make it halfway across the road when something hits me – literally hits me. As I fall to the ground in what feels like super-slow, *Matrix*-esque motion (although it probably doesn't look quite so graceful to the people around me), my impressive coffee-handbag-phone balancing act comes to an abrupt end. Landing flat on my back, right there in the middle of the road, I feel like I've been hit by a bus. Was I hit by a bus? I can hear people fussing around me and the impatient blaring of car horns. They can piss off, I could be dead – although if I'm thinking that, chances are I'm probably still alive, right?

As I run my hands down my body to check for major injuries, I feel that my skirt is up around my waist. I have never been happier to be wearing such thick tights, God bless the crappy, cold weather we have up north.

There's a strong smell of coffee coming from the double-digits'-worth of Starbucks puddle on the road next to me, which thankfully hasn't trickled towards me, although I am tempted to roll over and lap it up.

Despite having the wind knocked out of me, I think I'm going to make it.

'I am so sorry, let me help you up,' I hear a deep, apologetic voice insist, as a hand reaches for mine.

Flat on my back and in the middle of the road, with my skirt hitched up around my waist, I am in no position to be declining help, so I grab the stranger's hand and let him yank me to my feet.

'Here's your phone, I hope it isn't broken. Shit, there are a couple of scratches on it,' the stranger informs me, as he hands me my fairly battered-looking phone. My phone is noticeably scratched, but I don't tell him that most of the damage probably occurred the time my phone took a tumble down the stairs, bashed against something in my handbag, magically escaped my grasp, etc. In fact, my phone has been dropped so many times it's a miracle that it still works. I prod it with a very shaky finger and my trusty phone springs to life as usual. What a trooper. Only after making sure my phone is OK, do I actually look the only person who stopped to help me in the eye. Ushering me back across the road (the side I *don't* want to be on) is an absolutely gorgeous man. Shit, I can't believe he saw me lying in the road like that. He's wearing a very flashy suit and clutching an important-looking file stuffed with papers. Oh, and he has one of my shoes tucked under his arm, which explains why I'm limping – I thought I'd snapped my ankle or something.

'Thanks for helping me. I'm not sure what happened, I was crossing the road and—' I stop mid-sentence. The truth is, I have no idea what happened.

The good-looking stranger sits me down on the nearest bench.

'Are you all right?' he asks me with a very concerned look on his face. He looks like every portrayal of Prince Charming I have ever seen in the movies, with an added (and well-used) gym membership thrown into the mix.

'I'm OK, just a bit shaken up. Did you see what happened?'

'Please, wait here,' handsome stranger insists. 'I have to get this file to someone in that building.' He gestures towards the offices behind us with his file. 'Just ... don't move. I'll be back in five minutes, I'll explain everything then. Get your breath back, OK?'

I nod my head and watch him dash into the building behind me, my shoe still tucked under his arm which means I couldn't leave if I wanted to – not that wearing only one shoe concerns me, but these ones are my favourites.

Whatever happened to me, I am so lucky that I landed on my bum because I think it broke my fall. I'll never complain about the size of it again, I promise.

I check my phone again and then my bag to make sure nothing is damaged – or even more damaged than it was before I fell. Everything seems to be OK, and despite feeling a bit achy and a lot embarrassed, I think I'm OK too. The only things that suffered are the coffees – the poor coffees! It breaks my heart watching cars driving over the empty cups in the middle of the road.

'Right, are you OK?' the gorgeous stranger asks when he returns. 'I feel like such a dickhead. I was in a bit of a rush; I completely knocked you off your feet.'

Ah, so that's what happened.

'No harm done. I'm fine,' I assure him, although part of me is thinking I should be a bit pissed off – but who could be mad at that silky black hair and those perfect teeth? To be honest, I just want to get another coffee (for medicinal purposes) and get to work.

'I feel terrible. Can I replace your drinks? It's the least I can do. I'm Tom by the way.' He offers me his hand for the second time, this time for me to shake.

'I'm Nicole, nice to meet you. I think,' I reply as I shake his hand. He has a tight, manly grip and I'm certain I'm blushing right now.

'Nice to meet you too, Nicole. Let's get those drinks.'

'Honestly, it's fine, I—'

'Please?' Tom flashes a smile that I can't bring myself to say no to and so I give in, but not before he gets down on one knee and delicately places my shoe back on my foot. If the smile didn't have me saying yes, then the Cinderella moment sealed the deal.

Soon enough I'm in Starbucks again, only this time it's much busier and we're forced to wait for our order. We chat for a few minutes and it turns out that Tom works for a firm of solicitors not far from where I work and – despite the fact that he practically assaulted me, and the fact we've only known each other for about twenty minutes – we're getting on really well.

As soon as the drinks are ready, we walk back towards our offices. This is the second longest time it has ever taken me to walk the short journey from my flat to where I work. My record was set a couple of months ago when I spied a sale at one of my favourite shops, or a 'dental emergency' as I explained it to my colleagues, bursting through the doors several hours late with lots of suspicious-looking carrier bags.

'This is me,' I say as we arrive at the revolving doors that lead to my office. 'I'm sure I can handle it from here.'

'I'm sure you can.' He smiles that smile again. 'I know this must seem a bit weird considering the circumstances, but I'd really like to see you again. I've already swept you off your feet.'

That's the kind of cheesiness that would normally make me sick all over a man's shoes, but being so gorgeous, even a line as lame as that sounds utterly charming as it leaves his lips.

'Erm, *knocked* me off my feet,' I correct him, and he laughs.

'I'll give you my card, give me a call if you want to go for a drink sometime.'

After thanking him again, I take the card and say goodbye. As soon as I am in the building and out of Tom's line of sight, I toss the card into the nearest bin, because there's no way I'm going to call him. Yes, he's good-looking, charming, funny and has a really good job, but that's just not my type. He may be any normal/sensible girl's type, but I've never been that normal. Or sensible.

Anyway, I'm late for work. Better get a move on.

Chapter 2

My name is Nicole Wilde, and I don't live in the 'real world'. Well, that's what my Great-Aunt Dorothy is always telling me. Maybe she's right. I guess I am kind of lucky with the way things have worked out.

As silly as it sounds, I have always kinda wanted to be a celebrity. When I was a little girl, as shy as I was, I wanted to be an actress, a singer, a dancer or a musician, and I tried my hand at each one – it turns out I was crap at all of them. My singing voice wasn't terrible but it wasn't amazing either, acting gave me the giggles, trying to make my hands do different things at the same time just wouldn't happen no matter which instrument I tried to learn and as for dancing, well that's pretty much just exercise, and who wants to do that for a living?

Fast forward a few years to my mid-teens. I rebelled. Black nails and make-up, rainbow-coloured hair, fishnet tights and Slipknot T-shirts – that was me. However, like any scary-on-the-outside, good-girl-on-the-inside teenage faux rebel, music was my life. I might not have been able to make it, but I could certainly surround myself with it. No more of the cheesy 90s pop that I loved growing up, instead I started listening to proper bands that played proper instruments.

I would go to the local venue a few times a week and check out unsigned bands from all over the country who were stopping by the quiet little Yorkshire town where I grew up, just to have another leg of their little self-funded tours.

I would watch the bands and then hang out chatting afterwards, and hitting it off with the musicians was just something that came easily to me. Maybe this was down to the fact that – as my Great-Aunt Dot put it – my grungy, punky outfits were 'suggestive' and gave off 'the wrong impression', but I think it probably had more to do with the fact that we shared a love of music.

Hanging around with these unknown musicians gave me a taste for the music industry (and a passion for rockstars) so I started following big-name bands around, doing anything and everything to meet them, have my photo taken with them and ask them to sign my CD/T-shirt/body part. This only increased my desire to be famous and to surround myself with famous people – or those who were headed for fame. Of all the friends I made back in those days, some quit their bands, cut their hair and got real jobs but others stuck with it – one of the bands I know is actually getting pretty big at the moment, which is very exciting.

By the time I was eighteen, I was tagging along on tours – low budget, of course – sleeping in the back of vans and converted old buses. I'm not even embarrassed to say it, but by the time I'd finished school, unlike most of my other friends, I didn't want to get a job or a house or a husband – I just wanted to have fun. So, after my A-levels I took a gap year and became a professional hanger-on and I just loved it. I also ditched the scary teen-rebel look, trading in my brightly coloured 'do for stylish blonde highlights.

Sadly, everyone has to go home sometime, and one day I arrived at my parents' house to find my mum and dad waiting for me, armed with a question: what are you going to do with your life? The truth was that I didn't know what I wanted to do, so I decided to go to university – because, as bad as it sounds, that would buy me three more years of messing around. I wasn't some ambitious teen, packing my bags for uni with big dreams of becoming an architect or an artist or an astronaut, so the selection process was a little random. I decided to do journalism, because it sounded glamorous and could potentially involve celebrities. It turned out to be the best decision I ever made, because during my third year I got to go to ByteBanter for my work experience. To this day I don't fully understand what they do – they're some kind of techy news website – but I enjoyed my time there and I really clicked with the editor, Eric Tucker, or ET as he's known around the office. When I turned up on my first day, it was like being transported to the future – or teleported to the future, as ET corrected me when I said this out loud. Everything was chrome and black leather, there were all kinds of machines making lots of noise, lights flickering like crazy and the desks were just a mass of gadgets – I had entered geek world, and it was everything I thought it would be. The first thing I noticed was that there weren't any female employees. I remember asking ET if any women worked there and he replied: 'most of these guys haven't ever spoken to a girl, let alone worked with one'.

They might not have realised it, but a lot of the guys working there were accidentally cool. They were rocking the geek-chic look – you know the one, braces, thick-framed glasses, bow ties – I'm fairly certain that if they walked into any highstreet fashion shop, they would blend right in, not that any of them would ever go near a highstreet fashion shop.

Most of them wouldn't talk to me at first but some were friendly. They didn't make me feel stupid for not understanding HTML or JavaScript (which, sadly, has nothing to do with coffee) and they could have easily put me in a corner sharpening pencils (I made a joke about this at the time, they don't have pencils) but they didn't. Instead they gave me things to write about like headphones and music streaming services and, unsurprisingly, I managed to write about my favourite thing: bands. To make a very long story very short, at the end of my time there ET was so impressed, and so happy that almost all of the office had at least spoken to a member of the opposite sex, that he offered me a job, starting as soon as I'd finished my degree. I didn't think he meant it, but as soon as I graduated I gave him a call on the off-chance and, just like he said he would, he set me up with my own little department. Two rooms of their huge office were assigned to my project – a main office for my team and a little private office for me. The ByteBanter guys would build and maintain an online magazine for me, but I was in charge of everything else.

If the ByteBanter office was futuristic, the rooms they gave me to use were practically prehistoric. The decor reminded me of a film noir detective office – old wooden desks, proper filing cabinets, frosted glass on the doors and even a coat stand. Anything that wasn't actually made of wood was a similar colour.

I managed to poach Jake – my favourite member of the ByteBanter team – to come and do the day-to-day techy stuff for me and recruited my best friend from uni, Emily, to help me with the writing and there you have it, that's how I became editor of *Starstruck*, an online magazine.

Chapter 3

Pushing my way arse first through the ByteBanter double doors, I dodge my way through the desks to where my office is, saying my good mornings to the guys as I pass through – although I think that ship has sailed now.

I have a go at opening the *Starstruck* door with my forehead, with no luck, but thankfully someone at a nearby desk notices and helps me out.

'I'm here, I'm here,' I chant victoriously, as I arrive with the new coffees intact.

'Well, look what the cat dragged in!' Emily teases.

'I'm late, I know, but you wouldn't believe what happened on the way over here,' I begin to explain, handing out the drinks.

'What could have possibly happened that would make the ten-minute walk from your flat to here take *two* hours? And is this a skinny latte?' Vicky asks rather rudely, and yes, I am technically her boss.

I ignore her question about my lateness, but as for the latte – what is the right answer? I'm so not in the mood today. It took me two attempts to get her that damn coffee and if she doesn't drink it she *will* end up wearing it.

'No?' I reply, although it sounds more like a question than

an answer.

'Excellent!' She snatches it from me without the same thank you that I received from Emily and Jake.

'You know what they say, Nicole,' Vicky persists, 'the early bird catches the worm.'

'Ah, but the second mouse gets the cheese,' I reply.

'Yeah, but it's covered in dead mouse,' she says, looking and sounding thoroughly disgusted that I'd suggest such a thing.

Vicky Mason is the newest member of the *Starstruck* team. She is an aspiring journalist with a BTEC in Photography, desperate to break into the world of music journalism. Emily met her at a gig she was reviewing and I guess Vicky just latched on to her. She didn't have a job, and we didn't have a proper photographer, so after a lot of persuasion from Em, I agreed to take Vicky on. Oh, how I have come to regret that decision now; the girl is impossible to get along with. She's bossy, she's rude and she is so argumentative – although she would argue that she wasn't.

Emily gets on with her and Jake gets on with anyone, but Vicky and I just clash in every way imaginable.

She's an averagely talented photographer – much better now that I'm constantly splashing out on new kit for her to use. Personally, I think she would be much more at home trying to trick drunk celebrities into flashing their underwear outside nightclubs, so that she can snap some photos and sell them to the tabloids for a big chunk of cash.

I tell them the story about my encounter with Tom, hoping they might think my fall had more to do with me being late than my hangover.

'He gave you his business card?' Jake chuckles. 'Did you say his name was Patrick Bateman? You know, he liked blondes.'

'Very funny,' I say sarcastically. 'Now hadn't you better get back to playing The Sims or updating your blog or whatever it is you do on there when you're pretending to work.'

I have a great friendship with Jake. He teases me about

supposedly being a groupie, I tease him about being a nerd. We are about as opposite as two people can be, but we get on like a house on fire.

'Nic, can I see you in your office, please?' Emily asks. She sounds serious, but her face isn't giving anything away.

My first reaction is to panic – on the inside though, I'm not going to let Vicky enjoy my potential misery. I grab my caramel macchiato – I can't hear bad news without caffeine in me – and make my way into my little office. I close the door behind us, just as Jake starts singing the chorus of Carly Rae Jepsen's 'Call Me Maybe' in an attempt to tease me. He's spending way too much time around me if he's learning the lyrics to songs like that; I almost feel sorry for him.

'Right, hit me with it, get it over with,' I babble. I've never been great at receiving bad news.

A smile spreads across my friend's face.

'It's good news. I was going through the emails …' Emily pauses for dramatic effect.

'Spit it out, woman!' I demand, unable to wait a second longer.

'We've had an email from Plastic Rap's manager, you're interviewing them tonight!' she tells me with an extra-loud squeal.

'No way! We managed to blag an interview? How? I thought they were all booked up.'

'They had some journo drop out at the last minute, so there's a slot going free. It's after the show though, so late. Do I confirm?'

'Erm, yeah! You're coming with me, right?'

'Can't. It's my mum's birthday party tonight,' she reminds me and I can see how disappointed she is. 'He said in the email that he could supply us with photos, so you don't even have to take Vicky if you don't want to.'

'I don't want to,' I whisper with a cheeky smile on my face.

'I am so jealous. You never know, one of the Plastic Rap boys might fall madly in love with you. You could get married and your groupie days would be over. Then you wouldn't have to worry about getting up for work on a morning – I told you that you'd be late today,' she teases.

'Oi, who are you calling a groupie? And when did you tell me that I'd be late today?'

'Last night ...' she prompts, and I cast my mind back. Em and I went to a gig last night and then partied with the bands until the early hours – let's just say things got messy. She's right though. I remember the taxi dropping me off, drunkenly fidgeting with my door key, thinking it was the funniest thing ever, and Emily yelling something out of the taxi window about how I'd be late for work as she was driven off. A guilty smile spreads across my face.

'And don't think I didn't see you with Troy Reeves, Miss Wilde,' she adds.

Troy was on one of those terrible reality TV talent shows. He didn't win, but when I interviewed him he told me that he was glad because he could make music without a super-strict recording contract holding him back – we got on like a house on fire, so I always see him when he's in town.

'So how come you didn't go back with him last night?' Emily asks.

'I'm a lady!' I protest, trying to give off Kate Middleton vibes, but my Yorkshire accent betrays me.

Emily gives me a look.

'He had to go,' I admit. 'They were travelling through the night.'

'You looove him, Nicole.'

'I do not looove him,' I reply with a laugh.

'Gosh, Troy Reeves last night, Prince Charming today – it's true what they say about men being like buses, isn't it?'

'Yeah, they're dirty, anyone can ride them and they're never there when you want one.'

Emily, a dyed-in-the-wool romantic, rolls her eyes at this.

Plastic Rap are one of the biggest bands around at the moment. They're mainly aimed at the teen market, but loved by young girls and mums alike. Even a few boys admit to liking them these days.

At the moment they are touring the UK, and when tickets went on sale all venues sold out within a couple of hours. I managed to score a place on the guest list months ago, but all their publicity time was booked up. As far as their music goes, they're not really my cup of tea, but this interview will be good for hits.

'Get some work done,' Emily says, leaving me alone in my office and closing the door behind her. There are only a handful of reasons why my office door is ever closed. One – when Vicky is driving me especially crazy. Two – when I am in on my own, and therefore scared something might 'get me'. Three – when I actually need to do some work. Despite today being a three, I have Googled Plastic Rap and now I'm casually clicking my way through their photos and mentally placing them in order of hotness. This takes up about ten minutes that I don't have and I manage to burn another five flicking through the photos from last night on my phone. It certainly was a wild one.

Now officially in the p.m., I click open my emails. The first one I open is from Dylan King. Subject: Uh-oh.

I quickly scan through the email which informs me Dylan is 'seventy-five per cent certain' he *didn't* pay a woman sex, although he is 'eighty-five per cent certain' he did 'bang her' and she maybe stole some money from him. The percentages make me laugh but somehow I don't think they were meant to.

Dylan is a mega-star, so stories are forever popping up in the press about him sleeping with someone – and most of the time he *has* slept with them; in fact, I'm ninety-nine per cent certain.

As well as being a super-famous rockstar, he is also my best friend. I met him on my gap year when I won a competition to meet his band, The Burnouts. Back then, the bands I hung around with were small-time, so it was pretty cool to meet one of the most famous bands in the country and get to hang out backstage.

I remember their manager came out to get me and as we were walking backstage he said: 'They're going to love you, darling.' Back then I wasn't the expert that I am now when it comes to bands, in particular the inner (and outer) workings of your typical band member, so I weakly asked him what he meant. 'Blonde hair, curves. You're just Dylan's type; you want to watch yourself with him,' he warned me, making me even more nervous than I already was.

When I was shown into the backstage room, it was Mikey King, Dylan's younger brother who is also in the band, who I was introduced to first and he was lovely. Dylan was always the one I'd had the crush on, but Mikey was just so down-to-earth and charming. It's no secret that Mikey is the real talent in The Burnouts, he's the guitarist and he writes most of the music, whereas Dylan is the egotistical front-man with the pretty face and the shocking reputation. After I'd chatted to Mikey for a while, Dylan came in and he was everything people had warned me about. His ego was in full swing and I could tell he was going out of his way to try to impress me – he even played me an exclusive clip of their next single. Until that moment, I'd loved everything him, but being around this mega-famous arsehole was really starting to get on my nerves. So, when he played me their new song, despite it being amazing, I told him it was crap – because that ought to bring him down a peg or two. Of course I instantly regretted saying it, but after a few seconds of straight-faced silence he burst out laughing.

'I think you're the only person in the world brave enough to say something like that to me,' he chuckled – apparently the kind of person who will tell you your music is crap is exactly the kind of person you want to have in your life if you're a musician – and we became pretty much inseparable. We've been best friends ever since – although nothing more, I hasten to add. We're both very much in the other's friend-zone. This works well for both of us professionally, because if I am having a slow week with news he will give me an interview, and he can always rely on me to give him a bit of good press when everyone is reporting the negative stuff – like him 'banging' a potential thief, for example.

With me living in Leeds and him down in London, we don't see each other as much as we'd like, but we talk almost every day and we always have a blast when he is on tour.

My mind darts back to the 'real world'. Sitting at my desk and staring at my computer, I realise that I'm not going to be able to concentrate today, I'm just too excited. I go through the rest of my emails, clicking my way through the masses of press releases we receive every day. There are a few good ones but nothing too exciting. I'll do them later.

One exciting email I have received is from a tour manager, asking to me to confirm that I will be joining a band on their tour. These guys are also my good friends; I used to tour with them when no one knew who they were, and now they're embarking on their first headlining UK tour as a signed band, which is pretty exciting. I send a quick message (something which feels weirdly formal considering they're my buddies) confirming that I will still be joining them on the road and then crack on with my work.

After four hours of replying to messages and writing items for the website, I am more than ready to go home. In what little time I have, I'm going to pull out all the stops for tonight. I only wish I had time to pick up something new to wear.

'Don't mind if I get off a bit earlier, do you, team? Big night tonight,' I say, making my way towards the door.

'Last one in, first one out,' Jake jokes. 'Lucky for some.'

'Of course we don't mind. If you do pull one of them, be sure to text me,' Emily says excitedly. I think she may be even more excited than I am.

'I don't think so,' I call back as I make my escape. It's not that they are a bad-looking band, but my priority is the interview and I'm certainly not going to mess this up by getting my goals confused.

Chapter 4

I feel so old right now, and I'm only twenty-five. I'm at the Plastic Rap gig and, apart from a handful of parents and their young kids, I am surrounded by excited teenagers, most of them female. Unsurprisingly, I haven't bumped into anyone I know, so I have been entertaining myself. I've knocked back a few drinks and messed around on my phone quite a lot. It's very important to keep the good people of social media up to date on what I'm doing – fans are obsessed with knowing every little detail they can.

Plastic Rap are playing their last song and for the millionth time since I got here I am checking my bag for my Dictaphone. Absolutely nothing can go wrong tonight.

Looking up at them on stage, I have to admit that I can see exactly what the thousands of screaming girls see in them. They're good-looking in a goody-goody pop kind of way, not a tattoo or piercing in sight, which is something I actually quite like; it's not that often you find a musician without one or the other these days.

When the gig is finally over, I make my way to the hotel next door where our interview is taking place. Before I know it, I am plonked down in front of the band, who are eagerly awaiting my questions.

All five of them are so chatty; they've got bags of character and they're definitely saying all the right things.

Sometimes the really famous ones are rude or awkward and I hate it when there's a particular subject I'm not allowed to ask about, but that's not the case with these guys.

I've asked all the music-related questions that we're expected to ask, so it's time to get down to the juicy stuff.

'So, are you boys allowed girlfriends? A lot of bands with large teenage fanbases are told to keep their girlfriends a secret.'

Sam is straight in there with an answer.

'Yes, we're allowed girlfriends and we all have a girlfriend at the moment. Our fans are the most loyal fans in the world, they certainly don't mind us having them. It's all about the music.'

Fantastic answer, although I have to disagree. It's partly about the music, but their fans are genuinely in love with them. Hearts will break when they read this, that's for sure.

Eventually we wrap up the interview. I pose for a few photos with the band and I'm not going to lie, these are for my socials. I'm still a band lover at the end of the day.

Sam moves to stand next to me and slides an arm around my waist as we continue to pose for the camera.

'We're having a bit of a party if you'd like to stick around,' he says between smiles. Before I have chance to reply, in walks the band's tour manager with a group of ten fans, probably here for a meet and greet and ... no, scratch that, Carl is kissing one of them. Then her mate. Then *her* mate.

Oh boy. Honestly, you would think I would expect the worst from the get-go by now. I mean, I know this is how it goes, this is what band boys are like, and some fans will do anything to be close to their heroes, but I thought with these guys having girlfriends they might be diferent. Silly me.

'Thanks for the offer, but some of us have got work in the morning.' I try to sound friendly, jokey – anything but shocked and appalled.

'I'll give you my number, yeah?' He's persistent, I'll give him that. 'We're back here again in a few weeks. We'll have to meet up, babe.'

This is the second phone number I have been given today that I have no intention of calling – unless we ever need another interview, of course.

As I gather my things and walk towards the door, I take one final look back at the band, just as they are working out which band member gets which fan. Ten women – that's two each. It reminds me of when we used to pick teams during PE at school.

The band's chunky, bald tour manager stops me on the way out to ask a few questions about the magazine so I answer and politely thank him for his time. As I go for the door, he puts his arm up like a barrier blocking an exit and it is weirdly intimidating.

'Don't go putting this in your magazine,' he warns me.

'Wouldn't dream of it,' I reply bluntly, waiting for him to move so I can pass him. Eventually he does. I can't wait to tell Emily about this, in fact I'm actually hitting call on her name before I've even left the building. It doesn't take me long to relay the night's events to her as I walk home.

'I cannot believe it!' she squeals.

'I know, right? No wonder their fans don't mind them having girlfriends, it *really, really* doesn't matter.'

'Well yeah, that *is* shocking, but I can't believe you didn't stay. You were in there, Nic!'

'No way! You'd have stayed? In the queue?' I reply. '*Everyone* was in there.'

Emily snorts.

'We need to keep our heads down, Em. Trying to ruin the reputation of a huge band like Plastic Rap would probably just get us sued. Right, I'm at my door. I trust we'll be keeping this little discovery between us?'

'Say no more. See you in the morning and try not to be late, yeah?'

Cheeky! Then again, I am always late.

Chapter 5

It's good to be home, and I'm so glad I escaped the orgy as I much prefer my own bed. The kettle goes on and so does my laptop because, as soon as I get some caffeine in my system, I'm going to make a start transcribing tonight's interview. I'm very much a night person, which is proving really inconvenient because people expect me to wake up in the a.m..

Kicking off my shoes and abandoning my gig outfit in the middle of my living room, I wander around in my underwear until I eventually find my dressing gown which, for some reason, is plonked on top of the cooker. It doesn't really matter because my cooker is super-clean – not because I am a domestic goddess but because I never, ever use it. Living in the city centre, there is a restaurant or a takeaway everywhere you look – who needs to know how to cook these days?

My butt finally hits the sofa at 1 a.m. I know I've got to be up in seven hours (five and a half if I want to wash my hair, which I probably should because I have post-gig frizz going on), so maybe I won't be typing up the interview tonight after all.

I'm just about to shut down when a message from Luke Fox pops up. Just seeing his name makes me go all weird and, at twenty-five years of age, I still feel like a lovesick schoolgirl whenever I see him.

Luke is, you've guessed it, in a band and I have had a crush on him pretty much since the day we met. Unfortunately, he is a bit of a ladies' man, so despite our flirty banter, I have mostly just stood back and watched him sleep with anything female that crossed his path.

It was Luke's band, Two For The Road, that I used to tour with in my teens, and now they're a proper signed band in the middle of their first headlining UK tour – this is the band that I'll be doing a few tour dates with later this week. I'm making out like it's a magazine feature – and it will be going in the mag – but, to be honest, I have been on every tour with these guys since we met, so I'm not about to stop now they've hit the big time. It's amazing how things have changed. I used to sleep in the back of their van; now they're being driven around in a huge tour bus.

Touring can really take its toll on your body. I've developed tinnitus from all the loud music (it turns out your ears need protection too, something I learned a little too late) and tendon damage from a particularly high pair of heels that I wore for too many days in a row, and while thankfully I've managed to protect myself from the cocktail of sexually transmitted diseases that I know several of my band friends have encountered, my priority has always been to protect my heart. No, I'm not talking about exercising on a regular basis and taking aspirin, I'm talking about not getting too involved with the boys. With Luke, this has always been a struggle.

It would be the biggest understatement of the century to say that I have a slight crush on him – I am crazy about him. I haven't wanted to be anybody's girlfriend since Robbie Williams ripped off his clothes (and then his skin) in the 'Rock DJ' music video back in 2000, but I could quite easily believe in monogamy for this man – something which troubles me because I'm not a commitment kind of girl and he certainly isn't a commitment kind of boy.

He's tall without being lanky, his dark hair is effortlessly perfect with his fringe falling over his gorgeous brown eyes, and he always seems to smells so nice, even when he's all sweaty after a show. See what I mean? I sound like a fifteen-year-old girl. The bottom line is that he is gorgeous, but I'm not the only one who thinks so. He has an even bigger female following since hitting the big time, and I can't compete with semi-naked, fanatic chicks that operate as a team.

Luke: Nicole?

As the message pops up on my screen, the butterflies in my stomach start fluttering like crazy, it's ridiculous. When we see each other at gigs, we get on so well and we flirt constantly but that's just the way he is. He definitely doesn't know about my little crush on him. It would be stupid of me to interpret his flirting as real feelings because he's such a ladies' man and a total charmer. He's the kind of guy your mother would warn you about and your father would want to kill – actually, he could probably charm your mum too.

After what feels like several minutes of panicky excitement, I manage to compose myself enough to type a reply. He tells me that he is currently sat in a hotel room, all alone and bored out of his mind. After we get past the hello-how-are-you stuff, things start to get interesting.

Luke: No party tonight. This is not what I signed up for.
Nicole: Well I'll be with you in a few days, we'll make up for it.
Luke: Looking forward to it. Are you seeing anyone at the moment?

Am I seeing anyone at the moment? That's a laugh. The truth is that it's been years since I had an actual boyfriend. It's not that I'm lacking male attention, but my type happens to be: musicians.

When you're on the road, all relationships are short, even friendships. You take 'relationships' where you can find them and they require about as much commitment as a pet rock. Having a guy ask you to be his girlfriend in the 'real world' is the equivalent of a band boy actually remembering your surname. But that's the way I like it. The sad truth is, that I'd rather have two nights with a rockstar than two years with your average bloke.

The fact that Luke is even enquiring about my love life is enough to make my heart race.

> Nicole: Nope. Are you?
> Luke: No, I'm single too.

I knew that. Luke totally subscribes to the musician way of life and a girlfriend would only cramp his style. Before I have chance to worry about what to say in response, Luke sends me another message.

> Luke: Can I ask you something?
> Nicole: Sure.

I'm trying to sound cool, like I'm not really bothered what he says next – I am though. This is so high school, I cannot believe that I am still playing these games.

> Luke: You know that I fancy you, don't you?

If I'm being honest, I'm waiting for the punch-line.

My first guess is that it isn't Luke at all. It could be Eddie, the TFTR front-man, messing with me. Or maybe it *is* Luke, but he's drunk. Then again, if he's drunk, how come his typing is so accurate? And Eddie being sober, or alone, at this time of night after a gig is about as probable as me using my cooker for something other than storage.

Nicole: You fancy everyone, ha-ha!
Luke: No, I really fancy you.

If this isn't a joke then I am gobsmacked. I'll have to reply with something or he'll think he's scared me away. Not only is this guy my crush, but he could have any girl he wanted. He might not be a superstar like Dylan, and TFTR aren't as big as Plastic Rap yet, but he's big enough to have an album in the impressive end of the Top Forty at the moment.

Nicole: Is this really you?

Better to ask than to make a total tit of myself and have the rest of the band tease me about it for the rest of time.

Luke: Of course it's me. You don't believe me?
Nicole: Are you drunk?
Luke: Yes, but that's not why I'm telling you. I can't get you out of my head, especially when I'm alone on the bus ;-).

He's taking a bit of a risk with our friendship here, but he is a musician. He oozes confidence and probably thinks every girl in the world finds him attractive – then again, they probably do. Luke can easily get away with hitting on his female friends and using tacky emoticons in his messages.

Luke: Am I making things awkward? I'm sorry.
Nicole: You're not making things awkward, don't worry.
Luke: We flirt all the time, why do you seem so surprised?
Nicole: Again, because you flirt with everyone!
Luke: Wait until I see you, we'll talk in person and then you'll know that I mean what I say.

I agree, before changing the subject from Luke's declaration of lust and we carry on chatting for a while. Before I know it, it's nearly 3 a.m., which means I should definitely be in my bed by now. I don't want to go, but I don't want to be late for work again either. I am both relieved and devastated when Luke says that he had better get some sleep, so we finish the conversation by saying that we'll see each other on tour in a couple of days.

Finally climbing in my bed, I rest my head on the pillow and try to get some much-needed sleep. My conversation with Luke is replaying in my head and I can't help but wonder how things are going to play out when I see him.

I'm *so* going to be late for work in the morning.

Chapter 6

Despite the exciting events last night, not only am I at work on time but I am also the first one to arrive.

I am in a fantastic mood today and my work is reaping the benefits. In fact, I am so busy flying through the emails that I don't even hear Jake arrive. I'm surprised I couldn't smell the coffee as he was coming up in the lift.

He makes me jump by dropping a copy of the *Daily Scoop* newspaper on the desk in front of me. Plastic Rap are on the cover accompanied by the headline: 'We're having a fan-bang'. Not only am I amazed by the speed these tabloids operate at, but I'd give anything to have been the person who came up with that pun.

'Oh my God ...'

'I take it you left before this went on?' Jake enquires.

'I did. Minutes before, actually.'

'Do you think they were just waiting for you to leave to get started?' he jokes.

Jake is so funny. He's not really that into the kind of music we write about, but he is so good at his job and he keeps us all in stitches while we're working.

I take a long, unladylike swig of my coffee and grab the paper to have a proper read.

It doesn't say who their source is, but they must have been at the hotel last night because they saw exactly what I saw. I can't believe this has made the front page.

I read the article out loud as Emily and Vicky arrive together.

'Plastic Rap, the squeaky-clean teen sensation, are proving to be just as artificial as their name. There has never been any scandal in the press about band members Sam, Carl, Mike, John and Simon, all aged between twenty and twenty-two ... until now, that is.' Looking up to make sure that I have Emily and Vicky's attention, I carry on reading: 'At a gig in Leeds last night, the band members sent one of their people out into the crowd to bring them back a gaggle of adoring fans to bed. Our spy claims there were at least two women for each band member. The band, who market themselves as being teen-friendly, should know better.'

I've read enough. I wonder who leaked the story to the press – it certainly wasn't me, I was far too preoccupied last night – but I don't remember seeing anyone else in the room. It must have been one of the fans; maybe one of them realised how wrong it was and decided to tell the press. Well, good for her – whoever she was – and she didn't even give her name so she's clearly not just after the fame. Poor Em has a concerned look on her face; I didn't realise she was so appalled by the story when I told her about it last night.

'Nicole, I'm going to go pick up the new camera. I've had a message to say that it's ready,' Jake informs me, before turning to Vicky and asking her if she wants to go with him – it is for her after all. Vicky jumps out of her chair and heads to the door. She doesn't even say goodbye to us, the girl is *that* rude. I'm just glad to get her out of the way so that I can talk to Emily properly about the headline and about Luke.

'I saw that paper on the way to work this morning, I thought maybe you'd tipped them off,' she says as soon as we're alone.

'Come on, Emily. You know me better than that. As if I'd give *my* story to trash like the *Scoop*. Anyway, forget that, I have something far more interesting to tell you.'

I tell her everything about my conversation with Luke. She already knows how much I fancy him, but she doesn't seem that pleased for me.

'Oh,' is her response.

'Oh?'

'Well, he's not the kind of guy you really want to be with is he, Nic? Can you imagine being married to someone like that?'

'Bloody hell, Em! I'm not planning on marrying the guy!'

'Well what about those rumours that he is always off his face on drugs since the band hit the big time?' she quizzes me.

'Who knows if there's any truth in that? And like it matters. Like I said, we're hardly planning our wedding.'

I'm slightly annoyed that I'm having to justify myself to her; her love life is just as chaotic as mine, if not more so. I may go for the band boys, but Em goes for the bad eggs out there in the 'real world'. Anyway, I've never seen any of the boys touch anything other than a bit of weed now and then on the bus (not that I approve) – certainly not the hard stuff like you read in the gossip columns. The press are just trying to trash the hottest new band on the scene, simply because they can.

'In that case I'm very happy for you,' Emily says, with a smile that I'm not entirely convinced is genuine.

'Yeah, well don't go hat shopping just yet, will you?' I joke, but things are suddenly a bit awkward.

I'm touched by her concern but, like I said, I'm not planning on marrying him, and she doesn't usually care about the moral character of the band boys I 'get involved' with. He's my big crush, can't I just enjoy this moment?

'I've got Vicky living with me, as of last night,' Emily blurts out.

Now *I'm* shocked. 'Why?'

'She had a huge fall-out with her mum and she turned up at my mum's party with her bags – what was I supposed to do?'

I don't know what expression is currently occupying my face, but it must be bad because Emily reacts to it straight away.

'I know you're not keen on her, but she's a nice girl and it's only temporary.'

'You're too nice, Emily Adams. Don't let her take advantage.'

Our conversation is cut short by my mobile ringing. It's Dylan King so I take it in my office.

'Hello, rockstar, how are you?'

'Fucked,' he replies.

'What's the matter?' I do worry about him, he's such a good friend to me and he gets such a hard time from the press for getting drunk and hooking up with women. In a weird way I'm quite proud to be female *and* his friend, rather than just another one of his conquests. He has a hard time trusting girls, so it's nice to be so special to him.

'To summarise,' he starts, sounding more serious than I have ever heard him sound in his life, 'I've knocked up some woman, about seven months ago apparently. She's having twins – fucking twins, Nicole. It's going to come out sooner or later, she's saying she'll go to the press. I don't know what I'm going to do.'

'First of all, calm down. I don't want to be rude, but are you certain it was you who … knocked her up?' I ask, using his words. 'You've been, erm, seeing a few women this past year and not the most committed kind …' I trail off, hoping he'll catch my drift. My point is that he's shagged a lot of random girls. Random girls who have probably shagged a lot of random guys too.

'The timing is right,' he says before a long pause. 'And there's a video.'

'A video? Bloody hell, Dylan, when those kids ask you where they came from, you're going to be able to give them one hell of an answer.'

He laughs, but he sound worried sick. I guess this was bound to happen sooner or later. I love Dylan to bits, but he really puts it about and he drinks a lot, which we all know is a recipe for disaster. I think he's been really lucky to not have this happen on a weekly basis. Even so, I feel sorry for him.

'What are you going to do?' I ask.

'I've got a meeting with a guy this afternoon, some publicity crisis specialist who's going to work it all out for me. I've just got to keep quiet about it until then.'

'Good luck. Try not to worry, OK?' I know it's easier said than done, but what do you say to a friend who has accidentally knocked up a girl he hardly knows? And with a video souvenir too. Hallmark certainly don't make a card for it.

All around me, glamorous, rich and famous folks' lives are going down the pan and at the same time mine is getting better and better. It's true what they say, money and fame don't make you happy. When I think about the scandal with Plastic Rap and their young fans, and now Dylan and his pregnant one-night stand, it makes me really glad that I'm not famous. I do stupid things all the time, but luckily no one cares enough for a newspaper to want to write about it.

I try to put myself in Dylan's shoes, but I just cannot imagine how it would feel to have everyone knowing every little detail about you; for your parents to see the details of your sex life on the front page of a newspaper along with the rest of the world – your dentist, the people you went to school with, the guy who serves you in Starbucks. Some of the things I've read about Dylan, true or otherwise, have been so embarrassing, I just can't imagine the entire country knowing the dirty little details of my life and me feeling comfortable carrying on as if nothing were any different. That's why I'm glad I became a journalist – no one cares what we do.

Chapter 7

I was about fourteen when I went to see my first proper concert and it was mesmerising. I think that's when my love of the music biz started – I was just so fascinated by all of it.

I remember not long after that, I was hanging around outside the arena in Sheffield with my friends. We would turn up at 10 a.m. and wait for the bands to arrive, just hoping to catch a glimpse. That time in particular, we were standing at the temporary metal fence in the huge, empty car park when the bus pulled in. I just stared in amazement as it drove past us. It seemed huge – like the band were travelling around in a hotel on wheels. It's funny, I've been on so many since then that these days they all seem so small to me – tour buses that is, not bands.

Peeping through the fence, I watched them unload the bus. After the roadies had done all the heavy lifting, the doors would open and out strolled the important-looking people like managers and publicists. Then my favourite bit: the band would step off the bus, usually surrounded by girlfriends and friends. I wanted to be one of those people, following them around like a puppy, being the envy of every girl standing around in the car park. Well look at me now, I'm living the dream. Well, almost. Let's just say things aren't exactly the way I imagined them to be. I thought it was going to be pure glamour, but the reality of it is rather different. OK, so the five-star hotels are pretty glam, but even the most beautiful hotel room can seem like a shithole when you add a gang of lads who invite thirty of their closest friends for an impromptu party. Without entertainment planned, people will make their own fun and that is when things get messy. There's nothing glamorous about a luxury bath when it's nearly full to the top with beer, vomit, piss, fag ends and anything else that happens to be within reach.

I like to think I'm rock and roll, but I remember seeing a huge flat-screen TV taken down off the wall and being promptly thrown off the balcony and into the river that our formerly beautiful room overlooked. The band thought this was hilarious – it was no skin off their noses because their record label would foot the bill – but I'd kill to have a TV like that at my place. It was such a waste.

When I find myself alone in a hotel room I'll order room service, throw on a fluffy dressing gown and see what the movie channels have to offer. The only things I have ever thrown off a balcony, well technically spat off a balcony, were orange Revels – abominable.

Don't get me wrong though, I *am* a party animal. Put me in a hotel room with a bunch of drunk band boys and a few friends and things will always get messy. I've thrown up in a bath or two in my time, but that will not be happening on this tour. I'm not going to be able to seduce Luke with vomit.

At the moment I am hurriedly packing my bags so that I don't miss my train to Manchester. That's where I'll be meeting up with Luke's band, Two For The Road, and joining them on the last week of their tour.

Packing for tour requires two bags. I have a small bag to take to gigs with me – big enough for my phone, purse, camera and make-up – and a huge bag that could rival a suitcase for space. Inside this bag I have successfully crammed enough items of clothing to at least create the illusion that I am wearing a different outfit every day of the tour, my vital grooming items like my hairbrush and the super-important things like my phone charger. I lift it up before I squash in the last few items, just to see if it's too heavy to carry. It almost certainly is, but I'll manage.

As I frantically cram the last few things into the two bags, I mentally tick them off my list of things to take with me. Of course, the problem with a mental list is that you have to actually remember the things on it, and you can guarantee I will always forget something.

Guess what? I'm running really late. It's nearly 7 p.m. by the time I am making the short journey from my flat to the train station. I probably should have checked the train times, but I know there is one every half an hour so it should be fine. I really am so disorganised, but I think I secretly enjoy the drama. A few taps on my phone would tell me what time the train is due and what time it arrives in Manchester, but that would be way too easy, and if I start messing around with my phone then I'll definitely miss my train.

After buying my ticket I check the departures board and learn that not only is my train due to depart in three minutes, but that it is departing from platform sixteen. Just brilliant.

I knew that I'd be running late, so I decided to get ready for the gig before I left home. The downside of this is that I'm freezing in my dress but on the plus side it will save me loads of time when I get there, and at least I'm wearing my cosy Ugg boots. My pretty shoes are in my bag. I'll make the swap when I get there.

Running down the steps to platform sixteen I hear the all-too-familiar whistle, the one that means the train doors are about to close, and I'm about to miss my train. Before I know what I'm doing, I am diving through the closing doors, landing upright and still holding my things as the doors shut behind me. The train is absolutely packed and all the people standing in the doorway cheer and applaud my James Bond-style manoeuvre.

That is probably the most energetic thing I have done in a long time, so I smile and curtsy for my audience, before composing myself and trying to find my phone. This is one of those moments in life that is totally social media-worthy, in fact I think it was designed with moments like this in mind.

Impressed with myself, I wonder how I managed to move so gracefully with my big bag and, of course, it is then that I realise I left my big bag at home. This means that I have no clean clothes, no hairbrush and, worst of all, no actual shoes. Shit. It's too late to do anything about it now, I'll just have to manage. I've survived on low-budget tours, sleeping in the back of dirty old vans and trying to make my face of make-up last for more than one day – I'll be fine. I'm touring with Two For The Road; they have a big, glamorous tour bus and we'll be staying in a few hotels. I guess I'll have to buy some new clothes, but that is hardly an idea I am against.

About an hour later, the train pulls into Manchester Piccadilly station and I hop off far more gracefully than I got on. My friend, Gemma, is stood waiting for me. She's a huge Two For The Road fan and I remember exactly what it's like to be a fan, desperate to meet the band, so I told her that if she wanted to come along I would introduce her.

'Are you excited about tonight?' I ask.

'I am so, *so* nervous. I don't know how you keep your cool being friends with all these bands! Just promise to introduce me to Eddie.'

Eddie is the lead singer of TFTR and like every frontman ever, he is gorgeous, charming and as shallow as a puddle.

I resist telling Gemma about Luke – it's not that I don't trust her, I'm just worried. What if he acts like we never had that conversation? What if he was just drunk? I am not going to make a fool of myself tonight – although I'm not sure how easy that is going to be if I get a little bit drunk.

Finally, outside the venue, a big, scary-looking doorman

ticks our names off the guest list. I can hear the music from out here, it's Two For The Road. I told you that I was going to be *very* late.

Our first stop is the bar, and it's only as we're ordering our drinks that I realise I am probably just as nervous as Gemma is tonight. It has been such a long time since I felt nervous about meeting a band, and I know these guys so well, but this Luke stuff is having a strange effect on me. I've always kept my crush on him under wraps, but now that he might actually fancy me back, everything is different. Oh God, I'm sounding like a schoolgirl again.

Armed with our drinks, we make our way towards the stage where the show is already in full swing. Eddie, the singer, is upfront and smack bang in the middle. He's very typically good-looking (think Alex Pettyfer, but brunette) and he really knows how to work the crowd. The only time he isn't surrounded by a crowd of girls is when he's on stage. He has his shirt fully unbuttoned, like he's in Whitesnake (circa 1980s) or something, and a guitar hanging off his body which I don't think I have ever seen him play – that's Ben's job. Ben is the lead guitarist, but he's probably the shyest member of the band. I'm not sure how old he is, but he can't be more than twenty. He's a new addition to TFTR (after their original guitarist walked) and hasn't quite acquired the same level of cockiness as the rest of them, but given time I'm sure he will. Then we have the bassist, Mark. Mark is probably the one I get on with the least because he's taken that cheeky cockiness that makes Eddie and Luke so likeable and mutated it into full-blown arrogance. Even before they were famous, you could tell he thought he was the shit. He's never been anything but nice to me though, so I can't complain, but there is something very unattractive about a man who thinks that he is God's gift to women. His short blonde hair always looks like it needs a good wash and I wish he would have a shave – I am not a big fan of beards at the best of times, but his definitely needs some attention. As I'm staring at him, I catch his eye and he gives me a wink, so I give him a smile in return. Then I look at Luke, he's sitting behind the drums with his shirt off, sweat literally dripping off him as he bangs away on his kit with real enthusiasm. I get that feeling again, that pang of something in my chest. I think my heart just skipped a beat – how lame is that?

We've managed to push our way to the front of the crowd, at Gemma's request. I'd be happier blending into the background and pretending I'm important. As their song comes to an end, Eddie chats to his audience. I look over at Luke who is downing a bottle of water and the moment he stops drinking, he spots me. Standing up behind his drum kit and grabbing his microphone off the stand, he interrupts Eddie.

'Nicole Wilde, I see you! Guys, we've got a very special lady in tonight, huge shout-out to Nicole from *Starstruck*. She's touring with us and we want her to write nice things, so if you see her at the bar then buy her a drink!' And with that, he returns the mic to its rightful place and sits back down behind his drums.

'This one is for you, Nicole!' Eddie shouts, as he bursts into their next song. I am both smug and embarrassed in equal measure. Shout-outs are great, but embarrassing, and because it was from Luke, I can feel my cheeks flushing. I'm hoping people will assume it's because it's warm in here.

The guys put on one hell of a show and, before I know it, they're about to play their final song of the night.

'So, this is our last song, guys.' Eddie stops talking to swig his beer, his audience will wait. 'Thank you so much for coming. We're going to party here for a while afterwards so come and say hello, and then we're going to a club. Where's cool in Manchester?' he asks in the faux-American twang he picked up somewhere along the way – I'm not sure where, he's a Londoner. His question is met by a series of shouted-out suggestions from the happy crowd, none of which are audible.

After they play their final song and go off stage, the nerves really hit me. I'm going to have to have an actual conversation with Luke, and I can't hide behind a screen while I think of cool and clever responses. I am so worried he'll bring up the other night, but I'm even more worried that he won't mention it at all.

After a quick trip to the bar for more drinks, I am chatting with Gemma when Eddie and Mark come over to say hello. Like the good friend that I am, the first thing I do is introduce Gemma to them, and if she is nervous then she isn't letting it show because she is so cool. As the four of us chat, I feel two hands on my waist and my heart jumps into my mouth because I know who it is. I spin around in his gentle grip to see a slightly sweaty and, unfortunately, fully clothed Luke Fox. He pulls me closer for a hug and plants a kiss on my cheek.

'Well hello, Miss Wilde,' he says, with the usual slightly flirtatious tone to his voice.

'Hello, Mr Fox,' I reply.

Someone needs to say something else. Oh shit, is this awkward?

'You guys were awesome tonight,' I tell him as the rest of the gang go back to their conversation.

'Thank you,' he says before pulling me close and whispering softly into my ear. 'I think you and I need a conversation tonight, don't you, Nicole?'

In my flat boots (which do not go with my dress at all) I have to lift myself up onto my tiptoes to whisper back to him, 'That all depends on what you want to talk about, Luke.' Now it's my turn to sound flirtatious. Before he can reply, I am dragged back to the other conversation by the band's tour manager who has now joined us. I was far too wrapped up in Luke to notice. Mick the tour manager hands me my laminated Access All Areas pass so that I can get in and out of venues without needing to be on the guest list or with a band member.

As we're all stood chatting, I think over what just happened with Luke. 'We need a conversation' doesn't really mean anything, does it? No matter how flirty he was acting when he said it. I am snapped out of my thoughts by Eddie, who asks me something about the magazine. As I am answering, I feel Luke's hand moving slowly down my back before resting softly on my bum. I'm trying to give Eddie an answer, but I feel like everyone can see it on my face, and I'm sure my cheeks are flushing again. My face cheeks that is.

Just as I start to relax, the band are called away to do some photos. Time for some more Dutch courage.

Gemma and I knock back a few more drinks as we watch the band chat with fans, pose for photographs and sign autographs.

Eddie is surrounded by girls, as always, and Luke and Mark have a fairly big crowd around them too, but Ben is sat to the side texting away on his mobile, probably to his girlfriend. It must be strange for him to go from being an unknown guitarist to being in a band like TFTR. I think he's handled himself really well though. It's great that he's still with his girlfriend, especially considering the attitude towards women that the rest of the band seem to share. Although I suppose Eddie has had several girlfriends, technically, it's just unfortunate that they have all been other people's girlfriends.

I see Luke walking over, so I jump up from my stool, but the alcohol doesn't seem to want me to and I stumble straight into him. He catches me and asks Gemma how many I've had.

'Enough,' I interrupt, and I'm pretty sure I just winked.

'We're going to some club down the road, are you ready to go, babe?' he asks, and I nod.

Gemma has work in the morning so she has to go. I drunkenly see her to a taxi and wave her off. I am caught by a pair of hands on my waist again, although they're not quite as gentle this time. I turn around and see Mark, the sleazy bassist, and he looks like he's had quite a bit to drink as well. I call him sleazy because Mark has always had an eye for sleeping with as many women as he can, by making out like he's the most important one in the band – even though he really isn't.

'Nicole! Let's go, we're going to party!' he slurs, his breath stinking of cider, as he grabs me by the arm. I'm not entirely sure who is holding up whom, but he is stuck to me like glue all the way to the club. I don't even get to talk to Luke on the way there. I'm going to have to up my game.

Chapter 8

Once we're inside the club, everyone heads straight over to the bar and Mark pushes a bottle of something colourful and alcoholic into my hand, which I happily accept. He is attempting to make small talk with me, but I am too drunk to focus on a word he is saying.

Luke walks over to us and grabs my hand.

'May I have this dance, Miss Wilde?' he asks.

The DJ is blasting out pop music – they'd never play a band like TFTR in a place like this, which is probably why we're here.

I am dancing without a care in the world thanks to the alcohol, and although it's a fast song, Luke pulls me close and stares into my eyes. There's something about him that makes you feel like the most important person in the world when you have his attention and it's making me feel all funny inside. Either that or it's all the booze combined with the fast movements.

The music is too loud to talk so we just dance, and after what feels like hours of shamelessly flirting through movement, Luke pulls me close and tells me he'll be right back. He gives me a kiss on the cheek and disappears into the crowd.

I decide to try to find the other boys, rather than stand here dancing on my own. I spy Ben sitting on his own, still messing around on his phone, and then I spot Eddie and Mark lining up shot glasses on the bar and filling them with something I can't quite make out. Noticing me, Eddie calls me over.

'Just in time, would the lady care for a shot?' he asks.

'Oh, I think I'll give this round a miss, boys. I'm starting to sober up.'

'Well it's only 1 a.m., so we can't have that,' Mark insists as he pushes the tiny glass into my hand.

'Why not, eh?' I never did have much willpower, which is probably why I go on to drink another three. Any chance I had of sobering up is long gone.

'Let's dance!' Mark shouts as he drags me to the dance floor. I don't want to offend him but I'd rather go look for Luke. I wonder where he's got to.

Not wanting to hurt Mark's feelings, I go along with it. Dancing with Mark is very different, he dances like a drunken maniac, although that is probably because he *is* one. He is spinning me around, dipping me – I'm feeling very sick but I have to admit that I'm having such a good time. Maybe I'm misreading the signs, but I could swear Mark is flirting with me. Some of his dance moves are a bit raunchy and his hands are all over me. If I were perfectly sober, I'd probably be worried that people could see.

There's still no sign of Luke and before I know it, Mark is dragging me to the bar for last orders where we have yet more to drink. I'm officially drunk, although not quite as drunk as Eddie, who throws his arms around me and tells me how much he loves me, licking my face before falling to the floor. At this point Luke reappears.

'All right, Nic? You look a bit tipsy, babe,' he says with a chuckle.

'Whaaat? I'm fine,' I protest, never one to admit that I'm drunk out loud.

'Well Ed certainly isn't, so we're going to get a taxi back to the bus.'

He and Ben grab one of Eddie's arms each and carry him outside. Feeling a bit unsteady on my feet, I lean against the bar.

'We'll see you outside,' he calls back.

'Don't worry, mate. I'll take good care of her,' Mark calls after him, grabbing hold of my hand as we follow them out.

Standing around waiting for the taxi, my body starts to shake. I can't really feel the cold but I must be freezing. Mark gallantly slips an arm around me and rubs my shoulders, so maybe he does have a sweet side after all.

Luke looks over at us and gives me a concerned look, is he getting jealous?

'You two look cosy,' Luke calls over.

'Poor little thing is freezing,' Mark tells him.

'Yeah, it is a bit chilly out here,' he replies, equally as cold. He gives me a strange look but then his gaze is redirected to my ear.

'Nicole, you've got an earring missing.'

I put both hands up to the sides of my head and he's right.

'Shit, it must have come out when I was dancing. Do you think they'll let me back in to look for it?' I slur as I wobble on my feet. I'm really regretting that last drink. I can't think straight and I can't walk straight. As I head towards the club, the taxi pulls up and Ben begins trying to squash Eddie inside.

'I can only take four of you,' the taxi driver calls out, noticing that there are five of us.

'Don't worry, mate,' Mark calls back. 'Luke, I'll take Nicole back in for her earring and then we'll walk back. It's not far and we're not that drunk, right, Nic?'

'Right, Mark!' I give Luke a thumbs-up – clearly not the actions of a sober girl. Luke reluctantly gets in the taxi and they drive off, leaving me drunk and alone with Mark.

'Are we going to get my earring?' I ask, actually remembering something that happened in the past ten minutes.

'Yes we are,' he says as he bends over and picks my earring up from the floor. 'Oh look, there it is. I must have been standing on it.'

My few remaining sober thoughts are telling me that maybe something is up here.

'Shall we get back to the bus then?' he asks, grabbing my hand and dragging me in what I assume is the right direction.

I don't know what time it is, but it must be after 3 a.m. as we make our way down the eerily quiet streets of Manchester.

'I think Luke reckons he's in there with you, he's probably waiting for you on the bus with his jeans around his ankles,' Mark informs me, like it's a done deal.

I laugh and shrug my shoulders. It's nothing to do with him, is it?

'We could always stay out for a bit,' he suggests.

'And go where? Everywhere is closed!'

'Not everywhere,' he says, leading me down a dark alleyway, and before I have time to take in exactly what is going on, Mark is pushing me up against the wall and kissing me hard on the lips.

As we kiss I open my eyes and take in our surroundings. This particular part of the city is practically silent and it's too dark to see anything, but I know we must be near some bins because they are all I can smell. Mark's horrible beard is rubbing against my face, making it itch, and I can feel him carelessly tugging at my clothes. At that moment an ambulance goes flying past, illuminating the alley with its bright-blue lights and making me jump with its loud siren. What the hell am I doing here? I don't fancy this guy – bloody hell, I don't even like this guy most of the time. My vodka goggles are abruptly ripped from my face and I push Mark away.

'What's the matter?' he asks breathlessly.

'We'd better get back to the bus. They're going to wonder where we are,' I insist, but he's having none of it, grabbing my hips and moving closer, squashing me against the wall.

'They won't give a shit. Come on, just relax!'

I can't relax because I really don't want to do this.

'Someone might see us,' I say, wriggling free from his grasp and making my way back towards the street.

'Nicole, come on,' he calls after me, but I keep walking and eventually he follows me. We walk the rest of the way in silence.

Finally through the bus doors safe and sound, I make my way up the stairs to the living area and realise everyone is already in their bunk – apart from Luke. He's sitting on the sofa, probably waiting for me.

'You guys took a while, is everything OK?' he asks, sounding concerned.

'Everything is great, man,' Mark tells him, giving him a wink that we all know the meaning of. Oh God, I want to curl up and die! I'm fairly sure getting it on with one of his band friends is not the way to his heart.

'Oh, right,' Luke replies. 'Well, I'm going to get to bed. Night, mate,' he says giving Mark a pat on the shoulder. And then he looks at me. His eyes look so red and tired. 'Night, Nicole,' he says, walking off towards the bunks without waiting for a reply.

'Night,' I call after him, but it's too late. I've really blown it this time. All I want to do is get in my bunk and pray that everything will be OK in the morning when we're all sober. What happened with Mark was nothing really; a few seconds of madness while I tried to figure out the safest way out of a potentially bad situation.

Mark stands up and, presuming he's going to his bunk, I stand up too. He puts his hand on my shoulder and pushes me back down.

'I'm going for a piss, don't go to sleep. I'll be back in a minute. We've got unfinished business.'

He walks off towards the toilet. Now I really do feel sick. There's isn't even a hint of sexiness in his request and I don't even want to be near him, let alone anything else. So I do what any girl would do in my situation, I fake it. I lie down on the sofa, shut my eyes and pretend to be asleep. I hear him come back and loudly whisper my name a couple of times to try to wake me, but I keep my eyes tightly closed and eventually he gives up and goes off to his bunk. Too scared to move in case he hears me, I pretend to be asleep on the uncomfortable sofa until tiredness takes over and I fall asleep for real.

Chapter 9

Oh my God, I feel terrible. I've got such a headache and I'm too scared to open my eyes properly in case the light makes it worse. The events of last night are bouncing around in my head, which is probably contributing towards my headache. How could I have been so stupid? Mark might have masterminded a pretty decent plan to get me alone, but I didn't have to go along with it. Yes, I was drunk enough to get caught up in things, but unfortunately I wasn't quite drunk enough to forget what happened. But nothing did happen really, did it? It was just a silly kiss. I kiss people all the time – although, not everyone I kiss tries to remove my underwear in the street.

I open my eyes ever so slowly and stare at the ceiling for a second, giving them chance to adjust. The bus is silent so I assume everyone else is asleep. Rolling onto my side I see that Luke is sitting on the opposite side of the sofa, in the exact same place he was last night. He's staring at me and his face is totally expressionless. I must look terrible; not only did I have such an awkward, uncomfortable night but I didn't take my make-up off and you can guarantee my post-club hair will be a frizzy mess.

'Good morning,' I say weakly.

'Hello,' he replies. 'Rough night?'

'Something like that … what time is it?'

'8 a.m. Want to go get a coffee?' he asks in an unusually blunt manner.

'Yeah, sure. I'll just smarten myself up,' I reply shyly. I really didn't want him to see me like this.

'OK. I'm going outside for a smoke, I'll see you in a minute.' And with that, he's gone.

As I slowly sit up, I take in my surroundings. The living area is just as messy as I am. Empty cans and bottles are littered all over the place, there's the odd junk food wrapper and cigarette packets scattered around and I am being overpowered by two smells – Lynx and sweat. Unfortunately the latter scent is the stronger one.

Grabbing my bag, I make my way to the tiny bus toilet. It's impossible not to feel claustrophobic in these bathrooms; there's barely enough standing room for one person. The small space consists of a toilet, a small sink and a shower head, none of which are very easy to use, even when the bus is stationary. I catch sight of myself in the dirty mirror and, just as I suspected, I have make-up all over my face and a hairstyle that would be more at home in the 80s. Thankfully my face wipes are in the bag that I actually remembered, although unfortunately I don't have a hairbrush or any clean clothes with me.

Winding my long blonde hair into a bun on the top of my head, I begin wiping off my make-up – only to start reapplying it seconds later. With my hair looking crap, I make the decision to wear even more make-up to compensate. Standing back to take in my appearance in the tiny mirror, I can only conclude that I look like a groupie. My hair is messed up, my make-up is over the top and I'm still wearing my gig outfit – or maybe I just feel like a groupie after last night.

I am distracted from my thoughts by a noise from my phone. Taking it out of my bag I realise it is the low battery alert and, guess what? I packed my charger in the bag I left at home. Now I'm feeling seriously out of my comfort zone. I'm horribly hungover, I look a complete state, I'm going to have to face both Mark and Luke today, and to top it all off, my only form of contact with the 'real world' will be cut off when my phone dies, which I'm guessing is going to be sooner rather than later.

As I leave the bathroom and make my way past the bunks, I can hear girls giggling, but I don't remember seeing any girls last night when we left the club. Maybe they found their way onto the bus while Mark and I made our detour.

As I pass Eddie's bunk, a girl climbs out and, looking at the state of her, I start to feel slightly better about the way I look this morning. She is definitely still drunk, her clothes are hanging off her and she's looking at me like I've just fallen out of a tree. She actually looks like she has just fallen out of a tree.

'Becky,' she calls, looking at me but failing to acknowledge the fact that I am standing there and that she is blocking my path. Becky sticks her head out of the bottom bunk which, as far as I remember, is Ben's bunk, but he must be in one of the spares because, as we all know, Ben has a girlfriend and he doesn't stop texting her for long enough to even talk to another girl. Becky looks equally as rough as her friend so I'm quite happy to walk off the bus after them, they can only make me look better. Neither girl speaks to me until we get to the bus door, which neither of them can work out how to open.

'How the fuck does this open?' Becky asks me politely. I don't say anything, I just reach forward and open the door. Becky and her friend fall about laughing and hop off the bus. As they walk past Luke, they both say 'Bye, Luke' in unison, laughing hysterically as they stagger off.

'Bye, girls,' he says and then turns towards me. 'They weren't with me you know.'

'No judgement from me,' I tell him, holding up my hands. I'm hardly in a position to say anything, am I? Feeling self-conscious, I let my hair down. Knots or no knots, my long hair is like my safety blanket.

'You know I care what you think,' he says, throwing the end of his cigarette to the floor and stamping it out. 'Shall we go get that coffee?'

I nod and follow his lead. I love Manchester, but with my rubbish sense of direction I find it impossible to find my way around, and it doesn't matter how many times I visit.

'Cold, isn't it?' I say in an attempt to break the silence with small talk.

'It is. You should have put something warmer on.'

I look down at my dress. Not only is it totally inappropriate for strolling around town at this time of morning, but it isn't doing much to fight off the chilly October wind. Oh, and there's a rather unattractive booze stain down the side that must have happened last night.

'I would have, but I forgot the bag with my clothes in. Don't laugh!' I warn him.

He does laugh, and it's adorable. His eyes light up when he laughs and he's got the most gorgeous smile.

'What are we going to do with you?' he sighs, putting his arm around me, and I wonder if he's doing it to keep me warm, or just to touch me.

'I'll be fine.'

'You'll freeze! Don't worry, I'm sure I've got something you can wear,' he says as he ushers me into Starbucks.

I don't think I have ever been so happy to be in Starbucks. I haven't been inside this particular branch before, but it all feels so familiar and I instantly feel more relaxed. I may have been feeling out of my comfort zone before, but this feels just like home.

We grab our drinks and take a seat on the sofa in the only dark corner of the room, something my hangover and I are very thankful for.

'So last night was a bit mad,' Luke starts. 'I'm sorry we didn't see very much of each other. Did you sleep on the sofa all night?'

'I did. I was tipsy, I must have fallen asleep there,' I lie.

'I'm sorry you had to walk back with Mark.'

What I'm thinking is that I'm sorry I had to as well, but what I say out loud is, 'Don't worry about it.'

The conversation feels forced and awkward, and it worries me that I still have to spend a few more days with these people, living in such a small space. Yes, it's a big bus, but not when you're trying to avoid people.

'Well you must have had a horrible night's sleep, but don't worry, we're booked in to a hotel tonight.'

Thank God! After one night of not sleeping in a bed I am absolutely desperate to climb into one, even if I don't get to sleep, even if it's just for a minute.

'We've got three rooms booked, that's all the hotel in Birmingham had. Management wanted to put us somewhere really nice though. They're kissing our arses because the album is doing so well.'

'Yeah, that's great. I'm missing sleeping in a proper bed already.'

'We've got three double rooms. Mick is going in with Ben, and Mark and Eddie usually share,' he tells me, waiting for a few seconds before he finishes his sentence. 'We could share if you wanted to?'

I hesitate and before I get chance to reply, Luke starts talking again.

'Unless you don't want to. I mean, I can go in with Mark and Ed, no problem.'

'No, it's fine. We can't have the celebrities squashed in the same bed,' I tease, secretly delighted.

'Good,' he replies, leaning closer to me and resting his hand gently on my leg. 'Maybe we'll finally get some time alone together,' he lowers his voice to a whisper. 'I can't wait to get you on your own.'

I smile and sip my coffee. So I haven't scared him off after all. There's nothing like a bit of jealousy to keep them keen.

Chapter 10

Back at the bus, I wait patiently as Luke searches around in the luggage compartment for something warm for me to wear. The dress I am currently wearing was perfect for keeping cool at the venue last night, but in the harsh light of day the alcohol stain stands out a mile and my pretty dress does not go with the big, clumsy Uggs I am stuck wearing – but hey, at least my feet are warm.

'No clean clothes,' Luke calls out, still waist-deep in the luggage compartment. 'Unless you want something that stinks of sweat.'

I laugh, although to be honest I'm a bit distracted staring at his bum.

'Don't worry, I'll be fine,' I eventually call back.

'There is this though,' he says, holding up the biggest Two For The Road T-shirt I have ever seen.

'We've sold a lot of merchandise this tour, which is lucky for us. Sucks for you though, only XXL T-shirts left – but it's got to be warmer than what you're wearing now, right? It will certainly cover more skin … unfortunately,' he adds with a wink.

Taking the huge T-shirt from him, I hold it up against my body; you could fit at least two of me in this, but I think I can make it work. Sadly I don't think I can do anything about the fact that it is bright orange, though.

'This will be perfect, don't worry.'

I head into the living area. No one is around, so I can get changed here if I'm fast. Mark and Eddie have gone to get something to eat and, as far as I know, Ben is still sleeping. I check that I am totally alone one last time before slipping off my beautiful dress and slipping on my huge, bright-orange replacement. I can't imagine anyone wanting to wear one of these T-shirts, even if they are a fan of the band. Bright orange? Seriously?

As I predicted, I look like I am wearing a tent, but I'm not finished yet. If there's one thing I learned during my short stint at Brownies (I thought I was way too edgy to cook, sew and collect things that I found on the floor in the park), it's that you should always carry safety pins in your bag. Pulling all the extra fabric from both sides, I pin them together in line with the small of my back before rolling up the sleeves a little. My huge orange T-shirt now looks a bit more like a dress. A bright-orange, TFTR-branded dress that thankfully doesn't really clash too much with my boots. To be honest, my gold accessories set it off quite nicely. I don't look too shocking and I'm definitely warmer.

Stepping off the bus, I see Mark, Luke and Eddie smoking, and they look very amused by my outfit – probably because it's free advertising for them.

'Wilde, what did you do to it?' Luke asks, astonished. 'It actually suits you!'

'That's the thing with our Nicole, she can make anything look amazing, can't you, babe?' Eddie says, taking a final drag on his cigarette and flicking it across the car park.

'You're too kind, boys,' I say, embarrassed but flattered to hear Eddie refer to me as theirs.

I look over at Mark, who is leaning against the bus. He hasn't spoken to me today and I don't think he's going to either.

'We'd better get a move on,' Eddie says, jumping aboard the bus way too energetically for someone who drank so much last night. 'Luke, get that lazy bastard Ben up, will you?'

'I'm on it!' he replies, giving Eddie a playful smack on the bum as he follows him up the stairs.

It's just me and Mark now. Awkward. If he's not going to say anything, then I guess I'd better try.

'How are you today?' I ask with a smile.

'Fine, cheers,' he replies without even looking up.

'Good,' I say undefeated. 'Not many dates left now, I bet you'll miss it when it's over.'

'Yeah, probably.'

This is impossible. I was hoping that last night he was either too drunk to remember, or at least too drunk to care, but I'm guessing he isn't my biggest fan right now.

'I'll see you on the bus, yeah?' I ask, but I don't expect him to reply, and he doesn't. Then, the second my foot touches the first step, he calls after me.

'I hear you're sharing a room with Luke tonight. There's a shocker,' he says with an extra helping of sarcasm, just in case I wasn't picking up the vibes.

It's my turn to do the ignoring. I could kick off, but where would that get me? He's 'the talent' and I'd be off this bus in a flash if I got in his face. Anyway, I'm not going to let him ruin tonight for me. So what if I'm sharing a room with Luke? It's nothing to do with him.

Back on the bus, I make my way to the living area. The guys already have a film on so I take a seat next to Eddie. Mark isn't far behind, and he sits down opposite me. I'm so not looking forward to the drive to Birmingham, all squashed up together in this small space.

'So, Nicole, this feature you're writing on our tour, anything interesting to report yet?' Eddie asks me, and I wonder if Mark told him anything when they were alone together this morning.

'Plenty,' I tease. 'You're going to wish you hadn't invited me.'

'Don't pull any punches,' he replies. 'What you looking so

worried about, Boy Wonder?' he adds, looking over at Ben. Ben is so quiet and, surprise, surprise, he's already texting away on his phone.

'Oi, I'm talking to you. Had fun last night, didn't you?' Eddie shouts at Ben – who looks embarrassed as hell right now – in a borderline aggressive manner.

That reminds me, I'm here to write a feature and not to groupie my way through the whole band.

Apart from the noise coming from the TV, and the odd text alert from Ben's phone, the bus is so quiet. The roadies have their own transport and do their own thing, and Mick, the band's tour manager, is also their driver, so it's just me and the boys here – and everyone is too tired or too hungover to chat.

Eddie yawns, stretching out his arms and wrapping one around me. As he does this, Mark sniggers and shoots me a filthy look. I'm finding it hard not to look at him because he's sitting opposite me. I take my phone from my bag and I only get to tap a few buttons before it shuts off. Bloody smartphones and their rubbish battery life. I'll just close my eyes for a bit, anything that means I don't have to look at Mark.

Awkwardness aside, I'm really looking forward to tonight. Sleeping in a nice hotel is always better than sleeping on the bus and it will be much easier to avoid Mark too. Why does drama follow me around wherever I go? I still can't get my head around what happened last night. We've never really been that close, not like I am with Ed and Luke, but he was hell-bent on getting close last night. One thing I do know for sure though, this won't be mentioned in the magazine.

I wish I could text Emily. I'll bet she's sitting at my desk with her feet up. I left her in charge and under strict instructions to call me if anything eventful happened. Obviously she can't do that now that my battery has died, but I'm sure she'll be fine. I hope Vicky isn't taking the piss – I still can't believe she's staying at Em's house. Not only is she taking advantage of her good nature, but she's making it impossible for us to chat like we usually do because she is always around.

How long does it take to get to Birmingham, seriously? This is the longest journey of my life. My head is resting on Eddie's chest and I realise I must have dozed off for a bit. I have no idea for how long, but we're still not there yet. Mark and Luke are playing a video game, Ben is still texting and Eddie is asleep. The living area looks a little tidier, which means someone must have been really bored.

Mess aside, I adore tour buses. Try to imagine a really glamorous caravan. This isn't the biggest one I've been on, but it has bunks for eight people so it's still pretty massive. The living area is amazing; you can't really tell that you're on a bus. There's a big table surrounded by sofas and blacked-out windows and a massive flat-screen TV on the wall with various games consoles connected to it. The kitchen has everything you could need – I imagine, you know I'm not a very kitchen-y person. There's a kettle, fridge, microwave and even an ice-maker. Just down the aisle is where the bunks are, four on each side. They're not the comfiest beds in the world, but they're certainly not the worst. I could so easily live on one of these buses – as long as I had more clothes with me, of course.

I'm still feeling tired and Eddie is so comfy to cuddle up to – despite the rock-hard muscles in his chest – maybe I'll just fall back asleep until we get there.

Chapter 11

The sun is shining brightly in Birmingham today, it's a shame it is so damn cold. As a result of waking up on the sofa yet again today, my back is killing me.

I don't know where everyone is. Eddie is asleep next to me, although with me leaning on him I doubt he could move even if he wanted to, and Mark is still sitting in the same place, glaring at me again. I wonder if he's moved at all.

Thank God, we are finally here. I don't know my way around Birmingham (don't act like you're surprised) but I'd really like to get to a decent clothes shop and get something to wear. The novelty is starting to wear off my bright orange dress.

'All right, Mark?' I ask brightly, giving him another chance to put what happened behind us.

'Yeah, fine. Worming your way in with Eddie now, are you?'

'She's been in with me for a long time, you grumpy fucker,' Eddie says sounding half asleep, his eyes still closed.

'I'm going for a shower,' Mark informs us, storming off.

'What's his problem?' Eddie asks me as soon as Mark has gone. 'You knock him back last night or something?'

'Not exactly,' I reply, hoping that will be the end of it.

'No way!' he says excitedly, sitting up straight and suddenly wide awake. 'You knocked him back? Tell me everything!'

'It's nothing really.'

'I'm going to get you so drunk tonight, you are going to tell me everything,' he laughs.

'Yeah right, *you're* going to be less drunk than me? Remind me, who had to be carried to the taxi last night?'

'Don't put that in your magazine,' he laughs. 'The chicks won't go for that.'

'It was only today you told me that I could write about anything,' I remind him.

'Yeah, anything but that. Write about how you knocked Mark back though.'

He's clearly finding this hilarious and I have to admit he's cheering me up.

'Oi, stop saying that!' I nudge him in the ribs. As funny as it is, I don't want anyone to hear – especially Luke.

'Anyway, I'm beginning to think it's the other guys who can't handle their drink,' Eddie tells me.

'And why is that?' I ask. This should be good.

'Because when Luke and Ben carried me to the taxi last night, they dropped me twice,' he jokes. 'And as for Mark, he had to be smashed if he thought he had a chance with you.'

The minute the tour bus pulled up outside the venue, the plan was for me to go pick up something to wear tonight. I'd hoped we'd be in the city centre but I've been told that we're nowhere near a clothes shop of any description. I had a little wander down the road but, not wanting to get lost, I had to admit defeat. I am just going to have to come to terms with the fact that this is the outfit I will be wearing to the show tonight. I'm either going to look like a crazy fan or a groupie who has lost her clothes in the throes of passion, and I'm not sure which is worse. This is also the outfit I am going to be wearing if I try to seduce Luke – a hideous orange T-shirt, branded with the name of his band. If he's vain enough, that will probably do the trick. Eddie keeps making dirty comments about how he's always wanted to get it on with someone wearing his band's merchandise. I think he's joking but you never know with Eddie. Some poor woman will probably be dressing up in the works for him tonight.

We are ushered from the bus, into the venue and straight to the backstage room, and what a dump it is. The dressing room is small, with no windows, bare walls and a bare floor. Walking over to the table where the food is laid out, I grab a can of Coke and a bag of salt and vinegar crisps and plonk myself down on one of the battered old sofas, trying to ignore the suspicious stains on the cushions.

The boys are fussing around and getting changed, apart from Eddie who is studying the food carefully. He's upset because apparently there are things that were on the rider that are not on the table, and he's shouting at Mick to do something about it. It doesn't matter that the table is covered with food and drink, what Eddie wants Eddie gets. Some poor venue worker is sent out to get the missing items. Maybe things would change if I were famous, but I can't imagine kicking off because someone forgot to buy me some ketchup.

When it is finally my turn to have a shower, I make it snappy before slipping my T-shirt back on. Now that I'm hanging around the backstage area, I have to have my Access All Areas pass on show, which leaves me no choice but to wear it around my neck. There's no doubt about it, I look like a total nerd.

All alone backstage, I examine the table of food again. I didn't eat much yesterday and I've decided that was the reason I got so drunk last night (although it probably had more to do with the fact that I just drank way too much). I make myself a sandwich and, suddenly starving, I take an over-enthusiastic bite. Just my luck, Luke walks back into the room as I'm struggling to chew a huge mouthful of food. I have managed to make myself look like an even bigger loser, but at least I'm making him smile.

'Bitten off more than you can chew?' he asks.

He doesn't know the half of it. He waits patiently for a reply.

'Done,' I say victoriously, putting the rest of the sandwich to one side because suddenly I'm not that hungry any more.

'Well check out that super-cool laminated pass hanging around your neck. Are you with the band?' he asks. He is obviously not done teasing me just yet.

Now is my chance. Toying with my lanyard, I give him my sexiest look, but as I take a step towards him I catch my foot on a guitar lead and fall into him, face first. Luckily, he catches me and doesn't let go.

'Easy, tiger,' he says with a laugh, before leaning in closer and whispering into my ear. 'At least wait until I've got you in my room.'

With his face still just inches from mine, Luke starts gently kissing my neck and it's lucky that he's still holding me because my legs instantly turn to jelly. Next thing I know, we're kissing. I don't want to sound all lame and high school again, but this is our first proper kiss and all that's missing is the firework display. As he pushes me back onto the tatty old sofa, I wrap my legs around his waist. Just as our kisses get heavier, I faintly hear the door open and things come to a sudden stop. I smile and try to look innocent, something that I have perfected over the years to get myself out of tricky situations. With that said, even the most innocent of innocent looks couldn't make this situation look like anything other than what it is because my legs are still wrapped tightly around Luke's waist and locked at the ankle. If it's anyone other than Mark then I might be able to live this one down. I dare myself to look towards the door and, of course, it's Mark. He glares at me before wandering over to fridge.

'Not interrupting anything, I hope,' he says, grabbing a can of something and plonking himself down next to us.

'Actually, mate ...' Luke begins, but Mark doesn't let him finish.

'Good, because I need something to eat and Eddie needs *you* on the stage. Now.'

Luke looks at me and gives me that cheeky smile I love so

much. He plants a peck on my lips and manages to free himself from my grasp, pulling up and fastening his jeans as he leaves the room – I didn't even realise he'd undone them, what moves he has! It's just me and Mark now, and as long as he doesn't speak to me then I'll happily keep out of his way.

'I knew you were a groupie, but fucking hell. You could at least wait twenty-four hours between shagging each band member,' he snaps at me.

I like to think I'm a pretty chilled lady, a lover not a fighter and all that, but I can't keep my temper under control any longer and I snap back.

'Excuse me?' I ask, standing up and trying to subtly pull my dress back down over my lower half. 'First of all, I haven't shagged anyone,' I yell. 'And second of all, I was very drunk last night, and you knew that, and I didn't want to kiss you, and you knew that too. OK, I might have kissed you back for a second but, as drunk as I was, I still came to my senses. Get the fuck over it!'

It's amazing how a little bit of anger brings out my inner northerner.

Mark looks gobsmacked. Friend or not, I probably shouldn't upset the celebrities, but how dare he call me a groupie? If I had shagged him down that alley, he probably wouldn't be calling me any names.

'Do what you want, write what you want, shag who you want!' he shouts, leaving the room and slamming the door behind him.

There are hundreds of girls queuing up outside the venue right now and, despite being a total arsehole in need of a good wash and a shave, he could probably have his pick of any of them. Why waste his time getting angry at me?

My eyes start to feel heavy and a huge tear falls from my right eye, rolling down my face and stripping my skin of every ounce of make-up that dares to stand in its path. I wipe it quickly and grab my foundation from my bag. I can't let anyone see me crying.

I should be buzzing after kissing Luke. Instead, I am sitting in a backstage room, all on my own, sobbing because some C-list bassist just called me a slapper.

As I smarten myself up and retouch my make-up, I take yet another long, hard look in the mirror. Tonight is going to be a long night.

Chapter 12

After an awesome performance (including an encore), I am clapping and screaming just as much as any other fan in the room – maybe more so.

'Are you their mascot?' a handsome older man asks me, nodding in the direction of the hideous orange dress I forgot I was wearing.

'Not exactly,' I tell him with a giggle. 'It's a funny story really.'

'I hope you're going to tell me it.'

'To summarise …' I take a deep breath. 'I am touring with the band, to write a magazine feature, but I forgot my bag and I spilt a drink on my dress, so Luke, the drummer, was kind enough to give me *this* to wear.'

'Wow, he must hate you!' the stranger says, insulting my dress.

'I know, right? What a bastard!'

He laughs.

'You said you're writing a feature on the band? I'm here to write a review for the local paper,' he informs me.

'Oops! Did I say he was a bastard? Because what I mean to say is, what a wonderful band this is, and how you should definitely give them a good review!'

'Don't worry, I'm impressed. My name is Kenny by the way.'

'Nice to meet you, Kenny.' I shake his hand, 'I'm Nicole.'

'It's nice to meet you too. Can I buy you a drink? We can swap notes.'

The band have only just finished and I know I'm going to be on my own while they do promo and meet fans, so I agree and we take a seat at the bar. Kenny seems like a nice guy and he's a music reviewer for the local press so I'm sure I can learn a thing or two from him.

'I think your friend is worried about you,' Kenny tells me, gesturing towards Luke with a swift movement of his eyes.

I glance over and he's right, Luke is giving us a filthy look.

'He needn't be worried, I'm more interested in him than I am in you, darling,' he says with a wink.

Poor Luke, if only he knew.

'I'll put in a good word for you,' I tell Kenny, winking right back at him.

'Don't worry about it, I think he's got his eye on someone else in this room and I think we both know who that is.'

I smile, but then something catches my eye.

'Excuse me for a moment,' I say, making my way over to the band.

The guys are surrounded by fans, but there's this one girl who caught my eye because she is wearing the same orange T-shirt as me.

I tap her on the shoulder. 'Don't you just hate it when someone wears the same outfit as you?'

'It looks better on you,' she replies with an unconvincing smile.

'Are you trying to meet the band?' I ask.

'Trying.' She holds up a poster. 'I wanted them to sign this but it's like I'm invisible.'

'I'm a friend of theirs, I'll get them to sign it.'

Taking the poster and marker pen, I start with Luke.

'Can you sign this for that lovely girl over there?' I ask him.

'Sure. Who's that guy you're with?'

'A journalist, so be nice,' I warn him.

Ben signs the poster next, and thankfully he gets Mark to sign it too. If I'd asked, he probably would have told me to piss off. Now all I need is Eddie, who is surrounded, and groupies are his favourite thing so it's going to be tough getting his attention. I push my way through a girl gang and hook my arm around Eddie's. You've got to get territorial and show them who is boss, it's the only way a girl can survive in this environment.

'Eddie, could you sign this for my friend please?'

'Anything for you, Miss Wilde,' he says, taking the pen and signing over his face on the poster. 'Give me a kiss,' he says before puckering up, and I'm not sure who he's showing off for but I'm happy to help.

'No way, I know where that mouth has been,' I tease as I reach for the poster, but he holds it out of my reach and makes kissy noises at me.

I peck him on the lips and give the girls a friendly smile before taking the poster and making my way back towards my new friend.

'Ta-da,' I say, handing her the poster along with a plectrum, a wristband and some stickers. 'And here's a few bits from the merch stand too.'

Bless her, she looks so happy. It really bugs me that Eddie only gives attention to the women he fancies. It's girls like this who pay his wages, not the ones who are only here to try to sleep with him.

I head back over to the bar where Kenny is sitting.

'I saw what you did. You're a real sweetheart, aren't you, Nicole?'

'Oh, I do try,' I say with a laugh, just as Luke appears.

I introduce them and Luke shakes Kenny's hand. I'm surprised he isn't doing more to soften up the guy who will be reviewing him for the entire city of Birmingham to read.

Luke tells me that they've got to head back to the hotel for an interview, which I'm guessing is my cue to say goodbye to my new best friend and go with them.

'Kenny, do you want to come and have a drink in the hotel bar?' I ask. 'I want to hear more of your stories, and if these guys are doing an interview I'll only have to sit and watch.'

'I'd love to,' Kenny replies, clearly annoying Luke by doing so.

'Right, well we're going now, so if you're coming get a move on,' Luke tells us, so we knock back the remainder of our drinks and follow his lead.

Chapter 13

The hotel we are staying in is absolutely gorgeous. I couldn't ever afford to stay in a place like this on my own, but that's the beauty of being a hanger-on; someone else always foots the bill. I know that I'm lucky to stay in such beautiful places, which is probably why I don't take any of it for granted, unlike most of the bands I know.

Tonight we're staying at the Hotel Regale. I've only just stepped through the door and I'm already in love with the place. Inside the lobby they have replaced one of the walls with a huge fish tank, which is absolutely mesmerising – even to an entirely sober person, I'd imagine. On the other side of the tank is the bar, which is where Kenny and I are heading. There's no point in me going up to the room and hanging around in the background while they do their interview, I may as well be down here sucking Dutch courage through a sparkly straw.

As soon as they're done, Luke is going to call Reception and have someone let me know I can go up. I'm suddenly really nervous again, but trying to keep it out of my mind while I'm chatting to Kenny.

It isn't long before a nice lady lets me know that 'Mr Fox' is waiting for me. It sounds so weird to hear Luke being referred to as Mr Fox, like he's a proper adult.

I say goodbye to my new friend and we swap details before I make my way to the lift. I hang back for a few minutes, spotting Mick the tour manager getting in the lift with a gang of giggly girls. No prizes what, or should I say who, Eddie is doing tonight. I'm so glad I'm in with Luke because I am *so* not in the mood for a party with giggly fan-girls – and I'm allowed to say that because I used to be one; I know how annoying we are.

The nerves finally hit me as I step out of the lift. Luke is standing outside the door waiting for me, and he must have had quite a bit to drink while they were doing their interview because he is wasted.

'Shall we go in?' he asks, fiddling with the keycard for the room. For some reason he can't get the door to open.

'Do you want me to do that?' I ask.

'I can do it,' he snaps.

I thought maybe he was just nervous too, but he looks terrible. His eyes are red and watery, and between attempts to get the door open he is rubbing his nose. If we were in the 'real world', I'd probably think he was coming down with a cold, but we're not in the 'real world', are we?

In a way, I am proud of myself; I've always been very anti-drugs and there's a huge amount of temptation in the biz. Well, I've never been tempted. Sadly, it looks like Luke has. I know a lot of bands are close friends of Mary Joanna (say it quickly), but I'm guessing Luke is on something much harder. So the rumours are true.

Finally he gets the door open, laughing as he falls through the doorway, only just managing to stay upright. Kicking the door shut, Luke puts his hands on the wall either side of me. I can't move and I'm being forced to look into his eyes. I'd imagined this moment being intense, but this just feels all wrong. Not only that, but he looks a mess – sexy doesn't spring to mind at all.

He starts kissing me but it doesn't feel like it did earlier. Earlier was great, this is awful. I feel uncomfortable and his constant sniffling is making me feel kind of sick, so I pull away.

'Everything OK?' asks the snotty-nosed man of my dreams.

'Are *you* OK?' I ask.

'I'm fine, let's just get on with it,' he insists, sounding slightly annoyed that I stopped him.

'Get on with it? You smooth-talker.'

He ignores my sarcasm and starts kissing me again, pushing me onto the bed. This is what I wanted, right? Perhaps it will get better again – like it was earlier. After five minutes of awkward – and to be honest, slightly snotty – kisses, he rolls off me and sits on the edge of the bed, facing away from me. He seems frustrated and he's swearing under his breath, banging his hands on the bed like some kind of madman.

'Fuck!' he shouts to himself. To be honest, I'm a little bit scared.

'I'll be right back, just going to the bathroom,' I tell him. I don't wait for a reply before heading into the huge bathroom and locking the door behind me. I close the lid on the toilet and sit down. The bath looks so inviting, I'd love to have a long soak with lots of bubbles, pull on one of the fluffy bath robes, eat room service, watch TV and then fall asleep in the big, comfy bed – rock and roll. With a wasted Luke waiting for me in the big, comfy bed, I can forget about relaxing tonight though, and even though I would rather sit here until morning, I know that I have to go back out there. I'm not sure what has happened to the man I was pretty much in love with, but that isn't him sitting in there waiting for me, and that definitely wasn't him throwing me around the room before. It's only a matter of hours since we kissed in the dressing room, but now it's like that perfect kiss never happened. His mood is all over the place: one minute he is the life of the party, the next he's losing his temper.

I check the time and realise I have been sitting in here for twenty minutes now. It's time to face the music or, in this case, the musician.

It turns out I have nothing to worry about. Luke is fast asleep, the wrong way across the bed, with his jeans and his boxers around his ankles. His mouth is wide open and even though his eyes are closed, they still look so sore. I don't think I've ever seen him look so unattractive. A lesser woman than me would take a photograph. Who am I kidding? If my phone battery wasn't flat I'd probably snap a quick one, if only to remind myself that I never slept with a coke-head. That has to be the reason he's acting like this, it makes too much sense not to be.

I can see his chest moving so at least I know he's breathing, but I still don't fancy sleeping in here with him. I grab the spare keycard for the room next door. I might as well head to the party, drink this out of my mind and try to get some sleep in there.

Opening the door to Eddie and Mark's room (with ease, because *I'm* not high), I realise there isn't a party going on because all is quiet. This room is much bigger than ours, and thinking I hear someone in the bedroom I walk though, only to be greeted by Ben's bare arse and a rather embarrassed-looking girl underneath him. From the way he described his girlfriend to me earlier, I can safely say this isn't her.

With no idea where anyone else is, I head back to the bar, plonk myself on a sofa and gaze at the fish. Maybe Eddie and Mark will appear, maybe Ben's female friend will leave and I can go back up, or maybe Luke will come looking for me.

The past couple of days have been so weird. I thought these guys were my friends – I've known them for years, I've got drunk with them a million times before, I've crashed on the bus and in hotels with them countless times – but these past few days I've seen another side to them. Their true colours or the side effects of fame? I just don't know. Eddie, the one who I expect the least of based on past experiences, is the only one who has pleasantly surprised me, or at the least remained consistent.

I thought this was going to be the best tour ever and I thought things were going to work out great between me and Luke, but after several bad experiences with boys in bands you'd think I'd know better by now. I guess I just thought things were going to be different this time.

I don't know how I'm going to face them all tomorrow. After this business with Luke, my argument with Mark and catching Ben in the act, I'll be avoiding everyone apart from Eddie. To be honest, all I care about right now is finding someone I know, getting to bed and getting some sleep. I'll just wait here and hopefully someone will come looking for me.

Chapter 14

Another day, another night sleeping on another uncomfortable sofa – Nicole Wilde, this is your life.

This morning I woke up on the sofa in the hotel bar. I slept there all night. I'm lucky a member of staff didn't wake me up and ask me to move, because I really don't know where I would have gone.

It's 9 a.m. now. I've just been in the toilets freshening up and before I have chance to worry about what to do next, I spot Mick at the reception desk – he looks stressed out.

'Everything OK, Mick?' I ask.

'Nicole, I wondered where you'd got to. Everything is not OK – one minute.'

He's on the phone, saying something about a hospital and cancelling the rest of the tour. All kinds of thoughts are running through my head. Was Luke definitely OK when I left him last night? I was sure he was breathing when I left him, but I'll never forgive myself if something happened to him after I left. I wait patiently for Mick to finish on the phone and tell me what's going on.

'Right,' he composes himself, exhaling heavily and running a hand over his bald head. 'There was a bit of an accident last night.' He stops again, this time to punch something into his phone. 'At some point, while I was fast asleep might I add, a couple of the boys took the party to the hotel pool.'

I feel momentarily relieved because Luke hasn't choked to death on his vomit, but *someone* has had an accident …

'Eddie was pissing around on the diving board, he tried to jump in and hit his leg on the side of the pool. He's at the hospital now; they say his leg is broken. We might have to cancel the rest of the tour. They're giving him some pain relief and putting a temporary cast on, and then we're heading back to London so he can see a doctor there. Are you coming back with us?'

'Don't worry, Mick. I think I'll head home.'

This is a blessing in disguise. I can go home without having to face Ben, Mark or Luke. I feel slightly guilty for being so happy when poor Eddie is in the hospital with a broken leg, but it's best for everyone if I just leave.

'Could you let me on the bus, please?' I ask Mick as I try to look at least a little bit disappointed. 'I just need to get a few things.'

'I've got a few more calls to make,' Mick tells me, then he spots Mark walking across the lobby.

'Oi,' he calls to him. 'Mark? Let Nicole on the bus to get her stuff, mate.'

'Sure,' Mark replies as Mick tosses him the keys.

I follow him reluctantly.

'It's just down the road,' he tells me. I wasn't expecting him to talk to me at all.

'Were you with Ed when he fell?' I ask.

'Yeah, I was. He was off his fucking head. That's him and Luke, always taking it too far.'

Don't I know it. If Eddie was half as wasted as Luke, then it's no wonder he had an accident.

'I'm sorry for calling you a slut,' Mark tells me as we approach the bus.

'Actually, you called me a groupie,' I correct him without thinking, and I instantly regret it.

'Whatever,' he laughs. 'You are neither of those things and no one has the right to call you either of them, remember that.'

I smile at him and he sighs.

'I liked you, and I thought you liked me, but then I realised you liked Luke. You do like Luke, don't you?'

'Sort of,' I reply sheepishly. I thought I did until last night.

'I shouldn't talk this way about my bandmates – my friends,' he corrects himself, 'but Luke is bad news, Eddie too. Anything they come into contact with they'll either shag or snort. You're a nice girl, maybe a bit naive and easily led, but nice all the same.'

He unlocks the bus door and gestures for me to get on first. As I collect up my things from the living area, he carries on talking.

'It's not my job to warn you off these guys, and yeah, they're my friends, but so are you and I don't want to see them mess you around. I only snapped at you because I was jealous. Will you forgive me?'

'Of course I will,' I tell him, and he offers me a hug which I accept. 'I'm sorry for shouting at you too.'

'Forget about it, I'm just glad we're still friends. Just tell me that I wasn't a bad kisser.'

'You weren't a bad kisser.' I smile at him. He actually was kind of a bad kisser, but that's probably not the best thing to say out loud right now.

'So are you heading for the train station?' he asks.

'Yeah. Wasn't expecting to have to do this today.'

'Do you want me to walk you there?'

'Don't worry, I'm sure I'll find it. You go help Mick, he's so stressed out. Give Eddie my love, won't you? Tell him I'm putting this in the magazine.'

'Oh I'll tell him, don't you worry about that.'

We laugh. I am so glad that we are on good terms again. We say our goodbyes and he gives me a kiss on the cheek. My next impossible task is to wander through Birmingham, trying to find the damn train station.

Chapter 15

Oh, Leeds, how I've missed you. My train journey back from Birmingham was absolute hell. I just couldn't stop thinking about the past couple of days and when I wasn't obsessing over every little detail, I was falling asleep, all under the watchful gaze of an elderly lady who clearly couldn't wrap her head around my dress.

Speaking of my dress, I'm going to drop by the office and show the gang – because I know it will give Emily a laugh and provide Jake plenty of piss-taking material for the foreseeable future – and then it's home to bed for some much-needed sleep.

Armed with the coffees I picked up at the station, I bumbarge my way through the ByteBanter doors with my usual baby elephant-like elegance. ET pokes his head out of his office door.

'Wilde, I thought you were on the road?'

'I was. I'm back!' I say cheerily, holding my arms out in a 'voila' kind of way. I'm glad to be home and it's really showing.

This explanation obviously satisfies my boss, who has vanished as fast as he appeared, so I trot on to my office.

'What's up, darlings?' I yell as I enter the room.

'Are you high?' Jake replies without missing a beat.

'High on life, Jake. High on life.'

'And wearing orange,' Vicky chimes in.

'Yep, you know me and secondary colours,' I say, still with a huge smile. 'Love them!'

At this point Emily walks out of my office with a very worried look on her face.

'Oh God, what's happened?' I ask.

Jake's face has fallen too but Vicky is still smiling, so I know it must be bad news.

'What are you doing here?' Emily asks me.

'Eddie broke his leg. What's happened?'

'We've been trying to call you, why was your phone off?'

'I forgot my charger, tell me what's happened!'

'Did you know about Dylan?' Emily asks me.

'What about him?'

'About him getting some random girl pregnant!' she squeals, holding up today's paper as evidence. The headline reads 'You must be joKING: Dylan to be a dad' – very pun-ny, I have to admit.

'He sprang it on me the day before I left for the tour,' I admit. 'He made me promise not to tell anyone until I'd spoken to his new publicist.'

'Well his new publicist guy has been trying to call you – non-stop,' Emily informs me, handing me a scrap of paper with 'Charles Pace' written on it, followed by his number.

'Is that all? I can call him, explain I was away. It'll be OK, Em.'

'That's not all,' Vicky says, raising her hand.

'Put your hand down,' I snap before turning to Emily. 'What's happened?'

Emily places a hand on my shoulder. 'You've been mentioned on Scott Hale's website.'

I laugh.

'I have? I'm a nobody, why would he bother?'

Scott Hale is one of those celebrity bloggers. Basically he's a loser with a computer and a few friends in decent places. Half of the things he posts on his website are completely fictional, but everything he posts is completely horrible. There are never any happy stories, it's all 'this person has a shoplifting problem, this person is on drugs, this person had a threesome'.

Vicky happily loads up the website for me, clearly basking in my misery. I lean over her and read the blog in question.

'What? That didn't happen!' I exclaim.

Scott and I have never interacted in any way, shape or form, but this blog is clearly a personal attack on me.

His blog, which went online last night, explains how I went on tour with TFTR. It then goes on to explain how, by the end of the first night, I had slept with no less than three members of the band. Oddly, my first reaction is to consider which three members he is referring to. My second is to work out which three members I would pick, in order.

I am snapped from my inappropriately timed thoughts by Vicky, who reads key parts of the blog, titled 'Nicole Wilde has Three On The Road', out loud.

'Claiming to be there for journalistic purposes, Nicole Wilde of *Starstruck* is currently on tour with Two For The Road. One of my spies at their Manchester gig claimed they saw Nicole getting up close and personal with THREE different members of the band.' She stops reading, and starts summarising. 'It says you had one in the toilets, one around the back of a night club and one on the tour bus. Is it true?'

'Of course it isn't true, Vicky!' I snap. She reads the last line to me to well and truly twist the knife.

'Why pretend you're there to work, Nicole? It's clear enough to us that you were only there for one reason only ... or would that be three reasons?'

I stare at the screen for a moment. TFTR *are* getting quite famous, but this just feels so personal. I mean, my name is in the headline! And while there are bursts of almost truth in there, it can only be a coincidence because, despite a couple of awkward kisses, I didn't 'have' any of them anywhere.

'I have to get him to take this down!' I insist. 'Is there a contact address on there?'

Vicky gives me the email address so I take a seat at Emily's computer and start typing.

'Dear Scott,' I say what I am typing out loud for everyone to hear. 'I'm not sure who gave you the information about my time on tour with Two For The Road, but I can assure you that none of it is true. I would appreciate it if you removed the post from your site immediately. Thanks, Nicole Wilde.' I hit send.

'Why did you say you were home early?' Emily asks, and I tell her the story of Eddie breaking his leg. I don't mention everything that happened, I'll save that for later. I am almost finished telling her my story when the computer makes a noise.

'It's a reply from Scott,' I tell the room as I click open. 'Oh, you little fucker!'

'What has he said?' Jake asks.

I read out loud. 'Dear Nicole, I have it on very good authority that events happened exactly as reported on my website—'

'Blog,' Jake interrupts.

I continue to read. 'My spies don't lie, Miss Wilde. The blog stays up. Scott.'

'What the hell?' Emily shouts in disgust.

'He really is a little fucker,' Vicky tells me, and it totally throws me to have her on my side. 'Send him another email telling him what a little fucker he really is.'

She is right for once. I can't just sit back and let him publish lies about me.

'She should do it, shouldn't she, Emily?' Vicky asks her, and Emily nods.

'I don't think he's gonna take it down, Nic.'

'Exactly!' Vicky continues. 'He probably thinks you're a pushover. Show him that you're not, and then he might take it down.'

I regret doing it the second I hit the send button, but I do as my girls suggest and send Scott Hale a shitty email. I don't feel better for sending it, and he doesn't reply in the time it takes me to finish my coffee and have Emily fill me in on what's been going on over the past couple of days.

Heading into my own office, I shut the door behind me. I'm determined not to cry, but I don't want Vicky to see me just in case I do. I'm feeling a little delicate after the past couple of days and the last thing I need is another person making me out to be a groupie.

My parents moved to France not long after I started working here. I don't get to see them very often and I know my mum keeps an eye on my work – she is forever Googling my name to see what comes up – and I will be absolutely mortified if she reads Scott's blog about me.

Rummaging around in my desk drawer, I find my spare charger and juice up my trusty yet battered phone.

It starts bleeping like crazy with missed calls, messages, emails and notifications for all my socials – aren't I the popular one? That reminds me, I need to call Dylan's new publicist. What was his name again? I glance at the scrap of paper on my desk. Charles Pace. It's a mobile number, so at least I'll get straight through to him.

'Charles Pace,' a rather serious-sounding man's voice says after several rings.

'Hello, Charles, it's Nicole Wilde. You've been trying to get in touch?'

'Hello, Miss Wilde.' He relaxes slightly. 'Yes, I'm Charles. Dylan King has hired me to take care of his extra press.'

'Extra press? Is that what we're calling her?' I laugh. He ignores my joke.

'While I'm sure Dylan has plenty of faith in my ability, he doesn't entirely trust me yet. He gave me your number because he'd like you to give me your opinion on my ideas. He has instructed me to do whatever I see fit, providing it's approved by you. A rather unusual request, but he's paying my wages.' It's his turn to crack a joke, and I laugh politely because that's what you do.

'Unfortunately I couldn't get in touch with you before we ran the article in the *Daily Scoop*, but we had to go ahead because Miss Slater wanted to announce the engagement as soon as possible. Magazine deals to sort out and so on.'

'Sorry, you've lost me. Miss Slater?'

'Crystal Slater,' Charles replies. 'Dylan's fiancée.'

'He's marrying her?' I squeal, totally horrified. The idea of Dylan getting married is shocking enough, but to a woman he accidentally knocked up! A woman he has only known for a few days! I'm just so shocked!

'I'm sorry, Miss Wilde. I assumed you knew.'

Well, that explains all the missed calls from Dylan.

'When are they getting married?' I ask.

'Next week.'

'You're shitting me!'

'I think he's trying to do the right thing,' Charles offers up. It sounds kind of like he's trying to make me feel better. 'Good for him, I suppose.'

'He's crazy! I think he's making a huge mistake!' I insist. Charles doesn't say anything in response to this, but I suppose he's working for Dylan, so it's not his place.

'Did you say magazine deal?' I ask.

'Yes, for *Bacci* magazine.'

I cannot believe I'm hearing this. Maybe it was me, not Eddie, who jumped in the pool. Maybe I bumped my head and this is all a crazy dream? First my press debut on Scott Hale's blog, now this. Dylan is forever harping on about 'the bloody media' and how he'd never sell his soul. He has also spent the last few years sleeping his way through his female fanbase and I could get you a stack of magazines featuring interviews where he says he'd never get married.

'So, what's the plan?' I ask Charles.

'I'd give him a call, Miss Wilde. Talk things over. I'll keep in contact over the next few days.'

'OK, but please call me Nicole.'

'Nicole,' he corrects himself. 'Have a good day.'

And with that, our call is over. One short phone call full of so much life-changing information.

My phone only moves far enough away from my head for me to hit call on Dylan's name. He answers after one ring, not giving me any time to plan what the hell I'm going to say to him.

'Hey,' he says sheepishly. He sounds like a little boy who knows he's done something wrong and that he's going to be in big trouble for it.

'Oh, hello,' I reply. 'I hear congratulations are in order.'

'I tried to tell you. I wanted to tell you first. I know what I'm doing, Nic.'

'You only found out she was pregnant a couple of days ago, have you really thought this through?'

'First of all, *she* is called Crystal. All I know is that there's this poor girl and she's heavily pregnant and scared to death. It's all my fault and I want to make sure she's OK. And that my kids are OK.' He adds that last bit as an afterthought. It's so weird hearing him say things like that.

'And you have to get married to do that?' I ask.

'Trust me, will you? I've dicked around for too long, it's time to do the mature thing. I'm going to have a family, Nic!'

He sounds almost excited. Even if I think he's making a huge mistake, what can I say? I'm his friend and I've got to support him.

'Then I'm right behind you. The wedding is next week?'

'Yeah. Well, we want to get married before our babies arrive,' he says. It's *so* weird hearing him talk about his kids and say 'we' when he's talking about what's-her-name. I remember a particular interview he gave a while back. He joked he'd considered having a vasectomy so that this kind of thing could never happen. The press will almost certainly drag this quote up at some point in the very near future. If he wasn't my friend, I know I would.

An awkward silence falls.

'You've got a magazine deal,' I say to fill the silence.

'Crystal wants to do it, and I want to make her happy.'

'Well if it's good enough for the premiership footballers and their wives,' I tease. I'll bet Crystal is just like a footie WAG. I can just picture it, the big, tacky wedding with the magazine deal, photographers everywhere taking pictures of every second of their special day. Actually, now that I'm over the shock, this isn't sounding so bad. Maybe I can get my face in a magazine? That's a step up from a trashy blog, right?

'Charlie seems OK, doesn't he?'

'Charlie?' I reply. 'Oh, Charles. Yeah, I think so. I was kind of in shock when I spoke to him.'

'Don't worry, OK? And expect your invitation to my stag do soon, because you're gonna be there. It'll be the night before the wedding.'

'How traditional of you,' I tease. 'And I'll bet you need me there to make sure you don't do anything stupid or end up naked and chained to something.'

'Exactly! And it wouldn't be right without you there, would it? You're my best friend!'

'Aww, you're getting all slushy! What has this girl done to you?' I laugh.

He laughs too, although it's a much more nervous-sounding laugh than mine.

I know it sounds weird, but I'm sort of excited now. I love a good wedding; I might get my face in a magazine and I get to go shopping for a new outfit. Oh, and the stag do! I love to party with the boys! I've had some wild nights with The Burnouts and, if this is Dylan's last night of freedom, I'll bet Mikey is planning something awesome.

Caught up in the excitement, I totally forget that I was on my way home for a wash and a sleep before all this kicked off. A huge, involuntary yawn reminds me of this, so I grab my bag and head towards the door.

'By the way, I have something to tell you, Nic,' Emily informs me with a grin.

'Can it wait until this evening, love? I'm so tired I think I'm going to fall asleep right here.'

'Oh, OK,' Emily says. An unimpressed look spreads across her face.

'Or you can tell me now?'

'No, it can wait,' she reassures me with a smile.

'Well, in that case, I shall speak to you later. Bye, team!' I tell the room before making my exit.

'Bloody part-timers,' I overhear Vicky tut as the door closes behind me.

Chapter 16

Sitting at my desk, I stare at the blank Word document on the computer screen in front of me. I was first in the office today. The others have since arrived, although I am yet to be disturbed; I must have my concentrating face on.

I am tackling – well, trying to tackle – my Two For The Road tour piece while it's still fresh in my mind. I'm having a little trouble because it's a little *too* fresh in my mind if you know what I mean. For me, all the moments I remember are the ones that involve me and my chaotic love life – absolutely not stuff that can go in the magazine. Listen to me referring to it as my love life, love doesn't even come into it. Then again, I can't really call it a sex life because none of that happened either. In a way I'm lucky Eddie broke his leg – it gives me something to focus on.

Vicky barges her way into my office – without knocking, obviously. She pops a cup of tea down on my desk, but seeing as Vicky never does anything nice, I am instantly wondering what she has done wrong.

'Oh! Thank you!' I say, trying not to sound too surprised.

'You're welcome. Any word back from Scott Hale today?'

Shit, I totally forgot about Scott.

I check my emails and there's nothing from him. There is a

message from Luke Fox though.

'Nope. No reply from Scott,' I tell her and she loses interest and heads for the door. Before she closes the door behind her, Vicky turns around.

'Emily and I are getting on really well you know.'

'Awesome!' I reply, with just a hint of sarcasm.

'She has a boyfriend you know.'

'What?' I'm unable to hide my surprise.

'Oh yeah. She didn't tell you?' She smiles. Oh she is loving this.

'I've been busy.'

'OK. Laters,' she replies, finally closing my door.

'Laters,' I say in a silly voice as soon as I'm sure she can't hear me.

So Emily has a boyfriend? I thought we told each other everything! I called her up last night (after Vicky went to bed) to tell her all about TFTR, every little detail, and she didn't tell me anything about a boyfriend.

Alone again, I read my message from Luke.

'Nic, what can I say? The past few days have been pretty fucked up. Ed's leg is going to put us out of action for a while, not sure when or if the tour will resume so I won't get to say this to you in person. I'm sorry for what happened, I wasn't myself that night. You know what it's like on tour, you get carried away. The way I feel about you hasn't changed. I hope we're still cool? Luke x.'

What an infuriating email. It's so like Luke to say so little with so many words. The way he feels about me might not have changed, but how does he feel about me? I guess it's something that he apologised though, so I'll send something back telling him we're fine and then I'll get any silly ideas of something happening between us out of my head. I was stupid to think anything more than a few awkward minutes on the tour bus was what he wanted from me.

Back to my Word document. It doesn't take me long to finish the article – after all, it's only about two tour dates and I put most of the focus on Eddie's accident. People would much rather read about a rockstar jumping into a swimming pool during a wild night on tour anyway.

I don't stick the working day out much longer before grabbing my bag, saying goodbye to the team and heading for the door. I'll ask Emily about her boyfriend later.

Chapter 17

It's been a few days since the tour, and everything seems back to normal. Well, everything except Dylan and his accidental wife-to-be, but to be honest I'm sort of coming around to the idea now. Well, maybe not coming around to it, but I'm certainly adjusting to it. I think this might be good for him, calm him down a little.

We've had a hectic couple of days in the office – hectic, yet uneventful. I didn't get a reply from Scott, and he didn't take the story about me down either. I guess I'll just have to try to forget about that and pray to God that my mother doesn't come across it when she Googles me, because that is her number one method of keeping tabs on me while she's away.

The reason the past few days have been hectic is just because there's so much to do. We've got a new issue of the magazine to get online and then I'm off to London for Dylan's stag do – oh and his wedding, mustn't forget that part – so everything needs to be ready.

Today should be fun, we've got a new band called Chillz coming in for an interview. They're a three-piece punk/metal crossover band, and as much as I loved the genre in my teens, I'm into far more commercial stuff these days. Two For The Road are very typical of the punk-rock genre with their faux-American singing accents, hilarious lyrics and dressed-down look – they're about as 'alternative' as I venture these days. The Burnouts are definitely a rock band, but the kind that gets in the charts and bags number one after number one because almost everyone loves their music, even if they're not a long-time fan. Their videos wouldn't ever be played on the 'alternative' music channels (unlike TFTR, who never seem to be off the 'alternative' channels *or* the pop channels these days), which probably makes Dylan a pop star and not a rockstar, but he never got that memo, and that's why he behaves in a way that would make Mötley Crüe blush.

One thing is for sure though, despite their different genres, both TFTR and The Burnouts are undeniably gorgeous and a huge hit with the ladies, but Chillz ... well, they're just plain scary. They've got that typical metal look about them, all hair, make-up and piercings – I'm just looking at photographs of them to try to learn their names before they arrive. The singer/guitarist is called Dominic, he has long-ish hair covering his face so I can't actually see what he looks like. I guess I'll know him by his stubbly beard and excessively pierced lips. The drummer and the bassist are twins, Kane and Killer – I'm going to hazard a guess that Killer isn't his real name. Facially these two are identical, but Kane has long hair down to his waist and Killer has a shaved head, making them look a little like a before and after photo. With Halloween at the end of the month, and with these guys being a scary hairy metal band, we thought we might do a tacky Halloween photo shoot. Jake and I went out and bought loads of dressing-up stuff and loads of spooky decorations to set the scene, so we've taken over the ByteBanter photo studio for the afternoon. Metal bands aren't always up for being a bit silly – serious artists and all that – but these guys were well up for the idea straight away.

We're all messing around with the Halloween supplies. Vicky, who is rather appropriately wearing a witch's hat, is whispering with Emily at the other side of the room. I finally got some time alone with Emily yesterday and I think I might have upset her.

She was getting worked up telling me all about what it's like living with Vicky, and poor Emily is too nice to throw her out. Apparently, Vicky had a huge argument with her mum and she's refusing to go home. End of. She also told me all about how much Vicky complains about things, and all the nasty things she says about other people, but it was when we started talking about Emily's new boyfriend that she got upset. Emily teases me about only dating musicians and I rip her about the boring, normal guys she goes for, but when I made a joke about her new bloke she got really upset.

'Oh, Nic, he's such a gentleman. I slept over at his and after it was 4 a.m., so he made sure I was safe in a taxi,' she told me.

'He kicked you out at four? Not much of a sleepover,' I joked.

'What do you mean?' she replied.

'He humped ya and dumped ya in a taxi in the middle of the night. Oh, you're so right, this guy is a keeper.'

Although what I was saying was basically true, it was all part of the usual teasing. She got super upset this time though. I put it down to her feeling wound up over Vicky, but she's been a bit quiet with me today.

I have opted for a pair of devil horns, although we all know I'm a perfect little angel – unless you happen to catch me on a bus with a bunch of fit lads with instruments.

Finally the band arrive, and I am pleasantly surprised to see them looking normal – although I'm told they have their make-up bags with them. In traditional lead singer style, Dominic is absolutely gorgeous. It's a shame he's going to cover his face, because I'd sure as hell buy his album, if you know what I mean.

As Emily and I arrange the backdrop for the photos, the band goes through the dressing-up stuff with real enthusiasm. I look over to see how they're getting on and spy Kane and Killer trying to talk Jake into letting them 'metal him up', which is something I'd love to see, but something that Jake isn't going for. I can also see Vicky trying to chat up Dominic as he applies copious amounts of eyeliner. I'm wondering just how unprofessional a person can behave, but then my mind is dragged back to a couple of days ago. Visions of Mark and Luke flash before my eyes and wipe the smile off my face.

With the band made-up and ready for action, I crack on with my interview. I love meeting upcoming bands – they're so genuine, so obliging and so honest. If they make it big, that will all change in no time at all. In my experience, bands turn into arseholes when they hit the big time. Take Dylan – the day I met him, he was such a poser, the big *I am*. I'd seen him doing interviews on TV and I'd always thought he was full of himself, and when I met him I realised he is actually his own biggest fan. It was only after we hit it off that he started treating me like a human being. I've seen other people interviewing him and he's always got that cockiness about him.

After the interview we do a few silly photos with the band, making full use of all the Halloween gear. As soon as they leave, it's straight back to work, and I'm not even back in my office five minutes when my phone rings. It's Charles Pace.

I answer his call and we chat politely. Thinking about it, he's got a very sexy voice. You can tell he's a Londoner, but he's not quite as 'apples and pears' as Dylan. I was in shock the first time I spoke to him, so I can forgive myself for not noticing.

'I'm calling on behalf of my client, Dylan King,' he tells me rather formally. Who else would he be calling about?

He continues, 'Basically, it's about the stag and hen parties the night before the wedding. We want everything to run as smoothly as possible.'

'Don't worry, Dill has already asked me about this. He said he wants me to tag along, as an honorary boy, and keep him out of trouble. It's nothing I haven't done before,' I assure him, and it's absolutely true. There have been a few occasions where I've had to undress Dylan and put him to bed, then stay by his side all night, wide awake, just watching him to make sure he didn't choke on his own sick. What are best friends for?

Dylan has absolutely no idea when to stop drinking. He thinks because he can afford it, that it's OK to blow thousands of pounds at the bar and drink until he can't drink any more. It occasionally crosses my mind that he might have a bit of a problem with alcohol, but I'm never really sure how to bring it up. Maybe I'm just being dramatic because I care about him so much.

Anyway, at least he isn't hitting the drugs hard, like certain band members I know. I am now certain Luke was on something the other night – how else could you explain his weird behaviour? He was aggressive and frustrated and I've never seen him like that before.

'Yes, about that,' Charles starts, and I know by the tone of his voice I'm not going to like what he tells me. 'Well, Dylan has invited me along to keep an eye on him – so you are relieved of that duty. He has asked if you would attend Miss Slater's hen party, and keep an eye on her.'

'What? He wants me to hang out with Crystal? I've never even met her!'

'Off the record, Miss Wilde, he trusts you and he doesn't trust her. You can keep her out of trouble and I'll keep Dylan out of trouble. We'll all be in the same hotel, it's where the wedding is being held the following day – did you receive your invitation?'

'I did.'

'Shall I tell Dylan you said yes, Miss Wilde?' he asks.

'I guess you'll have to, but please call me Nicole!'

'Sorry, Nicole.'

'So why didn't he call me and ask me himself?'

'To be honest, I think he's a bit scared of you,' he laughs. 'I think he cares a great deal about you and about what you think. He clearly has a great deal of trust in you.'

I'm glad he trusts me, of course I am, but babysitting a heavily pregnant stranger on her hen do does not sound like my idea of fun. Getting trashed with Dylan, Mikey and the band, now that sounds like fun, and the perfect way to celebrate the end of the poor bastard's life.

'Tell him I'll do it. No, tell him I'll be happy to do it. Tell him that my present doesn't need to be anything too big, though,' I say, only half-joking.

'Big present, I'll tell him. So we'll finally get to meet at this wedding. It will be nice to put a face to the lovely voice.'

I wasn't expecting Mr Formal to say anything like that; I'm a little taken aback.

'Likewise,' I reply, in a much higher voice than usual.

He laughs. 'OK then, I will see you in a few days. Any more problems, I'll give you a call.'

'Great, and if Dylan wants to ask me anything else you tell him to man up and ask me himself.'

After our call, I can't help but think about meeting Charles face to face for the first time. I wonder if he has a sexy face to match his sexy voice. There's only one thing for it, I'll have to Google him.

No luck finding a photo on his company website, although there are plenty of photographs of his office and … wow! It's bigger than my office, it's bigger than my flat and it's bigger than my office and my flat combined. Next stop, Facebook, because everyone has a Facebook account. The good news is that I have found him – and I know it's him because we have Dylan as a mutual friend – but the bad news is that Mr Pace has a super-private profile and I can't see his photos. Damnit! I have exhausted all my resources, I'd make a pretty rubbish secret agent. I wonder if MI5 use Facebook? If they don't, then they probably should. As long as they don't stumble upon a private profile, they'll be fine.

Time for some work. Closing Facebook, I grab my Dictaphone and begin playing back the interview. The sooner I type this up, the sooner it'll be the big day.

Chapter 18

Yesterday I had a bit of an accident. The kind of accident you have in Harvey Nichols when you spend more on one outfit than most people do on their rent.

I don't usually go this crazy, but I'm going to be in a magazine with a bunch of people who have way more money than me, so I have to at least try to compete. For the past couple of days I have been dropping the fact that I am going to be in a magazine into every conversation possible, even when it has been entirely irrelevant.

I bought a dress, shoes and a clutch bag – I won't tell you how much it cost, but let's just say it wasn't entirely out of choice that I bought the rest of my accessories from Primark. Anyway, I'm hoping that everyone will be a bit too flash to know that's where my jewellery has come from – so long as no one asks me where I got any of it.

If I'm being honest, the magazine deal isn't the only reason I'm trying to look my best. I seem to have developed a bit of a thing for Charles – for his voice, at least. We've chatted on the phone quite a lot over the past couple of days and last night our call lasted over an hour. I'm dressing up to impress a man with no idea what he looks like *and* he isn't even in a band. I'm sure the novelty will wear off when I meet him and there's no sign of any instruments.

I place my outfit carefully in my case, which I must absolutely not forget to take with me. I resist the urge to try it on one last time because, you've guessed it, I'm running late.

I'll be arriving in London this afternoon and then heading straight to the hotel to be introduced to Crystal, something I'm not exactly looking forward to. The wedding is being held at The Trenton hotel. I'm booked in for a couple of nights and I do love my big, glamorous hotels – especially when I'm alone – so at least I have that to look forward to.

Big glam hotels, magazine shoots, celebrity weddings – this is the life. My job may only be glamorous in certain areas, but it's fascinating how I've become accustomed to certain things. Soon after making friends with Dylan, I realised I could live like a rockstar without actually being one, and that suits me just fine. I get to sleep in the hotels and attend the fancy parties and, when I'm with Dylan, I get to enjoy all the perks of his fame without any of the crap he has to put up with.

I know how weird my life must seem to outsiders. I'm fairly sure my dad – who is a big, serious businessman who deals in big, serious business – thinks I'm playing office with my friends, and my friends from school really do think I'm a groupie. I think the fact that I'm not doing what they're doing baffles them. They're all married or have kids (never a combination of the two) and their only window into my life is via social media, which only shows me partying with bands, it doesn't show me sitting in my dressing gown writing until dawn. I don't know why I don't want the boyfriend or the husband or the kids, but I just don't. I feel very much stuck in the middle as far as my life is concerned. I'm not a child, but I'm not an adult either – I'm like a teenager that has been left home alone while her parents are away for the weekend. That makes sense, my life is one big party. It probably has something to do with the people I hang out with. They get paid a shit-load of money for a few hours' work, which means they can spend their days doing what they like and have women falling at their feet, so why would they stick to just one girl? People like Dylan, Luke and Eddie are a bad influence on me. I've spent pretty much all of my adult life living by their rules and the consequences are that I have no idea how to behave in the 'real world' now. It's got to a point where I wouldn't know what to do with a boyfriend; I've forgotten the rules of the game. I'm pretty sure sharing beds with band boys is a no-no, even in an entirely platonic way, but in my world it's totally normal – we've all got to sleep somewhere. You can sleep where you like, dance with who you like, flirt with who you like and no one cares. Everyone is happy.

So what if I don't have a boyfriend … I'm going to be in a magazine!

Chapter 19

Thankfully, when I arrived in London I didn't have to travel very far to get to the hotel. I decided to get a taxi anyway because I almost always get lost in London and the last thing I need is to get lost the day before Dylan's wedding. He'd probably think I'd done it on purpose to avoid babysitting Crystal on her hen night. I really can't hide the fact that I am not looking forward to that, but I do plan on getting very drunk, so hopefully it won't matter.

I am currently sitting in the lobby of The Trenton Hotel, the most jaw-droppingly gorgeous hotel I have ever seen. If, for some reason, I had to get married (for example, if someone put a gun to my head), I'd want to do it here.

All the wedding guests are staying here and I can't even begin to imagine how much this wedding must be costing Dylan, but I'm pretty sure it's more than I'll ever see in my lifetime. Everyone around me looks important and expensively dressed, and then there's me in my grungy train outfit looking like the love child of Ke$ha and Jon Bon Jovi (circa 1986). I stick out like a sore thumb. In fact, I feel a bit like Julia Roberts in *Pretty Woman* – although hopefully I look less like I'm here to work.

Before anyone gets chance to show me the exit, the lift doors open and out steps Dylan, looking every inch the rockstar he is. Oh, and the girl he knocked up is with him – I mean his fiancée, Crystal Slater.

It's weird, I had expected to feel awkward, chubby and scruffy standing next to Crystal. But I don't. Crystal look even more out of place than I do.

Despite being heavily pregnant, she is wearing a pair of bright-pink hot pants and a halter-neck vest, her massive belly poking out between the two. Even if she wasn't pregnant, her outfit is a little inappropriate for a hotel like this – and that's without mentioning the fact it's October and we're in London, not the Bahamas.

I mentally tell myself off for judging her before she's even opened her mouth, making a pact with myself that I won't hate her unless she gives me reason to do so.

'Oh, *you're* Nicole.'

And there it is.

'Erm, yes,' I reply, not entirely sure what she meant by that.

'Well I didn't expect you to look like *that*.'

Is she taking the piss? Well, two can play that game.

'Really? Because you're exactly what I expected,' I reply, turning to Dylan to kiss him on the cheek.

'Hello, you.'

'Hey, Nic, thanks for coming. In case you hadn't guessed, this is Crystal,' he says, gesturing towards the blonde, fake-tanned and now angry-looking woman next to him.

I smile and nod in recognition and she scowls at me. Tonight is going to be just wonderful.

'So, are you looking forward to tonight?' Dylan asks me. It's as though he's reading my mind.

'I cannot wait. Super-stoked!' I exaggerate. 'What have you got planned, Crystal?'

'My sister Daisy has organised it all, we'll soon find out. Alcohol-free fun – are you coming dressed like *that*?'

Yep, tonight is going to be a blast.

'I'm going to head up to my room now and get changed, don't worry.'

'About that ...' Dylan starts, and I know I'm not going to like what he has to say. 'Small problem, Crystal solved it.'

'We didn't book enough rooms and the hotel is fully booked,' she starts brightly, 'so I suggested to Dilly – what with you being so cool about partying with the girls tonight – that you wouldn't mind sharing a room. So we've put you in with my sister, Daisy.'

'Right.'

'There are two beds, and it's a big room,' Dylan offers. 'Is that OK?'

'Yeah, fine,' I reply. It's not like I have much choice.

'Well, Dilly, you had somewhere to go, right? I'll take Nicole to her room,' Crystal suggests, kissing Dylan goodbye.

'You girls have fun tonight. Behave, yeah?' Dylan teases us.

'I'm sure I can keep her under control.' I laugh, amusing Dylan but definitely not Crystal.

'The next time we all see each other, I'll be getting married!' he yells, attracting a lot of attention and consequently getting a few dirty looks – not that he cares, he seems on top of the world.

So here we are, Dylan's best friend and his pregnant one-night stand, about to embark on a teetotal hen night in a bar that's only a few floors from where my real friends will be having fun at a stag do. I know where I'd rather be.

'Who does your hair extensions?' Crystal asks me as we head up in the lift.

'I don't have hair extensions,' I tell her honestly.

'Fuck off!' She tugs on my hair until she is convinced. 'How do you get it that long?'

Do I let her in on my secret, you know, the one about hair growing?

'I soak it in urine,' I tell her as the lift pings, stepping out first and leaving her there for a moment to process what I just said. She sniffs the hand she was touching my hair with and catches up with me, which is fortunate because I don't know where I'm going.

We stop outside a door, Crystal knocks and we wait several minutes before a grumpy looking girl with a mass of curly ginger hair and an ill-fitting hotel bathrobe answers.

'Daisy, this is Nicole. Nicole, this is Daisy,' Crystal says unenthusiastically. 'Right, I have to go get my hair done. Laters.'

'I suppose you'd better come in then,' Daisy welcomes me. Sort of.

The room is an absolute tip, but I can just about make out the one and only double bed underneath a pile of clothes and towels.

'You don't snore do you?' Daisy asks.

'Erm, no …'

'Good, because I require perfect silence to sleep,' Daisy replies before dropping her robe. 'Apart from my white noise.'

I have no idea where to look as she tries on various outfits – and white noise all night sounds like a nightmare.

'Am I OK to use the bathroom?' I ask.

'Yeah, I've already used it.'

Wow, she really *has* used it. The bathroom is even messier than the bedroom, with empty bottles of complimentary bath products scattered around, along with all the towels. There's a hand towel still on the rack, I guess that one is mine. As I start to tidy up, I realise that she has also made use of the other bath robe.

I'm not going to let her ruin my plan to have a nice long bath, and now I'm looking forward to it more than ever, especially because it means I don't have to be in there with Daisy.

Leaning over the huge bath to turn the taps on, I spot the huge clump of hair clogging up the plug hole. I'm squeamish at the best of times, but other people's hair in plug holes makes me feel physically sick. I can't touch it. There goes my bath.

Instead I have a shower, careful to avoid the clumps of hair and empty bottles scattered around the room.

Massaging the shampoo into my hair, I am interrupted by a bang on the door.

'Nicole? Are you going to be long? I need the toilet.'

This is going to be a long, long night.

Chapter 20

I have made friends with a lovely barman named Liam and he has agreed to sneak vodka into each one of my cocktails, despite Crystal's 'if I can't drink, then no one can' rule. I love Liam. Although no matter how drunk I feel, the Slater sisters are still doing my head in.

Crystal's friends are basically clones of her, all with similar hair and outfits – although Crystal is the only pregnant one as far as I can tell.

'This is the number one woman in Dylan's life,' Crystal tells her friend, pointing at me. 'Well, she was. I'm her replacement.'

She laughs, walking off and leaving me with one of her clones.

'So what are you going to do now?' Clone asks me.

'What do you mean?'

'Are you going to find another boyfriend?'

'Dylan wasn't my boyfriend,' I tell her, super-confused.

'Oh.' Clone looks confused too.

'We're just friends, and I'm a music journalist so I help out with some of his band stuff.'

'You have a job?' Clone looks even more confused.

It's like talking to a child, which is weird because she looks a lot older than me.

'Yes, I have a job. Do you have a job?'

'No!' She laughs hysterically, and I wonder if Liam is giving her alcohol too. 'I'm just waiting for my rockstar.'

I stare at her blankly.

'You know, like Crystal. We're all looking for them, so they can take care of us.'

'Why don't you just get yourself a footballer? They have more money,' I joke.

'Oh no, being a WAG is so 2008,' she replies, totally straight-faced. Oh God, she's actually serious – I'm out of here. It's late, I've babysat for long enough, I am going to bed before Daisy comes up and tries to make me sleep in the bath.

I walk towards the toilets before making a dash for the exit. Hopefully they won't notice I'm gone.

Maybe it's because I'm a bit drunk, but I can't remember what number room we're in – I think it ended in twenty-five. Maybe. I'll just try my keycard in all rooms ending in twenty-five, there's only like a billion floors here.

I'm not sure how long I've been trying my keycard in various doors, but none of them have opened.

Unable to spot the lifts, I make my way to the stairwell. After wobbling down one or two levels, I spot someone sitting on the floor. It's Dylan, and he's *so* drunk.

'Dylan?'

'Nicole! How are you? Are you having a paaaaarty?' he screams.

I plonk myself down next to him and ask, 'What are you doing here?'

'I don't know, I don't know. But listen, come here.' He looks around to check the coast is clear, before gesturing for me to lean in.

'I'm drunk,' he whispers, although not that quietly.

'I can smell that, Dill. Where are your mates?'

'Tomorrow I'm getting married!' he unhelpfully replies.

'Dylan, listen,' I hold his face with both hands so that he is looking into my eyes and hopefully listening. 'Do you know which room I am staying in?'

'I know what room I'm staying in – Mikey wrote it on my hand.' He laughs manically, clamping my head in his hands like I am doing with his. 'Let's go there!'

Dylan has two different room numbers on his hand, one written in pen and the other is a tattoo from a drunken night a little while ago. I'm sure it made sense to him at the time, but these days it just confuses him.

Before I have chance to say anything, he plants a kiss on my lips – just a peck, but probably not the smartest thing to do the night before your wedding.

'I love you, you know,' he tells me.

'I love you too,' I reply. 'I wouldn't be friends with you if I didn't – you're a pain in the arse.'

He laughs. I need to get him to his room and I need to get him sobered up. He's going to have one hell of a hangover tomorrow.

'Let me help you up.' I stand up and offer Dylan my hand.

'I can walk.' He springs to life, jumping to his feet. I'm not convinced he is sober enough to take care of himself – and I'll do anything to avoid the slumber party from hell – so I'll get us some coffee, just to make sure he sobers up properly.

'Do you have coffee in your room?' I ask.

'We do not.'

'Right, go to your room, I'll go get us some coffee from Reception. I'll knock on the door so let me in, OK?'

'Take my key, I have two. Just in case,' he says with a wink, before planting yet another kiss on my lips. It's still a peck, but this one lasts a little longer.

I take his keycard and head downstairs as Dylan climbs up the stairs towards his room. I probably should have taken him, but he seems a bit more alert now.

Making my way down the empty stairwell, I jump at the sound of Dylan's voice echoing down from a few floors up.

'I love you, Nicole,' he shouts.

'I love you too,' I reply in a loud whisper. He's definitely conscious, he'll be fine.

After collecting packets of coffee, milk and sugar from the bar in Reception, I head back up to the room.

Pushing the card into the door, it opens and I'm thankful I remembered the number of at least one room tonight, even if it wasn't my own.

The room is in darkness and I have no idea where the light switch is. There's just enough light coming in from the windows for me to see that Dylan is already in his bed – his huge bed. It's probably about three times bigger than the one I'm supposed to be sharing with Daisy.

Maybe I could sleep here … or maybe I should go. It's a bit of a dodgy idea, the night before his wedding. But then again, this bed is huge and I've shared a bed with him a bunch of times before, this isn't really that different. Someone needs to stay with him and make sure he isn't sick, and anyway it's not like anyone will ever know. All I know is that my head feels fuzzy and I'm really tired. Slipping off my dress, I climb into the huge bed. I'll have to think of an excuse to explain to Daisy why I didn't spend the night where I was supposed to – that's if she even noticed.

Chapter 21

Mmm! That was one of the comfiest night's sleep I've ever had. Maybe it's this bed? I don't feel the slightest bit hungover, although I imagine I still look it. It's not a miracle bed.

The sun is shining in through the massive windows and it takes my eyes a while to adjust to the light. Rolling onto my side, I realise I've made my way to the middle of the huge bed.

'Morning,' I say to the semi-naked, complete stranger in bed next to me.

'Good morning,' he replies.

I double-take. I have no idea who this man is, but I'm in bed with him, in my underwear. Screaming seems like the practical response but I can't get one to come out. Instead I whimper a little.

Sensing my alarm, the stranger gets out of bed and pulls on a pair of jeans and a T-shirt.

'I'll go grab us some breakfast and then when I get back, maybe you can tell me your name,' he smiles. 'Tea or coffee?'

'Tea,' I reply weakly. And with that, he's gone.

As soon as the door closes, I jump out of bed and grab my dress, putting it on as quickly as possible. How drunk was I last night? This has to be Dylan's room, because it was Dylan who gave me the keycard that definitely opened this door … I think.

Looking around the room for clues, I see a suit hanging up. Dylan sent me a photo of his wedding outfit, and the one hanging here looks just like it. Examining the desk I see Dylan's phone, this has to be his room – so who was that man?

Searching frantically for my other shoe, with every intention of making a run for it before the stranger returns, I hear the door open again. In walks the stranger, carrying a tray with two cups of tea and a plate of croissants.

'So who are you?' he asks, taking a seat at the table and sipping his tea.

'Is this Dylan's room?' I ask, ignoring his question.

'It is indeed. Sugar?'

'What?'

'Sugar,' he waves the sachet at me. 'For your tea. It's Nicole, isn't it?'

Now I am really freaked out, how the hell does he know my name?

'Yes,' I reply cautiously.

'I recognised the accent,' he tells me, standing up and offering me his hand to shake. 'A handshake seems a bit formal considering we just technically spent the night together. It's Charles. Charles Pace.'

Oh, I am mortified. I shake his hand as I try to get things straight in my head. So last night I tipsily bumped into Dylan (who has very drunk), took his keycard from him (probably his only one), decided I would share his bed with him, and ended up sleeping next to the man who is in charge of his public relations – AKA the man whose job it would have been to clear up the mess I would have caused if anyone had found out that I'd shared a bed with Dylan the night before his wedding.

'Sorry, this must be weird for you,' Charles begins to explain. 'Dylan asked me to keep an eye on him, so I went along to his party and said I'd sleep in here with him tonight. I didn't even realise he had left the room – I was pleasantly surprised to wake up next to you instead. It's nice to finally put a face to the voice.'

'Yeah, you too – and in your underpants, no less,' I reply, managing to find a little of that Nicole Wilde cheeky charm, despite our awkward situation. He blushes.

'So this *is* Dylan's room?' I'm still confused.

'It is and it's also the honeymoon suite.' A cheeky grin spreads across Charles' face. 'I'll be sure to tell him we road-tested it for him.'

'We didn't ... did we?' I can't even say the actual words, but it always pays to check, right?

'No, no. We didn't. I just woke up this morning and there you were. Anyway, it wouldn't be that great if we had, would it? What with you thinking you were in bed with Dylan.'

It's hard to be sure if that was a dig or just a polite way of warning me off. I must look like a proper little scandal magnet.

'I was drunk, I was tired, I didn't have a room of my own – all Dylan's fault really,' I offer as some sort of explanation.

'You secret is safe with me, Nicole.'

'So where is Dylan now?' I ask.

'I was hoping you could tell me that,' he replies calmly. I'm not sure if he's being professional or if he just doesn't know Dylan well enough yet – I remember one time we lost him for twenty-four hours, and you wouldn't believe what I had to go through to find him.

'Well, when I left him he was on his way here.'

'So the groom is missing,' he says, still totally calm. 'Shall we go look for him?'

I try to give off the same calm vibes, but it's impossible. How can anyone be calm on the morning of a massive celebrity wedding when the groom is missing?

Chapter 22

I've had some pretty weird weekends in my twenty-five years, but this is one of the strangest ones yet. I am currently searching the public areas of the hotel for Dylan – the last man I ever thought would get married – because he's due to tie the knot in a few short hours. That's weird enough for me, without the whole sleeping-in-the-same-bed-as-Charles thing. Speaking of Charles, he's gone to the lobby to see if the hotel staff can help us locate the elusive Mr King. Hopefully he hasn't left the hotel, or we've got no chance of finding him in time.

Now that I'm alone – and clothed – I'm realising how hot Charles looked in just his pants. I was a bit too freaked out to notice it at the time, but the more I think about it, the more my cheeks flush. Looking at my reflection in the mirror in the women's toilets (which is why I'm in here, not to look for Dylan … then again, you never know with him), I realise just how bad I'm looking right now. My make-up is smeared all over my face, my hair is absolutely massive and when I hurriedly put my dress on … let's just say it's not hanging on me as nicely as it did last night, more like hanging off me to be honest. What a fantastic first impression I must have made on Charles. Sexy, sexy Charles. I may have only spent a few minutes with him (awake at least), but I think I've got him figured out. I'll bet he goes to the gym every day – working out when he isn't working, which I'd imagine is the rest of the time, he seems to be constantly in professional mode – and I doubt he's short of female attention with that perfectly styled dirty-blonde hair, those deep-blue eyes and that sexy designer stubble he's sporting. I wonder if he's married. I didn't think to look for a wedding ring – clearly I'm off the ball this morning.

All I want is to go to my – sorry, Daisy's room and smarten myself up so that no one else has to see me looking like this. Can you imagine if Crystal saw me in this state? She'd have a field day.

As I attempt to scrape off some of last night's make-up with toilet roll, my phone rings. Even with a tiny handbag like the one I'm carrying, I struggle to find it.

Eventually grabbing hold of it, I see that Charles is calling me. I hope this means he's found Dylan.

'Hey!' I answer, trying to sound cool, calm and collected, but achieving none of the above.

'Hey, I'm on my way to the security room. We're going to look over the CCTV footage from last night, so if you want to meet me there and show us where you saw Dylan last, we can follow him and see where he ended up … hopefully.'

'Yeah, of course. Where is the security room?'

'On the ground floor. Ask at Reception and they'll show you.'

'OK, see you in a sec.' I click off the call and return my phone to my bag.

Taking out my lipstick, I try to make myself look a little more presentable. I definitely can't stroll around the swanky lobby looking like this. I apply a thick layer of red lipstick, by way of a distraction, and dab a little onto my eyelids. It seemed like a good idea but, in hindsight, maybe not. My eyes look sore now; in fact I'm looking a little cokey, à la Luke Fox. Crystal may have stolen my *Pretty Woman* crown yesterday, but I'm about to win it back. I not only look seriously out of place in this dress (last night it looked hot, at this time in the morning it looks tacky) but I also look like I've been partying all night. As I approach the front desk, the look on the face of the woman sitting behind it confirms everything I just thought. As she escorts me to a room with 'Security' stuck in big letters on the door, I can't help but think how bad this must look.

Inside, Charles is sitting in front of a bunch of monitors with a big, burly security guard. It's kind of scary, all these monitors – you don't realise just how many cameras there are on you in the hotel. Apart from the rooms, obviously, I don't think there is an inch of space in this hotel without a camera pointing at it.

'So, where was he last?' the security guard asks me, looking me up and down, taking in my trashy get-up.

Things are a little hazy, but I do my best to give him a rough time and a place so that he can check.

'I think we've got him, one moment.'

Looking at the big monitor, I can see Dylan lying on the stairs and me walking towards him.

As I see myself approach Dylan, our conversation silently plays out before my eyes. I remember the events of last night a second before I see them on the screen. I grab Dylan's face, he grabs mine, and there's that kiss. Without audio this is looking pretty bad. We stand up, about to head our separate ways.

'That looked pretty intimate,' Charles observes. I don't respond, mainly because I don't know how to.

'OK, so now we can follow him and see where he ends up,' says the security man.

Then we get to the part where Dylan hands me his keycard and then there's that second kiss – I'd forgotten about that one. It seems to go on for much longer than I recall, although perhaps it just seems that way because this is so awkward.

As Dylan climbs the stairs, the security man pushes buttons to follow him.

I can feel my cheeks flushing again. I know how it looks, but that's not how it was, so I'm not saying anything. Instead, I just stare at the big monitor, waiting to see where he stops.

'There you go, tenth-floor reception room.'

'Cheers, mate,' Charles thanks the security guard before turning to me.

I don't give him chance to say anything, instead I suggest that I go look for Dill, and Charles agrees that would be best.

In the sober light of day, I remember my room being on the eighth floor, so I can grab Dylan, send him on his way and then go get myself ready. The only way this weekend can go from here is up.

When I eventually find the reception rooms and walk through the door, the first thing to catch my eye is Dylan, lying face down on the floor in between the tables, an empty bottle of champagne still in his hand.

'Dylan, it's Nicole. Wake up,' I say in a hushed voice, shaking him gently. It only takes a few attempts and I hear him groan and move slightly. He's alive; so far so good.

'What time is it?' he asks.

'It's time you got your suit on. What the hell are you doing in here?'

'Who knows?' He rolls over and sits upright.

'We need to get you to your room and – oh my God!'

'What?' he asks, and I'm scared to tell him. Dylan has one hell of a black eye and a cut on his lip – injuries he definitely didn't have when I saw him last.

'Where did you get the champagne?' I ask, avoiding his question.

'I think I found it. Why did you say what you just said?'

'Don't worry about it, because we can fix it, but you have a black eye and a burst lip.'

'What?' he shouts. I hand him the little mirror I keep in my handbag so he can see the damage.

'Oh, fuck, fuck, fuck! Crystal is going to slaughter me.'

'Crystal Slaughter – isn't that her name?' I snigger, but it's clearly not the time.

He touches his lip and winces.

'Look, calm down. I've got loads of make-up in my room. We can cover it up and no one will know,' I assure him.

'I think I had sex last night,' he tells me frankly, changing the subject.

'With who?' I ask, surprised but not *that* surprised.

'I don't know, but I think that I did.'

'Are you sure? You were alone when we met up.'

'We met up? It wasn't you, was it?' he asks seriously.

'No!' I laugh.

'OK, but it happened. I never forget that.'

'Dylan, you've forgotten more sex than I've had in my lifetime, just calm down. Let's go cake you in make-up.'

'OK,' he says, taking a deep breath and exhaling slowly. 'Looking at the state of you, if this is what you normally look like, then your make-up must be the stuff of miracles.'

'Watch it, or I won't let you use it and then you'll be in *Bacci* magazine looking like a dick – and that's if Crystal will still marry you with a face like this.'

He laughs and winces with pain at the same time. 'You know, I thought the headache was because of the hangover, but my face kills.'

'I'll bet it does,' I sympathise. His face is a mess; I'm hoping my make-up bag is up to the challenge.

'Am I doing the right thing?' he asks me.

'Lot of men wear make-up. Some make it obvious, some don't.'

'Oi, you know what I'm talking about. Getting married. Am I doing the right thing?'

This is my moment, the last chance I'll get to talk him out of going through with this. When I first found out, I thought it was a bad idea. I mean, who marries some girl they don't know, but knocked up one drunken night? And now I've met Crystal, and she's just horrible, how can I let him go ahead and marry her? He's my best friend, I love him to bits. I sometimes think to myself that, in another life, we could have been so much more, if things were different. But I know he'll be miserable, not only being married, but married to a girl like Crystal – who has just been waiting for a rich and famous mug to marry – it'll ruin his life.

Looking into his eyes, I see that rare softer, entirely genuine side to Dylan that he likes to keep hidden. He's not worrying about what anyone thinks, there's no act. He actually looks worried – scared even. Then I remember how excited he was in the lobby yesterday. Maybe I'm just scared to lose him? If he's just nervous, it wouldn't be right to talk him out of it.

'Do *you* think you're doing the right thing?' I ask.

'I thought I was, but something just doesn't feel right, you know?'

It's now or never, Nicole, speak now or forever hold your peace.

'I think you're just nervous,' I say. I can't ruin his day and it's not my place to tell him whether or not I think he should get married.

'Do you think so?'

'Dylan, I don't think I've ever seen you surer about anything for as long as I've known you. You seemed so happy yesterday. If you think you're doing the right thing, then you do it.'

'I thought I was sure,' he says, and we sit in silence for a few seconds, neither of us knowing what the hell to say.

'Well there's always divorce,' I joke.

'There is. And she did sign a prenup,' he adds with a laugh.

'Come on, we'll stop by my room and grab my make-up bag. I met Charles, by the way.'

'Oh really?'

'Yeah. I'll tell you all about it on the way.'

Chapter 23

I don't think it matters how gorgeous my dress is; I had to get ready in such a hurry and my hair and make-up could have done with at least twenty minutes more attention.

I helped Dylan to get ready first, straightening his tie, covering him in make-up – typical groom stuff. He looks absolutely gorgeous and the make-up has really done the trick; you'd never know his face was such a mess underneath it all. I've got extra make-up in my bag in case he needs a touch up later. That won't seem weird at all.

Looking at him standing up there waiting to get married in front of his family, friends and random A-listers who will look good in the photos, I feel a pang of jealousy – I'm not sure why though. Did I feel jealous that night on the tour bus when he was having alarmingly loud sex in the bunk below me? No – I just wanted it to stop so that I could go to sleep. It was 4 a.m., none of us had slept in over twenty-four hours and the gentle rock of the bus was making me feel seasick. That's pretty standard procedure on tour though – if you can't stand the sex, get off the tour bus.

So why is this different? I certainly don't want to get married, not to Dylan or anyone else for that matter. Right?

'So, what do you really look like?' Charles asks, sitting down next to me. He's another man that scrubs up pretty nicely.

'What do you mean?' I ask.

'Well looking at Dylan, you'd never know his face was black and blue under all that make-up. It makes me wonder what you actually look like.'

'Oh, cheers!' I smile.

'Dylan looks a bit more relaxed.' He gestures towards the altar.

'I'm not surprised, he's still drunk.'

Charles looks surprised. 'He's still drunk and about to get married?'

'That's Dylan. Shouldn't this show be on the road?' I ask.

'It should, Crystal just sent a message saying she will be slightly late.'

'Late? She's only upstairs! It's not like she has to race across town, is it?'

Charles laughs. 'You don't like her, do you?'

'She doesn't like me either,' I reply, a little too defensively.

'I can't think why not, you're lovely,' Charles whispers to me, and before I have chance to work out if he's being sarcastic again, the music starts. Her ladyship must be here.

Chapter 24

Considering the groom was drunk and the bride was the Bride of Chucky, the wedding went without a hitch. Well, apart from when Dylan said, 'I, Kylan, Ding' by mistake. Charles and I very much enjoyed his slip up, laughing together and nudging each other like a couple of naughty school kids. He's good fun, is Charles – we're getting on really well.

After the ceremony we posed for photos together and I can think of far worse people to have on my arm in a huge magazine like *Bacci*.

The photographer took a lovely photo of me and Dylan and I really hope they print it, although I doubt they'll publish a snap of the groom and his female best friend. They might print the photo of Charles and me though, which also has massive dress-showing-off potential.

After sitting next to Charles during dinner, my mini-crush on his voice has turned into a full-blown crush on his everything. It's only now that we're listening to the speeches that we've finally stopped chatting.

Mikey's speech is up next – I'm really looking forward to this one. I spoke to him earlier and he warned me not to miss it, so I'm expecting great things. Of course, this *is* his brother's wedding so I'm sure he'll take the honour seriously and not use it as a platform for his cheeky lyrics.

'If I can have your attention, please?' a voice bellows over the PA system. 'It's time for the final speech. Give it up for the best man.'

Applause and cheers fill the room as Mikey takes the microphone, a mischievous grin plastered across his face.

'Hello, ladies and gentlemen, I'm ...,' Mikey pauses, and the entire room falls silent. 'Sorry about that,' he says sincerely, 'I'm just so nervous. This morning Dylan told me that if I did a good job at being his best man today, that I could be best man at his next wedding too.'

The room erupts with laughter – well, everyone apart from Crystal is laughing, she doesn't look too impressed. Mikey carries on regardless.

'For those of you who don't know me, I am Mikey, Dylan's little brother. I'd just like to point out to the bridesmaids that the term "little brother" refers to our difference in age, and not our physical characteristics.'

Still no reaction from Crystal, but the crowd love it and one of the bridesmaids gives him a cheeky wink.

'I don't want you thinking that just because Dylan is my brother that I'm going to go easy on him,' Mikey continues. 'It is tradition that I give him the most uncomfortable five minutes of his life. For the record, Crystal, the most uncomfortable five minutes of your life will be later on this evening, courtesy of the groom. Or did that happen eight months ago? I'm not sure. That said, I'm not standing here in front of you now to make a fool out of my brother. Why should I take all the credit? He's been making a fool of himself for years.'

Dylan is taking the speech as intended – as a joke – but Crystal has a face like a slapped arse.

'I hope you've all had plenty to drink and that you're having a good time,' Mikey continues. 'I could tell you a few stories about Dylan having plenty to drink and having a good time on tour, but it seems a shame to ruin the wedding.'

Charles and I are in hysterics. I don't know what is funnier, the speech or the fact that Crystal isn't laughing at all. Dylan is laughing his head off. I wouldn't like to be in his shoes tonight.

'I can't believe you two got married today and you're not even touching,' Mikey points at the happy couple's hands. 'Come on, Dylan, she's not that big. I'm joking, I'm joking, I know she's pregnant. Well, that's what she told us anyway. Crystal, place your hands on the table and Dylan, place yours on top, show the girl some affection.'

Mikey knocks back half of his champagne prematurely as Dylan and Crystal do as instructed.

'I'd like to take this moment to tell Crystal that she looks stunning.' Everyone in the room takes a moment to make sighing noises at Crystal. 'Dylan, you just look stunned. But seriously, Crystal you look beautiful. Bridesmaids, you did a great job with her this morning. Dylan, what can I say? We tried our best.'

Crystal isn't laughing at the jokes, she isn't smiling at the compliments and she isn't even laughing at the jokes that are only about Dylan, but to be honest I think the fact she isn't amused is what is making Mikey really go for it.

'He has got himself a beauty though, and she's definitely his type. I've always said that my brother likes his women like he likes his cars. He's currently driving a convertible Mercedes-Benz which is a really nice car, and confirmation that he loves topless models.'

I'm laughing so hard my face is hurting.

'Time to be serious,' Mikey insists. 'I think marriage will be good for my brother. It will teach him loyalty, self-control, responsibility and a load of qualities he wouldn't have needed if he'd just stayed single.'

Mikey glances around the room. 'Do you all have a drink in your hand? I am about to propose a toast. I've actually congratulated the groom already, I said to him, "Dylan, you will always look back on this time as the happiest day of your life" – and that was just the stag do.'

Mikey pauses for laughs.

'Ladies and gentlemen, there are two very important people here today, without whom very little of this would have been possible. As the evening goes on, I'm sure you'll spend more time with them, I know I will. So if you'll join me in raising a glass. To the bar staff,' Mikey says, raising his glass.

'To the bar staff,' the rest of the room echoes.

'Seriously, though,' Mikey says, fooling no one this time, 'they say a man is incomplete until he is married, and after that he is finished. Dylan, you are finished from today, my brother. A toast, to Dylan and Crystal.'

'To Dylan and Crystal.' We all raise our glasses.

'Before I go,' Mikey nods towards Dylan and Crystal, 'I see you're still holding hands, that's nice. Dylan, you should enjoy that. It's the last time you'll ever have the upper hand again. Thank you and good night!' he yells into the microphone like he's just finished a show at the O2 Arena.

That has to be the funniest speech I have ever heard in my life. Charles actually has tears in his eyes from laughing so hard – in fact, so do most of the guests. Crystal, however, is a crazy shade of red. She must have found some of it funny, surely? OK, maybe not the part where he called her big (that one was never going to be funny), but the rest of it was just brilliant.

'Let's go congratulate Mikey,' I suggest to Charles. 'That was amazing.'

We have to push our way through the crowd of guests gathered round him, but we finally get to the front.

'Oh my God!' I give Mikey a playful shove. 'That was so funny!'

'Maybe you could tell Crystal that,' he suggests, grabbing me for a hug. 'Apparently she didn't like it.'

'Everyone's a critic,' Charles jokes, offering Mikey a hand to shake.

'Ah, but not all critics go to the toilet to cry. Dylan has just had to run after her,' Mikey informs us, 'which was difficult because he can hardly walk.'

'Maybe it's her hormones, mate. She is pregnant, after all,' Charles suggests.

'Or maybe she's just not very nice,' I chime in, without really thinking about what I'm saying. Charles looks at me, shocked.

Mikey throws down another glass of champagne. 'Don't say anything to Dill, but I'm with you on this, Nic.'

It's good to know I'm not the only one who doesn't like her – for a while I was worried I might have been possessed by the green-eyed monster. Speaking of monsters, as Charles and I make our way back to our table, we are stopped by Daisy.

'Where were you last night?' she asks bluntly. I had planned on thinking up an excuse, however I was distracted with other things this morning. Thankfully I had time to tell Charles all about her during dinner, so he's well prepared.

'And who is your friend?' she asks, looking him up and down and licking her lips like she genuinely wants to eat him.

'Charles. Nice to meet you,' he says, shaking her hand. 'I'm sorry, Nicole stayed with me last night. She will be tonight as well, I hope that's OK? At least you'll have the room all to yourself.'

'Oh, so this is your boyfriend?' she asks me. I stare at Charles blankly.

'I am,' he replies confidently.

'Oh, OK,' she says before losing interest and walking away.

'I hope you will accept my offer,' Charles says.

'Really?'

'Of course. I do only have the one bed, but it's not like we haven't shared before.'

I laugh. I guess that's true, although I don't remember it. Perhaps tonight will be more memorable though …

Chapter 25

I like to think that, deep down, I am a nice person. However, I felt a weird sense of satisfaction watching Dylan and Crystal go off to the honeymoon suite, knowing I've already spent a night in their bed. Can you imagine what Crystal would say if she knew? She'd probably insist on changing sheets or rooms or hotels.

I tried to talk to Crystal earlier. I went up to her and told her she looked lovely. She replied with, 'Thank you, and thank you for not making much of an effort to try to upstage me.' End of conversation.

I was really hoping that we'd be able to get along. Dylan is such a huge part of my life and I don't want that to change. I suppose it will though. She'll be there on all the tours – on the bus, backstage, at the hotel and with two screaming babies. Fucking wonderful. So, in the past week I guess I've lost my two favourite bands to tour with.

I swing by my/Daisy's room to collect my things on the way up to Charles' room. I plan on leaving fairly early tomorrow, and I don't want to have to face Daisy or anyone else for that matter. Another quick getaway. To be honest, I just want to get the hell out of London. As silly as it sounds, I'm scared I'll bump into Luke. I know London is huge, and it's very unlikely, but that's how awkward I'm feeling.

Now in Charles' room, I can't help but feel a little scandalous – sharing a bed with a man I hardly know. On tour it's one of the most standard, day-to-day things you can do, but Charles isn't someone on tour, Charles is from the 'real world'. The 'real world', where you only go to bed with someone if you want to … oh God! You think you're so streetwise and socially blessed when you spend a lot of time with musicians. Instead it's making me forget how to behave like a regular human being. What am I supposed to do? If I leave now it will seem strange, and I'm sure I'll have to work with Charles in the future – is that a reason to stay or to go? This is so messed up. Yes, Charles is gorgeous, but I don't want to have sex with him. Regardless of what my brain is telling me, my body is kicking off my shoes and sitting on the bed. It clearly has an agenda that I am not aware of.

This room is nice – it's not as big as Dylan's, but it's a hell of a lot bigger and nicer than Daisy's.

'Can I get you a drink? It's pretty late, I think I'm going to get in bed if you don't mind,' Charles says, and now it definitely feels real.

'Sure, I think I'll do the same. I'm kind of tired and I've got a long trip ahead of me tomorrow.' Plus, if I'm asleep then I don't have to have sex with you – hopefully.

'It's only a couple of hours on the train, isn't it?'

'Yep,' I reply awkwardly, killing the conversation.

'So, drink, what can I get you?' he asks after a few awkward seconds.

'Surprise me. Am I OK to get changed in the bathroom?'

'Go ahead,' he says with a smile.

I disappear into the bathroom with my case. This is going to be fine, I'll get through this. Searching through my case I find my pyjamas, and the startling reality of what I have done hits me. To sleep in, I packed a black vest … and my SpongeBob SquarePants short-shorts. Smooth move, Nicole Wilde.

Brushing my teeth and taking off my make-up (and if I'm totally honest, putting quite a bit of make-up back on), I venture out of the bathroom.

'Oh God! Sorry!' I squeal, throwing my hands over my eyes. Standing at the end of the bed, wearing nothing but a pair of black socks and a tight-fitting pair of black boxer shorts, is Charles. 'I didn't realise you were still getting changed.'

'No, it's OK. I'm changed.'

I slowly move my hands away from my eyes and try to focus my gaze on his eyes and absolutely nothing lower down. There's a little voice in my head (although I believe it originates somewhere further down my body) begging me to look down, but I'm stronger than that.

'This is how I sleep,' Charles tells me. 'I didn't bring pyjamas.'

He nods towards my super-sexy night-time attire and appears to be stifling a giggle. 'Anyway, it's all you saw me in this morning.'

Charles hops on the bed, settling right in the middle with his hands behind his head.

'You getting in?' he asks with a cheeky smile.

I nod nervously, pull back the covers and climb into bed, staying as close to the edge as possible. As I lie back, in one swift movement Charles places an arm behind me and scoops me towards him, resulting in my head resting on his chest.

'So tell me a bit about yourself,' Charles says, squeezing me tightly.

'Erm ...' I always blank when people ask me these kinds of questions. It's hard when you're put on the spot, especially being a writer. People think words come easily to us, but that's usually after a few sleepless nights at the keyboard and a scary amount of coffee. 'Well I live in Leeds, on my own. My parents and my brother are living in France at the moment – some work thing of my dad's.'

'Are they coming back?' he asks, actually sounding interested.

'Oh yeah, definitely. Soon, I hope. We have a house in the

country, but I didn't want to stay there on my own so I rent a flat in the centre. It's OK, but I haven't ever really adjusted from family life to being on my own.'

'I live alone too, although I've always been a loner. Only child, busy parents. Do you have a boyfriend?'

'Nope,' I reply – I'm never sure how to answer this question. No, I haven't had a boyfriend for years, but that's not to say I don't have boyfriend-type characters in my life. The problem has always been that the kind of guys I am attracted to don't have much willpower when it comes to girls throwing themselves at them, so they don't have girlfriends, which in turn means that I don't have boyfriends. It's gone on for so long that I wouldn't know what to do with one now. To try to put this point across to a practical stranger is impossible without looking sort of bad, so hopefully he won't ask any questions.

'Do you have a partner?'

'No, but I'm still looking. Tell me about your last boyfriend.'

'Gosh, I wasn't expecting to have this conversation tonight. I haven't had a boyfriend in years.' I instantly regret this confession because now he's going to wonder what is wrong with me.

'That surprises me.'

I told you.

'It's a long story,' I say in self-defence.

He smiles. 'You're beautiful, any man would be lucky to have you.'

'You're only saying that because you're in bed with me,' I joke.

'No, I'm not,' he says rather bluntly, and as I turn to look at him he kisses me. It's only for a few seconds, but it takes my breath away.

'Well, good night then,' he says, reaching over and turning the light out.

So there I am, in the dark – and in more ways than one. I'm a little confused because I just kissed a normal boy, and I think I liked it.

Chapter 26

I woke up in the exact position I fell asleep in – cuddled up to Charles. This must mean I *really* love him, or at least that's the soppy line that Emily fed me during our five-minute phone call. When I woke up, Charles was already awake. He kissed my forehead and then went for a shower – that's when I called Em.

It took me a little while to fall asleep last night. I felt such a buzz from that kiss and I'm still feeling it now.

Stepping out of the bathroom with nothing but a towel around his waist and a smile on his face, Charles stares at me and I feel a bit awkward.

'Good morning, you,' I say to break the silence.

'Good morning, Miss Wilde. How are you today?'

'I'm OK – not looking forward to getting the train home.'

'Well I'm free all day. I could walk you to the station?'

I smile. 'That would be great, thank you. Oh, and thank you for letting me sleep here, I don't think I could have survived another second with Daisy.'

'It was no problem – and I really enjoyed your company.' Charles runs a hand through his wet hair and I battle to maintain eye contact again.

'Do you mind if I use your shower?' I ask.

'Sure. Cup of tea after?'

'Oh, that would be great.' I haven't had any caffeine in twenty-four hours and I'm really starting to feel it.

I climb out of bed as ladylike and as sexily as possible – something my SpongeBob jim-jams are making very difficult. As I pass Charles, he plants a kiss on my cheek before watching me make my way to the bathroom, giving me a little wave as I close the door behind me.

Unlike in Daisy's room, there is a nice fluffy robe and towels galore waiting for me. The bath is much bigger too.

I hear Charles click the TV on, so as soon as I get in my warm, bubbly bath I get straight back on the phone to Emily.

'Can you talk now?' she asks excitedly when she answers.

'Yes. How are you?'

'How am I? Are you joking? Tell me what happened, what is he like?'

'Like a younger Daniel Craig with the charm of Michael Bublé.' I'm teasing her, although that's actually a fairly accurate description.

'If that's true then you marry him! I don't care if he isn't in a band,' she teases me in return, although she probably means that as well. 'Imagine if we both had boyfriends, things are going really well with—'

'Shit, Em, I'd better go,' I interrupt her. Charles must have turned the TV off and I'm worried he might hear me on the phone.

I place my phone down carefully on the bathroom floor (the last thing it needs is a bath) and grab the bottle of complimentary body wash – this is the life. It's flashy hotels like this one that remind me of touring with Dylan. Now that Two For The Road are pretty famous they're staying in much nicer hotels, but that wasn't always the case. When I hit the road with them in the early days – when they were supporting any band that would have them – they couldn't even afford to stay in hotels, not even the odd night in a Travelodge. Instead we slept in the old banger of a van we drove around in, everyone in their sleeping bag on the floor surrounded by all their gear. I know I complain about the bathroom facilities on the big tour buses, but they beat the ones in the van – there weren't any. It's easy enough for the boys to hop off the bus and pee up a tree – or do it out the window as you're flying along the motorway if you're Eddie – but for girls it's difficult and that's why to me that tour will always be known as the Hold It In Tour.

I used to be terrified sleeping in that damn thing – the back door didn't even lock. What we would do is, on a night (or let's face it, early morning), we'd all pile in and then the last person would reverse the van against a wall so that no one from outside could get in. It also meant that no one inside could get out in a hurry, so if there was a fire you'd be screwed – luckily the fires only happened while the van was moving. Thankfully they signed a record deal before the van had chance to kill them.

I stop daydreaming and examine my hands. My fingers are sufficiently wrinkled and I wonder how long I've been in here.

I wrap the fluffy robe around my body and start putting on my make-up. To be honest with you, I'd rather he saw me without the robe than without the make-up, and that might actually happen because it didn't occur to me to bring any clothes in here with me.

Emily seems to think I should make a move on him and while I'm not that great at the emotional stuff, if there's one thing I know how to do, it's make a move. Wearing nothing but a towel will certainly help me in my quest.

Charles is sitting on the bed playing with his phone, so I sit down next to him.

'Sorry, do you want to get dressed?' he mutters, jumping to his feet, keeping his eyes on his phone. 'I'll take a walk to Mikey's room.'

Rejected. A quick flash of his smile and he's gone. I guess I will be getting dressed after all.

Chapter 27

I waited with Charles as he checked out, deciding not to pop up and say goodbye to Daisy, or Dylan and Crystal who I'm certain would not want me popping my head around the door to say goodbye.

We're making our way to the train station, Charles dragging my pink suitcase along behind him.

'So how did you get into music journalism?' he asks me.

'Well, I was a total Bander when I was a teenager and—'

'What?' he interrupts me.

'What?' I ask, confused.

'You were a what?'

'Oh, a Bander. Sorry, it's easy to forget you're not a teenage girl,' I joke. 'A Bander is just a fan I guess – an extreme fan – but not in a weird way. Banders follow bands around, turn up at hotels, queue outside venues for hours on end … just to meet the band and hang out.'

'So you were a groupie?' he asks.

'No! No sex!' I laugh. 'I was probably about fourteen when I started following bands around.'

'A stalker, then?'

'I suppose you could liken the actions of a Bander to stalking, but it was always a friendly act. Well, most often a friendly act,' I correct myself.

'Most often?' he asks with a confused laugh.

'Oh, you don't mess with Banders.' I laugh to myself, a million memories bouncing around in my head. 'Banders can be brutal, and sometimes you have to do extreme things to meet bands – lots of lying to lots of people …' As well as flirting with security guards and breaking and entering, but we won't tell Charles that. He looks shocked (but slightly amused) as it is. 'All you need is one boybander and twenty or thirty Banders trying to get a photo and you've got a Royal Rumble right in front of your eyes.'

'Well who knew that sort of thing happened,' he chuckles. 'So when you hear stories about fans going crazy at gigs …'

'Banders.'

'And you were one of them?'

'I was. If I weren't a Bander, I wouldn't have made as many friends as I have, I probably wouldn't be doing journalism – I wouldn't have met Dylan! I was a fan of The Burnouts for a while before meeting them and that's when we hit it off.'

'Did you and Dylan ever get together?' he asks rather bluntly, and with a very serious look on his face.

'Oh God, no!' I insist, without a moment's hesitation. I don't think anyone would be surprised if I had slept with Dylan – who hasn't these days? – but I honestly haven't.

'You didn't ever, you know, get it on?'

I laugh loudly. 'Get it on? Who says that?'

'Don't dodge my questions,' he replies sternly, instantly wiping the smile from my face.

'No, of course not, we're friends – best friends. We've never even come close to—' I stifle a smile, '—getting it on.'

'Like *When Harry Met Sally*?' he asks, sounding a little sarcastic.

'Not really, they get together in the end of that film.'

'Exactly.'

We carry on walking in silence. So Mr Perfect does have a

bit of a dark side.

'So,' I eventually break the silence. 'You've seen *When Harry Met Sally*? Men like you are hard to find.'

'We're a dying breed,' he says, back to his usual charming self.

Finally at the train station, the familiar whiff of Starbucks fills my nostrils and I can't resist it.

'Well, thank you for walking me here – and carrying *that* suitcase. I'm going to pop in Starbucks to kill a little time.'

'I'll come with you,' he suggests, ushering me in the right direction. 'What can I get you?'

'Caramel macchiato, please.'

'I'll have a caramel macchiato and a cappuccino,' he tells the girl taking our order.

I insist he lets me pay, after everything he's done for me this weekend, but he's having none of it.

As we wander out of Starbucks, I check the time – I really ought to be boarding my train now.

'Well, I had better get going,' I tell Charles, and I could swear he looks disappointed. 'Thank you for the coffee. And for the room. And for the alibi.'

He laughs. 'You're welcome – especially for the room.'

Oh, there's that smile again. We stand and stare at each other for a moment – what is the proper etiquette for saying goodbye to a man you hardly know, but have shared a bed with twice?

'It was nice to finally meet you,' I tell him sincerely and wrap my arms around his neck for a goodbye hug.

'It was nice to meet you too.'

Charles loosens his grip around my waist and I move back slightly, leaving us face to face.

It's an intense moment and I can't think of anything to say, not that it matters, because before I can utter a few awkward silence-breaking words, Charles pulls me closer again, only this time for a kiss. A long kiss.

'Wow,' I say out loud, although not intentionally, when he

finally lets me go.

'Wow indeed. You had better go, you're going to miss your train.'

'Goodbye then.'

I turn around and make my way towards the barriers. As I walk through, my phone beeps and I fumble in my bag to find it.

It's from Charles. 'Miss you already.'

'You too,' I reply.

Chapter 28

Lying on my sofa, nursing a cold cup of tea, I can't help but feel a little pissed off. After what felt like the longest train journey of my life, I was looking forward to coming home and having a night in and a catch-up with Emily. Instead I am sitting here bored and alone because Vicky is still living with Em and apparently she needed her tonight.

I called Emily when I got home and we managed to chat for a few minutes while Vicky was in the shower. I think she's driving Emily mad. Today Vicky went through Em's wardrobe, pulled out all of her clothes and concluded that they would all be too big for her to borrow – that's Vicky though. She makes these little comments that don't seem so bad, but you know exactly what she means. She may as well have jumped up and down on Emily's bed shouting 'look how big your clothes are on me, fatty!'.

I don't know what could have possibly gone wrong in the shower, but Vicky came out crying so Em had to take care of her tonight. So here I am, alone and bored, and without any work to keep me busy because I did all I had to do before I went to London.

I grab my laptop and type a parent-friendly version of the weekend's events in an email to my mum, who is even more excited about the photos being in *Bacci* magazine than I am. Then

I go through the motions of replying to emails, checking socials, that sort of thing. Then I open Messenger and glance down the list of names and my heart skips a beat at one of them – Luke Fox. So much for telling myself that I didn't care.

Luke: Hello?

I suppose I could close Messenger and pretend I didn't see his message, but then again I don't want to sever ties with the band.

Nicole: Hey.
Luke: How are you?
Nicole: Fine thanks, you?

Wow, this is awkward.

Luke: I'm great, just bored backstage. We're back on tour, as of today.
Nicole: Really? Is Eddie OK?
Luke: He's fine. His leg is in plaster, but he's loving all the attention.

I bet he is. This is probably the best thing to ever happen to Eddie. The groupies will be all over him – even more so than usual. I don't really know what to say, so I say nothing. The ball is totally in his court.

Luke: We're in Leeds on Friday, I can put you on the guest list if you like?
Nicole: Thanks, that would be great.
Luke: +1?
Nicole: Please. I'll bring Emily.
Luke: Great. Looking forward to seeing you, so sorry about last time.

Nicole: Don't worry about it, honestly.
Luke: We'll talk about it properly on Friday?
Nicole: Sure.
Luke: Well I'd better go get ready.
Nicole: OK, say hi to the boys for me.

Now there's a conversation I'm going to do everything I can to avoid having. I'll take Emily with me, under strict instructions that she doesn't leave my side for a second. I remember doing something similar at school when I knew that a boy I didn't like was going to ask me out. I asked one of my friends to promise not to leave me alone with him. Then again, as soon as he asked her to she walked off and left me alone with him and I ended up being his girlfriend for six months, but Emily would never do that to me.

I'm feeling really nervous about going, but I don't want to end up out of touch, especially now I'm probably out of Dylan's loop. At least we'll be in my home town, which means I can go home afterwards. If Luke thinks I'll be sharing a bunk or a room with him, he can think again.

Chapter 29

'So come on, how was it?' Jake asks me.

'It was OK, I guess,' I tease, amused by his interest in popular culture and the gossip from Dylan's wedding. Jake couldn't have cared less about all this stuff until he met me, and although he pretends he still doesn't care, I know better.

'Tell us everything,' Emily insists.

'It was *so* glamorous,' I spill. 'Well, ninety-nine per cent glamorous.'

'What do you mean?' Emily looks confused.

'Crystal Slater – sorry, Crystal King.'

'You didn't like her?' Em asks me.

'Honestly? She's horrible. I went down there with an open mind and I gave her a chance, but I really didn't like her.'

Emily and Jake are both staring at me, absolutely fascinated by my story. We wouldn't be able to have this conversation if Vicky were here, because I don't trust her one bit. We've sent her on the lunch run, which gives us a chance to have a decent conversation.

'She was horrible to me from the word go, I didn't stand a chance. If she wasn't going to try, then why should I?'

'She probably feels threatened by you,' Jake tells me frankly. 'We've all seen you with Dylan, you're his right-hand woman. He hangs off your every word. She's not going to like that.'

'Well I can't imagine I'll be his right-hand woman any more, not now he has a wife.' I say the word wife in a silly voice.

I go on to tell them all about it, everything from Daisy to Dylan going missing, although I'm careful with what I say about Charles – it's not that I don't trust Jake, it's just more of a girly conversation.

I've only just finished telling my story when Vicky comes barging through the door. As she does, our conversation stops rather abruptly, none of us thinking fast enough to pretend we were talking about something else. Vicky dramatically throws the bags containing our lunch down on her desk. My initial concern is with my sandwich.

'Don't stop on my account, carry on,' she yells, already in a full-blown strop.

'We weren't talking about anything in particular,' I tell her with a forced smile, although judging by the look on her face she isn't buying it.

'Bullshit!' she shouts.

'Vic,' Emily speaks to her in a hushed voice, 'don't forget who you're talking to, Nicole is your boss.'

Vicky screams before turning on her and walking straight back out the door.

'Oh, for God's sake! Talk about overreacting,' I say.

'Shall I go after her?' Emily asks me. I'm thinking no, but I tell her yes.

'She's taking advantage of Em's good nature,' I tell Jake when Emily has left the room.

'I know, but she won't listen. You've been away a lot recently, so the two of them have been together a lot. Can't you just sack her, Nic? We don't need her really.'

'I want to, believe me. I don't think I have a real reason though.'

To be honest, I have no idea about that side of things, but it didn't really matter when I was only employing my friends. I'll have to have a word with ET.

I walk over to Vicky's desk and inspect my lunch. Panic over, my sandwich is fine, so I head into my office with it. Jake is back at his desk happily tapping away at something I probably couldn't understand, so I shut my door behind me. That way I don't have to face Vicky when she comes back – if she comes back.

I scroll through some of the press releases in my inbox to see if there's anything special. This is the most stressful time, just after we put an issue online, because we have to start finding things to fill the next one. There's nothing jumping out of the screen at me, but I don't need to worry just yet.

I am stopped in my tracks when I notice a new email come through. It's from Charles.

I click the message instantly. I haven't heard from Charles since that text just after he left me at the station.

'Thought you might like to see a couple of these – strictly for your eyes only.'

I download the attachments excitedly. The first one I open is a photo of me and Dylan from the wedding. Wow, what an awesome photo! It pains me that I can't show anyone yet, but I know that the magazine is out later this week. The second photo is the one of me and Charles, and I can't help but think about what a cute couple we make – not that we are a couple. Oh dear, there's that crazy talk. You know, those little things you hear other girls say right before you thank God you're not one of *those* girls. I look so happy in this photo. I'm not drunk, I'm not hanging off a celebrity, I'm not in some random club, I'm just myself, standing next to a normal bloke, and I'm smiling. I feel vain just thinking it, but my dress looks amazing, and despite not having enough time to finish my hair, it still looks pretty good. I'm so proud of these photos and I can't wait to see the rest. I want to show Emily as soon as she gets back, although I already feel a strong sense of loyalty towards Charles, and if he says they're for my eyes only then I plan to keep it that way.

I can hear Emily and Vicky chatting with Jake – Emily must have been able to talk her into coming back, what a shame.

Deciding to keep out of her way, I stay in my office until 5 p.m., but unfortunately, I can't go home without walking through the main office. Let's say I could fit my arse through the window, we're way too high up for that to be an option.

When I walk out into the main office, despite the fact that it is 5 p.m., everyone is hard at work and in total silence.

'Jake, are you OK switching everything off?' I ask, trying to avoid eye contact with Vicky although I can feel her eyes on me.

'Yeah, no problem. See you tomorrow.'

'I'll call you later.' Emily smiles at me.

'Yeah sure, see you all later.'

'Wait,' Vicky calls after me. I take a deep, calming breath before turning to face her.

She makes her way across the room to me with a smile on her face, but she's still got that look about her, the kind of evil look that would make you think twice about leaving your children or small animals with her.

'I'm sorry about earlier, Nicole. I thought you were talking about me but, don't worry, Emily told me everything.'

I look over at Emily, hoping that she didn't actually tell her everything. She probably made something up.

'Oh good,' I say as sincerely as I can manage. 'Forget it ever happened.'

'I will,' she says, and then she does that last thing I would ever expect her to do. She hugs me. I have never seen Vicky show anyone any kind of affection, and here she is, giving me a hug.

'There,' she says, finally letting go. I can see Jake sniggering behind her back.

'Well,' I say, still rather shocked, 'see you all later.'

How weird was that?

Chapter 30

Maybe it's because the past couple of weeks have been so eventful, but this week has been so bloody boring.

Work has been quiet, Vicky has been behaving, I haven't heard anything from Dylan – I wonder when I will hear from him. Is he even allowed to talk to me? I can't say I've had much experience with pregnant women but, going by what I've seen in the movies, hormones can make them a little touchy, right? I don't know how true that is, but I can imagine Crystal being a total nightmare, sitting on her arse, demanding weird things in the middle of the night.

I haven't heard from Charles either, not since he emailed me those photos. Not a call, text or email. You know what they say, you don't miss something until it's gone. A week without drama, and I'm missing it. I get the feeling that's all about to change though because Luke messaged me this morning to say he was excited about seeing me. The poor bastard, he probably thinks he's going to get lucky tonight. I sent him a polite reply, but nothing is going to happen between us. It's not that I'm going soft but he isn't just another band member, he's been my friend for years and I'm not about to ruin our friendship by sleeping with him. The worst thing I could do would be to demote myself from friend of the band to just another conquest. I have always believed that it's the ones they don't sleep with who they care about the most.

Today is going very slowly. It's 4 p.m. now; at five I can go home and get ready which will take a couple of hours – I'll probably be late, but what's new?

Spinning around in my chair as I often do to pass time, I stop to face the window and gaze out over the busy streets of Leeds. I have such an amazing view from my office window and yet I rarely stop to appreciate it. I'm really lucky the ByteBanter team took me on, because I could never afford the rent on an office like this – or on my flat to be honest, my parents pay for that. They told me they were moving to France for my dad's job, my brother too, and after all their efforts to talk me into doing a degree, we decided it would be best if I stayed here. They weren't supposed to be gone very long – a year or so – but things took off over there and the years soon piled up. I'm not sure when they're coming back, but in the meantime I get lots of free holidays.

Our family home isn't actually that far from Leeds, but I haven't been back since they left. I didn't fancy living alone and village life just isn't for me. So everything is as I left it – well, it should be. My auntie and uncle are house-sitting for us, but I don't visit them. Mainly because we're not that close, but also because it would remind me of how much I miss my mum and dad. I even miss Jack, my little brother, but most of all I miss our dog, Harley. I haven't seen any of them since July when I popped over for a few days. My Mum is always trying to talk me into moving there, and, believe me, it's tempting – particularly on a cold and gloomy day like today – but I've come so far with the magazine, it would be a shame to give it all up to live it up in France. I think.

My phone rings, which is lucky because I was on the verge of feeling lonely, abandoned and emotional. I spin my chair meaningfully until I am facing my desk again. It's Charles.

'How are you?' he asks me.

'I'm great, thank you. How are you?' I neglect to tell him that I am bored, lonely and missing my mummy.

'I'm good. What are you doing tonight?'

'I'm going to a gig – just one of the bands I work with.'

'Oh,' he says, clearly disappointed.

'What's up?' I ask.

'I'm actually on the train at the moment, I'll be in Leeds in about ten minutes. I thought I'd surprise you. I should have checked that you were free, I'm sorry.'

'Don't apologise,' I insist, suddenly feeling like the bad guy. 'I'll text you directions to the office, come straight over.'

'Are you sure? I don't want to ruin your plans.'

'You won't be, I'd really like to see you,' I tell him honestly.

Panic stations! I jump out of my chair and fly towards my office door, slamming my brakes on just in time to stop myself crashing face-first through the glass.

'Emily,' I try to call her name calmly, but that child-at-Christmas squeak in my voice is a little obvious. 'Do you have a moment?'

'Come on then, who's put that smile on your face?' she asks, and I feel my grin widen.

'Charles,' I tell her as calmly as possible. 'He'll be here any minute.'

'What? Here? *Here* here?'

'Yep, he just called. He wanted to surprise me.'

'Oh my God, Nicole, that's great. He must really like you. You give this man a proper chance, none of your usual bullshit about him not being a musician.'

I laugh, mainly because she's being serious.

'What am I going to do about tonight? The gig is sold out and I can't really call Luke and ask him to put another bloke on the guest list, can I? But I don't want to miss the show …'

'You should go. Take Charles – you want Luke to see you with another guy, it'll sort out your friendship, set some boundaries.'

'Or you could take Vicky,' I suggest, but the look on her face says no.

'Give Charles my ticket, it's fine.'

I'm not sure exactly how fine it really is, but I kiss her on the cheek and tell her what a good friend she is.

'Ah, Nicole, what if life isn't about sleeping with rockstars? Maybe life is about being with a nice guy who travels two hundred miles just to surprise you.'

I smile. Perhaps she's right.

'It's so romantic,' Emily continues. 'I can't wait to meet him.'

Jake knocks on the door.

'Nicole, there's a bloke here for you.'

This is it. I stand up, adjust my dress (it must have worked its way up around my waist when I was playing with my chair) and head towards the door. Emily follows close behind me.

There he is, and even hotter than I remember, standing there in his suit. He must have come straight from work. He greets me with a kiss on the cheek and I introduce him to everyone. The look on Vicky's face has made my life, she's totally jealous and she can't even hide it. Despite it being my choice not to date the conventional way, she's always teasing me, saying I can't get a man. Usually I'm not this smug, but I just can't help it when it comes to Vicky.

'I actually came to show you this,' he tells me, rummaging around in his bag. He pulls out the issue of *Bacci* magazine with Dylan's wedding feature on the cover. It doesn't hit the shops until Monday.

'Oh my God,' I exclaim, carefully taking the magazine from him and delicately flicking through the pages. The photographs are amazing and I'm in quite a few of them, which delights me.

'Wow, look, there you are again,' Emily points out.

Vicky leans over. 'You can hardly tell it's her in that one, it's so small.'

'Give it a rest, Vicky,' I hear a male voice say. I have to look to double-check that it is actually Jake who said this, because he's usually so laid-back and never confronts anyone. Vicky folds her arms in a strop and sits back at her desk while the rest of us chat about the wedding.

'Well, I'd better make a move, you've got a gig to get to,' Charles eventually says.

'I have a plus one, you're welcome to come with me.'

'Are you sure?' he asks with a huge smile on his face.

'Of course. I just need to pop home and change.'

I head back into my office and shut my computer down. I'm so nervous I feel sick, but I just can't stop smiling. I certainly don't feel bored or lonely now.

Chapter 31

'Nice place,' Charles says as we walk through the door of my flat.

I was so bored last night I actually tidied up the place a bit – I'm glad I did.

'Can I get you anything?' I ask.

'I'm fine, thank you.'

'Well make yourself at home,' I gesture towards the sofa. 'I'll just get changed.'

He sits down and I rush into my bedroom. I can't actually believe he's here. He's travelled all this way just to see me, I can't get my head around it.

I fling open my wardrobes and gaze across everything I own. I feel under extra pressure to look amazing now. My original plan was to show Luke what he's missing, but now I really need to dress to impress. Grabbing my black boots, I decide to work my way up. Black tights next, and then an AC/DC T-shirt that's just about long enough to pass off as a dress. I finish the look with my biker jacket, countless accessories and a ton of black eye make-up and red lipstick. I backcomb my hair a little and I'm good to go – not only has this got to be a new record, but for once I don't think I am going to be late.

Grabbing my phone and bag, I stroll causally into the living room.

'Wow. You look great,' Charles tells me.

'So do you.'

While I was getting ready Charles has changed too. He's going to leave his bag at mine to save taking it to the gig. He's wearing jeans and a tight-fitting T-shirt. He grabs a jacket not unlike mine.

'Shall we go then?' he smiles.

I gesture towards the door but, instead of passing me, Charles takes hold of my hand.

'Let's go.'

Chapter 32

We're standing outside the venue as the security guy looks down the list for my name. Charles is still holding my hand – he hasn't let it go since we left the flat, not for a second. We chatted all the way here; it's nice when you meet someone who the conversation just flows with.

'Nicole Wilde, plus one. In you go,' the doorman as he ticks my name off the list. We finally stop holding hands when it's time to get them stamped on the way in and I'm way too nervous to initiate contact again, so we walk in side by side.

It's really busy here but we eyeball a space at the bar and push our way through. As Charles orders our drinks, I scan the room for familiar faces, but I fail to spot anyone.

'A screwdriver for the lady,' Charles says, handing me the vodka and orange I asked for. For some reason it makes me cringe a little.

Charles is just sipping his pint when his phone starts ringing.

'I have to take this, I'm really sorry. Back in a moment,' he says, kissing me on the cheek and disappearing outside.

I scan the room again. I know TFTR are a bit too famous to hang around in the venue beforehand now, but this is my turf and I usually see someone I know.

I'm suddenly feeling really nervous. Maybe it was a bad idea bringing Charles here. Should I really be trying to make Luke jealous? I don't want to piss him off by rubbing his nose in it.

I throw my drink back and lean over the bar to get the barman's attention.

'Another please,' I say when he finally makes his way over to me. 'And with a straw, please.'

As I sip my drink, I feel a familiar pair of hands on my hips. I'd know that pervy yet sweet touch anywhere. I put down my drink, turn around. It's Luke.

'Hello, gorgeous,' he says, taking hold of my hands and kissing me on both cheeks. He keeps hold of my hands and looks into my eyes and I feel all tingly and my heart is pounding in my chest – a feeling I only ever experience around him.

He gestures towards the pint on the bar behind me. 'Well I know that isn't yours because you hate beer,' he laughs.

I've gone from feeling lovesick to actually sick. I pray that Charles doesn't come back in and I consider making an excuse to leave. Maybe Emily is right, maybe Luke does know how to play me, but it's the look in his eyes. He looks so pleased to see me and I feel like a huge bitch. I open my mouth, hoping a believable reason to leave will come out, but I am stopped in my tracks by the return of Charles. Oh shit.

'Hey,' Charles says bluntly. I notice him give Luke a funny look as he puts his arm around me, tearing my hands from Luke's. I feel absolutely terrible. I need to remember to tell Emily what a terrible idea this was. She is usually spot-on with her advice.

'Well, I'd better go set up,' Luke tells us, but I know he's lying. I hate myself for making him feel so uncomfortable. I almost hate Charles for making things even worse, although I guess this is my fault. I just want to go back to being friends, instead I think we're going to fall out. Luke doesn't wait for a reply, he just walks away.

'Who was that, then?' Charles asks, with a slightly aggressive tone to his voice.

I hesitate for five seconds. Five seconds too long.

'That's Luke, he's the drummer in the band we're here to see.'

'I know that, Nicole. I work in music PR,' he says almost angrily. 'He was holding your hands.'

'Yeah, we're old friends,' I reply defensively.

'Old friends, like you and Dylan?'

I know exactly what he's getting at.

'I have to go to the bathroom, back in a minute.'

I walk off towards the toilets. I know exactly where that conversation was going and I really don't need it right now. I feel terrible enough, I don't need some guy I hardly know giving me a hard time.

Barging my way through the doors, I make my way down the lonely corridor towards the toilets. I have an overwhelming urge to cry (don't I always these days?), but I don't – if only because I'm aware of exactly how much eye make-up I'm wearing.

As I get to the end of the corridor, the men's bathroom door opens and out walks Luke.

'Hey,' I blurt out, over-enthusiastically.

'Hey. So who's that dick?' he asks, and I laugh.

'That's Charles.'

'Right. You seeing him then?'

This is all so high school.

'Sort of.'

'Right.'

This is weird. He looks genuinely upset. I'd go as far as to say heartbroken if I didn't know him so well.

'Well I hope he realises what a fucking lucky guy he is.'

'I don't get you, Luke,' I tell him, unable to handle any more game-playing. 'You keep making these comments that seem so sweet, and then acting like a bit of an arsehole. Just put me straight, please.'

'What do you want me to say, Nicole?'

'Why is he a lucky guy?' I ask, hoping for an honest answer.

He stares at me for a moment, thinking over my question.

'Because …' his expression changes from sincere to smug, '… I was hoping you could bunk up with me tonight. But I guess you'll be in his bed instead.' He winks at me before walking away.

Unbelievable. Just when I think I am seeing a softer side to that man, he turns around and shows me that he only has a hard side – literally.

Inside the toilets I stare at myself in the mirror, pleading with my eyes not to let any tears out. I'd better get back out to Charles. I'll bet he was only trying to protect me. He knows the music industry, he knows musicians. He could probably tell what Luke was after the second he laid eyes on him. I'm really lucky he was here tonight or I probably would have ended up with Luke.

Peering through the door, I check that the coast is clear and head back into the gig. The first band has just come on stage. Walking over to Charles, I link my arm with his.

'Let's forget about that,' I tell him, but he gives me a puzzled look and I realise he can't hear me because of the music. I lean closer to him.

'I said, let's forget about all that. He's just a friend, I promise you.'

'Don't worry,' he smiles, and rests a hand gently on my cheek. Then he leans closer and kisses me on the lips. Neither of us says anything after that, we just watch the band.

Chapter 33

After the gig, I introduced Charles to Mark and Ben, and we all chatted for a while. I'm just waiting for the gang of girls to disperse from around Eddie and Luke. It was weird seeing Eddie on stage with his broken leg, mainly because he never usually stands still on stage.

As soon as Eddie and Luke are alone, we walk towards them. They're looking right at us and talking, and I can't help but wonder if they're talking about me.

'Eddie, you are a real trooper,' I tell him.

'I try. Got to keep the fans happy.'

I introduce him to Charles. I don't introduce Luke, it seems weird.

'So what's happening tonight?' I ask. 'Are you guys partying here, or are we going somewhere else?'

It is a TFTR tradition that after every gig, we party. In fact, that's the reason they're called Two For The Road, they're total party animals.

'We're just going to head back to the bus tonight. Probably drive through the night,' Luke replies.

'Really?' I ask, astonished.

'Eddie's leg is giving him shit, isn't it, mate?' Luke nudges

Eddie, who dutifully replies.

'Yeah, my doctor told me not to push myself, so …' his voice trails off.

'Oh, OK.' I don't really know what to say.

'We're actually going to head off now, so we'll see you next time,' Luke tells me, walking off without so much as a goodbye.

I look at Eddie for some sort of explanation.

'Well you'll have to come here and hug me, I'm an injured man.'

Forcing a smile, I lean towards him and wrap my arms around his neck.

'He's upset, he'll get over it,' he whispers in my ear.

'Go put your feet up, see you soon hopefully,' I tell him, and I really hope I do see him soon, but I doubt I will. This is the end of the road for me.

'Shall we get out of here then?' I ask Charles, and he nods.

Once we're outside, we start walking back in the direction of my flat.

'They were lying about calling it a night you know,' I tell him, unable to disguise my disappointment.

'I know, I guessed as much.'

I sigh.

We walk the rest of the way in silence. I can't believe Luke has ruined this evening for me, whether he meant to or not. Of course, I ignore the little voice in my head telling me that it's all my fault.

We stop outside my flat.

'Well, I'll pop up and grab my bag and then head to my hotel.'

'Where are you staying?' I ask.

He laughs awkwardly as we get in the lift.

'What? Where are you staying?'

'I haven't actually booked in anywhere,' Charles admits. 'I was sort of hoping I could stay with you tonight.'

I look at him surprised, and he gives me a cheeky smile.

'What? We've already shared a bed twice, don't look so surprised.'

Stepping out of the lift, we walk towards my door and I mess around with my keys for a moment.

'I had a great time tonight, despite your angry male fan club,' he tells me, running the back of his hand gently up and down my back.

'So did I,' I reply, finally getting my key inside the lock. Charles is leaning on the wall in a cool, don't-give-a-shit manner as I turn to face him.

'You can stay here tonight if you want to,' I tell him as he moves his face much closer to mine.

'Really?' he whispers.

'Well, I owe you for putting me up in London. So yes.'

Before I have chance to change my mind, Charles kisses me passionately. After a few minutes of kissing in the hallway, he picks me up, fireman-style, before unlocking my door and carrying me inside. The door closes behind us and we're in total darkness, apart from a little light shining in through the windows.

'Where's the light switch?' he laughs.

'Over there.'

'You do realise I can't see where "over there" is, don't you?'

I laugh, unable to offer any assistance slung over his shoulder.

'Forget it, bedroom is this way,' he says, carefully walking through the dark living room which, once again, I am so thankful that I tidied.

As Charles carries me through the bedroom door, he loses his footing. Luckily we are next to my bed and both land on it in a heap.

This feels weird – good weird though. I'm in my own bed, I'm sober and Charles … well he's just Charles. A really nice guy that I met and not some person from some band. We start kissing again and it makes me realise something. Normal guys are good at this stuff too.

Chapter 34

This morning I woke up next to Charles for the third time, and while it was a lot less frightening than the first time, it was no less special than the second. The difference this morning is that we didn't just sleep together, we *slept* together.

I'm still in bed, but Charles went for a shower not so long ago. If I'm being honest, I did get up at 7 a.m. and put on a bit of make-up (just in case I looked terrible) before creeping back to bed and waiting for him to wake up and see what a natural beauty I am.

He might have travelled two hundred miles to see me, but it was only a flying visit and Charles is booked on a train back to London which leaves in a couple of hours. Yes, it's Saturday morning, but he has some big event tonight that he has to attend. I wish he didn't have to go, especially after last night got off to a bit of a bumpy start. It ended a bit bumpy too, although for a much better reason.

I need to get out of bed and get some clothes on, having promised I'd walk Charles to the train station (via Starbucks of course), but I just don't want to get up. The sooner I get up, the sooner we'll leave and the sooner we leave, the sooner I have to say goodbye.

Rolling over, I grab my phone from next to my bed. My hand slips and my phone falls on the floor, bouncing on the carpet a couple of times. Too lazy to get up, I dangle my upper body off the side of my bed and reach out to grab it. I hold my position and glance at my phone screen. Thankfully my phone is still working despite taking a tumble yet again – but the even bigger surprise is that the message is from Dylan.

'Thanks for everything last weekend. We'll speak soon, I promise.'

I cannot believe that this is the only contact I have had with Dylan since the wedding and I can't help but wonder if this has anything to do with Crystal.

At this point Charles walks back into the room with nothing but a towel wrapped around his waist and a smile on his face.

'You all right there?' he asks, laughing at me.

'Oh I'm fine, just dropped my phone. I had a text from Dylan, first one since the wedding.'

'Speaking of Dylan …' he gestures at my walls and I can only presume he's referring to my posters. I wait for him to say it though. 'You have posters on your wall – how old are you?' he asks, mocking me slightly.

'Twenty-five-year-olds can't put posters up?'

'Is it not a little odd to have Dylan on your wall?'

'I don't, I have The Burnouts on my wall. The whole band.'

Is that weird? Can't I be a friend and a fan? And why is he picking on me for having the bedroom of a teenage girl? Fluffy cushions, fairy-lights, swoonsome men all over the walls – maybe I'm trying to make up for my teen years, I didn't exactly have the teen dream bedroom then, it was more of a gothic dungeon. Forget good-looking guys, I had the likes of Slipknot gracing my walls.

Charles inspects my walls further.

'Maybe I'm a bit old for it all,' I admit, 'but my walls are just covered in memories; stuff that I can look at, remember where they're from and feel happy. You should see my room at my parents' house.'

He walks over to my dressing table, examining my mirror.

'That's a perfect example,' I insist. 'You see all those plectrums? They're all from different guitarists I've met over the years.'

I have an impressive collection of plectrums and drumsticks, considering I can't play an instrument. My plectrums are stuck neatly along the edges of my mirror, and my drumsticks are in a plastic vase, arranged like flowers.

He examines a drumstick and rolls his eyes.

'Hey, I'll have you know that some of those belong to music royalty.'

'I'd stick them on eBay if I were you.' He smiles at me, but I think he's being serious.

'So what time is your train?' I change the subject.

'Oh, so now you're trying to get rid of me? Because I don't approve of your little Dylan King shrine?' he teases. 'And what's this?'

'Please don't touch that,' I beg, seeing the photo album in his hands. It's too late though. I think the fact I begged him not to open it only made him want to look even more, because he flicks through it, regardless of my wishes.

I should probably explain. You see, Dylan and I have been friends for a long time now and I've travelled with him a lot. On tour you start traditions and you have your in-jokes and Dylan and I have this thing … there's only one way to put it really, we go to different cities, we locate one of their 'you are here' maps and we hook something we are wearing on it, before posing for a few photos, and then leave it there. Sometimes the easiest thing to leave is your underwear. I suppose the hope is that one day someone will realise this has been happening all over the country and it will go viral. I don't even remember how it started, and it's funny to us – of course, no one knows it's us, there isn't another person on this planet who knows about our silly little tradition – well, apart from Charles, as of now.

'You realise this is a terrible idea, don't you?' he says, still flicking through.

'It's just a bit of fun,' I insist. 'And no one ever sees, we're not stupid.'

'If these got out, some poor bloke like me would have to try to clean up the mess, and there is no positive spin to put on this. It's a very disrespectful thing to do, Nicole.'

Once again, I've shown him what a walking, talking PR disaster I really am. He's probably not crazy about the fact I take my underwear off around Dylan either – not that he ever sees anything.

'I should put some clothes on,' I tell him, unsure what else to say.

'If I had my way, you'd never put clothes on.'

And, just like that, Charles is charming again. I smile. He must see me and imagine all the different ways I could make his job a nightmare; it can't be easy for him.

Keen to impress, I look for an outfit that I can put together quickly – it's harder than it sounds.

'Mind if I go make myself a drink?' Charles asks after getting ready in a matter of seconds.

'No problem, I'll be ready in fifteen minutes.'

Forty minutes later, and we're walking to the train station – a little bit faster than I'd like in these shoes, but I think we're running slightly late.

'Before we go, there's something I wanted to talk to you about,' Charles tells me in his serious voice.

'Oh?' I ask, worried and out of breath from the fast walking. It's embarrassing how unfit I am.

'Don't look so worried!'

Oh, but I am worried. After last night with Luke, and this morning with my, and I quote, 'Dylan shrine', I dread to think what he's going to say. It's pretty sneaky of him to leave the awkward conversation until minutes before he jumps on a train.

'Will you be my girlfriend?'

'Yes,' I say without a second thought.

'Great! That's great.'

We smile at each other, and I'm not sure anything could ruin this moment.

'Crap, my train,' Charles blurts as he checks his watch. He must be running seriously late if he's swearing, because I don't notice him swearing very often, unlike me, Nicole-fucking-Wilde.

'We're going to have to run,' he concludes. I give him a worried look. 'What's wrong?' he asks, and I nod towards my feet.

'OK, *I'm* going to have to run.'

The heels I am wearing are beautiful, but they weren't designed with running in mind. To be honest, I'm not sure they were designed with walking in mind either.

'We're nearly there anyway. Go home and go back to bed for a bit … girlfriend.'

I smile. It's been a long time since anyone has called me that.

'You'd better get going then … boyfriend.'

Even though he is running late, Charles drops his bags and kisses me.

'Right, now I have to dash but I'll see you soon,' he promises, before running off towards the station.

I manage to walk four steps before it hits me – I have a boyfriend. Oh God, I have a boyfriend. I'm panicking because I haven't had a boyfriend in years and I'm not entirely sure how they work anymore. One thing that's really freaking me out is the fact he is a – shock, horror – normal guy. You know what? I'm not going to over-think it, I'm just going to go with the flow and enjoy being happy.

Despite my already achy feet, I think I'm going to walk the long route home – the one that will take me past the venue we were at last night, just to see if the bus is still there. It will be interesting to see if they did drive through the night, because I'm pretty sure they were bullshitting me about that.

The buses might seem small when you're living on them, but

hiding them is not an option – they are huge. Clear as day in the venue car park, there is the tour bus. Do I care? Do I balls! If Luke is going to be that immature, that's fine by me, I don't care. If I cared then I'd be banging on the bus door right now, bellowing for an explanation. Instead I decide that the best thing to do is walk straight past and go home. Home where I can have a nice long bath and think about how lucky I am to be with a nice, sweet guy instead of some horny musician who picks me up and puts me down, and alternates me with God knows how many other girls. I'll hold my head high and walk straight past. I don't need them.

'Oi,' I hear a voice call from behind me. It's Eddie, who is propped up against the bus smoking a cigarette. When I'd spotted the bus I was on the opposite side, so I didn't notice him standing outside.

'Hello, you,' I call back, walking over to see him. I can't ignore Eddie, can I? He hasn't done anything wrong. 'How's the leg?'

'It's not bad. They're keeping me drugged up, I can't feel a thing.'

So much for him being in too much pain to party last night. Eddie's face drops when he realises the conclusion I have come to.

'He'd have me for saying this, but Luke really likes you. Seeing you with that guy just got to him.'

I don't get chance to say anything else because the bus door opens and three women stagger off, complete with messy hair, smeared make-up and the-night-before clothes.

'See you next time, ladies,' Eddie says with a wink. 'Don't roll your eyes, Miss Wilde,' he chuckles. I didn't realise I had. 'You know that walk of shame better than anyone.'

'Well not any more. I'm a changed lady.'

'Changed? How so?' He lights up another cigarette.

'Because I have a boyfriend. No more walks of shame for me.' I may as well tell him, but I neglect to mention that I've only had a boyfriend for about twenty minutes – he doesn't really need to know that little detail.

'Wow. Nicole Wilde. A boyfriend. I never thought I'd see the day, congratulations.'

'Thank you. So where are you guys heading now?'

'London. Last night of tour, the party is going to be huge. You should come!'

'Really?' I ask, shocked to be invited.

'Yes, you were supposed to be with us anyway. It wouldn't be the same without you, you're one of the gang.'

I can tell he genuinely wants me to be there, and I really want to say yes. Will things be awkward with Luke, though? It's Saturday, I'll be back tomorrow lunchtime so I won't miss any work. Luke is my only reason not to go … fuck it.

'OK, I'll go pack a bag! How long have I got?'

'We're leaving in an hour – and not without you, so hurry up. I know what you're like.'

'Will Luke mind?' I ask.

'Fuck Luke!' he laughs. 'I need a nurse and you're the lady for the job. Go pack your bag, I'll break the news to Luke. Actually, I'll stay here propped against this bus until someone comes to help me back on, but then I'll break it to him.'

'OK, don't leave without me.'

I walk off as fast as my heels will allow. I'm going on tour.

Chapter 35

Hovering at the tour bus door, I wonder if this really is a good idea. I just want everything to go back to normal – to be able to sort things out with Luke and carry on touring with them – but I worry this is asking for trouble. I've got two choices, I can get on the bus or I can turn around and go home. It isn't too late to spare myself the drama.

The bus door opens, and tour manager Mick steps off.

'They're expecting you, climb aboard,' he tells me out of the side of his mouth that isn't occupied by a cigarette.

OK, maybe it is too late. I climb the stairs and take a deep breath before making my way to the living area – where a lot of noise is coming from.

'Hello, boys!' I smile nervously.

I am greeted by an echo of hellos, although I'm not entirely sure whether or not I heard one from Luke. Everyone is on the sofa, apart from Ben who is rummaging through the fridge.

Less than five minutes on board and I'm reminded just how much I love the bus.

'Give it up, Benjy. You're not going to find anything,' Eddie yells at him. 'We're all out of everything,' he tells me. 'We've sent Mick for supplies. Then we're off.'

Ben obediently slams the fridge door closed.

'Get her that thing while you're up,' Eddie orders him.

'What thing?' I ask, rather worried.

'You'll see.'

Ben comes back with a little nurse's cap on an elastic headband. It's white with a blue cross on the front, and from the looks of it I'd guess they got it from a branch of Ann Summers rather than an actual nurse.

'Get it on, Nurse Wilde. You promised you'd look after me,' Eddie chuckles.

I think myself lucky I don't have to wear the whole outfit and dutifully put it on, adjusting it in the mirror behind me. I decide not to ask where it came from – or who wore it before me – because I'm certain I do not want to know.

'Nurse Wilde. Sounds like a porn star,' Mark suggests.

I laugh. 'You should be so lucky!'

Even quiet little Ben looks me up and down and tells me it suits me – he even winks at me! I'm not sure quiet little Ben is that quiet any more – he has officially been corrupted – but who didn't see that one coming?

'And you have to keep it on until I say otherwise,' Eddie informs me.

'I will. You OK, Luke?' I ask, because he's being awfully quiet.

'Yeah, not bad,' he tells me bluntly. 'You?'

'Yeah, I'm great.' I sit down next to him.

Eddie grabs the Playstation controller and throws the other one at Mark.

'Game on!' he bellows, and they resume their game.

Ben is hunched over an acoustic guitar, alternating between strumming and jotting things down in his notebook. With everyone suitably distracted, I lean closer to Luke.

'You sure you're OK? You seem a bit quiet.'

'Yeah, I'm fine,' he says, still cold as ice. 'You have a good night last night?'

'It was great! You guys were great. It felt weird leaving you and going home so early though.'

'Yeah, well, Ed was in a lot of pain. I'm sure your boyfriend was glad to get you home early too.'

Oh, so Eddie told him then.

I ignore the latter part of his reply. 'Well it felt all wrong going home, but we'll make up for it tonight.'

'Yeah, it's going to be a big one.' Luke rests his head on the back of the sofa and closes his eyes. I think the conversation is over.

'Supplies are here,' tour manager Mick calls out, dumping the shopping bags on the table and wandering off in his usual blunt manner.

'Beer!' Eddie yells.

'I suppose that's my job,' I laugh, although somehow it ends up being my job to put everything away too.

'Mmm! Put that on the bottom shelf,' Eddie shouts in a pervy yet jokey way. This causes Luke to open his eyes, but only for long enough to give us a disapproving look.

'Crap!' Mark yells, throwing his controller across the bus. They're playing some football game, and Eddie is wiping the floor with him.

With everyone occupied, I grab a can of Coke from the fridge (Mick always picks some up when I'm with the boys because the only liquids they drink on the bus are water and beer), hand Mark the controller that I picked up on the way over and take a seat next to Eddie. Ben is still attached to his guitar. I don't know what he is playing but it sounds familiar.

'What song is that?' Eddie asks him.

'Just something I'm working on,' he replies.

'I've heard it before, I'm sure.' Eddie pauses the game. 'Play some more.'

'No, I just made it up,' Ben says defensively.

'I'm telling you, I recognise it. Someone back me up.'

'It does sound a little familiar,' I say truthfully.

'Come on, Ben. Keep playing,' Eddie demands, and Ben does as he is told.

Everyone stops and listens carefully to Ben's 'new' tune, trying work out where we've heard it before.

'I've got it!' I jump up, rather pleased with myself. 'That first part, it sounds like "Basket Case" by Green Day.'

'Yes!' Eddie claps his hands. 'That's it! She's got your number, boy wonder. Come on, play it properly this time.'

Defeated, Ben starts to play the song again, this time actually playing 'Basket Case' and it isn't long before everyone joins in. Even Luke has perked up, tapping the drum beat on the table with his hands.

'A sing-a-long is just what this bus needs,' Eddie concludes afterwards. 'What are we singing next?'

It's amazing how a little sing-song has changed the mood of the entire bus. Ben – who can play anything you ask of him – takes a few requests and plays a few more songs.

'Oi, Nurse Wilde,' Eddie shouts out, right in the middle of our take on Bon Jovi's 'Wanted Dead or Alive'.

'Yeah?' I reply.

'I need a piss, help me out.'

'You must be joking!' I squeal, and he gives me that cheeky smile of his that tells me he *is* joking. It isn't hard to understand why girls fall at his feet – these days I think he's tripping them up with his crutches.

'You really are taking the piss with that one,' I reply.

Chapter 36

We finally arrive in London and are swiftly ushered into the venue through the back door. There was a huge crowd of fans waiting for the band and no security in place yet, so Mick had to try to drive through them.

We are shown into a very nice dressing room and the boys are straight over to the food. Rather than risk my life trying to get through them, I sit down. I can eat while they're doing the soundcheck. I consider texting Charles to tell him I'm in the area. I consider it, but I don't do it. How desperate would that seem? He travels all that way to see me, asks me to be his girlfriend, travels all the way back to London and then I turn up on his doorstep. Anyway, he's at an event tonight so I couldn't see him if I wanted to.

Mick walks through the door with a skinny brunette. She doesn't look very old – I'd guess about nineteen or twenty – and she has an excited look on her face.

'Ben!' she calls out, running over to him, wrapping her arms around him and giving him a sloppy kiss on the lips.

'This is my girlfriend, Carla,' he says proudly. He has a massive grin on his face – that is, of course, until he makes eye contact with me. His smile vanishes and the colour drains from his face.

He's probably having flashbacks from that night in Birmingham when I walked in on him with some girl. Whoever that girl was, she isn't this girl. There is an awkward moment where everyone just freezes and says nothing, apart from Eddie who is cramming Quavers into his mouth and chuckling.

Probably thinking he's doing the right thing, Mick gestures towards me. 'Go sit with Nicole, she'll keep you company.'

If it's even possible, Ben's face goes even paler as Carla does as she is told and sits next to me. Ben reluctantly goes back over to his band mates, where he carefully monitors the situation.

'Hi, I'm Carla.' She offers me a hand to shake.

'I'm Nicole.'

'I've never been backstage before,' she confesses. 'It's not what I expected at all.'

'Really?' I ask, curiously.

'Yeah, I thought it would be dead glamorous!'

'Would you believe me if I told you this was one of the nicer backstage areas I've been in?'

'No way! So do you do this a lot?' she asks, clearly fascinated.

'Now and then.' Never one to brag.

'How come?'

'I'm a journalist.'

'Oh wow! Do you have any famous friends? Apart from these guys obviously. Oh my God, I was so shocked when Ben got the job in this band, they're dead famous, aren't they? Who else do you know?'

'I don't like to name-drop,' I laugh, genuinely embarrassed.

'She's best mates with Dylan King,' Luke interrupts, having crept up on us unnoticed.

'Oh my God, are you really? He is dead famous, and so gorgeous!'

'It's true.' Luke sits down. 'I keep asking her to introduce us, but she never does.'

'I'd thought about inviting him along tonight,' I say

unenthusiastically.

'Oh my God! Do it!' Carla cries. 'I am in love with him.'

'Really?' Luke asks.

'I was going to, but I haven't really heard from him since the wedding. I don't think Mrs King is overly keen on him contacting me.' Another awkward silence. 'I'll text him though,' I say, rummaging in my bag to find my phone.

'Yeah, that would be dead good,' Carla enthuses. 'Tell me more about your job!' she demands, grabbing my hand.

Before I have chance to say anything, a guilty-looking Ben wanders over.

'Can I borrow you, Nicole?' he asks without a trace of his new-found confidence.

'Sure.' I jump to my feet, forcing Carla to let go of my hand. Ben ushers me towards the door, and we walk along the corridor in silence until we reach the back door.

Once outside, Ben waits for one of the roadies to walk out of earshot before letting me know what he wants to talk to me about – as if I didn't know.

'Nicole. Carla is—'

'—a very sweet girl,' I interrupt.

He looks down at his feet, examining his Vans trainers – anything to avoid eye contact with me.

'Please don't tell Carla about that girl you saw me with,' he pleads, suddenly straight to the point.

Looking back into his sad eyes, I'm not really sure what to say. It's not really my place to tell Carla. I don't know her and, to be honest, I don't know Ben that well yet.

'I admired you, you know,' I tell him sincerely. 'You weren't like the rest of the guys. Don't get the wrong idea, because I love them all to bits, but when it comes to women … well they're not that great, are they?'

'No,' he says softly, still looking at his trainers. 'This is pretty new to me, and when the band is together, especially now we're on tour, it feels like … I don't know.'

'A different world?' I ask, completely able to relate to all of this.

'Yes, exactly!'

'None of it feels real, does it?'

'That's exactly what it feels like!' His eyes fill with emotion. 'How did you know?'

'Because I only hang around with these people and I get caught up in it. But you know what? I'm turning my life around. I have a boyfriend now, no more messing around with bands.'

'I'll never do it again. I can't believe I did it in the first place.'

'I won't tell her.' I place an arm around Ben, who is looking closer to tears by the second. He must feel really bad. 'You are an awesome guitarist, and you're going to do well, be it with these guys or another band. There's going to be loads of girls throwing themselves at you, but if you really like Carla …'

'I do,' he insists.

'Then you know what to do. Don't be so hard on yourself though, Ben. You're young and it's a hell of a lot of temptation.'

'I was terrified about talking to you, but I'm glad I did.'

This is what happens when you're a female and you tour with a bunch of guys, you end up fulfilling all the female roles they're missing from their lives while they're on the road. It doesn't matter that I can hardly look after myself when I'm at home, suddenly I'm playing mother, taking care of them, putting away their shopping, comforting them and looking after their things. When people think of groupies they see 80s-style, coke-sniffing, orgy-having, good-time girls, but that isn't the case at all – although I do admire their fashion.

Ben hugs me and as he squeezes me tight, he whispers in my ear, 'For what it's worth, I think Luke really likes you.'

'Well isn't this cosy?' Mark interrupts. 'Moved on to another band member already, Nicole? And with his girlfriend just inside.' Mark smiles and I presume he is joking.

'Something like that.' I smile back.

'Eddie wants you, Nurse Wilde. Something about getting changed.'

'You're kidding me, right?'

'What do you think?' Mark laughs, lighting his cigarette. 'Run along.'

Back in the dressing room, Carla is still sitting on the sofa. She's fiddling around with a digital camera and a laptop is open in front of her. As soon as I walk in the room, she calls me over.

'I sent you a friend request on Facebook. You can use Ben's laptop to accept me if you want. I'm so excited that we're going to be friends!' She pushes the silver MacBook towards me and I dutifully log in and accept.

'Oh, Nurse Wilde!' I hear Eddie calling out. I am still, of course, wearing my nurse's cap and therefore must report for duty.

'Coming, sir,' I call out cheerily, although there's a slightly flirtatious tone to my voice that I hadn't originally intended – this is well received by Eddie, who replies with, 'You will be.'

Eddie struggles to his feet. 'I can hop to the bathroom, but can you hold my bag please, nurse?'

'Oh, I'm sure I can manage that,' I reply with a giggle.

This is like something for a Carry On film. It's nice. Nice and normal. Luke is the only one being weird with me now. He's still lurking by the table, looking over at me every now and then. It's kind of embarrassing. You know the look I mean: I look up and see him looking at me, he pretends he wasn't looking at me, so I pretend I wasn't looking at him etc.

I follow Eddie into the bathroom as instructed, carrying his bag. I'm not entirely sure the whole Nurse Wilde thing is a joke, you know. Carrying his bag in from the bus meant leaving mine on there – to be honest I'm just glad I remembered it this time.

'Unbutton my jeans for me please, darling,' he asks with a cheeky grin.

'I'm fairly sure you can do that yourself, sweetheart,' I reply.

'Yes, but I have to hold my crutches while you pull me off – I mean pull *them* off.'

A loud and exaggerated coughing noise comes from the other room. It has to be either Luke or Carla, and it sounded a bit too manly to be the latter. I share a silent look of recognition with Eddie. He raises his eyebrows.

'Shut the door first, nurse. There are ladies out there.'

'There's a lady in here too,' I protest, doing as I'm told.

The bathroom is very small. There is a shower cubicle taking up half the room and Eddie and I are currently squashed quite close together somewhere between the toilet and the sink.

'Bit of privacy, much better,' he says, before nodding down towards his jeans. 'If you don't mind.'

Despite the flirty banter, I decide that he probably really does need my help to change his jeans. This is probably just his way of dealing with being dependent on other people. It can't be much fun being a twenty-something year-old man and needing help to get dressed.

I crouch down and fiddle with the button on his jeans. Should anyone walk in now, this would look seriously suspicious.

'While you're down there …' he jokes. This makes me hurry back to eye-level.

We just stand for a few seconds, Eddie in his underpants, me with my silly, adult store issued nurse's cap, our bodies are just about touching and our faces are only inches apart.

'I hate making promises.' He bites his bottom lip and abandons one of his crutches so that he can place a hand on the back of my neck.

'What promise did you make?' I ask. 'And look at that, you could've taken your own jeans off!'

'You know the day we met you, Luke took one look at you and said "That one is mine".'

The expression on my face must say it all because he quickly backtracks.

'Not in a disrespectful way, but he actually liked you and, band law, well that means more than the actual law, as you know. None of us could touch you.'

I don't bring up the fact that Mark tried it on with me, although I'm pretty sure he'd be out on his arse if the matter went to band court.

'Why are you telling me this?' I ask.

'Because we're in here alone and my trousers are down.' He strokes my cheek and I cringe internally – although I can't say I'm not flattered or tempted (if I were single). 'But I know how much Luke likes you. Actually likes you. He hasn't even looked at another girl on this tour, you know. It pains me to say it, but I think you had better put my jeans back on.'

I laugh and oblige, unsure what Eddie's point was in all this. I feel a bit freaked out about the fact that Luke put a claim on me. Bloody band law. The phrase gets knocked around a lot. I think it's an attempt to create some kind of order in a world where real laws and morals are ignored. So you can take lots of drugs and sleep with anyone and everyone – as long as your band mate hasn't put first dibs on them. You can trash a hotel room, put the phone in the toilet, throw the kettle out of the window and replace the contents of all the bottles in the mini-bar with urine, but you never sleep in another band member's bunk without permission. You know, the important stuff.

For Eddie to use the words 'actually likes you', well that must mean something, right? For Eddie to sleep with someone they only need to have a pulse, so to really like someone must mean something.

As he hobbles out of the bathroom, I hang back, thinking about what he just said. It probably didn't mean anything; maybe he realised I had a boyfriend and would probably reject him, maybe that was his way of backtracking?

Luke is standing in the bathroom doorway.

'Can I, erm …' he gestures towards to toilet.

'Oh yes, sorry. Go ahead.'

I squeeze past him through the narrow doorway, smiling at him as our eyes meet. For a second he smiles back, but then it quickly vanishes and he closes the door behind him. Ben and Mark are back in the room, sitting on the sofa chatting with Eddie. Carla is standing next to them, snapping photos as they chat which they occasionally pose for, mid-sentence.

'Nicole, quick, get in the photos! I'm going to take so many pictures tonight!'

'That's awesome!' I reply, sitting down next to Eddie.

'Hey, Nic, guess what?' he says to me in a hushed voice.

'What?' I asked, ready for some gossip.

'Mick has a date!' he replies, falling about laughing.

'No way! With who?'

'Some chick he met out front; she works here. Apparently she looks just like Mark's mum.' Eddie laughs even harder, even Ben is laughing – Mark of course isn't finding this funny. Carla is still snapping away, not even noticing what we're actually talking about – bless her, she just looks so pleased to be here.

Tour manager Mick isn't the best-looking bloke in the world. He's completely bald, but what he lacks in hair he more than makes up for in tattoos. There is a big spider tattooed right on the top of his head. A big hairy tarantula – oh the irony. Years of touring and drinking free beer have left him with a belly to be proud of and it can often be seen poking out from underneath his beaten rock band T-shirts. If I remember correctly, today's T-shirt is a Guns N' Roses tour T-shirt, circa 1987. I remember glancing at the dates on the back and thinking to myself how the shirt was even older than me. Before he was a tour manager he was a roadie for some of the big bands in the 80s – that scruffy T-shirt is probably worth something. I'll bet he has some amazing stories to tell, but Mick is a man of few words. That's why I am surprised that he has managed to bag himself a date, we can't have been here more than an hour or so.

'And get this, he's waiting for her to finish work, and then fucking off with her! He's not staying for the gig, he's going to miss the after-party and everything,' Eddie continues. 'Nic, come on, let's go have a look at her. Ben saw her before, reckon she really does looks like exactly like Mark's mum.'

Poor Mick. I'm happy for him – if he wants to have a little end of tour party of his own then he should go for it. After weeks of running around after these guys, he deserves it.

We walk down the corridor and out onto the stage. In front of us we see Mick, propped against the barriers, watching a rather lady who is bent over in front of him picking up empty plastic cups. Eddie grabs my arm in suspense as we wait for the woman to turn around. I feel a pang of guilt just standing here, waiting to catch a glimpse of the Mick's latest squeeze

The woman stands up straight, and while I can't say that I've ever met Mark's mum, this woman must really look like her because Eddie, unable to contain himself, erupts with laughter. I dig Eddie in the ribs with my elbow and his laughter blends seamlessly into wails of pain.

'Bloody leg, it's giving me hell today. Just came out to check out the set-up, keep doing what you're doing.' Eddie looks over at them and salutes. 'You're doing a great job, ma'am.'

She gives him an unsure look before walking off. Eddie looks over at Mick and pushes his tongue against the inside of his cheek, he's unable to do the accompanying hand gesture because of his crutches but Mick knows exactly what he's getting at and flips him the bird.

'So when's the soundcheck, you old dog?' Eddie asks him.

'Get the guys, I'll see if we can do it now. I'm getting off in twenty minutes,' Mick announces, walking off towards the sound booth.

'Oh I'll bet you are,' Eddie replies so only I can hear.

'Oi, don't be a dick.' I give him a playful push, careful not to knock him off his crutches.

The rest of the band appears to do the soundcheck so I make

my way off the stage and into the crowd which consists of Mick, his new lady and Carla. Carla is still taking photos – some of the band during the soundcheck, some of me and even some of Mick and his lady friend. I'll bet Carla doesn't have a bad bone in her body. I really hope Ben will start treating her better. I'm rather enjoying having her around, it's nice having another girl with us. Usually there is a strict no-girls rule (unless they're just stopping by the bus), excluding journalists and merch girls (a funny name, really, given that they're always grown women) – although you don't see quite so many women tagging along to sell the bands merchandise for them these days. There is no way I would ever be a merch girl, although I bet some people assume I am one when they see me going around with the guys. The no-girls rule also extends to girlfriends. Of course there are always women on and off the bus, but never for more than one date. It's different with Carla though, she isn't some drunk girl who I'll never see again after she disappears with Eddie for a few hours. I have the chance to chat to her, I can spend the gig with her and she'll be at the big party later. I meet lots of girls when I'm on the road with the guys, but I rarely learn their names, or even find out their names in the first place. The same goes for the band; I don't think they're too fussed about taking names either.

Once the soundcheck is done, Mick says he is leaving and that he will meet the band at the hotel in the morning. We're staying in a hotel just down the road from here, and because it's the last night of tour we have the biggest suite the hotel had to offer. It's going to be one hell of a party tonight. After a few minutes of chatting I decide to go get changed, as it's not long before the gig starts.

'Hey, Eddie, do you have a key for the bus?' I ask. I left my bag on there so that I could carry his instead.

'I don't, babe. They don't trust me with anything while I'm on these things,' he lifts his crutches as he speaks, quickly putting them back down to regain his balance.

'We don't trust you with anything, period,' Mark chips in and everyone laughs. 'Try Luke, he's backstage. I think he has the spare.'

They carry on chatting as I make my way backstage again. Luke is there alone and I feel nervous about talking to him.

'Luke?' I call as I walk through the door. It's probably best to get straight to the point, just in case he doesn't want to talk to me.

'Yeah?' he replies.

'Do you have a key for the bus? I need my bag to get changed.'

'I don't. Mick has them both.'

'But Mick has gone …'

'I know. Did you need anything important?'

'Oh, only my clothes.' I laugh, making a mental note to keep the clothes I am wearing very clean because I'll be wearing them all night and all morning. 'Another gig of yours where I'll be looking like crap, eh?'

'You look beautiful, don't worry about it,' he tells me as he turns back towards his laptop.

There's that funny feeling in my stomach again. What is it with this guy? They say you don't miss something you never had, but less than twenty-four hours after becoming Charles' girlfriend, I am still wishing I was Luke's.

Chapter 37

I officially love Carla, she is so much fun! We've spent the whole gig together drinking, dancing, and drinking more. And she meant what she said earlier, she really is taking a *lot* of photos – I can't even begin to imagine how many snaps of me she has, I've been posing like a supermodel all night. My lips actually ache from pouting so much.

The crowd is huge tonight and there are so many people squashed at the front of the stage which is why we decided to stay at the back, so that we can dance.

I messaged Dylan earlier to see if he wanted to come down, but he replied saying he couldn't because Crystal needed him – whatever, I'm having too much fun to care. Maybe I've realised that most of the friends you make in this industry are very short-lived and easily replaced … or maybe I'm just drunk.

'This is our last song, but you guys have been fucking amazing! Our best crowd yet!' Eddie yells into his microphone followed by a huge cheer from everyone in the room. He may well say that at every gig, but tonight I think he really means it. I have never seen such a big audience turn up to see them headline and I feel strangely proud of my boys. Having known them since before they were famous, it's like watching your kids grow up well – I'd imagine.

'Nurse Wilde, where are you?' Eddie calls out, holding a hand over his eyes to shield himself from the bright spotlights as he examines the crowd.

'Woo!' I call out, hopefully not sounding as drunk as I feel.

Eddie looks over in my direction, but he's just following the sound of the 'woo', I don't think he can actually see me.

'Nurse Wilde has been looking after me while my leg is broken. You should be able to spot her, because she should still be wearing her nurse's cap.'

'I am, I am,' I call out, fully aware that he can't hear a word I am saying.

'If you see her, buy her a drink – I couldn't have changed my jeans if it wasn't for Naughty Nurse Wilde. This last song is for her.'

The band burst into one of their best-known songs to finish the gig.

I feel a tap on my shoulder and spin around to face the barman. He says something, but I can't hear a word he is saying.

'What?' I shout, leaning over the bar to try to hear.

'I said, these shots are for you.' He pushes two little glasses overflowing with a bright-red liquid towards me. 'I'm a big fan of the profession.'

'Thank you!' I shout, picking them up and pushing one into Carla's hand.

Without saying a word, we knock back our drinks, perfectly in sync with each other. I am at that rather pleasant stage where you realise you are drunk and can therefore try to keep a lid on the stupid behaviour. It's that point just after tipsy, but just before the stage Carla is at. I don't think Carla can hold her drink as well as I can, despite having the exact same amount to drink as me. More and more of her photos are of the floor and every few minutes she throws her arms around me and tells me that she loves me. I laugh and tell her I love her too. I really hope we stay friends. I might even be able to convince the guys to let her come on the next tour with us.

After the gig, various people stop by the bar and say hello to me, Naughty Nurse Wilde as I am so lovingly being called, and a few people buy me a drink and ask me to tell the guys how wonderful they are. As the crowd clears out, a few people hang back hoping for a chance to meet the band, and I spot a few journalists hanging around waiting for the band to come out and do their interviews.

Eventually Eddie comes out, looking slightly worried.

'I've had a call from the label, they have been trying to get in touch with Mick but he's turned his phone off. I've got to give them a ring back once we're all back at the hotel,' he tells us, leaning close so that no one else can hear. I smile at him in an attempt to calm him down but he looks really worried. He hobbles over to the group of adoring fans waiting for him with a big smile on his face, he's such a professional.

Luke, Mark and Ben walk out and Carla runs straight over to give Ben a big kiss. Luke is walking straight towards me. I try to look cool, but my face feels weird. The more normal I try to appear, the weirder it feels. I pick my drink up and suck on my straw in an attempt to force my face to do something normal, although it is probably the drink that is causing my problems.

'Hello!' I hiccup. 'Great show!'

'Thank you. Listen, I've told Eddie we'll see them at the hotel later. I was hoping we could go now and have a chat.'

I look over at the rest of the band who are chatting to fans and journalists. 'But don't you have to …'

'I'm gonna pose for a couple of photos, but then we can go. We really need to clear the air, Nic.'

'OK, sure. Do what you gotta do.'

He walks off towards his band mates and I turn around to face my barman. 'Can I get a vodka, please?' I ask him.

'Sure. On its own?' he asks, and he sounds rather surprised, probably because I haven't drunk anything tonight that wasn't a bright colour, or claiming to have something to do with a fruit.

'On its own,' I insist. 'It's medicinal.'

Chapter 38

After a short yet awkward walk to the hotel, I am currently sitting on a sofa that is twice the size of the bed in my flat, and my bed is a double. We are finally in the suite, but it wasn't easy getting in because Luke didn't know what name the room was reserved under. The boys have a selection of fake names which they use when booking hotels, just in case any Banders try to track them down. Back in my Bander days we would to do that all the time, just try our luck and call up every hotel in the city and ask if we could be put through to whoever we were looking for, and you know what? A lot of the time it worked. That's why the smarter bands use fake names.

It took Luke several attempts at guessing, naming various characters from *Family Guy* and *South Park*, but when we finally worked out that there was a reservation in the name of Mr E Cartman, things moved much quicker. So here we are, me sitting in the middle of the giant sofa and Luke rifling through the mini-bar to fix himself a drink – a drink which he informs me is his first of the night, which is very unusual. Then again, he's probably on something harder these days. He seems normal tonight though.

Luke climbs across the sofa, carefully clutching his drink, until he is next to me.

'This is one big sofa,' he laughs nervously.

'It is.' What else can I say?

'So that guy ...'

'Charles?'

'Charles. He's your boyfriend now?'

'Yes.'

'Since?'

'Since this morning,' I tell him, honestly.

'He asked you?'

'He did.'

'Right. I thought so, because last night you said ...'

I wait for Luke to finish his sentence, but he doesn't. We sit in silence for a few seconds.

'If I had behaved differently last night, you might have said no to him.'

I'm not sure if that is a question or a statement.

'Luke, I do really like him.'

'Did you like me?' he asks bluntly, knocking back the remainder of his strong-smelling drink in one go.

I place a hand on top of his and look at him, but he doesn't meet my gaze.

'I thought something might happen between us,' he admits.

'Oh, I'll bet you did,' I tease. Thankfully he laughs and I instantly feel at ease again.

'This is weird, isn't it?' he says.

'Just a bit.'

'Can we go back to being good friends?'

'I'd really like that,' I reply, resting my head on his shoulder.

'Good. Forget the weirdness, things can go back to normal. I think you're sobering up, can I get you another drink?'

'Oh, yes please.'

'As soon as the lads get here, the party can start. I wonder how Mick is getting on.'

'Mick,' I say. 'Mick is in my bad books. I want my damn clothes!'

'You and your clothes,' he laughs. 'Well if you can't get changed, then I won't either. And I stink.'

'The groupies won't like that,' I tell him.

'Well tonight I'm not really interested in the groupies, so it's OK.'

Luke's phone rings.

'It's Ed,' he tells me before he answers. 'Mate ... Yeah, we're in, bloody Mick nearly dropped us in it ... We'll tell him he's fired, he doesn't need to know we're joking,' he laughs down the phone. God, he looks gorgeous. He's very typically good-looking, undeniably gorgeous in fact. You can tell he is a bit of a ladies' man just by looking at him, he oozes charm. He's definitely got the face for fame – I always say that about Dylan, too. He's good-looking, in that Robbie Williams sort of way. He's got that rough and ready, bad-boy look. Charles ... Charles is good-looking but in a plain sort of way. The first thing I noticed about him (after I'd calmed down) was how muscular he was, I'll bet the girls go wild for that – I know I did. Luke is really skinny and Dylan, well, he doesn't give a damn. He's not skinny, he's not fat and I don't think he'll ever care either way. It's his don't-give-a-damn attitude that attracts the women, I think.

'They're on their way, and with a shit-load of booze,' Luke tells me once he has finished on the phone. 'I'm going to go down and meet them, you OK up here?'

'Of course.'

'Over there,' Luke says pointing to the stereo. 'Set up the music for when we get back.'

'Yeah, I can handle that,' I call after him. At least I thought I could – it turns out the more expensive the stereo system is, the harder it is to operate. There's only one thing to do – call Jake.

'Jake! You have to help me!'

'What's wrong?' he asks, sounding concerned.

'Oh, it's nothing bad.' I laugh, feeling guilty for worrying him.

'I need IT support.'

'I accept that when we are in the office it is my job to give you IT support, but you have me on standby 24/7.'

'Aww, but you love me for it,' I reply, knowing that he is only joking.

'Go on, what's up?'

'I'm in a hotel room and the stereo system is too confusing for me. I can't even work out how to turn it on.'

Jake laughs a little harder than I'd like. I am very tech-savvy with the things I care about, but things like this go way over my head.

'Describe the stereo to me.'

'Erm ...'

'What can you see?'

'Lots of buttons?'

More laughter.

'OK, take a photo and send me it.'

It only takes me a matter of seconds to take a photo and send it to Jake. Instantly he knows which buttons I need to push.

'That is one hell of a sound system. Where are you?'

'Oh shit! I forgot to tell you, I'm in London.'

'London?' he asks. He sounds surprised, but not that surprised. This kind of thing happens a lot.

'Yes, with Two For The Road. I'm at the hotel, it's after-party time.'

'I thought you sounded a bit drunk. Will you be at work on Monday, young lady?'

'Yes, boss.'

'Before I hang up, is there anything else you haven't told me?' he jokes, but it reminds me that I do have something to tell him.

'Oh! Charles is my boyfriend. I have a boyfriend.'

'No way! Nicole Wilde, with a boyfriend. Congratulations. We never thought we'd see the day.'

'Thank you. Does it give you hope that you might find a girlfriend one day?'

Jake laughs because he knows I don't mean this.

'Right, I have to go. Tell Emily for me.'

'I will, have fun tonight. But not too much, remember you have a boyfriend now, although he's probably there isn't he?'

'Erm, no he's not actually.'

'Oh dear!' He laughs at me again. 'Behave.'

I hang up the phone a matter of seconds before the guys walk through the door, followed by Carla and a bunch of people I don't know.

'Look what I got,' Luke holds up two bottles of champagne and I notice that Mark has another two. 'Geezer behind the bar was a fan, he gave us these. I told him to come up when he finishes.'

Eddie eases himself onto the sofa next to me.

'I've got to give the label a ring, we may not feel like drinking them after we hear what they have to say.'

'Just do it, man. Get it out the way and we'll get pissed afterwards,' Luke tells him, but he is looking worried too. This is the band's first proper headlining tour since they signed their record deal, so everything is riding on the success of this tour. The fact that someone at the label wants to speak to them now – it's probably going to be really good news or really bad news.

'Fuck it. I'm calling them,' Eddie declares, and everyone quietens down to listen in. It's hard to get an idea of what is being said because we can only hear Eddie's side of the conversation. His voice and face are emotionless, and what he's saying is giving nothing away.

'OK, well thanks for calling us tonight, I'll let the band know. Thank you. Bye.'

Eddie presses a few buttons on his phone and eventually he looks up, still with a blank expression.

'Come on, spit it out,' Luke insists.

'It's bad, isn't? Just tell us, man,' Mark adds after a few more seconds of silence. Everyone in the room is looking at Eddie, waiting for him to say something. Whether he's singing on stage or standing in a room of people, he knows how to work a crowd.

'Get that fucking champagne open,' Eddie says before a huge grin spreads across his face, 'because next year we are going on a fucking arena tour of Europe!' he yells, no longer able to control his excitement. The rest of the band look on in amazement before erupting with happiness and the rest of the room quickly follow.

'Mate, get on the phone to room service, we're going to need more champagne,' Luke says to a man I don't know. 'We really do have something to celebrate tonight.'

Eddie fidgets with one of the bottles we already have, shaking it vigorously.

'Is that a good idea?' I giggle.

'Of course it fucking isn't!' he says, popping the cork and spraying champagne everywhere. Stuck on the sofa with Eddie, I scream – mainly with delight – as the champagne flows all over us. As the spray calms down, Eddie holds the bottle to his lips and starts necking the remaining contents. He doesn't get far before he starts coughing, and passes the bottle onto someone else.

'Wooo!' he screams. 'I am on top of the fucking world!'

I have never seen him so happy. The music starts playing, and despite not being able to move, Eddie dances – from the waist upwards anyway. Looking down at my white top, I realise that not only is it soaking wet, but it is also see-through and my bright-pink bra is on show for all to see. In fact, everything I am wearing is soaked in champagne. Bloody Mick. I can't spend the night in these wet clothes. My clothes are still locked on the bus. Why does this stuff always happen to me? Still, this is a celebration and I'm not letting anything get in the way.

A random person pushes a glass into my hand and we all toast the band.

I search for the bathroom, although I'm not entirely sure what I'm going to do when I get there, to try to dry my clothes. Maybe a towel? I laugh at myself and conclude that I am drunk enough to think I can towel-dry my clothes, but sober enough to laugh at it. At the rate I am drinking, that won't last very long. Perhaps I should slow down.

I bump into Luke, who looks me up and down.

'Hello!' he says to my chest. 'Nice bra.'

'Oh God, don't,' I insist, folding my arms. 'I can't believe this has happened, and when I don't have anything to change into. Again.'

'I've got a band hoodie if you're interested?'

'What band?' I ask seriously. Luke grins and I realise that it will be *his* band.

'I'm nothing but advertising space to you, am I?' I joke.

'Well, if you wanna keep that on, be my guest.'

I give in. 'Give me the damn hoodie.'

He rummages around in his backpack and tosses the hoodie at me. I thank him, mainly because it's not bright orange or way tooo big.

'When you're changed, meet me by the table, we're doing celebratory shots.'

I continue my search for the bathroom and change my top. I feel better already, despite another makeshift dress.

I find Luke with Mark, Eddie and a few other people who are all introduced to me, but I don't remember a single name. The glasses are being lined up with a variety of different liquids being poured into them.

'It's better you don't know,' Luke laughs, reading my mind. I am temporarily disorientated by a blinding flash of light. It's Carla and her camera, and she is gone as fast as she appeared.

'Right, come on then,' Luke says to everyone sitting at the table. 'This one first.'

I hesitate.

'Come on, Nicole, you can drink most of these guys under the table.'

'Yeah, well, I've had one hell of a head-start,' I insist, but everyone is looking at me so I reach for my glass. We'll put this one down to peer pressure.

A few shots later, I feel much less aware of what is going on, but I keep drinking anyway. I feel great! Everything is coming together nicely and everyone is happy. Luke grabs my hand.

'Come on, let's dance.'

I have no idea what the song is – things are starting to get fuzzy – but I somehow manage to get onto my feet. It's party time!

Chapter 39

My hangover has hit me like a ton of bricks. I woke up on the huge sofa, so I guess I slept here ... along with six other people, none of whom I know. I sit up slowly because my head is throbbing and I feel dizzy as hell. I must have gotten so drunk last night because I only remember up to a certain point, although I imagine this is for the best. Resting my head in my hands, I finally find the courage to open my eyes again and find myself looking down at my bare legs. Where the hell are my trousers? What was I even wearing last night? A skirt, I think. I remember the impromptu wet T-shirt competition, and changing into the hoodie which, thankfully, I am still wearing.

As far as I know, I am the first one to wake up. It's light out, but I have no idea what time it is. I scooch along the sofa carefully, trying not to wake anyone up. I am equally as careful as I tiptoe across the room to the bathroom because I wouldn't want to stand on anyone. There are bodies everywhere, all alive hopefully.

I peer around the open bathroom door slowly – something I learned to do the hard way. The only person in there is Mark, who is asleep in the bath. I glance around the room for my clothes and spot them on the towel rack. I feel them and not only are they dry, but they are warm too. I change into them carefully, putting the hoodie back on over my stinky top, hoping it will mask the smell of champagne so I don't smell like a drunk on the journey home. I wash my face and rinse my mouth under the tap, after using my finger as a toothbrush with the help of the complimentary toothpaste. I am bursting for the toilet but I'm not sure I want to have a wee with Mark in the room, even if he is asleep. Lifting the toilet lid, still unsure if I should risk it or not, the decision is made for me because it's full of random things. At a glance I can see a trainer, a toilet roll and everything is covered in sick. I don't think I will ever need the toilet badly enough to reach in there and fish them out.

I bravely look in the mirror and instantly wish I hadn't, but it does amuse me to see that I am still wearing my nurse's cap.

Back in the main room, I search for my handbag. The place is well and truly trashed, but the TV is still on the wall and none of the windows are broken – they would have been Dylan's first port of call if he were here last night, he's like a magpie when it comes to shiny, breakable things.

I start to count the empty bottles of champagne, but lose interest by the time I reach number eight. Let's just say there are lots. Ben is sleeping upright in one of the big chairs with Carla sitting on his knee, who is also asleep with her mouth wide open and her camera still in her hand. I carefully take the camera from her, snap a photo of the two of them and then place it back in her hand – well she took plenty of photos of me last night.

Searching through the piles of empty bottles, cans, glasses and random people, I look for my handbag but can't find it anywhere. I'm going to have to look in the bedrooms, so I creep quietly into the nearest one. Eddie is in there with a girl either side of him. He's got an arm around each one and, despite being asleep, I could swear he had a smile on his face. As I look for my bag, I considerately glance around the room for his crutches but I don't see them anywhere. I hesitate before I walk into the next bedroom because Luke must be in there and I'm not sure I want to see who he's with. I feel jealous, but remind myself that I have a boyfriend. Luke can do what, or who he likes, I'd just rather turn a blind eye to it. I tell myself I am being stupid and take a deep breath before opening the door. I don't look at the bed and I won't unless I absolutely have to. I begin to search over the opposite side of the room and it takes all my strength not to look behind me, but despite the huge strain on my tired eyes I manage to resist. I spot my bag on top of a set of drawers and grab it a little over-enthusiastically, knocking a lot of other stuff onto the floor. With the curtains closed, it is still quite dark in here, but I search the floor for the items I knocked over and begin to pick them up. I'm not sure why I'm doing this, because the entire suite is a total tip. A little box hits the floor and its contents spill out at my feet. As I start putting things back inside, I realise what I am touching, even in this poor light. I've watched enough TV to realise this is Luke's little drug box with all his various bits and pieces in – little bags of powders and pills and some other things I don't recognise. Just holding it in my hands makes me feel sick and I quickly drop it.

'Nicole?' Is that you?' Luke asks me. I suppose I'll have to turn around now.

'Good morning,' I say, trying not to sound suspicious. 'I was just looking for something. I found a bag.' Why did I say that? 'My bag, I mean. I found my bag. The bathroom is in a bit of a state, I'm going to go downstairs and use the one in the lobby, freshen up my make-up and stuff.'

'I'll come with you. Wait there.' Luke slowly sits up and moans. 'Shit, we really overdid it last night, didn't we?'

'Just a bit.' I smile, although some of us overdid it more than others in my opinion.

Luke stands up. He is wearing nothing but his underpants but it doesn't take him long to find his bag and put on some clean clothes.

'Let's go, but don't get too close, my breath stinks.' He laughs, but I'll keep my distance just in case.

Once we are in the bright light of the main room, I can see how terrible he looks. I mean, I know I don't look so hot this morning, but Luke looks really ill. His skin is white and his bloodshot eyes are only made more obvious by the dark circles below them.

'You OK?' I ask him quietly as we walk through the sea of people towards the door.

'This hangover will go down in history,' he laughs, before wincing and putting his hand to his head.

'Maybe we should grab a coffee too, I think we need it.'

Chapter 40

Having made myself as presentable as possible (thank God I keep make-up in my handbag), I head to meet Luke in the bar. He is already there, waiting for me with two cups of coffee in front of him. As I sit down next to him, he pushes one towards me and I thank him.

'Last night. Oh man.'

'I know just what you mean,' I reply. 'How much do you remember?'

'Not nearly enough. How about you?'

'I only know the things I don't remember,' I tell him, and he looks confused.

'How do you mean?'

'Well, I don't remember taking my skirt off.'

'I'm sure I'd remember if you took your skirt off.' He winks.

'Honestly, I woke up without it.'

'Well I don't remember that, and for that I will never forgive myself.'

'I don't even know what time it is,' I say as I suddenly realise.

'Wow, it's 11 a.m.,' Luke informs me after checking his phone. 'And I have a few missed calls from Mick.'

'Oh, can you call him back? I really need my clothes! I smell like pure alcohol.'

'I know, it's turning me on,' he jokes. 'But if you insist, I will call him.'

Mick must have answered the phone after one ring, I think he's been waiting for this call.

'Right, he's on the bus outside. He can wait until we've finished these though.'

I notice that Luke has nearly finished his coffee, whereas I have hardly touched mine because it's way too hot for me.

'So what's the plan for today? Are you heading home?' Luke asks me.

'Yeah, I'm going to head over to the train station as soon as possible, hopefully there will be a seat available.'

'Well if you can't get a train you can always come and stay at mine.'

'Thank you, but if I'm not at work tomorrow I'll be in serious trouble.'

'And you're the boss?'

'I'm the boss.'

We both laugh.

'Well, the offer stands, if you ever need a place to stay in London, just let me know.'

'Thank you,' I tell him, squeezing his hand.

Luke has finished his drink, so I knock back the rest of mine a little faster than I would usually.

'Ready to go?' he asks.

I nod, but as we stand up I come over all dizzy and wobble on my feet slightly. Luke notices and takes me by the arm.

'You OK?'

'Yeah, just hungover. It will be a long time before I drink again,' I tell him.

'Of course it will. Well, I'll keep hold of you, just in case.'

We walk, arm-in-arm, to the bus where we find Mick sitting in the doorway smoking a cigarette.

'Mick,' Luke acknowledges him with a nod.

'Hello,' Mick says sheepishly. 'I've had a call from the Simon at the record label—'

'I know,' Luke interrupts him. 'He called us last night, we celebrated without you.'

'And don't we know it,' I add.

'Brilliant,' says Mick, standing up to let us on the bus. He is surprisingly quiet and I wonder how his date went, but I don't think he'd appreciate me asking.

Once on the bus I grab my clean clothes and a bottle of water from the fridge and take them into the bathroom. I wash my face and brush my teeth properly using the bottled water, because the water from the bus taps never seems clean. I change my clothes and apply lots of make-up, but no amount of perfume can truly cover the smell of champagne coming from my body. Still, it's better than smelling like beer I suppose.

I always hate the last day of tour. I hate saying goodbye to everyone and hanging around, waiting to go our separate ways. Usually I try to leave as soon as possible, which is odd considering the reason I do it is because I wish I didn't have to.

Luke is waiting for me in the living area.

'I might head over to the train station now, I'll have a better chance of getting a ticket.'

'Yeah, sure. Well it's been great seeing you, it wouldn't have been right without you last night. I'm glad we're OK.'

'Me too. I'd hate to lose you as friend.'

Luke stands up and I wrap my arms around him. He gives me a gentle kiss on the cheek.

'I'll miss you, though.'

'I'll miss you too,' I tell him, honestly, 'but I'll see you soon. Congratulations again.'

'Thanks. Maybe you could come with us.'

'Around Europe? You don't want me cramping your style,' I tease.

'It wouldn't be the same without you, you've been with us since the beginning.'

'I'll think about it,' I smile. It's hard to tell if he's being serious. 'Say goodbye to the guys for me. And Carla too, it was great to meet her.'

'Yeah, she's a good girl.'

'And what am I?'

'Bad to the bone, Nurse Wilde,' he tells me with a cheeky grin.

'Which reminds me.' I grab the nurse's cap from my handbag. 'Can you give this back to Eddie, please.'

'Keep it,' Luke insists. 'It was always meant for you anyway.'

I smile and put it back in my bag – I have a spot on my dressing table where it can go, along with the rest of my groupie treasure.

I give Luke a little wave as I head for the door. As I step off the bus, Mick asks me if I am going.

'I am. I hope you had fun last night,' I tell him and, for the first time ever, Mick actually blushes. 'See you next time.'

Chapter 41

Not only did I manage to get a train home, but I got to sit on an actual seat too. Anyone who travels by train will know what a novelty an actual seat can be. I turned up at the station and joined the queue at the ticket office straight away. I was ecstatic when the woman working there told me that I could get a seat on the next train – I wasn't quite as happy when I saw the price. Still, it's better than hanging around.

I thought about giving Charles a ring to see if he fancied meeting up, that way I could see him and I wouldn't have to kill time alone. It was probably for the best that I didn't, though. It's way too early in the relationship for Charles to see me looking how I looked this morning and I don't think that the hungover look (complete with champagne-sticky skin) is one that a lot of men go wild for.

After a nice long bath, I am sitting on my sofa in my pyjamas, despite the fact that it is only 6 p.m. To be fair, I didn't get much sleep last night because we partied until God knows what time and I didn't get much the night before because Charles was here and, well, we didn't do much sleeping.

Speaking of Charles, I'd better call him and let him know that I am home (and that I went to London in the first place). I pick up my phone to call him but it rings before I have the chance. It's Emily.

'London?' she says as soon as I answer the phone.

'I take it you've spoken to Jake,' I reply with a giggle.

'I have, we went out for lunch today. Vicky too,' she informs me. 'Jake told me everything! You and Charles ... I can't believe you didn't tell me!'

Is she mad at me? She sounds a little pissed off.

'It all happened so fast, Em.'

'I love that you bag yourself a boyfriend and then go off on tour with the band that you are head groupie for.'

'I am not head groupie,' I protest. 'And just because I have a boyfriend, it doesn't mean I'm going to stop touring. Why would I have to do that?'

'Most guys wouldn't be happy about it,' Emily informs me, before backtracking a little. 'You don't have to stop, I was only joking.'

'Let's hope I never have to choose between the two, eh?'

'Yeah, that boy would be out on his arse.'

'Speaking of arses, have you got rid of Vicky yet?'

'No. You should have seen her face when Jake was telling us about you, Charles and London. She couldn't hide her jealousy.'

'Why does she hate me so much? I'm always nice to her, aren't I?'

'You are always perfectly nice to her face.'

We both laugh. It doesn't matter how horrible or annoying Vicky is, I could never be nasty to her face and neither could Emily – which is probably why she is still living at her house.

'I think she likes you really.'

'Why would you think that?' I ask, totally baffled.

'She is always asking me questions about you. She is really interested in everything you're doing.'

'I'm not convinced. If you like someone, you're nice to them. I don't think girls do the whole treat 'em mean, keep 'em keen thing.'

'You gave her a chance, that's all you can do. Not many people can see her good side, but she is really quite sweet.'

Emily really cannot see the bad in anyone. Vicky could kill a kitten, and Emily would still think she was doing the right thing. Emily and I have so much in common, it's the reason we get on so well, but she is just far too trusting. I know better, but I found out the hard way.

'I'll be at work in the morning – on time,' I tell her optimistically.

'What a novel idea,' she teases.

'I will,' I insist. 'I'm ready for bed now. I'm knackered.'

My body must be listening to me because I yawn right on cue.

I feel bad for not telling Emily about Charles first of all, but everything happened so quickly. I know I've been neglecting her a bit recently, but now things are calming down I can make it up to her.

I fluff up the big pillows behind my head and slouch down further. I am so comfortable here, I never want to move again. I'll call Charles and tell him about my weekend and then I'll get in bed, that way I can catch up on my sleep and be up nice and early tomorrow. What a great plan.

Chapter 42

Well, what a terrible plan that turned out to be.

I must have fallen asleep minutes after getting off the phone with Em. Not only did I neglect to call Charles, but I must have dropped my phone in my sleep because there's a new little scratch on the side. Just brilliant.

Despite my very early night, I have managed to sleep in. Yes, I'm going to be late, but they expect it of me these days. That said, I don't want to push my luck so I quickly grab whatever clothes are scattered across my bedroom floor and hop into them, pile on some make-up and untangle the plaits I lazily pulled my wet hair into last night.

I'm halfway to work and rummaging around in my bag for more lip-gloss when I realise that I have left my mobile at home. I hate being without my phone – it's usually a permanent extension of my hand and I genuinely feel like I am missing a limb without it. It's too late to go back for it now, though.

Finally inside the office, everyone is hard at work – even Vicky – and it takes a few seconds before anyone notices I have walked in.

'Good morning, darlings. I know, I'm late, I'm sorry. Vicky, I'll get you some money, go to Starbucks and get whatever you guys want.'

'Fine.' She snatches the money from my hand and I take a deep breath to stop myself from saying something. A nice girl deep down, my arse.

As soon as her butt is out of the door, I walk into my office and plonk myself down at my desk. Emily follows me inside.

'Charles has called for you.'

'Yeah? I left my mobile at home. I forgot to call him last night, he's probably wondering what's happened to me.'

'He's called a few times actually, he sounds a bit pissed off.'

'Really?' That surprises me. I know we haven't spoken for forty-eight hours, but I didn't think he'd be the needy type. 'I guess I'd better call him back now then. Cheers, doll.'

'I'll leave you to it. If Vicky gets back with your coffee, I'll keep it out here until you're done,' Emily says, closing the door behind her – she really must think something is wrong. I search my desk for the little pink Post-it with Charles's number on and punch it into the phone on my desk.

'Charles Pace,' he answers in his usual serious tone.

'Hello, boyfriend, how are you?'

'Fine, and you?'

'I'm great, thanks. I've had one hell of a weekend—'

'Oh, I know you have,' he interrupts me.

'What do you mean?'

'I can't believe you've done this to me, and so soon after agreeing to be my girlfriend. It's disgusting.'

'Charles, what are you talking about?' I ask, entirely confused now.

'Are you seriously pretending you have no idea what I'm talking about?'

'I seriously have no idea what you are talking about,' I tell him honestly. Why is he shouting at me?

'Then I suggest you have a look on Facebook and call me back.' He slams the phone down.

I'm a little taken aback by his aggressive tone, but I do as he says and start up my computer. I haven't been on Facebook for a few days what with everything that has gone on – what could be so bad? I don't immediately see anything that might upset him, but then I click on my notifications. I have been tagged in an album called 'TFTR TOUR'. My heart sinks. Carla and her bloody camera! I get the feeling that big blank gap from Saturday night is about to be filled in. Taking a deep breath, I click on the first photo and flick through. There are a few backstage ones from before the gig and an awful lot of me at the gig looking a bit drunk, and, despite a few unflattering angles, I don't see anything that would immediately put Charles off. I'm beginning to wonder what the hell his problem is, but as I carry on clicking I finally learn how the night progressed. There are a few of me playing the drinking game – I remember that – and then suddenly, there it is, the moment I took off my skirt, or rather, the moment Luke pulled it off for me. I carry on flicking through the photos and I feel sick. There's one of me wearing nothing but my underwear and my borrowed hoodie, champagne bottle in one hand and giving the camera the finger with the other. Another of me pouring champagne into Luke's mouth. Another of me taking off Luke's wet T-shirt. Another of me sitting on his knee. I'm sure I told Carla that I had a boyfriend, why would she upload these? I know that I'm not really doing anything wrong, but I can see how they might look from Charles' point of view. I have to call him and explain, so I relocate the pink Post-it and dial his number.

'Charles Pace.'

'Charles, the photos are not what they look like.'

'What else could they be, Nicole? You tell me.'

'You work in music PR, you must have been on a tour or to a wrap-party?'

'Never. You may be surprised to hear this, but proper jobs don't involve getting drunk with bands.'

'There were at least thirty people in that room, you can tell from the other photos.'

'Oh, very classy,' he snaps.

'Please let me finish.'

He doesn't say anything and I take this as my cue to carry on.

'We were just having a laugh, nothing happened. I took my clothes off because Eddie sprayed me with champagne by accident. I'll admit I was very drunk, but we were celebrating.' I sigh. I don't know what I can say to make him believe me. 'This is just what happens. I wouldn't cheat on you.'

'You think getting drunk, taking off your clothes and sitting on some other guy's knee is just what happens?'

On tour it is.

'What kind of world do you live in? Seriously. Normal girls don't behave like *that*, having their photo taken all over other boys.'

'Whoa! Hang on a sec,' I say, suddenly relocating the confidence to stand up for myself. 'Don't make out like I've done something worse than I actually have. Those guys are my friends and I can sit on them if I like. I will admit that, in those photos, we do look a bit close, but nothing happened. Are there any photos of me cheating on you? No. Because I didn't. So you can believe me, or—'

'Nicole, calm down. I believe you. But you have to stop acting like this with other guys. It's just not acceptable.'

And, just like that, he's calm again. He's like the Incredible Sulk. I don't want to agree with him because I don't believe that I did anything wrong, but the last thing I want is to fall out with him.

'You didn't even tell me you were in London. Why didn't you tell me that?'

'It was really last minute, and I knew you had a work thing. I was going to call you last night, but then I fell asleep.'

'I need to know that I can trust you.'

'You can trust me.'

'Promise me that I can trust you?'

'I promise, Charles.'

'I like you a lot, Nicole. I'd hate for a bit of silly behaviour to get in the way of what could be something special. I've got work to do, but I'll call you tonight, OK?'

'Sure. I'm sorry, Charles. Speak soon.'

He puts the phone down.

Bloody hell, I wasn't expecting this today. I have another flick through the photos. I look so happy in them, the happiest I have looked in a long time. I can see why Charles is upset and I do feel a bit bad now. I guess I would have reacted in the same way if it had been the other way round. I flick back to the photo of me sitting on Luke's knee and notice that there is a comment from him and one from Carla. Luke's says: 'I love this one' and Carla's says: 'Me too! You guys make a great couple' – shit, I really hope Charles didn't notice that.

Maybe I do need to sort out my behaviour. I may not remember what it's like to have a boyfriend, but Charles is probably in the right. I make enough jokes about my world vs. the 'real world', but they have never seemed more different. I'm going to have to do everything I can to fit back into the 'real world' or I'm going to lose Charles. No more touring and no more after-parties, not until I know how to behave at them without getting overly familiar with the bands. I've been hanging out with these people for the whole of my adult life, so I suppose their behaviour was bound to rub off on me eventually. I guess I'm going to have to make a big decision: I can carry on having fun and messing around with my silly band boys or I can change my life entirely to try to be more like the kind of girl Charles expects me to be. Decisions, decisions.

Chapter 43

'But they don't have a drummer, and yet I can hear drums in their music,' Vicky protests. Her voice is way louder than she realises because she's wearing headphones.

I'm having a bit of trouble reviewing an album so I've got everyone in the office having a listen to see what they think of it.

'Yes, there are drums, but they have a session player record them. It doesn't matter. What do you think of—'

'But it doesn't make any sense,' Vicky cuts me off mid-sentence. 'How can they have drums in their music, but not play them?'

'Who's your favourite musician?' I run my hands through my hair and sigh. We've been having this conversation for way too long already. At first Emily was acting as the middle-woman, but even she has given up now. And Jake, well he's just sat behind his computer (on his fence) trying not to laugh.

'I like Pink.' She folds her arms and smiles smugly.

'Of course you do, and do you hear drums in Pink's music?'

'Yes.'

'Right, and is Pink a drummer?'

'No. She has someone play them for her.'

'Exactly.' I nod my head as she processes the thought, any minute now she's going to crack on to what I'm saying.

'Yeah, but she's just a singer. This band play instruments, so why don't they have a member play the drums?'

Jake cracks up, unable to control his laughter a second longer. 'Give it up, Nic, it's impossible.'

Vicky shoots Jake a dirty look and then turns back to me, waiting for an explanation. She thinks she's got me beat and I can't help but laugh too because I don't have an answer for her.

'This isn't helping at all.'

'Play it out loud, maybe if we all listen together ...' Emily suggests, ever the diplomat.

I watch the three of them for a moment. Emily and Vicky messing with the CD player, Jake sat back watching them and chuckling to himself. It's good to have things back to normal. It's only been a few days since the drama with Charles and the Facebook photos, but we've talked a lot and I've made him some fairly big promises. I think we're going to be OK, and I'm so pleased because I like him a lot. I spent years without a boyfriend, thinking that I was happier with casual encounters, but the idea of having someone always there for me and always on my side is one that I could really get used to.

We're all rather enjoying the quiet days at work, the ones we always have just after we put an issue online. Everyone is always in a much better mood and even Vicky has been known to smile and say nice things on these quiet days.

As the album plays – for the fifth time – I ignore the music and chat with the gang.

'I am *so* looking forward to tonight!' I say excitedly. 'A night out that doesn't involve bands – I don't remember the last time that happened. It's been a bloody long time though.'

'About that,' Vicky says, spinning around on her desk chair so that she is facing me, 'I'm thinking maybe we should give it a miss. Do something else.'

'Do something else!' I echo. 'Like what? I've been looking forward to this for ages!'

Tonight is Halloween and to celebrate we are going to a foam party. I have my outfit ready and waiting for me at home. Rather originally, I have opted for a devil costume which, if I am being honest, is just my own red clothes with a clip-on tail and horns. I love Halloween and I love foam parties, so I'm not too impressed with Vicky's sudden change of heart. If she doesn't like it, she can always stay at home.

'The foam really irritates my skin!' she protests, clearly appalled that I had dared to suggest she go near foam.

'But we planned this ages ago, and you knew about the foam – it's a foam party!'

'It's just not worth it. You really should take better care of your skin, Nicole.'

Looking over at Emily, I give her my best please-deal-with-her face. You can always count on your best friend to side with you in situations like this.

'Maybe we could do something else,' Emily suggests.

Or not.

'What?' I look over at Jake and, surprise, surprise, he gives me his best I'm-not-getting-involved face.

'We could watch scary DVDs at my place.' There is a look of desperation in Emily's eyes as she says this, like she is willing me to agree. I am fighting a losing battle here because if Vicky doesn't want to go, then Vicky won't go, and Emily won't go if her new roommate doesn't want to.

'Yeah, fine,' I mutter, walking into my office and slamming the door behind me.

It is 6 p.m. and I'm still at work. Emily and Vicky have gone home and Jake has gone to his place to get changed. I am here all alone finishing off this damn album review. To be honest, I don't have to do it right now but I'm a bit pissed off and I don't want to go over to Emily's just yet. I just can't face a whole night of Vicky.

So here I am, pretending to write a review. I don't know if it's because it is Halloween or because I am here alone, but I feel really freaked out. It's dark out – nature's little reminder that winter is nearly here – and the lights in the main office are dimmed, so I think I'll stay here in my office until Jake comes back to pick me up. I am cursing myself for telling him it would be at least 7 p.m. before I would be finished, but it seemed like a great idea at the time when I just wanted everyone to piss off.

The office has never seemed so creepy and I actually find myself fully opening the blinds and looking out of my window, just to see people. This settles my nerves for a few minutes before I start feeling vulnerable again – in my well-lit office anyone in the dark street, or the dark rooms in the office across the road, could be watching me ... Oh God! I swiftly fiddle with the cord that closes the blinds, letting out a bit of a whimper – pathetic.

Sitting back down in my desk chair, I let out a sigh. It's no use, I'm going to have to call Jake and get him to come for me now because I'll drive myself crazy sitting here. I grab my phone and begin to search for Jake's name when I hear a loud clatter in the main office. My eyes dart up from my phone and focus on the door. I stay absolutely still and listen to the silence for a few seconds – did I imagine that? I really do know how to freak myself out. I am snapped from my reassuring thoughts by a second loud noise and it is definitely coming from the office. Panic sets in. I can't just sit here and wait for it to come and get me. What am I thinking? It's not an it, it's a person. Was my first thought really that it might be a ghost? No, it's a person, and I'm going to go out there and defend myself. I am far too cool to die like this! Just imagine what people would say: 'Oh, she died working late.' Oh no, if I'm going down, I'm going down fighting.

I laugh to myself (very quietly, of course) at the idea of me going out there to face whoever it is, because I am the girl who once spent a night at Emily's house just because there was a moth in my bathroom – a big, hairy moth with designs on flying into my mouth, I'm sure of it.

Another clatter. Right, that's it. I grab something from my

desk to arm myself with and walk slowly towards the door, gently placing my free hand on the door handle. I look at my weapon of choice – a can of hairspray. What the fuck am I going to do with that? Spray the person to death? Glancing back at my desk, I spy a heavy-duty hole-punch (I'm not even sure why we have a hole-punch because I don't think we've ever used it), why didn't I grab that? I've come too far to go back for it now though.

I can definitely hear someone moving around and they sound much closer to the door now. Flinging open my office door with such force I almost rip the handle off, I charge through with my hairspray in one hand, frantically searching for the light switch with the other. Seeing the dark, shadowy figure of a man walking towards me, I close my eyes and scream as I fumble for the switch. Finally clicking it on, I open my eyes and prepare to spray my opponent.

'Whoa! Whoa! Don't spray me!' he cries out, shielding his eyes.

They say that most victims know their attacker, well I certainly know mine – although I'm not entirely sure he's here to attack me.

'Is that pepper spray?' he asks with a relieved, yet still slightly cautious look on his face, walking towards me, holding his hands up in the air.

'Extra-hold.' I hold up the hairspray can for him to see and we both laugh before hugging one another.

'Dylan, what are you doing here?'

His smile drops as I ask this. I sit down on the sofa, ready to listen.

'It's just everything,' he says as he sits next to me. 'I'm sick of everything. Married life is shit, people tell you it's going to be shit and you think they're just having you on, but it's shit, Nicole. A huge pile of shit.'

As he drops his head into his hands, I place a comforting arm around him.

'And do you know what the worst part is?' he asks. 'You tried to tell me this was a dick thing to do, and I didn't listen. I was so caught up in doing the right thing.'

He says the 'the right thing' in a silly voice.

'No one can tell you what the right thing is, Dill.' I rub his shoulder sympathetically.

'I spoke to Charles today, he told me about you two.'

'I was hoping to tell you myself, but you haven't been answering my calls.'

'It's her.'

Oh, I know it's her all right. I'm just hoping it's her hormones that are making her act this way.

Standing up, Dylan puts his hands behind his head and stares at the ceiling, exhaling loudly.

'I don't want this, Nic. I don't want any of it. I don't want her, I don't want kids. How did I get into this mess?'

'Look, calm down. It might seem bad now, but once the babies are born—'

'No!' he cuts me off. 'This isn't me, and you know it. You know it, Nicole.'

'Have you been drinking?' I ask.

'No.'

'Would you like one?' I rummage around in the little office fridge, trying to find something to mix with the vodka that I keep in my office – for emergencies, and this is most definitely an emergency.

'There we are.' I push the glass into his hand and he takes a big drink without giving the contents a second glance.

'What's this crap in my vodka?' he asks, his face scrunched-up in disgust.

'It's orange juice,' I tell him with a giggle. 'It's a fruit.'

'Give me the bottle.' He knocks back the rest of his drink reluctantly and pours himself a large vodka.

'What are you doing in Leeds?' I ask, cutting to the chase.

'I ran away.' He laughs like a maniac.

'You ran away? How old are you again?'

'I couldn't take another second of her, Nic.'

'You mean your wife?'

'Don't rub it in, please.' He pours himself another drink, and tops up what I have left with even more vodka. I sip it politely, but it's strong enough to remove my nail polish.

'I was supposed to be going out tonight. Mikey was throwing a big Halloween party, but Crystal said she couldn't go, so I couldn't go.'

'Well it is Halloween, she probably has to work. Actually, she's on maternity leave, isn't she?'

'Oi, that's my wife you're talking about,' he laughs. 'Anyway, what are you still doing at work, you loser?'

'My plans were ruined too. I'm going over to Emily's to watch scary movies, probably nothing scarier than *Hocus Pocus*. Want to come?' Imagine Vicky's face if I turn up with Dylan, a proper celebrity.

'You make it sound so appealing,' he says sarcastically, 'but I think I'll pass, not really my scene.'

'Well let's go to the party I was supposed to go to then,' I suggest, because that is definitely his scene and it's mine too.

'Can you imagine the headlines if I am papped on a night out in Leeds with another girl, while my wife is stuck at home, pregnant and alone? Man, I wanna quit the business so bad right now.'

'You can't do that, just think of all the fans you would be letting down.'

'Think about it, if I wasn't famous there's no way Crystal would have wanted to shag me. I wouldn't even be in this mess. When I stormed out, I thought I might go to a club, but I couldn't risk having my picture taken. I'd look like a total dick.'

'I know things seem shitty right now,' I down my drink for confidence, because I'm not entirely sure that I truly believe what I am about to say. 'You're just panicking because it's all different. You just need to chill out, have a night off, and everything will seem better in the morning.'

'You're probably right,' he reluctantly admits. I know I'm probably wrong, but what choice does he have now? Trying to divorce a pregnant woman a couple of weeks after your rushed wedding is bad enough, but for a celebrity like Dylan, it would ruin his profile completely, he'd be hated.

I grin at him. 'I'm always right.'

'I'm being a selfish shithead, aren't I?'

'You're not being selfish, Dill. You're just not used to this stuff.'

'I'll go back early tomorrow and beg for forgiveness, I guess.'

'Good idea. Do you need a place to stay?'

'I booked into The Chater – something.'

'The Châtaigne?' I ask, excitedly.

'That's the one.'

'Oh, flashy!' I say this to tease him, but it really is a nice hotel. All of the really big stars stay there when they come to town.

'Don't take the piss or I'll get you with that hairspray. We could go back there and get drunk?' he suggests with a sigh.

'Way to make a girl feel welcome!'

'Well we can't go anywhere else, can we?'

'Perhaps …' I skip towards my office excitedly. 'I'll be back.'

I grab my phone to make a quick call.

'Emily, hello,' I say breathlessly as soon as she answers. 'Listen, something has come up and I can't come over tonight, can you let Jake know not to pick me up please?'

'Yeah, course. What's going on?'

'I'll tell you, but it's top secret. Don't even tell Jake.'

She promises, but it goes without saying that I can trust her.

'Dylan is here! He needed to get away so he's come here, but he's going back in the morning.'

'Oh my God!' Emily squeals. 'Is he staying at yours?'

'No, no, he's staying at The Châtaigne.'

'Oh, flashy!'

'That's what I said!' I said over-enthusiastically, quickly lowering the volume of my voice again in case Dylan hears me. 'I'm going to take him to the foam party, cheer him up a bit.'

'That's nice but it won't look very good if anyone sees him out partying, will it?'

'Don't worry, I've got it covered.'

'How?' she ask curiously.

'A disguise!' I announce proudly.

'Won't that look a bit weird?'

'Emily, it's Halloween.'

'So?'

I laugh. 'So everyone is dressing up tonight, you ditzy cow!'

'Oh,' she replies, sounding slightly offended. 'Well I'll let Jake know, have fun.'

The call ends abruptly, but she knows I'm busy.

Skipping back out into the main office, I grab the big box from underneath Jake's desk and plonk it down in front of Dylan. 'We're going to a party! A foam party!'

'We've been over this, I—'

'Look inside the box,' I insist.

'Halloween costumes? Nicole Wilde, you beauty!' he rubs his hands together and begins searching the box for something suitable.

'We had them leftover from a photo shoot, I knew they would come in handy for something.'

Dylan pulls out a rubber Frankenstein's monster mask and puts it on. It covers his head, eyes and nose and he is instantly unrecognisable. I grab the witch's hat that Vicky wore during our Halloween photoshoot with Chillz. As far as witches' hats go, it's really pretty. It's black, with a big, black, glittery bow and a black lace trim. This will do nicely.

I hand Dylan my compact and he checks out his disguise.

'I think we might actually get away with this, you know.' He grabs the bottle of vodka and fills our glasses. 'We may as well finish this and then we'll head over to the club. It's a long time since I've been anonymous. I'm excited.'

He looks excited – well the bottom half of his face does, at least. I'm excited too. This feels like a chance to act like it's the good old days. It might even be our last chance. I'm going to make sure we have a really good time, because as soon as the babies are born he won't be able to do this anymore. To be honest, after my conversation with Charles, I'm not sure I'm supposed to be doing this anymore either. Not if I want to keep him.

Chapter 44

I am covered in foam, I am drunk and life is good.

Dylan is also covered in foam, drunk and still wearing his mask. I can still see his mouth though, and I don't think he has stopped smiling for a second tonight.

We've spent the entire night drinking and dancing in the foam. It's been great hanging out in public with Dylan without being approached by anyone. No one has given us a second look all night, we just blend in with all the other monsters and witches.

I'm waiting for Dylan outside the little boys' room and dancing in a way that a sober person couldn't get away with. Dylan staggers through the doorway and falls into me, pinning me against the wall.

'Caught you!' I shout and we both find this absolutely hilarious.

'I'm so hungry! There's a seriously stacked mini-bar in my room.'

'What are we waiting for?' I yell.

As we make our way towards the exit, Dylan wraps an arm around my waist.

'Don't want you falling,' he yells over the music, but he isn't exactly steady on his own feet right now. We stumble out onto the street, which is crawling with people all wearing different costumes.

'Sorry, mate,' Dylan says as he stumbles into a lamp-post.

'There!' I point down the road towards the little side street where the hotel is located. 'That's where we need to be.'

We walk down the road slowly but surely. It's for the best in these (drunken) circumstances.

Dylan is singing to himself in a high-pitched voice and we're both laughing uncontrollably. I try to shush him as we approach the hotel because it's so quiet outside. There isn't a soul around, not even a doorman outside the hotel.

Just when I think we've made it in one piece, Dylan topples over and, because he is holding on to me, he drags me down with him. We fall really awkwardly and somehow Dylan manages to land right on top of me. We freeze for a few seconds before carrying on with our hysterical laughter. Dylan's mask has fallen off and his hair has gone all flat so I run my hand through it to make it look less sticky and to make him look less like a drunk as he walks through the hotel lobby.

'Are you OK?' he whispers.

'I am, but you're squashing me. And your mask has come off.'

'Shit.' He stands up, still laughing, and looks around the floor for his mask, almost taking another tumble. 'I think it went under that BMW.' He points towards the car parked next to us. 'I'll get it.'

'No, no, no, no,' I beg. 'Leave it. You might set off the alarm or something. I'll never wear it, I assure you. It doesn't go with anything I own.'

'OK, let's go eat!' he announces, slapping his hand across his mouth when he realises just how loud his voice is.

'Shhhh!' I tell him, giggling and taking him by the arm. 'Try to act sober, OK?'

Chapter 45

I've had some hangovers recently, but this one really takes the alcohol-soaked biscuit.

My memory of last night is hazy. Come to think of it, I'm having a lot of trouble with my memory at the moment. I'm beginning to think it has something to do with alcohol.

I'm right in the middle of a king-size bed and it's oh-so-comfortable. If only I didn't have this banging headache; it's like my brain is trying to bash its way out of my skull – I think it's had enough of me.

There's a massive TV on the wall facing me, already switched on. I never get to watch much daytime TV because I'm always either asleep or at work, but for a moment I am totally captivated by a guest who reckons he's set a world record for eating crumpets. I hear a groaning noise coming from the bottom of the bed, which is so huge I actually have to crawl to the bottom just to see what is on the floor. Face down, sprawled out across the carpet (which looks surprisingly comfortable), is Dylan.

'You all right?' I extend a leg and give him a prod on the shoulder with my big toe. He doesn't say anything, he just laughs at me.

'Say that again,' he demands.

'What?'

'What you just said, say it again,' he insists, still lying face down on the floor.

'You all right?'

'I fucking love your Yorkshire accent.'

'Oh God, what do I sound like?'

'Yo'rite!' he teases.

'I don't sound like *that*!' I insist, with a sneaking suspicion that I do sound exactly like that. 'You all right?' I say to myself, smiling because I see exactly what he means.

'Listen, you want to visit the village where I grew up and hear an old farmer talk with a proper Yorkshire accent, you'll fast go off it.'

'Go on then, how would they say it?' He rolls over onto his back and puts his hands behind his head.

'Y'alreyt?'

He laughs. 'Sounds the same to me, Nic.'

I give him the finger and he sticks his tongue out at me.

'It's hearing that dodgy accent that reminds me how much I miss spending time with you. Last night was fun.'

I've missed him too.

'How much of last night do you actually remember?' I ask, standing up and adjusting my outfit. There is nothing quite like the pain of falling asleep in an underwired bra.

'Well, none of it, but it was good fun, I'm sure. Thank you for looking after me.' He smiles sincerely.

'You're welcome. Can I use your bathroom?'

'Sure. You leaving me?'

'Yeah, I'm late for work, and you have to go home and grovel to your wife, remember?'

'Ah, shit. I remember.'

I close the bathroom door behind me. Another nice big bathroom to remind me of how small and crap my own is, no pun intended.

'What the hell are you watching?' I hear Dylan shout.

'God knows! It was on when I woke up.'

'Watching him stuffing food into his mouth is making me want to throw up,' he groans.

'Turn it off,' I laugh. 'You're determined to get blacklisted from every hotel in the country for making a mess.'

Looking in the mirror, I am half-tempted to wear my witch's hat on the way home, because not only does my hair look awful, but it might distract people from my make-up-smeared face. I wet a towel and try to wipe the smudges off, careful not to wipe it all off because that would be as bad as going outside naked. Despite being late for work, I have no choice but to go home and smarten myself up, even though work is much closer.

'How do I look?' I give Dylan a twirl.

'Like you spent a night in a hotel room with a rockstar,' he says with a wink.

'That's what I'm afraid of. It's like the walk of shame, without the shame.'

'Would it really be a shame?' he teases.

'Shut up you!' I lean forwards and give him a peck on the cheek. 'Right, some of us have proper jobs to get to, so I must leave you here in your five-star hotel, poor you. Maybe you should tidy up a bit, the room is a tip.'

'It looks like we gave the mini-bar a good bashing. I'll see you soon, I promise,' he calls after me as I walk towards the door.

'I hope so,' I tell him with a smile, but I'm not convinced. I really hope I do, but I think I have to let him go and do what he needs to do for a while. He'll regret it, if he doesn't give it a try.

As I go down in the lift, I look at my reflection in the mirrored walls and fidget with my hair and clothes until I look as presentable as possible. Stepping out, I look across the lobby and see a huge crowd gathered outside the hotel entrance. As I walk closer, I notice that that it's the paparazzi with only a couple of hotel security guards to stop them coming inside. Armed with super high-quality looking cameras, I selfishly hope that whoever they're waiting for doesn't come out at the same time as me because I'd hate to get caught looking like this in the background of one of the photos – knowing my luck it would end up on the front of a national newspaper.

I wonder which celebrity they are waiting for. Whoever it is, I can't help but feel a bit sorry for them. This is exactly what Dylan was telling me about last night. Dylan! As soon as I'm out of earshot, I'll give him a call and warn him. They wouldn't be able to believe their luck if they were waiting around for someone else and Dylan King strolled out. Two for the price of one!

I manage to walk out of the door and down the steps before one of them calls out, 'There she is!'

I spin around to see which mega-star they are waiting for, only to have them all point their cameras at me.

'Nicole, over here,' one man calls out. I don't know what to do so I turn around and run towards the main road. Looking over my shoulder, I realise they are all chasing me but I don't have the energy or the right shoes to escape them. Shit, shit, shit. As I get to the main road I look left, then right. I don't know where to go. The photographers catch up with me almost instantly and carry on snapping. Standing here helplessly with them all surrounding me, I have nothing to do but panic. They're all shouting things at me, but I can't work out what anyone is saying. I instinctively hold my witch's hat over my face.

'Out the way! Move!' I can just about make out a broad Yorkshire accent booming over the rest. I feel a pair of hands on my shoulders and sense myself being ushered away from the photographers.

'Get in here. Quick.'

With the hat still held firmly over my face, I get in the car. I don't know who this person is, but if he had both hands on my shoulders then he can't have been one of the men trying to take my photo.

As I feel the car moving, I finally let go of the hat and gaze out of the back window, only to see the crowd of photographers try to chase the car for a few seconds before admitting defeat.

'You OK?' I hear the driver ask. Oh thank God, he's a taxi driver.

'Yes. I think so.' I let out a sigh of relief. 'Thank you for saving me.'

'Wasn't gonna stand by and watch them harass a young lass.' I see him smile in the rear-view mirror. 'Where can I drop you where you'll be safe, love?'

I give him the name of the street where my office is because it's closer than home. 'What do I owe you?' I ask.

'You don't owe me 'owt, happy to help.'

I key his driver number into my phone. He saved me so I'll have to think of a way to thank him, although I'm not sure of the etiquette when it comes to saying, 'thank you for saving me from the paparazzi,' because this type of stuff isn't supposed to happen to me.

'Love, if you don't mind me asking, what is it you've done to have them chasing you?'

Looking into the rear-view mirror again, I make eye contact with my hero.

'I wish I knew.'

Chapter 46

I leg it through the ByteBanter office without making eye contact with any of the staff. Finally through the *Starstruck* doors, I am greeted by Jake and Emily and they look like they know something I don't.

'What the hell is going on?' I cry out, assuming they already know.

Emily and Jake look at each other in a which-one-has-to-tell-her kind of way.

'Tell me!' I try to calm down. 'Please.'

Emily hands me a copy of today's *Daily Scoop*. I take the wretched tabloid in my hands and examine the headline.

'Dylan goes Wilde!' I read out loud. There is a large photograph underneath the headline showing me lying on the pavement with Dylan on top of me. We're gazing into each other's eyes and I'm running my hand through his hair.

'Fuck!' I throw the paper as far away from me as possible. 'It's not what it looks like.' I feel tears roll down my cheeks.

'We know,' Jake puts his arm around me, but I noticed that Emily keeps clear. 'Maybe if you just explain what actually happened—'

'Are you kidding?' I snap. 'I was there, I know that nothing happened, and even I think it looks fucking dodgy!'

I'm not sure how I'm going to talk my way out of this one. The photos from last night show me arriving at the hotel and the photos they took this morning will show me leaving the hotel – it's going to look like I spent the night with Dylan. I mean, I know I *did* spend the night in his room, but nothing happened. Neither of us did anything wrong, we didn't even share the bed!

'Why are you looking so sheepish?' I ask Emily, noticing her picking up the paper that I threw. She's being awfully quiet, or maybe I'm just being over-sensitive.

'Tell her,' Jake insists, and I've never heard him sound so forceful or so angry.

'Tell me what?'

Emily fidgets with the newspaper, sorting the pages back into the right order.

'Tell me what, Emily?' I yell, making her jump. Never in my life have I shouted at Emily and doing so makes me feel even sicker than I already do.

Still not saying a word, she hands me the newspaper and points to the by-line.

'Words and pictures by Vicky Mason,' I read out loud. I can't believe my eyes.

'How?' I look at Jake and follow his gaze towards Emily.

'Emily, no. You didn't.'

'I thought I could trust her.' Emily falls back into her chair and bursts into tears.

'Why on earth would you think you could trust *her*?' I yell. 'And I asked you not to tell *anyone*! I trusted you!'

It breaks my heart to shout at her when she's crying like this, but look what she's done. She's made me look like a homewrecker and she's made Dylan look like a cheat.

'You think you're entirely blameless in all of this?' Emily says as she wipes her eyes. 'You brought this on yourself, Nicole.'

I don't know if they were crocodile tears before, but they are fast drying up now and her voice is getting stronger again.

'How on earth did I bring this on myself?' I ask.

'I hardly see you these days. We're supposed to be best friends, and you're never around. Vicky was always around and she was just so easy to talk to.'

'She was always around because she was living at your house, and she was easy to talk to because she was trying to get dirt on me. How could you be so stupid?'

'I'm stupid?' she replies, standing up and walking towards me. 'If you didn't get yourself in these situations, then there wouldn't be a problem.'

'So you thought that made it OK to tell Vicky one of my biggest secrets? What else have you told her, eh?' This isn't a serious question, but then I noticed the look on her face and I can read her like a book. 'Are you fucking kidding me? What else have you told her?'

'Back when the Plastic Rap story broke, I panicked and thought maybe she'd blabbed, but then you said you thought it was one of the girls there, and I realised I could trust her.'

So it was Vicky who leaked it.

'Anything else?'

'I might have mentioned some stuff about you and Luke being close – but that was before anything happened.'

'Did you not think it was a bit suspicious when we read that article about me?' I ask, unable to believe she could be so stupid.

'There's no smoke without fire, Nicole,' she tells me, like she is so perfect and I'm so terrible.

'So let me get the straight. Vicky has been living in your house and you've not only been doing everything possible to make her happy, but you've been telling her all my secrets?'

'I didn't plan on it, it just happened.'

'You don't even care, do you? You've probably ruined my career because no one will trust me now. You've probably ruined Dylan's marriage – he's got twins on the way, for God's sake.'

Emily casually shrugs her shoulders. I can't believe she's done this to me.

'I thought I could trust you with anything,' I tell her quietly.

'Nicole, you have been able to trust me with a million other things,' Emily says in self-defence.

'It doesn't matter how many times I've been able to trust you,' I tell her. 'It matters how many times I haven't.'

'Whatever.'

'I can't believe you've done this to me,' I tell her. I really can't believe it, up until this moment I would have trusted Emily with my life.

'Oh my God,' she yells angrily. 'You are *so* selfish!'

'Look—' Jake starts, but Emily cuts him off.

'Stay out of this, Jake, we all know whose side you'll be on.'

'Oi, leave Jake out of this,' I snap.

Before we have chance to continue scrapping and getting nowhere with it, ET barges into the office.

'My phone is ringing off the hook,' he shouts. 'What the hell is going on?'

'That will be because we unplugged ours,' Jake tells him.

'Vicky has set me up, made me look bad and sold the story to a tabloid,' I squeak at him.

'You made yourself look bad,' Emily snaps.

'Oh my God, shut up, you—'

'Everybody quiet,' ET bellows, stopping me mid-sentence. 'The ByteBanter team are being bombarded with calls and emails about this, and all you're doing is arguing like school-children in here. You can all go home until we sort this mess out!'

'Nice one, Nicole,' Emily says sarcastically.

'This is more your fault than it is mine,' I insist.

'Girls, please,' ET shouts. He's so used to dealing with men, he probably doesn't know how to cope with two pissed-off females screeching at each other in front of him.

'I'm out of here,' Emily says, storming off and slamming the door behind her.

'Good riddance,' I call after her.

ET rubs his eyes and exhales deeply with exasperation before leaving the room. For a second, Jake and I just stare at each other in disbelief, because neither of us expected a drama today. As I think about everything that has happened, and the consequences that will surely follow, I can feel myself getting more and more upset. It's bad enough that mine and Dylan's reputations will suffer, but the magazine is paying for it too. As my mind races and I wonder what the hell I'm going to do, I can't help but burst into tears.

'Come on, Nic,' he says softly. 'Let's get you home.'

Chapter 47

I've always craved a celebrity lifestyle, but if this is what it's like then I think I'll pass – although it might be too late for that, because this morning I was chased by the paparazzi! I'm on the front of a national newspaper!

Having made it home safely (our office has a back door – who knew?), the first thing I did was call Dylan to warn him, but he didn't pick up. I got a text a few minutes later saying Charles had called him to tell him and that he was trying to get out of the hotel unseen. That's when I realised – Charles! I'm going to call him and explain, just as soon as I work out what to say. The important thing to remember is that I haven't done anything wrong, but I'm a bit worried after our last misunderstanding. He knows me, he knows Dylan, he'll be fine about it … so why am I worried?

I pour myself a large drink – alcohol is absolutely the right thing to do. Having a hangover is only making my situation worse, and vice versa, so if I can get back to being tipsy then things will be a lot easier. As I lean forwards to pick up my phone, I catch a strong whiff of chemicals – it's my post-foam-party hair. My head suddenly feels unbearably itchy. Perhaps I'll have a bath before I call Charles, give myself a little time to calm down.

My hair is washed and I feel considerably less foamy, but I can't bring myself to get out of the bath yet. My phone is on top of the drawers next to me, staring at me, reminding me that I should call Charles. No more putting it off, I'm going to do it right now and get it out of the way. I dry my hands and pick up my phone. His mobile is switched off, so I call his office and it rings for ages, in fact I'm just about to hang up when he answers.

'Charles Pace.'

'Charles, hey, it's Nicole.'

He doesn't say anything, forcing me to speak first.

'How are you?'

'I'm a bit busy actually, Nicole. One of my married clients has been caught having spent the night in a hotel with another woman.'

I giggle before realising that he isn't joking.

'I can't believe people are thinking that! You know this is Vicky trying to ruin my life. The bitch even used *my* camera to take the picture.'

'What is it your lot say? A picture is worth a thousand words.'

'Something like that.' I giggle nervously.

'Nicole, this isn't funny,' he snaps.

'Charles, I'm really sorry.'

'You're sorry? It's going to take a bit more than sorry, you stupid little girl.'

'You're not the first person to have a client get a bit of bad press, you know,' I reply, raising my voice slightly.

'You think that's what's bothering me?' he asks. 'Disgusting. Nicole, you not only shagged someone else behind my back, but you shagged one of my clients. You've humiliated me!'

I try to speak but my voice fails me.

'You don't honestly believe that?' I eventually manage to whisper. 'You don't think I'd do that? He's my best friend and he's married. What kind of girl do you think I am?'

'I know exactly what kind of girl you are,' he says coldly. 'Plus, you don't think everyone around you can see the chemistry that the two of you have? The attraction between you both that for some reason you're both trying to pretend isn't there? Now if you'll excuse me, I have a lot of work to do today.'

'Charles, wait. Please, I don't know what to do. I'm being chased by photographers, Vicky has set me up, I've fallen out with Emily. What do I do?'

'I'm sorting things out for Dylan because he pays me. If you want a bit of damage control, then I suggest you do what all the other kiss-and-tell tarts do and hire someone.'

'What did you say?' I ask, regaining a bit of my confidence. My mind instantly goes back to that conversation I had with Mark on tour. He told me that no one has the right to say things like that about me and he's right. Charles might not believe me, but I haven't done anything wrong.

'You heard me. You know, after I saw those photos online, with you all over that boy,' I can hear the disgust in his voice as he speaks, 'I thought that maybe it was a one-off, especially when you promised me that I could trust you and that it wouldn't happen again. Well, look where it's got me. I should have stuck with my instincts and ended things between us the second I saw those photographs.'

I am not usually very good at controlling my temper, and today is no exception.

'Oh, go fuck yourself!' I shout, throwing my phone. As soon as it leaves my hand, I realise what I have done. My phone lands in the bath with a big splash. It's only in the water a matter of seconds, but I fear the damage has been done. Jumping out the water, I grab my towel and dry the phone. I prod a button but it fails to light up this time. I panic because my entire life is in this phone and I can't remember what you're supposed to do with them if they get wet. I wrap it back up in the towel and run out of my bathroom. Maybe if I blow it with my hairdryer it will help to dry it out. I grab my dryer from my bedroom and hurriedly plug it in. I'm just about to switch it on when I hear my front door open. Suddenly very aware that I am naked, I grab the towel from my phone and wrap it around myself. No one can get in without a key, so it must be Jake.

'Jake, is that you?' I shout.

'Yeah, you OK?' he calls back.

'No,' I cry. 'Can you come in here please?'

'Whoa! I'm not looking!' he says as he walks through the door and realises I'm wearing nothing but a towel.

'I dropped my phone in the bath, what do I do?'

'Not that!' he says spying my hairdryer. 'That will only drive the water in further.'

He grabs my phone and does something I wouldn't have known how to do.

'Put this somewhere safe,' he instructs, handing me my SIM card. 'Do you have a vacuum cleaner?'

'Do *I* have a vacuum cleaner?' I echo with a laugh.

'Do you have any rice?'

I stare at him blankly.

'Right. Of course you don't. I'm going to pop back to mine with this, don't go anywhere,' he calls as he runs towards the door. 'It's crawling with photographers out there.'

'Thank you,' I call after him.

Ruining my phone is just the shit-flavoured icing on the cake today. I feel so alone, and I have no one to talk to. I glance over at my telephone, my proper telephone that is. The only reason I have a landline is for the internet, I hardly ever use this phone. I need to talk to someone, but all of my numbers are in my mobile. I know Emily's number off by heart, of course, but I don't want to speak to her. I can't believe she's done this to me. If she told me a secret and asked me not to tell anyone, I would never ever blab. Especially not to someone she hated. Has this been Vicky's intention from the beginning? I feel sick at the thought of her scheming behind my back all along. At least I know where Scott

Hale got his story from. Oh my God, that day when I read the story, it was Vicky who egged me on and told me to send Scott a nasty message. If I wasn't feeling so devastated, I'd probably be impressed.

Part of me thinks that I should forgive Emily, but today I have lost everything. My boyfriend, my credibility, my phone ... I may as well add a back-stabbing best friend to the list. I pick up the house phone as I consider whether to call her or not. There's a card poking out from underneath the phone and, as soon as I see it, I realise what it is and what I should do.

I punch the number in and sigh with relief when it is answered straight away.

'Hello, Mum,' I say as cheerily as I can.

'Hello, darling, what a nice surprise. How are you?'

'Not so good actually.' I burst into tears.

'Nicole! What's the matter?' she asks me. I try to reply but once again my voice fails me. 'You sounded so happy in your last email. Have you had a row with your new boyfriend?'

My mum waits patiently for me to stop crying and I explain to her what has happened, in parent-friendly detail.

'That's horrible!' she exclaims. 'I'm sorry I'm not there to help you, darling. Do you want me to get your dad to book you a ticket over here? You could be here by this time tomorrow.'

'I don't want to run away, Mum. I have to fix this. I have to keep the magazine going and I have to make people see that I haven't done anything wrong.'

'You're a brave girl but I don't like to think of you upset and alone. I thought better of Emily.'

'She just got caught up in it, I guess. I don't know how I'll be able to forgive her though.'

'Give it time, love. Oh, my poor little girl!' It sounds like my mum is crying, which makes me feel even worse.

'Jake is looking after me, Mum. Don't worry.'

'You could do a lot worse than him, you know.'

'I know, but we're just friends,' I remind her.

'I know, but maybe he's the kind of man you should be going after.'

'No more southerners,' I hear my dad call out. I'm not even sure he knows what is going on yet, but as far as he is concerned, it always pays to remind me of that little snippet of advice.

'Say hi to Dad for me,' I say with a laugh, instantly cheered up just hearing their voices. 'I'm going to go, Jake will be back with my phone soon.'

'Well take care of yourself, and remember we're not that far away, you could be here in a matter of hours if you wanted to. Let us look after you,' she teases. 'You're still my little girl.'

'I know. Thanks, Mum.'

'Why not go back home for a few days. It's the perfect place to hide,' she suggests, but the idea of going back to the village and staying with my uncle, auntie and perfect cousins is not one I'm overly keen on.

'I'll be fine, Mum. It'll blow over in a couple of days.'

'OK, love. Well, I'm off to Google you.'

'You do that,' I chuckle.

It's at times like these that I really miss my mum.

I peep out of my window and see that Jake is right, a gang of photographers are hanging around outside the door, the bloody vultures. It angers me that these people are harassing me just to get a photo to go with a story. My privacy feels majorly invaded, but isn't this basically what *I* do for a living? Although in my case, I can safely say that the story is absolutely not true. I'm going to have to find a way to make people see that.

First things first, I'd better put some clothes on before Jake gets back; he looked mortified before when he walked in and saw me in my towel. Did I even wash my conditioner off? I've nothing better to do so I may as well get back in the bath.

After warming up the water and adding a shot of something expensive and purple that is supposed to make me feel relaxed, I lie back and let the water cover my face for a moment. I feel safe under here – a million miles from the outside world.

I dread to think what people are saying about me as they're picking up the morning paper and seeing those headlines and that misleading photo. That bloody photo that Vicky took on my own camera. Despite only looking at it for a few seconds, the image is burned into my mind and it's all I can see whenever I close my eyes. I pull myself up out of the water suddenly and gasp for breath. I can't hide forever, can I?

Chapter 48

'I've tried them, Jake. Their publicist doesn't want to know.' I snap my laptop closed in temper. 'Don't worry,' Jake says, pushing a cup of tea into my hand. 'We'll find someone – anyone.'

'Like who?' I ask, flinging my arms in the air and spilling my tea down my onesie. It's been a few days since my ordeal – maybe even a week or so, I'm not sure. When you don't leave the house for a while, all the days just merge into one.

Unfortunately what happened is still big news. The paps are still hanging around outside my flat and although there aren't as many now, the few that remain are playing the long game because they know I'll have to leave at some point. Well let them wait, because I can sit here in my tea-soaked clothing forever if need be.

Dylan is supposed to be making some big statement soon, not that it will do any good. On the day the news broke, Dylan hadn't even made it back to London before some more news broke – that Crystal had gone into labour.

Jake has been my knight in shining armour through all of this. He's been looking after me, shopping for me and he's even set up a little office in my flat so I can work from here. I never need to go outside ever again.

For the first few days I had him buy me every tabloid and

trashy magazine on offer, keen to keep an eye on what was being printed. I've cut that out now though, because not only was it working out quite expensive, but the more I read, the more the story changed. It wasn't true to start with, but one paper in particular is just making things up – the one Vicky appears to be working for now – the bloody *Daily Scoop*.

Do you know what, though? This is great. It's getting really cold out, so being able to work from home in my pyjamas is awesome. Well, that's what I'm going to have to start believing anyway, because I've been sitting here for the past couple of days trying to get an interview with anyone at all and no one wants to know. I've tried every contact I have. My band friends don't want to be associated with me right now, and all the publicists in the world are worried I might try to shag their clients and ruin their careers in the process.

'I know!' I yelp with delight. 'Plastic Rap! I think Sam took a shine to me, he gave me his number.'

'It's worth a shot,' Jake replies with a shrug of his shoulders.

I grab my phone – not the one I dunked in the bath, that one is finally toast. Instead I have one of Jake's old ones, but it's not as easy to use as my previous phone. Eventually I work out how to call Sam.

'Yo!' he answers cheerfully.

'Hello, Sam? It's Nicole Wilde from *Starstruck*.'

'Wow!' he says, sounding totally surprised. 'Didn't think we'd hear from you again.'

'I was just wondering if you fancied another interview,' I ask, straight to the point.

'Do we want another interview with you? Hmm, let me think about that one. Fuck off!'

'Look, I know you're probably a bit put off by what you've read in the papers—'

'What we've read in the papers?' he interrupts me. 'What we've seen in the papers is your little story about us shagging our fans.

We know it was you, Nicole. You were the only other person there.'

'Sam, listen to me. That wasn't me, I promise you.'

'Save it, Nicole.'

I don't get chance to explain myself, Sam has hung up.

'Didn't go that well?' Jake asks, although he already knows the answer.

'Bloody Vicky! She has well and truly fucked me.'

I feel tears run down my cheeks and, before I know it, I am sobbing again. There's that look on Jake's face, one that I've come to know these past few days. I cry and he looks like he has no idea what to do with me.

'Come on, Nic.' He takes the phone out of my hand to save it getting soggy like its predecessor. 'How long have you been wearing that thing now?' he asks, nodding at my adult babygrow as he sits down next to me. I wonder if it's/I'm starting to smell.

'I don't know.' I hold my sleeve up to my nose, smells OK to me.

'This isn't the Nicole I know. The Nicole I know has rules about these things. Never wear the same outfit twice in the same week, right? You need to get changed, it'll make you feel better.'

'I doubt it will. Who's going to see me?' I ask. 'Just you. I'm stuck in here. Can we listen to "Somebody That I Use To Know" again, please?'

Jake laughs at me. 'No, and I'm a little worried about your obsession with that song. Gotye should be paying *you* royalties.'

I laugh half-heartedly, safe in the knowledge I can sing it until I pass out as soon as he leaves me unattended. He's got me on some kind of break-up ballad ban.

'Go have a bath,' Jake suggests with a little too much enthusiasm. 'Do that thing with your hair that always makes you late for work, get some nice clothes on and I'll go pick us up a pizza or something – did you know that all you have left in your fridge is moisturiser and a cucumber?'

'That's not for eating,' I tell him.

'Filthy,' he jokes with a laugh. I give him a playful punch.

'It's for my eyes, pervert,' I tell him, not that he didn't know that.

'Well you could do with using it on those puffy eyes right about now. Forget work.' Jake grabs yet another tissue and dabs my eyes dry.

'OK,' I say rather pathetically.

Despite everything that is going on, I do appreciate all Jake is doing for me and I can't help but feel amused by how much Nicole-like behaviour he has absorbed over the years.

'I need to go to into the office,' he says. 'Will you be OK for a bit?'

I nod. Jake kisses me on the forehead, grabs his coat and leaves.

I touch my head where he kissed me, pleasantly surprised by his tenderness. Then I run my hands through my greasy hair – I'd be mortified if anyone else saw me like this.

After having a bath and washing my hair, I dry it half-heartedly. I can't be bothered to put any clothes on, so I lazily pull on my dressing gown and flop back down on the sofa, clicking on the TV with the remote. I don't pay too much attention to what's on – I just want to hear noise – but a familiar-sounding song catches my attention. It's Two For The Road, they're on some chat show. I well up with pride, it's nice to see them getting the recognition they deserve. I don't suppose they'll want to be associated with the likes of me anymore, bad for their reputation I'd imagine.

As I watch them perform their new single, my phone starts to ring again. It's barely stopped ringing for days; Jake has made me promise to ignore it. We have a special code, so if Jake or my mum wants to call me they ring three times, hang up and then call again. It's ringing more than three times, but I grab it anyway. It's Luke, and before I know what I'm doing, I've answered.

'Hello, you're on TV!' I answer cheerfully.

'Hello, you're on the front of my newspaper!' he replies in a similar tone, reminding me of my current situation.

'Oh yeah? What have I not done now?'

'A lovely photo of you and Dylan King at his wedding, and

yet another revelation about your affair – apparently you crazy kids are into some strange role-play.'

'Who isn't?' I joke. We laugh together, but only briefly. 'It's not true,' I tell him.

'If you tell me that it's not true, then I know it's not true. So that's cleared that up.'

'Well I'm glad someone believes me. That makes you, Jake and my parents.'

'Who else matters?' he laughs. 'Boyfriend doesn't believe you, then?'

'Boyfriend thinks I'm a tart.'

'Boyfriend knows you quite well then.' He laughs again and it makes me laugh. It feels good to laugh properly after days of being a miserable cow.

'He didn't deserve you, Nic.'

'Nah, I guess not. So how come you're live on TV and on the phone to me at the same time?'

'It's not live, they're lying.'

'Bloody media, it's all a lie, isn't it?'

'I just called to see how you were – I've got a pretty good idea now.'

'It's horrible, Luke,' I confess. 'I'm stuck in my flat, Jake from work is looking after me but I don't see a soul otherwise. I'm too scared to go outside. I want to clear my name, but I don't know how to go about it.'

'What has Dylan said?'

'Four-fifths of fuck all. I can't get in touch with him, his phone is always off.'

'Do you know where he lives?'

'Yeah.'

'Well come to London. You can stay with me, clear your name and then we can hang out for a bit. Like a bit of a holiday,' he suggests with a laugh, but I think he's being serious.

That might be a good idea. Well, what else am I going to do?

Slip my tea-stained onesie back on and sit here calling people who are only going to tell me to fuck off? I need to go down there and see Dylan, perhaps together we can set the record straight.

'Luke, that's actually a pretty good idea. You're sure you want me staying with you, though? I mean, I could damage your reputation by association.' I say this in a jokey voice, but it's actually true. No one else wants anything to do with me – with good reason – maybe Luke should stay away.

'I don't think there is anything you could do that would damage my reputation further,' he assures me with a laugh. 'And anyway, you're my friend so that always comes first.'

My heart does a little dance inside my chest and I know that my crush on him is still tucked away in the back of my mind somewhere.

'You're too good to me, Luke. Thank you.' A slightly awkward silence follows.

'Well I'm not that good to you, I'm afraid. I'll have you cooking and cleaning and washing my clothes for me.'

'Honey, I don't cook or clean for myself and I certainly don't wash my own clothes.'

'Aww, you'll make someone a crap little wife one day.'

We both laugh and, for the first time in days, things don't seem quite as hopeless as they did. I finish up on the phone and begin to pack my suitcase. I've always been pretty fashion-conscious, but now that I have photographers on my case I need to up my game. I've published enough photographs of stars with their fashion faux pas and wardrobe malfunctions pointed out to know that I need to put extra thought into what I pack, and what I wear on my journey down there. The next photograph they take of me will be the first since *that* morning, so I don't suppose I'll have to try very hard to look better than I did with my foam-irritated skin, messy hair and night-before outfit. Just listen to me! I think I'm a celebrity when really I'm no better than a kiss-and-tell girl in the eyes of the press – even though I didn't do any kissing or telling.

Jake arrives later, pizza in hand.

'You're not doing a bunk, are you?' he asks, gesturing towards my case and the huge pile of clothes and shoes currently taking over my living room.

'Nope, I am off to London. I'm going to stay with Luke—'

'Oooh!' he interrupts, giving me a wink.

'Not like that. I'm going to see Dylan, and we're going to set the record straight and then maybe we can get back to normal,' I announce excitedly.

'And you're sure this is the right thing to do?'

I pause for a few seconds. Of course it is, and why wait? I'll go first thing tomorrow.

Chapter 49

I feel ashamed to admit it, but for a few moments this morning I actually enjoyed my current situation a little too much. Yes, the same horrible situation I have spent days crying over.

Jake spent the night on my sofa so that he could help me sneak past the few remaining paps. They must be working in shifts because there are always a couple of them waiting for me – and all I did was allegedly sleep with one of the most famous people in the country.

After spending a couple of hours getting ready, I put on my over-sized sunglasses, grabbed my case and got ready to make my escape. I know I'm only going for a few days, but I had a rather emotional goodbye with Jake. He is the only person who has been there for me through this, and I really do appreciate all that he has done for me. He truly went above and beyond the call of duty today, by putting on my bright-pink dressing gown and creating a diversion on my balcony while I made my escape. It must have worked because I made it to the train station and here I am, sitting on the train, completely unnoticed. See, this is what I'm talking about; I feel almost disappointed that no one is recognising me.

The train is surprisingly quiet; there are only four other people who can see me from where they are sitting. There's a rather intimidating-looking goth couple – the boy goth keeps looking at me and smiling and I am smiling back because it's not that long since my questionable teenage get-up bagged me a few funny looks from the general public. People assumed I was a sixteen-year-old serial killer rather than a teenage girl with a penchant for studded apparel. There's a little old woman blatantly staring at them over her battered Mills and Boon book – she looks terrified. The person closest to me is a middle-aged man in a suit and he's fast asleep with his mouth wide open. I guess I've been lucky. Dylan might be a mega-star, but I'm fairly sure I am sitting in a carriage with the four people who are least likely to give a shit about pop music and celebrity culture.

I am bored out of my mind. It's not that I'm not used to the journey, it's just normally I wouldn't dream of tackling it without a Starbucks and huge pile of magazines next to me. I couldn't even look at WHSmith in the station, let alone pop in and face my own face.

Taking my phone out of my handbag, I make the brave decision to check the social networks. So far I have avoided them, but now curiosity is getting the better of me. I log into Facebook. Clicking my messages, I notice quite a few of them are from people I don't know. As I open Instagram, I can't believe my eyes – in the space of a few days my number of followers has gone from a three-digit number to a five-digit number. I feel that rush again, that pang of excitement. I resist the urge to post, because these people could just be waiting for me to say something so they can send me abuse. I'm sure Dylan's young, female following will have a few choice words for me. Not long before the original Crystal scandal broke, some model Dylan had slept with sold her story to a tabloid, saying he was a drunk and crap in bed. Her name was DeeDee, and so Dill's fans took to their socials to get the hashtag #DieDieDeeDee in the trending topics and they succeeded – it was there for a couple of days. I feel sick at the thought of them saying things like that about me, especially when I don't deserve it. That's what this trip is for though. I'm going to go see Dylan and we're going to tell everyone that it isn't true. I look up from my phone to see goth boy smiling at me – again. I smile back. Things can only get better.

Chapter 50

Hello, London, I have arrived. There's a real spring in my step as I hop off the train, I've just got a really good feeling about today. I'm going to clear my name, I'm going to spend time with Luke and it's going to be fun.

Luke is meeting me here because I am notoriously bad at getting from A to B, and with London being quite big I will almost certainly get lost.

As soon as I have my caramel macchiato (aren't my priorities fantastic?), I make my way to our arranged meeting point and wait. The station is so busy but no one gives anyone a second look. Thinking about it, this would make a fantastic hiding place.

My phone rings – it's Luke. He's slept in and won't be able to come and meet me. Apparently he needs a shower and to wash his hair, otherwise he might be photographed looking dirty. I guess now he's famous, even he is worried about what people think.

'If you wanna get the Tube …'

'I *don't* want to get the Tube, no Tube,' I insist.

'It's the quickest and the cheapest way,' he laughs at me, silly northerner that I most likely am.

'I don't care, what if it gets stuck?'

'It won't get stuck!'

'It might! Or someone might see me.'

'Oh, Nicole,' he laughs and then sighs. He's defeated and he knows it. 'You do make me laugh. Right, go outside and get a taxi.'

'OK, stay on the line though,' I make my way outside, somehow managing to hold my case, phone *and* coffee.

'Right, I have a taxi.'

'OK, you want to come to—' he starts telling me the address.

'Whoa, whoa, whoa, stop right there,' I tell him. I tap the driver on the shoulder. 'Excuse me, could you speak to my dad and he'll tell you where to take me.'

I hear Luke laugh as I hand the phone over. The driver dutifully takes my phone and talks to my 'dad'.

'Hello? … Oh yes … Right … Of course … Oh, thank you.' He laughs and I imagine what Luke is saying to make him laugh.

The driver gets out and hands me my phone.

'Come on,' he says grabbing my case and putting it in the back of the car. 'Let's get you where you need to go.'

I shuffle awkwardly into the car and when the driver gets back in, I see him look at me in his rear-view mirror.

'First time in London, is it?' he asks.

'No, I come here a lot actually,' I admit.

'Bloke said you were from Yorkshire.'

'I thought he might have.'

'How do you get around in Yorkshire then?' he asks.

'On horseback usually,' I say, deadpan.

He looks at me in the mirror again and then laughs, hopefully realising that I'm joking.

The car comes to a standstill at the traffic lights.

'This would have been a lot quicker by Tube, you know.'

'So people tell me,' I reply, mildly annoyed at Londoners and their bloody Tube agenda. 'But if I got the Tube, then you wouldn't get my money, would you?'

'Under strict instruction not to take money off you, your bloke will be waiting.'

'Oh.' Well that's nice of him.

Eventually the car comes to a standstill.

'Here we are, darlin'. Bet that was faster than horseback, eh?'

I jump out the car, dragging my own case out behind me.

'Hello,' I hear Luke's voice behind me.

'Daddy!' I call out, throwing my arms around him, fully aware the jig is up because he is clearly way too young to have fathered me.

'Cheers, mate,' he says to the taxi driver who thanks him very enthusiastically – that must have been one hell of a tip.

'Your bird is funny,' he tells Luke with a chuckle before driving off.

Still messing with my suitcase (trying to get the handle thingy to go up so I can drag it along properly), I feel Luke's hands on my hips.

'Allo, my bird,' he says in a put-on cockney accent.

I turn around. 'Hello, my—' I am stopped in my tracks, words escape me.

He laughs and flashes me that cute smile that makes me go weak at the knees, but there's something different about him.

'Luke, you look terrible,' I eventually blurt out, without a hint of tact.

'Ha! Well I told you I needed a shower. If you think I look bad, you should smell me,' he jokes, grabbing his sunglasses from the top of his head and putting them on to cover his dark and bloodshot eyes. He looks tired, messy and like he hasn't had a decent meal in months, and yet it's only been a few weeks since I saw him last. I've never seen him look so pale and ill.

He grabs my case in one hand and my hand in the other.

'This way,' he says as he leads me towards a huge apartment building.

'Wow! You live *here*? Who knew you guys were doing so well?' I tease.

I have been friends with TFTR for so long, and I've seen

exactly how hard they have worked for their success, and yet it still seems weird to see them so famous so quickly. I find it hard to see them as celebrities, although they undoubtedly are now.

'Wow!' I blurt out as Luke opens the door to his apartment.

'You like?' he asks. 'I tidied up a little because I knew you were coming.'

He kicks the few remaining pieces of junk out of sight.

'This place is beautiful, Luke.'

'Thanks. Listen, make yourself at home, I'm going to jump in the shower.'

He disappears into another room and once the door is closed behind him, I twirl around, taking in my surroundings. This place is like a dream, it makes my shitty little flat look so … shitty. As you walk through the door you are greeted first by the huge kitchen – it looks untouched and I can't imagine he uses it very much. I'm currently standing in the middle of the living room. It's a typical lad pad: leather recliners, huge TV, games consoles, pool table. It must be so much fun living here; it must kill him having to leave this place to live on the tour bus for weeks at a time.

There are hundreds of framed photos on the walls, all of which are of the band, photos from tour and stuff. As I make my way across the room looking at them, I am taken aback by my own face on so many, and there's one photo in particular that catches my eye. It's the picture of me and Luke that Carla took, the one that caused all the trouble with Charles. It's actually a really beautiful photo and it captures the two of us perfectly. I wish I could go back in time to that night. It's not that long ago, but it's before everything went wrong. I'd go back and stop myself getting so drunk, I'd stop Carla taking photos of me – or at the very least I'd ask her not to upload them – and then I'd be able to stop myself getting papped with Dylan. Things would be fine with Charles, and Dylan would go back to playing happy families with Crystal. It's funny how things work out sometimes. It only takes a handful of events to reshape lives so drastically.

The door to the balcony is unlocked so I step outside and take in the scenery. He has a perfect view of the O2 Arena just across the river.

'Looks even better from up here, doesn't it,' I hear Luke say behind me. He steps out onto the balcony with me. Despite it being a cold November day, he's out here in nothing but a pair of jeans, with his hair still wet. My eyes instantly look towards his body and although I quickly force myself to hold eye contact, I can feel them trying to glance down, like they have a mind of their own. The eyes want what the eyes want.

'It really is beautiful,' I say, glancing out over the river, anything to stop me perving.

'So do I look much better now?' he asks.

'Much,' I assure him. He doesn't though, he looks terrible, but I can't say that to him again. I cast my mind back to the tour and the drugs – I really hope that isn't the reason he looks so rough.

'You look worried.' He leans on the railing next to me. 'Then again, I'd be worried if the entire country thought I was a marriage-wrecker.'

'Well hopefully I'm going to get that sorted.'

'Hopefully. In the meantime, feel free to stay with me for as long as you like. I've got some time off, I can show you the sights.'

'Oh, I'm sure you'll show me the sights.' I give him a cheeky smile.

'It just so happens I'm one of London's biggest attractions, haven't you heard?'

'Hey, mister, step out onto the street with me, we'll see who gets the paparazzi all up in their face first.'

'You not enjoying your fifteen minutes, then?' he asks me as we head back inside.

'It's a roller coaster, that's for sure. I always wanted to be famous you know,' I tell him.

'I think most people do these days.'

'Yeah, but not famous for anything in particular.' I laugh at how ridiculous this must sound. 'I guess, I grew up watching Paris Hilton in shows like The Simple Life, and I thought: yep, being a socialite looks like fun. I didn't want to be famous for my writing or anything like that, I just wanted the lifestyle. I've always looked at socialites and I wanted to be like them – not really famous for anything in particular.'

'I don't know, Paris Hilton is pretty famous for her sex tape.' He flashes me a grin.

'Don't you be getting any ideas. I mean it though – I wanted it all, right down to the tiny little doggy.'

'You wanted a tiny little doggy?' he laughs.

'I still do, I want a tiny little doggy. A Chihuahua – preferably one that will fit inside a designer handbag. Although I'm not sure I would actually put it in a bag, that never seemed like a good idea.'

'Oh, that would be awesome.' He laughs and takes hold of my hand. 'You know what though, it would suit you.'

'I know, right?' I joke.

'Well you could always marry Dylan now his current marriage has gone tits up. He's got more than enough money to give you that lifestyle.'

'Don't even joke about it, I am sorting that out as soon as possible. Now that I'm living the lifestyle, I'm not so sure I want it after all. Actually, I'd better start making calls.' I pull my hand from his and it feels really sudden and forceful; I hadn't meant it that way.

'I'll give you a bit of privacy. Can I get you a drink?' he asks.

'Sure, surprise me!'

He laughs and heads for the kitchen, and I begin the impossible task of trying to get hold of Dylan King.

Chapter 51

For as long as I have known Mikey King, he has always been exceptionally nice to me. When I first started hanging around with Dylan, I felt a little intimidated by it all. We'd be at parties and Dylan would wander off and leave me on my own, and back then I didn't really know anyone or how to behave in those kind of situations, but Mikey would always look out for me. If he saw me standing on my own, he'd be over in a flash. I've always felt that he gets overshadowed by his big brother. Dylan is the frontman with the just-above-average voice, but all the charm and sex appeal to get away with anything, whereas Mikey is the genuinely talented guitarist who, despite being good-looking, doesn't have quite as much confidence as his brother. He definitely makes the most of his rock and roll lifestyle though, just like his brother – sorry, just like his brother used to. His brother who currently has his phone turned on, but seems to be ignoring my calls. I tried him a few times and he didn't pick up, then I tried him again and he rejected my call. That's when I called Mikey. He was so sweet to me; there were no questions about what went on, he didn't even need to ask. He knows us both well enough to know that nothing happened and I think he must have felt a bit sorry for me because he agreed to help me – behind his brother's back.

Dylan is hiding from the press in his massive house, and Mikey is staying with him, being Dylan's Jake I guess. In the morning I am going to Dylan's house and meeting Mikey at the back entrance. He's going to smuggle me inside so that I can talk to Dill. He's making his statement in the afternoon. Maybe I can be there with him, help back up his story. I think he's avoiding me because he's worried about being in contact with me, but we can put that right.

'So you're doorstopping him?' Luke asks.

'You mean doorstepping,' I laugh. 'And no, I'm not. I'm invited, well, technically invited.'

'You journalists love to twist shit, don't you?' Luke teases, melting my heart with his cheeky smile.

'Hey, I am a victim of shit-twisting.'

'I know, I know. Shall I get us some dinner?' he asks, changing the subject.

'Sure. Do you need a hand?' I ask, knowing full well that I can't cook. To be honest, I just want to play in his kitchen, it looks fun. He has gadgets that I didn't even know existed.

'I'm sure I can handle it, dinner is just one quick phone call away.'

Running my hand across the worktop, I examine the kitchen. It looks like it's been used even less than mine.

'Don't you cook?' I ask, surprised. He's a few years older than I am, I assumed he was a proper adult.

'No,' he says with a laugh. 'Why, do you?'

I shake my head. It's amazing I manage to survive on my own.

Luke drops a pile of takeaway menus in front of me.

'I'll let the lady choose.'

I am stuffed full of pizza and more than a little bit drunk. Luke has enough alcohol in his apartment to seriously consider supplying one or two of the fancy bars that are in the area and we're currently working our way through some of it. However much I've had to drink, though, Luke has easily had double that.

'Would your Chihuahua wear clothes, then?' Luke asks me.

'Of course! Dogs deserve clothes too. You can even buy shoes for them.'

'What? Shoes for dogs?' He laughs manically. 'Lies.'

'I'm not lying. One day I will have my tiny dog, and he'll be wearing tiny shoes, and you'll owe me an apology.'

'We'll see, Wilde.'

I let out a huge sigh and rest my head on Luke's shoulder. 'Have I made a mess of my life, Luke?'

'Most girls would kill for your life.' He strokes my cheek.

'Maybe I should have got a proper job, a proper boyfriend – do you know how many of my school friends are married or have kids?'

'Married *or* have kids?' he asks, confused.

'Yeah, one or the other, sometimes both.'

We both laugh.

'Don't say things like that,' he demands. 'I don't have a proper job, or a proper girlfriend. My life is as bullshit as yours.'

'We live bullshit lives, Luke.' I pour the remainder of my drink into my mouth, and the questionable cranberry:vodka ratio catches my throat. 'That's what I need, another drink. I'm going to numb the pain, sort the Dylan crap tomorrow, and worry about the rest after.'

'You know, if you want to forget your troubles, I have something even better for us,' Luke tells me.

'Oh aye?' I ask, no idea what he's on about.

'Aye, farm girl,' he teases. 'You up for it?'

'Up for what?' I smile.

'A bit of coke.'

'Coke? Oh.' I suddenly realise he doesn't mean the kind you drink.

'It helps, Nic.'

'You shouldn't take drugs, they're bad for you.'

'Ha!' he laughs. 'Says the girl with the triple vodka. Everything is bad for you these days.'

Does he really think that doing drugs will solve all my problems? Is that what he does? I knew he'd done a bit on tour, but I thought that was just a tour thing.

'How often do you do this?'

'Now and then. It's all right, Nic.' He drags himself to his feet and offers me his hand. I let him pull me up and he leads me into his bedroom.

'Sit there,' he instructs me, nudging me towards his bed. 'Just watch me do it first, it's fine, honestly.'

'What? No! Please don't do that in front of me,' I protest.

'Nic, it's fine.'

'It's not fine,' I insist, panic in my voice. Luke sits down next to me and I look into his eyes. I'd always thought his eyes were so beautiful, before they started looking all sore and puffy. I place my hand on his face and despite his tired eyes and bad skin, I can still see his kind face and his lovely smile.

'Luke,' I sob.

'Shit. Don't cry, Nic.' He holds my face gently in his hands.

'Promise me you won't take anything,' I whisper.

'I want to,' he says as he runs his hands through his hair. 'My God, I really want to. But I won't, OK?'

I nod and, before I realise what I'm doing, I lean forward and kiss him softly. Tears still streaming down my face, I stop kissing him and wipe my eyes.

'I wasn't expecting that to happen,' he tells me with a confused smile.

'I think I just wanted to shut you up,' I laugh. I know we were trying to be friends but, from the moment I laid eyes on him earlier today, all the old feelings came flooding back, no matter what state he's in.

'I think we should go to bed.' Luke stands up.

'Oh. OK. Where am I sleeping?' I feel so awkward – why did

I kiss him?

'There's a bed in the spare room, but I think you should come in with me tonight, keep an eye on me, you know?' he pulls off his T-shirt and unbuttons his jeans.

'OK.' I stand up, not entirely sure if I'm reading the signals right. No one has ever tried to sleep with me when I've been a crying, snotty mess before.

Luke places a hand on the back of my neck and feels for the zip of my dress before pulling it down and letting it fall to the floor. He's so close I can smell the beer on his breath, but I really don't care.

'Bedtime I think, Wilde.'

Chapter 52

'I'm sorry about last night.'

Waking up in Luke's bed with him, that is the last thing I expected him to say.

'Don't apologise, you weren't that bad,' I tease, snuggling closer and resting my head on his chest.

'You know what I mean, and I'm sorry. I never should have tried to pressure you into doing … that. I won't ever suggest it again, and you won't ever see me do it again.'

I don't know whether that means he's going to stop doing it, or he's just not going to do it in front of me, but it's progress for now.

'I know,' I say, sitting up to check the time on my phone. 'I'd better go, I'll be late to meet Mikey.'

'You've got ages,' Luke says after checking his watch and realising that I'm not meeting him for a few hours.

'Yes, but I have to get ready and I have to get there.'

'How are you getting there?' he asks.

'Taxi,' I tell him, knowing exactly what his reply will be.

'A taxi? In London? That will be expensive, you know.'

'Why do people who live in London always say that? Do you think they're free up north or something?'

'Something like that,' he laughs. 'It's your money, Nic. If it were me I'd—'

'—get the Tube,' I say in unison with him, mocking his accent slightly.

'OK, fine. Do you want me to come with you?' he asks.

'No, stay in bed. You look tired. I'll come back straight after and we'll go out to celebrate, yeah?'

He nods and flashes me that smile. God, I love it when he smiles. I grab my toilet bag and walk towards the bathroom, pausing in the doorway.

'You won't do anything silly while I'm out, will you?' I ask.

He laughs. 'You worry too much, Nic. Go get ready.'

Chapter 53

Currently hiding in the bushes at the bottom of Dylan's massive back garden, I feel like a secret agent or something. Hidden in the eight-foot tall fence that surrounds his house is a secret gate that only opens from the inside. I know that Dylan uses it to sneak in and out of his house sometimes, but this is the first time I've done it. So here I am, standing in the mud, waiting for Mikey to come and let me in.

'Everything is going to be OK,' I reassure myself out loud. Well, it has to be. Nothing happened with Dylan and that's the truth. If something had happened, then we'd have something to hide and people would find out that we were lying, but if we're telling the truth then who can catch us out?

'Good morning,' I smile as Mikey opens the gate, but then I catch the worried look on his face.

'What's happened?' I ask instantly.

'Quick, come in. I told Dylan you were coming about five minutes ago. He's worried about you being seen here, but there's only one pap out front. Podgy git – you could have come in the front door, he wouldn't take much out-running.'

His joke calms me down a little, but the idea of Dylan not wanting to see me, no matter what the circumstances are, makes me feel physically sick.

Once inside the house, we make our way to the living room where Dylan is sitting in his boxers. I didn't even realise Dill was in the room until Mikey flicked the lights on.

'Mate, leave the lights on or I'm opening the curtains,' Mikey insists.

Dylan ignores him and cranks up his music. He's listening to 'She Hates Me' by Puddle of Mudd – on repeat, I'd imagine.

'Hello,' I say, approaching him with caution, like he's a bomb that could go off at any moment. 'Great song choice. I have Eric Carmen's "All By Myself" if you'd prefer it.'

I gesture at Mikey to turn the music down, and sit on the sofa next to Dylan. For the first time since the day we met, he doesn't give me a kiss on the cheek.

'All right,' he says unenthusiastically. I don't think it's a question, but I answer anyway.

'Yeah. How are you?'

'Oh yeah, I'm great,' he mutters sarcastically. 'Where are you staying?'

'With Luke. From Two For The Road.' I name-drop the band because he doesn't react to the name Luke.

'What are you doing here?' he asks, cutting to the chase. 'You could get me in even more trouble, Nicole.'

'Dylan, you wouldn't answer my calls, what was I supposed to do? We have to sort this out.'

'I'm sorting it out today. I'm going to make a statement to the press this afternoon.' He chuckles to himself. 'Charles will be over soon to help me write it, so you might want to get out of here before then.'

'Dylan, Charles thinks we're lying!' I squeal. 'How can he help you write this if he doesn't even believe you?'

'Nicole, I just want to see my kids – and get my wife back.'

I notice he adds the wife part as an afterthought, but I don't mention that.

'I know it must be hard for you, I'm sure you're desperate to see what they look like—'

'I've got a picture,' he interrupts, rummaging around on the table next to him.

'Dill, they're gorgeous,' I say when he shows me the photo of two tiny baby girls. Well, I assume they are girls because they are dressed head to toe in hot-pink.

'That's Char – short for Chardonnay,' he says pointing to the baby on the right.

'Of course it is,' I reply, and he shoots me a filthy look.

'And that's Lamb on the left.'

'Short for Lambrini?'

I laugh. I can't help it.

'Don't take the piss, Nicole.'

'Sorry. But honestly, they're beautiful.'

'I know, that's why I have to make this right, so I can see them properly.'

'Of course. Look, I can make this statement with you, we can set them straight together.'

'Nicole,' Dylan says, finally looking me in the eye, 'I'm going to apologise.'

'To who?' I'm confused.

'To Crystal. She says that if I make a public apology for everything I've done, then she'll come home and she'll bring the babies with her. I just want them back, Nic.'

Still confused.

'You're going to apologise for what?' I ask.

'She doesn't believe me, she's never going to believe me. If I own up to sleeping with you and publicly apologise, then they'll come home.'

'But you didn't sleep with me, Dylan,' I remind him, just in case he has forgotten.

He shrugs his shoulders. 'It's the only way to get them back. You could apologise with me, that might help.'

I cannot believe what I'm hearing.

'Dylan, the only thing I am willing to apologise for is ultimately being the reason your children are named after alcohol!'

'Nicole,' he says softly, but I continue my rant, pacing around the living room as I speak.

'I am not apologising for something I didn't do, and you shouldn't either. The Dylan I know didn't even apologise for the stuff he *did* do. What's happened to you?'

He says nothing.

'How do you think this is going to make me look? Everyone hates me, they think I'm a home-wrecker!'

'So apologise too,' he says, unable to look me in the eye. 'It's easier to get forgiveness than it is to prove what really happened.'

At this point Mikey walks back in the room, closely followed by Charles.

'Get her out of here, she's going to ruin this, Dylan,' Charles demands as soon as he claps eyes on me.

I look over at Dylan. He has his head in his hands.

'Dylan,' I call his name to get him to look at me. He doesn't.

'Mikey, please can you show Miss Wilde out of the back door,' Charles mutters.

'Don't worry, Mr Pace. I was leaving anyway.' I push myself past him, giving him a cheeky wink as my body brushes past his – childish, I know. Before I leave, I turn around and appeal to Dylan one last time.

'Don't do this, Dill. You know it's wrong.'

He doesn't say anything. He wants his kids and this is the only way he's going to get them. There's nothing left to say.

Mikey follows me out into the hallway, closing the door behind him.

'Go on, Mike. Throw the home-wrecker over the back fence,' I joke, although I half suspect that's what he's expected to do.

'I know you didn't do it,' he whispers, 'and I know he's making a mistake doing this. I understand why he's doing this, but it's wrong. You don't deserve this.'

We hug and I feel touched that he would side with me over his own brother, even if it is only secretly.

'Thanks.' I wipe away the one tear that has managed to escape from my left eye, despite me trying so hard to keep my emotions under control. 'I'd like to leave out the front door,' I tell Mikey, remembering that there is a photographer outside.

'Maybe I accidentally left the key in the door when I let Charles in,' he says with a wink.

I kiss him on the cheek and turn towards the front door. I feel like a total cow for possibly ruining any chance Dill has of seeing his kids, but I won't let him ruin my reputation without a fight. Maybe if I do this he'll be forced to tell the truth.

I open the door and begin my walk down the driveway. As I get to the bottom, the photographer looks at me, and I smile back at him. The expression on his face is wonderful, like he knows who I am but he can't quite believe his eyes. Surely the woman Dylan King had an affair with wouldn't be leaving his house days later, having not been seen entering his house this morning at all. He fumbles awkwardly with his camera, but I move slowly enough for him to get a couple of photos (a couple of good photos – that last ones were *so* embarrassing) before running off down the road. I don't think he's chasing me, but I don't stop to find out.

As I hurriedly do my best to lose the pap, I am instantly hit with a wave of regret. I know that I am right in thinking that Dylan shouldn't own up to something that he didn't do – especially because he will drag me down with him, and the female is always looked upon as being worse than the male in these scenarios – but I'm not sure I've done the right thing. I'm fighting to protect my reputation, but at what cost? Don't Dylan's kids deserve their dad in their lives? God knows they need him. I mean, just look at what Crystal named them. Fuck! I shouldn't have done that. There's no turning back now though.

Chapter 54

I slip my shoes off in the lift of Luke's apartment building. I ran for way longer than I had planned to – who knew the paparazzi were so agile? I suppose they have to be in their game.

I grabbed a coffee and a copy of the *Daily Scoop* from one of the cute little shops downstairs. I didn't want to buy that trashy excuse for news, but curiosity got the better of me, especially when I saw the headline 'Where is Nicole Wilde?', accompanied by a photograph of Jake flashing his arse from the balcony of my flat. I called him as soon as I saw it and he couldn't be prouder to have his backside on the front of a national newspaper – I'm just glad I could help him achieve his life goal.

'Hello,' I call out as I let myself into Luke's flat with the spare key he gave me. 'Luke?' I call again, but there's no sign of him. I check his bedroom but he isn't there – his phone is though, so I guess there's no point calling him to see where he is.

Walking back into the lounge, I make myself at home. Reclining in one of his leather armchairs, I sip my coffee and read the paper. This is the life. The whole scenario feels weird, but strangely comfortable, and it scares me just how much I'm starting to enjoy it. That doesn't mean I'm happy with the whole country thinking I'm a home-wrecker, though.

The headline makes me laugh because I know that tomorrow's paper will have an answer to that question, and that Dylan won't like it. Poor Dylan, he looked so proud of his babies – even if they were named after their mum's favourite drinks. I suppose I'll just have to wait and see what happens; there's nothing I can do about it right now. I should probably have a nap, I don't think I got much sleep last night. I could drop off right here, but after that huge coffee I'm going to have to go for a wee first. I'm so showbiz.

I hop up to go to the toilet, relieved that Luke is out because he doesn't have a lock on his bathroom door and I am terrified that he is going to walk in on me while I'm on the loo.

As I open the bathroom door, I am totally shocked by what I see. I can't speak, I can't move, I can hardly think. Luke is lying on the bathroom floor with blood running from his head, flowing along the cracks between the floor tiles. I say his name but he doesn't reply, so I try to find a pulse in his neck. I'm trying to keep calm but as I struggle to find a pulse, panic sets in. I have no idea what to do and I don't want to make things worse so I call an ambulance. Luckily I have his address written on the back of my hand (a trick I learned from Dylan).

The super-calm lady on the phone tells me not to touch him and to wait for the paramedics. She keeps me on the phone while we wait for the ambulance to get here. I glance around the room to try to work out what has happened. There is blood on the side of the toilet, and while I'm no Adrian Monk, I'm guessing he must have hit his head on it. Then something catches my eye next to the sink. Oh, Luke, you stupid boy. I scoop up the perfect little white line of powder and flush it down the sink before doing the same with the little bag of (what I'm assuming is) coke sitting on the side.

Eventually the ambulance arrives and I stand back and watch them work quickly to help him. The male paramedic looks at me.

'Has he taken anything?'

'I don't know,' I reply. I'm not lying, I really don't know. I'm scared of getting him into trouble if he hasn't taken anything – from what I saw it didn't look like he had.

'Right, let's move him,' he instructs the female paramedic.

I stand back as they carefully lift him onto the stretcher. He's still unconscious and his arm drops off the side. A perfectly rolled twenty-pound note falls out of his hand and rolls towards my feet.

The male paramedic walks over to me and calmly asks me again, 'Has he taken anything? It's important you tell me.'

'I *really* don't know. There was some stuff at the side of the sink, I flushed it away. Is he going to be OK?'

'We're taking him to hospital, are you coming with us?'

'Please.'

As they wheel him out to the ambulance, I look for things to take to the hospital but I have no idea what he might need and even if I did, I'd have no idea where any of it is.

I grab my handbag and my keys and follow them out. Judging by the speed they are operating at, this must be serious.

Chapter 55

I hate hospitals. Just sitting here in the waiting room is making me feel sick – something I'm sure is the exact opposite of what the hospital is supposed to do.

I am sitting with Frank, who is Two For The Road's manager. I had no idea who to call when we arrived at the hospital, so I called Mick, their tour manager. He didn't sound half as surprised as I had expected him to, he simply passed the information on to Frank.

I've heard lots of stories about Frank but I've never had the pleasure of meeting him. I was expecting a podgy, balding, grumpy old man, but I couldn't be more wrong. Frank is probably in his mid-forties and is good-looking in an older, George Clooney kind of way. I remember Eddie telling me what a hard-ass he was, but he seems genuinely concerned about Luke and he thanked me for calling the ambulance. He is actually from Sheffield and I'm finding his strong South Yorkshire accent weirdly comforting right now.

A nurse is walking towards us in what seems like super-slow motion, her face expressionless. All kinds of things are running through my mind.

'How's he doing?' Frank asks.

I'm not sure why, but I get up and walk away, leaving her to talk to Frank. I mess around with the vending machine and watch them chat from down the corridor. As I make myself a hot chocolate that I have absolutely no intention of drinking, Frank comes to talk to me.

'He's had stitches in his head and he's got concussion. He's lost some blood, cracked a couple of ribs too. He's spoken to the doctor, thinks he might have blacked out over the sink, bashed himself up on his way to the floor.'

'He's awake?' I ask, surprised.

'Yeah. He's been lucky. He's asking for you, lass. Nurse says you can go through.'

I glance over towards the nurse who is looking at me; she must be waiting to show me the way.

'Have this.' I thrust my watery hot chocolate into Frank's hand.

'Cheers,' he says with a chuckle. He doesn't strike me as the kind of man who drinks hot chocolate.

I am shown into the private room where Luke is. He is propped up slightly in his bed and despite looking beaten up, the first thing he does is smile when he sees me.

'Now then,' I say cheerily. 'What the hell have you been getting up to? I leave you alone for a couple of hours … There are easier ways to meet nurses, you know.'

What I actually want to do is shout and scream and swear at him for being such a fucking idiot, but now probably isn't the time.

'My hero.' He forces a smile.

'Erm, heroine,' I correct him, instantly biting my tongue. That's probably one of many things hidden in his medicine cabinet.

I take his hand and squeeze it tightly. We have our ups and downs, and he can be a very silly boy, but I really care about him.

'How did it go with Dylan?' he asks. I would have thought that would be the last thing on his mind – if he even remembered.

'Don't worry about that.'

'That bad?'

'That bad.'

'Shit, Nic. I'm sorry.' He quickly lets go of my hand, and as I look up I see that he is crying. I hate to see people cry but seeing Luke cry is just something else. I've always seen him as this big, strong man, and right now he looks like a helpless little boy and it is breaking my heart.

'Come on, don't get upset. You're going to be all right, the doctor said so.' I feel a tear run down my face too.

'Karma's a bitch,' he laughs. Well, half-laughs, half-cries.

'Oh, Luke.' Now I'm sobbing too. 'Come on, Eddie will be here any second and he'll laugh at us.'

'If he's on his way in, he's coming to laugh anyway,' Luke concludes, and he's probably right. It's not that Eddie doesn't give a damn, he just won't know what else to do. The fact he's coming straight over shows just how much he cares.

Frank joins us, slowly and cautiously entering the room.

'All right, lad?' he asks in the same fake cheery tone that I used.

'Yeah, just keeping you on your toes, mate. It's about time you did some proper work.'

'I've just spoken to the doctor, he says they're going to keep you in for a few days and then you can go home.'

'Yeah, but cracked ribs. Will I be able to drum? We've got the tour!'

'You'll be right, lad,' Frank assures him. 'You'll be back on your feet by then, doc said.'

Oh, it really is so nice to hear a northern accent.

'I hate hospitals. Let's just go home, Nic,' Luke says with a straight face, so I can't tell if he's joking.

'After you then,' I say, nodding towards the door, well aware of the fact he can hardly move.

In an attempt to take his mind off things I tell him – and Frank – all about what happened with Dylan.

'I'll kick his arse,' Luke says angrily, trying to sit up.

'You can't even wipe your arse, lad,' Frank laughs, easing him back down. 'You're not supposed to be moving.'

'Oh, who cares?' I say. 'He's going to tell everyone that I slept with him and wrecked his marriage – his bullshit marriage to a girl whose name he didn't even know until after he knocked her up – and everyone is going to think I'm some evil woman … but who cares?'

'That's the spirit!' Luke says sarcastically.

'Why don't you put a statement out, too?' Frank suggests. 'Give your side of the story, tell everyone what really happened. Your word against his.'

'Who would believe *me* over Dylan?' I ask. 'We got caught in a compromising position, everyone thinks something happened and he's going to tell them it did.'

'But it's not true,' Luke insists.

'Since when did anyone care about the truth? Dill is doing this to get his wife and kids back, he's pretty much telling them what they want to hear. Anyway, there's probably going to be a photo of me in some paper tomorrow because I was snapped leaving his house.'

'If there's anything I can do to help, just let me know,' Frank tells me sincerely.

'Thanks.'

'Are you two OK if I get off?' he asks.

'Yeah, we'll be fine. I'm sure Nicole won't be leaving me just yet.'

'Erm, I'm not going anywhere at all,' I insist. 'I'll sleep here in this chair.' The chair I'm talking about is an old armchair. I suspect, once upon a time, it was a nice lemon colour, but now it's a yucky shade of brown.

'Nic, you don't have to do that. You can stay at mine, whether I'm there or not.'

'No, I'm staying here.' I look over at Frank, who is hanging around by the doorway, waiting for one of us to tell him what's happening. 'Thanks, Frank, you can go.'

'Well you are a nurse,' Luke jokes as soon as Frank has left us alone.

'Unfortunately, I left my cap at home. But yes, I am a nurse of sorts.'

He starts laughing, but this quickly turns to tears again.

'Am I going to be OK, Nicole?' he sobs.

My heart breaks for him. I take hold of his hand.

'Of course you're going to be OK,' I reassure him. 'I'm going to stay here with you, I promise. And then I'm going to go home with you, and I'm going to look after you until you're back on your feet. Literally,' I laugh, holding back my own tears this time. I mean it though, as soon as he knew I was having trouble he offered to help me, so that's what I'm going to do for him.

'I love you, Nicole. I mean it.'

'Well that's the painkillers talking.' I wipe his eyes.

'No, I mean it. I really love you. I've been a dick, but I'm going to turn this around, OK?'

'Excuse me,' a nurse interrupts us. 'I've got an Eddie Baker here to see you, if you're feeling up to another visitor.'

'Yeah, send him through.'

'I know I shouldn't be saying this, but I'm a huge fan,' the nurse says excitedly.

'Really?' This puts a smile on Luke's face. 'Remind us to sort you out with some signed CDs before I leave.'

The nurse goes bright red and leaves the room.

Luke loves me, yeah right. It's amazing what a bump to the head can do to a person.

Chapter 56

If I've learned one thing over these past few weeks, it is that my body absolutely does not agree with me sleeping on any kind of chair. I woke up in my uncomfortable armchair to see Joanne fussing over Luke – she is one of the lovely nurses working on the ward. Most of the nurses have taken an instant liking to Luke, which is lucky because Luke has taken an instant liking to most of the nurses. I spent yesterday evening watching Eddie find reasons for them to come in and check on Luke, which was just *so* much fun for me. To be fair, they are all really nice ladies and they're really taking care of Luke – and me, his temporary roommate, even though I'm certain that isn't in the job description.

'Good morning,' Joanna whispers to me.

'Hey. How's he doing?'

'He's doing OK, I'll be bringing him his breakfast through in a minute. Can I get you anything?'

I ask her if the gift shop is open because I plan to head down there before Luke wakes up. I can grab a toothbrush and something for my breakfast because I'm not sure when the last time I ate was, and I'll pick up a copy of that horrible newspaper which will most likely have a photo of me outside Dylan's house on the front, along with some horrible, yet terribly funny, headline.

Creeping out of the room so that I don't wake Luke, I make my way to the gift shop. It doesn't matter what time of day it is, hospitals are creepy places. I pass one of the hospital porters on my way down the corridor. Luckily there is nobody on the bed that he is pushing and we exchange good mornings. As he passes me, my eyes are drawn to the bottom of the sheet which appears to be covering a big silver box and I shiver. Don't even think about what is in that box, Nicole.

There is a lovely little old lady working in the gift shop and we chat as I pile the things I want on top of the counter. I tell her that I am here with my friend who had a fall – I spare her the details.

'I hope that's not what you're planning on eating for breakfast,' she gasps, in the same way a loving grandma would.

I look down at my can of Coke and packet of peanut M&Ms.

'Erm … peanuts are good for you, they're full of protein,' I reply. Something I'm fairly sure is true, although them being covered in chocolate probably isn't that great for you.

She gives me a look, a 'come on, young lady, you know I'm right' look, so I swap the Coke for a carton of orange juice, laughing at my submission.

'Wait there,' she says, tottering off into the back room. While she is in there, I blindly grab tabloids off the shelf and dump them on the counter. I don't even glance at them, I'm going to wait until I'm with Luke because I reckon I'll need the moral support.

'We don't usually put these out for another couple of hours,' the little old lady tells me, placing a sandwich on the counter, 'but you have to take care of yourself, or you'll end up in the bed next to your friend.'

I open my mouth to protest, but she stops me.

'And it's on me, so no excuses.'

'Thank you. I'm Nicole,' I tell her, offering a hand for her to shake.

'Nice to meet you, Nicole. I'm Doris.'

'Thank you for looking after me, Doris.'

'You're very welcome, darling.'

As I bag up my shopping, I promise Doris that I will be back at lunchtime.

Luke is awake when I get back, being propped up in his bed by two nurses so that he can eat his breakfast, which looks absolutely disgusting. I'm guessing it's porridge; if it isn't then it's cement for sure.

'Good morning.' He smiles. I don't think I've ever seen him look more pleased to see me.

'Hello.' I take the newspapers and the orange juice from my bag and sit myself on the plastic chair next to Luke's bed.

'You shouldn't bother reading those,' he tells me as soon as the nurses have left the room.

'But I want to see if my picture looks good.' I try to sound like I'm joking when I say this, but to be honest this is the first photo I was ready for, so I'm hoping it looks OK.

I grab the *Daily Scoop* first because not only is it the highest-selling tabloid in the UK, but they just love writing about Dylan King.

'Sit up here, we'll look together,' Luke says, carefully patting the spot next to him on the bed. After sitting down as lightly as I possible – because at the moment even breathing is causing him pain – I mentally psych myself up to start reading. With everything that has gone on over the past few weeks, I have had to re-evaluate all aspects of my life. I've learned that I can't trust people, how even innocent situations can be made to look bad and, most importantly, I've learned to expect the unexpected, because anything could be around the corner. Even so, nothing could have prepared me for the latest chapter in the messed-up story that is my life.

Neither of us speaks, we just read in silence. The headline reads: 'Nicole Wilde – house parties, heroin and hospital' and underneath is a photo of me and Luke, one of Carla's from the end of tour party, the one of me sitting on Luke's knee, wearing nothing but that hoodie. We both look totally wasted – if the article were about anyone else, I'd probably believe it looking at that photo.

I glance at the name underneath the headline. Vicky Mason. In my attempt to avoid the world at all costs, it didn't occur to me to unfriend her on Facebook.

Reading the article, it explains how – in one of many 'heroin-fuelled house parties' – I got up to 'all sorts' with 'Luke Fox, drummer of hot new band Two For The Road'.

'You know,' I say quietly, breaking the silence, 'I know that I'm no angel, but if I went outside and it was raining heroin, I wouldn't know what it was.'

'You would if you inhaled.'

'Luke, this is not the time for jokes.'

He snatches the paper from me as assertively as he can, dropping it on the floor and wincing in pain at the sudden movement.

'Don't read that shit. We'll get Frank here and he'll tell us what to do. OK?'

'OK.'

'On the bright side, it's promotion for the band that money just can't buy,' Frank says as he joins us, overhearing our conversation. 'I mean, it's an awful story, but a pretty blonde lass wearing nowt but a band hoodie in a paper like this ...'

I can practically see the pound signs in his eyes.

'Are they allowed to use a photo from a private Facebook account and make up a story to go with it?' I ask.

'Nicole, you're in the business, you must know this happens all the time?' Frank says unhelpfully.

'I don't care,' I reply. 'None of this is true at all. First of all, I didn't tell anyone that Luke was in here, and no one knows I'm here.'

'Well that could have been anyone. Famous face takes drugs, found unconscious, rushed to hospital. It could have been the paramedic or one of these nurses.' He picks up the paper and reads through the story again. 'Right,' Frank claps his hands. 'From what you've told me, Nicole, it sounds like they knew you were in town from the photo of you at Dylan's house, and they know you are friends with Luke if your mate is writing for them.'

'She's not my mate,' I snap.

'Whoever she is. When they got wind of what happened to Luke, it would be more valuable to them to put you with Luke instead of Dylan, especially after the statement—'

'The statement!' I interrupt. 'What did he say?'

'That he shouldn't have cheated on his wife, that he panicked about settling down and had one last fling. He begged for forgiveness.'

I nod. So he did what he said he was going to do and now he looks like a reformed character, and I look like an even bigger groupie with a drug problem.

'I'll release a statement on behalf of both of you, telling them what nonsense this all is.' Frank grabs his notebook and starts scribbling things down.

'Tell them the truth, I don't give a shit,' Luke insists.

'That's very noble of you, Luke, but it will ruin your career before it's even properly started. You boys might be doing well, but you're not famous enough to get away with a drug problem.'

'I don't give a shit,' Luke repeats, overpronouncing each word.

'You don't need to, lad. Look, enough of this is made up for us to rubbish it, after that no one will believe a word of it. Nicole, you say those photographs were uploaded the day after the party?'

I nod.

'Well then, anyone who goes on Facebook will see the date they were uploaded and that will prove your version of events.'

'Right,' I say, but I'm not so sure about this.

'Leave it with me, OK?'

I guess for now that is all I can do.

Chapter 57

With Eddie, Ben and Mark showing up to keep Luke company this afternoon, I decided to get out of the hospital for a while. Desperately in need of a proper wash, I headed back to the flat. Either the paparazzi have given up on us or I managed to exit the massive hospital through a door without a snapper waiting behind it.

Whatever buzz I was getting from all the press attention before has fast worn off, and at this stage I couldn't give a fuck who is or isn't waiting for me outside.

No one was waiting for me outside the flat when I arrived there, which made life much easier, and as I travelled up in the lift, the thought of a nice, long, relaxing bath was enough to make me feel a little less stressed. Of course my stress levels went through the roof when I walked into the bathroom and saw all that dried blood all over the floor. When I went in the ambulance with Luke on the day of his accident, I simply closed the door behind me. Well, it was an emergency. I completely forgot about the bloody mess that would be waiting for me when I did eventually return, but cleaning isn't something that crosses my mind on a normal day, so it's even less likely to occur to me during an emergency.

I got down on my hands and knees and scrubbed the tiles until there wasn't a trace of blood left. It was harder to clean up than I had imagined and the smell was just the worst. I did it though, and I did a good job. I have surprised even myself.

I have been in the bath for ten minutes now, and while I wouldn't go as far as to say my stress is melting away, it's certainly being chipped away at.

Luke's bathroom isn't exactly well stocked for female guests, and as I look through what few products he has to try to find something I can wash my hair with, I hear my phone vibrating against the hard floor. I dry my hands and answer it carefully, because the last thing we need is another accident involving this bathroom/my phone.

'Hello,' I say cheerfully after seeing that it's ET calling – my boss from ByteBanter.

'Hello, Nicole,' he replies without the same enthusiasm. 'You sound cheerful, all things considered – is that the drugs?'

ET has always had a very dry sense of humour, but I'm not entirely sure if he was joking there or not.

'Just trying to keep positive,' I tell him.

'Great. That's great. Hopefully you'll be able to see the positive side of what I'm about to say.'

Oh crap, why do I get the feeling this is going to be bad news.

'Go on,' I prompt him, hoping we can get this over with quickly and painlessly.

'After everything that has gone on, we think it might be best to disassociate ByteBanter from *Starstruck*.'

'Look, ET, I know I'm not there at the moment, but the magazine isn't involved in any of this.'

I can hear my own voice sounding more panicked as I force out each word. *Starstuck* is my world, without it I'm just some unemployed groupie. No one in the industry will trust me enough to employ me, and there's no way I'd be able to do any other kind of job. I'm useless at everything else.

'Nicole, I like you, so I'm going to be honest with you. I don't care who you slept with, who you didn't sleep with – I haven't even heard of half of the people you go around with – but it's you we feel we should disassociate from. The magazine is your baby and you're free to pursue things alone if that's what you want, we hold no claim over the format or the name, we just can't back you any more, not now it's affecting *our* business.'

So they get a few phone calls from reporters or a few shitty emails, big deal. Am I really getting fired over a silly rumour?

'What about Jake? This isn't his fault.'

'We've given Jake his old position back, and we've found something for Emily.'

'Oh good, I'm so glad Emily is OK,' I reply sarcastically.

'Wilde, you sound upset.'

I am upset, but I'm not going to let it show. If he doesn't appreciate me enough to stand by me in my time of need, then fuck him.

'I'll be fine,' I tell him bluntly.

'That's the spirit,' he cheers. 'You're a smart girl. Look at this as a new opportunity, we're setting you free. Spread your wings, the sky is the limit.'

'Yes, OK, I'll do that. Thank you.'

I rush ET off the phone before my emotions – or my temper – get the better of me.

If there's one thing that I have learned throughout all of this so far, it's that you should never make the mistake of thinking that things can't get worse. Things can get worse, and they have gotten worse for me ... Much worse.

Chapter 58

It's been little over a week since Luke's accident and I am like a regular Florence Nightingale. OK, maybe that's a slight exaggeration, but I have officially moved into Luke's spare room and I am looking after him. With no income or savings, I don't even have any money in my pocket these days. I'm so lucky to have my parents paying the rent on my flat while I figure things out, but when my mum asked me if I needed money, I said no. If I told her I'd blown what little money I had saved on an outfit for Dylan's wedding, she wouldn't be too impressed. So I am staying here, nursing Luke back to health and living off his money which, to be honest, is making me feel like a bit of a loser.

Life is weird now. I hardly leave the flat, unless I'm going to the shop or the coffee bar just downstairs, and we're pretty much living off takeaway food. Right now this suits us just fine because neither of us is getting very good press. No one seems to care about the little details that prove the things in the press aren't quite what they seem; people would much rather hate me for being a home-wrecker. The nasty headlines still upset me, but I guess that's what you get when you sleep with one of the country's biggest stars. I say sleep with, because that's all we did. Sleep.

'So what culinary delight are you preparing for us tonight?'

Luke asks me with a cheeky grin.

'If by preparing you mean opening the container and putting the contents on a plate, then we are having Chinese, and any more sarcastic comments and you can get your own,' I reply, sticking my tongue out at him to make sure he knows I'm only joking.

'Touchy. Is it nearly time for my bath?'

'You wish. Surely you must be getting better by now? I'm sure you're milking this.'

'What kind of nurse says that?'

'The kind who really doesn't want to bathe you,' I tease.

'Why not? I'm clean!' Luke insists, sounding mildly offended.

'If you're clean, then you don't need a bath, do you?'

'We could take a picture for the *Scoop*. Just you, me and my rubber ducky.'

I shoot him another dirty look.

'Seriously though, I think they're starting to lose interest,' I tell him. 'I'm just going to keep my head down, let this blow over and then—'

'And then what?' he interrupts. 'Nic, they've ruined your life. You've lost friends, they've damaged your reputation, trashed your website. Let me talk to the press, I can at least clear up my accident.'

'But Frank said—'

'Fuck Frank!' Luke winces with pain.

'Calm down.' I rest a hand on his shoulder so gently I'm not even sure if I'm touching him.

Everything he just said is right, but there isn't anything I can do about it.

'Forget about things for tonight, I'll go order our tea.'

'OK, but you're in London now so stop calling it tea. It's dinner.'

I almost preferred him unconscious.

Luke and I are sitting in his bed, eating Chinese food and flicking through the channels on a TV that makes the one in my bedroom look like a toy. It's so big that if I were to stand next to the damn thing, the people on it would be bigger than me. Normally I'd say that could only be a good thing, but it turns out that stress is the best diet going. I've shifted a few pounds over the past couple of weeks, but now things are getting back to normal and we're living off takeaway food, I expect I'll quickly put the weight back on, times two.

'Wait, go back.' Something catches my eye and Luke clicks back a channel as instructed. I thought I saw Dylan, and I'm right. The show, rather creatively called *We Four Kings*, appears to be some sort of fly-on-the-wall documentary filmed at Dylan's house.

'Bloody sell-out,' Luke mutters, but I'm too fixated on the screen to say anything.

'This is Char,' Crystal points at a baby in the arms of an older woman – I'm assuming she's the nanny.

'No, this is little Lamb,' the woman corrects her with an awkward smile.

'How embarrassing is that?' Luke laughs. 'Your boy Dylan isn't saying much, is he?'

'OK, well this is Char,' Crystal says, pointing to the tiny baby in Dylan's arms. To the people watching, he probably looks like the proud parent, but I know better. He hasn't uttered one word yet, which isn't like him at all. He just looks so miserable. When he came to my office to see me, he told me that this wasn't what he wanted and I talked him into it.

I'm not sure what I'm supposed to think or feel when I see babies. I think there might be something wrong with me. I have no maternal instinct whatsoever. Most women look at babies and they think they're adorable, it makes them want to have their own. I look at babies and I panic. I don't even find them cute, they're like little machines constantly firing out piss, crap, snot and sick. I remember when one of my cousins brought her new baby to meet us just before my parents moved away. 'You're doing that look, Nicole,' my mother told me with a subtle nudge. 'What look?' I asked after they had gone. 'That look you do when you see small children, it's like you've caught whiff of a bad smell, it's plastered across your face whenever a baby is in the room.' I thought perhaps she was exaggerating until I saw the photos later on. If I didn't know better, I'd think Dylan was fighting off a similar look.

We watch for a little longer as Crystal shows the cameras around the house – Dylan's house, the one I was in not long ago.

'You OK?' Luke asks me.

'I guess.' I'm not sure what I'm feeling really.

'You miss him?'

'A bit,' I lie. I miss him like crazy. I know it hasn't really been that long, but it feels like he's dead. I doubt Crystal will ever let him see me again.

'You've still got me,' he says with a smile.

'Only just. No thanks to that crap you shove up your nose or wherever you put it,' I snap.

'I guess I deserved that,' he says, looking embarrassed.

'Luke, I'm so sorry. I was just so worried about you and what you were doing to yourself. Why did you do it?' I ask.

'I don't know.'

'Does it feel good?' I don't mean to question him about it, but I've never really understood what could possibly make someone want to take drugs.

'At first, yeah. It's like being in love. At first it's amazing, you know? You're on top of the world.'

'And then?'

'And then you end up alone, feeling like shit and wondering what the hell just happened. And skint,' he adds with a laugh. 'I was having to take more and more to hit the spot,' he admits seriously.

'That's what you think of love?' I tease in an attempt to change the subject. 'Anyway, you've never been in love with anyone but yourself.'

'I have been in love actually,' he insists and an awkward silence follows.

Finally, I break it. 'Well you're far from being skint if you're living in a place like this. And you're not alone, you've got me. So no more drugs, OK?'

'No more drugs, Nicole. I promise.'

I'm not sure whether or not I believe him, but that's the best I can hope for right now.

Chapter 59

As I queue with my basket of shopping, I wonder what inspired me to buy the coffees first. I like to think I'm pretty smart, but I can be so stupid sometimes. I sigh with relief as I dump my basket down at the till, sitting my drinks down at the end of the checkout so that I can pack my bags. It's as I do this that I spot the latest copy of *Bacci* magazine, the front cover occupied by the King family. It pains me to do so because I know this is just Crystal cashing in, but I buy a copy. I can obsess over it as I drink my coffee.

As I pack my bags, I glare at the cover. 'Our plans for a family Christmas' the cover reads, and I am reminded that it is nearly December. I wonder what Luke does for Christmas? I imagine I'll end up back in Leeds, all alone.

I pay for my shopping and head back to the flat. It's starting to get pretty cold. I need to go to the proper shops and buy more clothes because I only have the few items I packed and it certainly didn't occur to me that I might need my scarf and gloves. With the way money is (me not having a penny – Luke gave me money for this shopping), I guess I'll have to ask Jake to send me some things from my flat.

As I approach the door, I see Frank, Luke's manager, buzzing to be let in.

'You'll be lucky,' I call out, 'he was fast asleep when I left and nothing wakes him.'

'Don't I bloody know it,' he chuckles, taking my bags from me.

'Thank you,' I say, once again comforted by his lovely northern voice. 'He'll wake up when he smells the coffee, don't worry.'

'Actually, I'm here to see you,' he replies.

'Me?' I say, shocked.

'Yes, you. I'll tell you all about it when we get inside.'

'Let's give him another half hour while we talk, eh?' Frank suggests as soon as we're inside, grabbing Luke's coffee from the cup-holder.

'Sure.'

'I've got a job for you,' he says proudly, sipping his stolen coffee.

'I don't think I'd make much of a musician, Frank,' I laugh.

'Neither do I, but I'm not just a band manager, you know. I'm a proper agent, I've got all sorts on my books. People know you're living with Luke, so I suppose they thought they could approach you through me.'

'So what does this mean?' I ask, confused. Who would want to give me a job?

'I want to be your agent, Nicole. We've gone about this all wrong. People clearly want to talk to you, why shouldn't you speak up?'

'Speak up about Dylan?'

'Yes. The offer came from *Chit-Chat*, do you know the show?'

Oh, I know the show – not that I watch it. It's a chat show involving two washed-up female hosts (plus special guests) sitting around and complaining about everything. It's on every Thursday afternoon so I never get chance to watch it – not that I would if I had the time.

'What do they want me for?'

'They're doing a special on adultery—' he doesn't get to finish his sentence before I cut him off.

'No, no, no, no, no. No. Because I haven't engaged in any adultery. I'm not going to be some kiss-and-tell girl that they can have a go at on TV,' I rant.

'It's going to be a big show. Kathy Saunders, who hosts the show, cheated on her husband with some bloke, reckons it's made her marriage better. Then there will be the other regular, Deborah Blake,' he takes his phone from his pocket and pushes a few buttons before reading aloud, 'and pop princess Kelly Parker, who recently found out her footballer fiancé had been playing away from home.'

'So why do they need me?'

'They want to talk to you because you have been caught up in an affair and, before you start, I know you haven't. But Dylan told the nation that you did. This can be your chance to set the record straight. Don't you want to have your say?'

'Well yeah, but not like this. I don't think I could go on TV and talk about anything, let alone this.'

'They'll pay you.'

'They'll pay me? To go on TV and talk about this?'

'Yes, and they really want you on the show so I've got you a pretty good deal.'

'How much?' I ask. I cannot believe I am entertaining the idea, but I'm jobless and I have no money to even get back home, so I'm in no position to turn this down.

Frank takes a pen and a pad of Post-It notes from his inside pocket, writes down a number and sticks it on the table in front of me. I'm not quite sure why he wrote it down, it's not like anyone can hear. It must be a showbiz thing that I'm not aware of. As I pick it up off the table and read the number to myself, my jaw physically drops.

'How much?' I squeal.

'And that's with my commission deducted. That would all go to you.'

'They want to pay me that much money to go on TV – for

how long?'

'It will probably be a fifteen-minute slot.'

'Oh my God!' I laugh in a slightly manic way. It may not be that much money, but I'd be stupid to turn it down now that I'm unemployed. Having no money or independence is really starting to wear me down. 'OK, tell them I'll do it,' I say.

'Great stuff, lass. I'll get on the blower to them and sort it out. It's next week so you'll want to start thinking about something to wear. Let me know if you need anyone to help you with that.'

'Erm, I can dress myself thanks, Frank.'

'I can see that, Nicole. I mean an image consultant. You want to put the right message across.'

Never in a million years would I have expected Frank to mention anything style-related to me. I see him out and run in to see Luke. I stop myself jumping on his bed at the last minute, remembering his injuries, although he's mending nicely now. I wake him and tell him all about the show.

'I though Frank was just your band manager,' I say, still unable to process what a big-shot he is.

'He's a big name, so are his clients. Google him,' Luke suggests, carefully sitting up. 'No coffee this morning?'

'Frank drank it. Luke, should I go on this show?'

'I don't see why not. People already hate you, and don't give me a dirty look like that, because you know they do.'

He has a point.

'Just go for it.'

So this is my fifteen minutes of fame. I suppose I should make the most of it.

Chapter 60

Sitting in my dressing room – yes, *my* dressing room – at the TV studio, I try not to think about what I'm about to do. At this point, it still doesn't feel real. Yes, I'm sitting here with my hair and make-up done, in my stylish yet demure dress, just waiting to be called, but I'm still not convinced someone won't realise what a terrible mistake they have made and show me the door.

I practice my voice again. When the woman on reception asked me if I was Scottish, I thought it best to practise sounding … not northern. When I'm up north I get teased constantly for my weak accent, but when I visit London people treat me like I speak another bloody language.

There's a knock on the door.

'Come in,' I call out, mentally kicking myself for sounding so northern. A man wearing a headset peers just inside the doorway.

'Ready for you in ten minutes, Miss Wilde.'

'Oh, right. Shit.' I kick myself again for swearing, but he's gone. No swearing. No northern terms. I absolutely cannot come across as the foul-mouthed, northern home-wrecker that I (kind of) am. No smart-arse comments, no silly puns – I just need to be myself. Well, a version of myself that doesn't swear, pun or have an accent.

Before I know it, I am being ushered towards the set.

'This is your seat,' he points to one of the empty chairs and then addresses the person I didn't know was standing behind me. 'Ah, Miss Parker, you will be seated to the left of Miss Wilde.'

'Brilliant,' she says unenthusiastically, walking straight past me. What a bitch. Then again, to her I'm probably just another girl like the one who ruined her relationship.

I take my seat as instructed and admire the set. Everything is red and gold – presumably because Christmas is coming, although I imagine their usual set is equally as garish.

'One minute to go,' Headset guy calls out.

I am taken aback by the studio audience, I didn't realise so many people were going to be here. I watched an episode of the show last night (for research) and presumed the enthusiastic laughter and other audience noises were canned. We're all sitting around a large table, shaped a bit like a banana, with one host on either end – guests go in the middle. I am sitting between Kelly and Deborah Blake. I don't know what it is Deborah is famous for, but I'm guessing she was someone back in her day and she's still very aware of that fact. I'd guess she's in her early sixties. I know that Kelly is twenty-nine, so I'm the youngest on the show. Then we have Kathy Saunders. She used to present a breakfast TV show, and I remember the scandal when she was caught shagging her co-host, who was also married. She's probably fifty-ish, but trying oh-so hard to look more like thirty. If people can forgive her, maybe they'll forgive me in time.

Headset man appears next to one of the cameras in front of us. 'And we're live in five, four, three …' he gestures the other numbers with his fingers, and then a big red light appears on top of the camera. I guess this is it.

'Hello, and welcome back to *Chit-Chat*. Today our topic of conversation is adultery.'

The audience make 'oooh' sounds.

'You've never cheated on anyone, have you, Deborah?' Kathy

asks across the desk. I wonder if I'm in shot. I don't know what to do with my face, smiling feels awkward, but I can't just sit there glaring at them.

'I haven't, no. Never cheated on anyone, and I've never been cheated on,' Deborah chirps.

'That you know of,' Kathy says with a chuckle and the audience roar with laughter. It's not that funny, is it?

'I've spoken about it many times on the show before, but for those of you who don't know, I *did* cheat on my husband, but it saved my marriage. If I hadn't cheated, we probably would have broken up eventually. So personally, I owe an awful lot to my affair. However, one of our guests today – Kelly Parker, everybody.' She gives the audience a moment to cheer and clap. 'Kelly, your footballer fiancé, Jed Ellis, cheated on you. How did that feel?'

'It ruined my life, Kathy,' Kelly tells her. 'I thought we were happy, we'd set a date for the wedding, and then it came out in the papers that he had been cheating on me with several other girls. It broke my heart. I'm not sure there is ever an excuse for it.'

'Oh, there is. In my case, it was a great thing, but when people get hurt …' Kathy trails off, and then looks at me.

'Our other guest, Nicole Wilde—' no pause for applause, not that I was expecting any, '—you had an affair with Dylan King, one of the country's biggest stars.'

'I didn't have an affair with Dylan, we're just friends,' I say weakly, feeling defeated already.

'You'd been friends for so long, and yet you didn't get together until *after* he was married.'

'Nothing happened between us. I don't think one suspicious-looking photograph in a tabloid is enough to prove otherwise.'

'He was on top of you, on the floor, your hands were all over each other,' Deborah interrupts, and then once again all three women stare at me, waiting for an explanation.

'Well come on, if we were going to have an affair do you really think we'd get it on in the centre of Leeds, right outside a five-star hotel? It has like 250 rooms, that's a lot of people that could have seen.'

'By all accounts, you were very drunk,' Kathy says, smugly. 'And men do tend to think with their … ahem.'

'Yes, and by all accounts,' I say, trying to copy Kathy's voice, 'at no point did take off his trousers. We were a bit drunk, fine. We fell over, he landed on top of me – if I was going to lie, don't you think I'd come up with a better one?'

I look at Deborah, she's not buying it and neither is Kathy. If I didn't know better, I'd think Kelly believed me, though.

'But Dylan confessed *and* apologised. Isn't it time you did the same thing?'

Ah, fuck it.

'Dylan only confessed to keep his wife happy, so that he could see his kids.' I hear the northern creeping back into my voice, big time. I didn't pronounce one 'h' in that sentence.

'Well, that's my next point. When I had my affair—' oh, shut up about your affair, you terrible person. It's like she's proud of it. 'No one got hurt. You nearly broke up a marriage, and a marriage with two new babies.'

'No one got hurt?' I ask. 'Don't you think your husband was hurt that you cheated on him? And what about the other guy? It didn't save his marriage, it ruined it.'

I'm so pleased I Googled that last night.

'Well, just a second—' Kathy's voice is raised, but I'm on a roll now.

'No, I won't wait just a second. I don't care if you believe me or not, I don't care if any of you believe me.' I wave my arms like a maniac at the cameras and the audience. 'I know what's true and I can sleep at night, no problem. But you!' I point a finger accusingly at Kathy, there really is no turning back now. 'You are *so* proud of the fact that you cheated on your husband, and you ruined another man's marriage, and poor Kelly here, well her fiancé really hurt her, and you sit there going on about how wonderful affairs can be. It's crap!'

The audience gasp at the word crap. No, really, they do.

'My word!' Kathy exclaims. 'In all the years we have been doing this show, not once has a guest sworn on air. You should be ashamed of yourself – for two reasons now,' she adds, giving me that last boost of confidence I need to really kick off. She turns to address the cameras. 'I apologise to those of you watching at home. I did say that I didn't want a common kiss-and-tell gold-digger on *Chit-Chat*, but no one listens to me.'

'Oh, we wouldn't want a common kiss-and-tell gold-digger on *Shit-Chat*,' I repeat, mocking her accent. Well, when did being mature ever get you anywhere these days?

'I came on here to set the record straight,' I continue, because there's no stopping me now, 'not to have you pick on me and big up affairs in front of a woman who has had her heart broken because of one. This show is a joke. You have a platform to address real issues, and yet you spend the whole time complaining about men and justifying adultery. What a fucking joke.'

A matter of seconds after the words leave my mouth, the red light goes off and two large security men enter the studio.

'You are a disgrace,' Kathy tells me. 'We invite you to be on our show, and you repay us by swearing three times.'

'Three times?' I ask, counting them in my head. 'I'll give you "shit" and "fucking" – but "crap" is allowed, right? I can say "crap" as much as I want.'

'Get her out of here,' Kathy instructs the security guards.

'Crap, crap, crap, crap, crap, crap, crap, crap,' I chant as they drag me out of the studio, one guard at either side of me, which seems a little excessive.

My fifteen minutes of fame didn't even last fifteen minutes, and as I walk down the corridor towards Reception (technically, I think they're carrying me, which is a bit extreme considering all I did was drop an F-bomb, *and* I was going to leave anyway), I can't help but laugh at my career suicide. I don't think Frank will want me on his books now.

The two big men walk me right outside the door.

'This one isn't allowed back in,' one of them tells a third big bloke who is guarding the entrance.

I straighten up my dress. 'I don't want to come back in … but can I have my handbag please? It's in the dressing room.'

'I'll send out a form, list the items you have left in the building and your address. We'll send them on,' one of the original big blokes tells me before heading back inside.

'But my purse and my phone are in that bag! Please?' I beg, but I am ignored.

If I'm being honest with myself, that probably could have gone better. I'm glad I stood my ground though. If that woman thinks she can call me a gold-digger on national TV … It's hard enough being labelled a home-wrecker, I don't need to give people another reason to hate me.

I plonk myself down on a bench. It's only then I realise how blooding freezing it is, and that my coat is still inside. I try to imagine how things could possibly be any worse and, to be honest, I can't. If my mum were here, she'd probably tell me that at least I had my health, and that there were people far worse off than me in the world – although I suppose after I walk across London in the freezing cold my health will take a hit too.

I put my head in my hands and try my hardest not to cry – if only because my tears will freeze on my face.

'Nicole,' I hear a female voice call out. Looking up, I see Kelly Parker with my bag and coat in her hands.

I'm speechless.

'Here.' She hands me my things, and I quickly slip my coat on. 'I went to the dressing room to see you and they told me you'd been escorted straight out. I grabbed these for you, figured you'd need them,' she says with a friendly smile.

'I don't know what to say. Thank you.'

'No, thank you. Everything you said about that show was

right. I only went on because I've got an album to promote, but I would have sat there and listened to her talk crap about affairs. You stood up to her, that's pretty cool.'

My life is so weird, I wish I was keeping a diary. Dear Diary, today I swore on daytime TV, and then pop princess Kelly Parker told me I was pretty cool.

'Well people already think I'm a home-wrecking bitch, it's not like my reputation can get any worse,' I laugh, but I know it's true.

'Not that it makes any difference, but I believe you. And I'm sure others out there do too.'

'Really?' I'm gobsmacked. Someone believes me, and that someone just happens to be a superstar.

'Yes. Look, I have to go, but let's swap numbers. Are you in London for a while?'

'Indefinitely,' I reply.

'Wicked, well we'll meet up. Go for coffee or something.'

'Great,' I say coolly. I never thought I'd be playing hard to get with a woman, but this is Kelly Parker! I so want to be her friend!

We swap numbers and she disappears back inside the studio. As I take my phone out to punch in her number – should I lose the piece of paper with it written on which, let's be honest, is highly likely – I see that I have sixteen missed calls from Frank. Another call comes through as I attempt to add a new contact, and I accept the call straight away by mistake. It's Frank again.

'Nicole, where are you?' he asks, without as much as a hello.

'Outside the studio.'

'Turn left, and walk down the road. There's a coffee shop, I'll meet you there. I'm on my way now.' He hangs up.

Oh dear. I think I might be in some sort of trouble.

Chapter 61

I took the liberty of ordering Frank a drink. That's the sign of a true bad girl, the instinct to try to sweeten the person you are in trouble with. When I was at school, my parents always knew when I had done something wrong because it was the only time I was helpful without being prompted. Like that time when I was eleven and old Mrs Atkins from down the road told me off for playing outside her house ... so I called her a bastard, which was probably the worst word I knew at the time. My parents knew something was up the second they saw me doing the dishes. Of course, they would have found out anyway because Mrs Atkins came over to tell them – a conversation that was particularly hilarious to listen in on, I have to admit. Do you think maybe I swear too much?

Frank walks in and scans the room for me. He's got a concerned look on his face. He spots me and hurries over to the table.

'Have you spoken to anyone yet?' he asks.

'What do you mean?'

'I mean, have you spoken to anyone yet?' he repeats the questions. 'Since the interview.'

'Only Kelly Parker, she came out to see me, said thank you for standing up for her. We're going to meet up,' I tell him excitedly, but my smile quickly fades as I remember I'm in bother.

'You befriended Kelly Parker?' he asks. I wish he just get on with bollocking me so I can go somewhere and cry.

'Sort of.'

'Nicole Wilde, you're pure gold.' He rubs his hands together and a huge grin spreads across his face.

'Erm, what?' Now I really am confused.

'First of all, you have a go at a TV legend, and if we're being honest you only said to her what thousands of others wanted to, you swear – you can't buy the kind of publicity we'll get from this. Oh, and the best bit, the icing on the cake, you make friends with Kelly Parker. The nation's sweetheart. We all know how she feels about cheaters, so if you're OK with her, you can't be that bad. This is going to show you in a very good light, Nicole. Well done.'

Did I just get praised for swearing and cheeking my elders? I've come a long way since I was eleven. This is possibly the greatest day of my life.

'Are you up for doing more interviews?' he asks. Not only can I not really think of a reason to say no, but if people are coming around to the truth then I've got to stick with the plan. What choice do I have?

Chapter 62

So, it's official – I am a Z-list celebrity. After my little flip-out on national TV, I appear to have divided the nation – well, the nation of people who give a shit. It's not exactly fifty-fifty, but there are people on my side now. The *Scoop* is still running crap about me, and they've managed to take a couple of the things I've said out of context and made up stories to go with them, but I expect no less of those bastards. I've spent the past week doing interviews, which is the strangest thing in the world. In all my years of being the one who asks the questions, I'm finally getting a taste of what it's like for the other person. My verdict? It can be quite fun if the person likes me, or is on my side at least. *Goss*, one of the weekly showbiz mags, has started a little campaign on my behalf which is really nice of them – but when I get someone who has decided I am guilty before they have even walked into the room, then I know it's going to be a bumpy ride. I'm toughening up, though. I don't go to the toilets and cry half as much as I used to.

It's amazing how quickly you can take to being a 'celebrity'. For starters, being paid while someone takes up a tiny bit of my time to talk to me is probably the best thing to ever happen to me. Oh, and who knew photo shoots were so much fun? One magazine had me dressed up like Shania Twain, surrounded by half-naked musicians, 'Man! I Feel Like a Woman'-style.

Frank is working really hard to get me some good press. He's a top man, although he is getting his cut. Luke is doing much better, too. Luckily his ribs weren't too badly broken and they are healing nice and quickly. He's moving around like normal, although he's been advised to take time off from performing. Apart from a few TV appearances, he isn't missing out on much work so he's taking the opportunity to rest before the big European tour next year.

Tonight we're actually going to an event together – a big, fancy music award ceremony. They're actually going to let me walk down the red carpet. I'm under no illusions, I know I'm not really a celebrity, but a girl could get a big head over the treatment I received today.

I've been given a proper make-over and a dress that I really don't deserve to wear, and the Two For The Road boys are all suited and booted too. Poor Eddie is still in plaster, but there's no chance of it getting him down. He is absolutely loving the attention, and his cast looks amazing – he's had some famous tattoo artist doodle all over it. Apparently he's a pretty big deal in the tattoo world, or so the guy told me. As soon as he realised I wasn't impressed by ink, he soon got bored of talking to me.

It's been nice spending the day with the guys. We all shared a car to the ceremony, and on the way there I told them all about what's been happening to me. Either they're really good actors, or they all believed me when I told them it was all lies. It's nice to have people just believe me without any extra effort on my part.

Finally pulling up outside the venue, Frank talks us all through the procedure. This is as new to the band as it is to me. In a way, it feels quite nice that I have Luke to share this with, if only because I can follow his lead. Frank must have realised I'd be scared, so we're all going to stick together, even for the photos.

'Luke, I'm bricking it,' I whisper into his ear, proving that it doesn't matter how pretty and expensive the dress is, there's no hiding a foul-mouthed Yorkshire girl.

He offers me his arm to link up with. 'Just hold onto me and you'll be fine. Don't let go, smile at the cameras, we'll be inside in a matter of minutes.'

I take one last deep breath and we begin our journey along the red carpet. Before we even reach the photographers, the flashes make me feel dizzy. The band stop to sign a few autographs, but I keep hold of Luke's arm rather tightly. Somehow he still manages to sign things and pose for photos. I'm used to seeing girls all over him, but this is insane. I usually only ever experience this kind of hysteria when I'm with Dylan; the girls (and quite a lot of the guys) go crazy for him.

As we approach the photographers, we pause while they finish up snapping photos of whoever is in front of them. It's only as we're standing still, waiting for our turn, that I realise they're taking photos of Dylan and Crystal. How stupid of me not to consider that they might be here – Frank must have realised, then again, he was probably counting on it.

Willing them to hurry up and go, I grip Luke's arm a little too tightly. Realising something is wrong, he only has to follow my trail of sight to work out what's bothering me. Crystal looks tacky as ever, she's dressed like a Barbie doll.

Dylan looks over in our direction; maybe he's just seeing who is next or maybe he can feel my eyes burning into him. It isn't long before Crystal catches sight of me too. The filthy look she shoots me is enough to alert the photographers to something, and one by one they turn to face me. They instantly start snapping photos of me and shouting my name to try to get my attention. Dylan and Crystal disappear and, sensing drama, Frank ushers me away from Luke and the guys, hurrying me into the building. As he does this, I hear a few of the photographers shouting horrible things at me to try to get a reaction, or my attention at least, but I don't look back.

'You knew they would be here,' I say to Frank once we are safely inside.

'You didn't?' he replies. 'These are music awards and he's one of the biggest musicians in the country.'

If I knew where the toilets were, I would go cry in them. Instead, I wait for Luke so that I can latch back onto him and I'm not letting go until we are back in his flat.

'Nicole?' a friendly female voice calls out. 'I thought that was you.'

As Kelly Parker greets me with a big hug, I catch sight of Frank over her shoulder, rubbing his hands together, pound signs rolling around in his eyes.

'I've been meaning to call you, I've just been so busy,' she says sincerely – I think. 'You've been busy too I see.'

'She has,' Frank interrupts. 'You could be too if you sign with me.'

Kelly ignores him.

'Nicole, are you all right?' she asks, obviously realising I haven't spoken a word yet.

'Dylan was outside with Crystal, it was weird. She looked at me like she wanted to kill me.'

'Babes, I've seen her in magazines, that's her day-to-day face.' She laughs briefly, then she looks at Frank and her expression changes to a serious one. 'Could you give us a moment?'

Frank obliges.

'Do you want to sit with me? Let's kick up a fuss,' she suggests, and I feel tears rolls down my cheeks. It means a lot to me to have her believe that I didn't do anything wrong, especially after all she's been through.

'Don't cry.' She takes a tissue from her tiny clutch and dabs my face in a way that doesn't affect my make-up.

'I'll be fine. Don't worry, you don't need to babysit me.' I smile, truly grateful for the offer. 'I'm here with some friends, I'm just waiting for them to come in.'

'Two For The Road?' she asks. 'I've read about you and that Luke guy. Are you two, y'know …?'

'We're just friends.' I smile. I've missed having a female friend to chat like this with.

'As long as you're sure you're OK, I'm going to go inside. We will absolutely meet up in the next couple of days, promise me?'

'I promise,' I say, although I'm not sure what Frank has lined up for me.

She hugs me again as Luke and Eddie walk over, or limp over in Eddie's case.

'Are you OK?' Luke asks me, not even looking at Kelly. I nod.

'Kelly Parker, I'm a huge fan.' Eddie takes her hand and kisses it. I think he is trying to be charming, but he's coming across a little creepy, bless him.

'Thank you. So did you win some kind of competition to come back here?' she asks slowly and, without waiting for an answer, she hugs me again before wandering off.

'Was she joking?' Eddie asks me, and I know that she was but I don't tell him that. Instead I shrug my shoulders, grab Luke's arm and head over to where Frank has been waiting.

'I've just checked the seating plan, you're on the table next to Dylan. Don't worry, they're big tables. You probably wouldn't have noticed, but I thought I'd best tell you,' Frank warns me, although I suspect this isn't much of a surprise to him either. I think he wants drama and headlines for me, when all I want is an easy life. The shine is wearing off being a celebrity pretty quickly. I knew there were downsides, but I didn't realise they would overpower the positives. Hopefully Frank is right, and I won't notice the happy couple sitting near me. We'll see.

Chapter 63

Frank is a massive liar. I'm practically back-to-back with Crystal, and the same goes for Luke and Dylan. When we went to sit down, I noticed Luke look at Dylan, and there was such hate in his eyes. He'd always joked about wanting to be mates with him – I'll bet it's because of me that he doesn't want to any more.

We've been sat here for an hour or so, and despite their public displays of affection, and Crystal purposefully saying things loud enough for me to hear, I am pretty much pretending my best friend and his horrible wife are not there.

'And now for the Female Artist of the Year award,' announces the host, who I vaguely recognise as being someone from some TV show.

As the video with the nominations plays, I feel a tap on my shoulder. It's Dylan.

'Where's your wife?' I whisper.

'Toilet. I'm sorry about this, I didn't know you'd be here.'

'Whatever.' I turn back around, but he grabs my shoulder. Not hard, but Luke is there quick as a flash to remove it.

'I don't want any trouble, mate. I just want to talk to her before Crystal gets back.' He sounds panicky, like maybe he thinks Luke might hit him or something.

'What could you possibly have to say to me that you can't say in front of your wife?' I ask. 'Unless you wanted to apologise for lying to the press about us having sex when we didn't.'

'I'm sorry about that, Nic—'

'You piece of shit,' Luke cuts him off. 'I didn't doubt for one second that she was telling me the truth, but hearing you say it out loud now just makes me want to smack you even more.'

Dylan looks at me, and I'm sure I can see tears in his eyes. 'I just wanted to see my kids, Nic.'

I do get that, but it still sucks.

He spies Crystal making her way back through the tables and quickly turns around.

I squeeze Luke's hand. 'Thanks for sticking up for me.'

He smiles, and we turn our attention back to the host.

'And the winner of Female Artist of the Year goes to ...' she pauses for dramatic effect. 'Kelly Parker.'

Oh my God, Kelly won! This time last week I wouldn't have cared, but now she's my friend and I'm so proud of her. She looks absolutely beautiful as she makes her way to the stage. Her dress puts mine to shame.

'Wow, this is such an honour, thank you.' She kisses the trophy triumphantly, and then goes on to thank all the people who helped to make it possible.

'I've had a pretty horrible year,' she says, and everyone in the room knows that she is talking about her cheating fiancé. 'But I want to put that all behind me and just get on with making music. I'd also like to dedicate this award to my friend, Nicole Wilde, who is in the audience. I know how harsh the press can be – I had to have my heart broken before they decided to like me – and I know that once this mess is cleared up you'll all like Nicole as much as I do. Thank you.' She holds her trophy high before leaving the stage.

Before the events of the past couple of months I wouldn't have said I was much of a crier, but that speech went straight to my tear ducts.

'That was seriously cool of her,' Luke says.

'Some people are so desperate for attention,' I hear a female voice say rather loudly from behind me, but I'm too happy to care.

Chapter 64

You know that feeling of relief when you're having a nightmare and you wake up to find it was all a dream? Well I just had that, but in reverse. In my dream we were all at work, even Vicky, and we were all getting on great – something which probably should have tipped me off that it wasn't real. I woke up from my realistic dream to read that I have allegedly resumed my romance with Dylan King. I've got to hand it to the *Daily Scoop*, when they set out to ruin you, they really go for it.

After last night's red carpet awkwardness, someone had the bright idea to dig out the photo of me leaving Dylan's house back when I first arrived in London – before Crystal had taken him back. Why am I making excuses? Nothing happened. I went over to try to sort things out and then he gave that false statement. Oh God, and I practically gave that pap his photo because I thought it might force Dylan's hand and make him tell the truth. Instead, I gave them ammunition. They have a photo of me leaving Dylan's house and I have no way of proving when it was taken. Even if I tried, who would believe me?

The new and exciting twist in the tale is that I am supposedly cheating on Luke with Dill. They dug up Scott Hale's blog about me and the TFTR boys, and because I am living with Luke now, in the world of journalism, that absolutely makes him my boyfriend. So, I'm cheating on Luke with Dylan, who is cheating on Crystal with me – what a small world. I would imagine Crystal knows Dylan and I haven't been getting up to anything because, as far as I know, she doesn't let him out of her sight, but I don't think she'll be rushing to defend me anytime soon.

The rumours of my sex life have been greatly exaggerated. Supposedly I've had sex with various members of TFTR in the space of a couple of nights on tour, I've been having an affair with Dylan King, I am in a relationship with Luke Fox and we spend our days smoking, snorting and injecting things. So, how much of that is true? Well, I didn't have sex with anyone on the TFTR tour, let alone multiple people, Dylan and I haven't had an affair, Luke isn't my boyfriend (despite our night of passion before he decided to split his head open and crack his ribs) and now, when we're not working, we spend our time watching movies and playing video games and caffeine is our drug of choice. If you believe what you read in the papers, then I'm having the time of my life. The reality is that I don't have a boyfriend, I'm scared to go out too much in case the paparazzi harass me and I spend most of my time chained to the computer, guest-writing articles for various magazines or replying to email interviews.

So, what is happening tonight? Well, Luke is ordering pizza while I scan his DVD collection for a movie. Then we're going to get an early night – in our separate beds. I wish I was having half as much fun as the press were making out.

Chapter 65

It is the most wonderful time of the year, so why do I feel so crap? I have always loved Christmas and, come December, I am usually up for anything remotely festive. It was only last year that Emily and I went to visit Santa in town. I sat on his knee and told him that I wanted Ugg boots (I got them, although they were from my mum and dad) and had my photo taken with him. I thoroughly enjoyed it – I think Santa did too, which was kind of creepy.

I have just completed all of my Christmas shopping, but as hard as I tried I just couldn't get into the festive spirit. This is, to put it simply, because my life is fucked. The grass is always greener – it's a cliché, but it's true. I spent so many nights sitting in my little Leeds flat writing about famous people and envying their lives, but now I'm getting a taste of it, all I want to do is spit it out. Here's another cliché: be careful what you wish for. I always thought I'd achieve my socialite lifestyle by falling in love with a rockstar, making me some kind of rock WAG – details that I should have made clear every time I wished for the high life because I may have the fame side, but my reputation is always going to precede me, and we all know what kind of reputation I have. That said, I do have supporters now. My fanbase is made up of people who love me for swearing on a show watched by their grandmother, or Kelly Parker fans – I suspect no one actually believes I'm innocent because they certainly didn't before my little flip-out on TV. Anyone who was starting to believe me certainly won't now, since the *Scoop* stepped up their little campaign against me, making out like Dylan and I had rekindled our romance – the one that never even started. Oh well. At least I have managed to stretch out my fifteen minutes of fame, because if it wasn't for the work Frank was getting me, I would be unemployed.

With few friends there and no job to rush back for, I'm not going back to Leeds anytime soon – suddenly there's not that much to go back for. Jake is forwarding me all my post and sending me the things from my flat that I need. Now that it's common knowledge that I'm living in London, my little flat has drifted back into anonymity, with not so much as a drunk idiot pressing the buzzer in the middle of the night. My flat is getting about as much action as I am – probably more, because at least Jake is popping in and out of my flat.

As much as I miss my flat, I'm loving living with Luke – although it was never going to be a long-term thing. He has been behaving, but only because at first he was too ill to misbehave and now because I am watching him like a hawk. I can't be around all the time though, and now he's back on his feet it won't be long before he'll be back on the blow (heard it called that in a film we watched the other night, can't stop calling it that now) and bringing girls home – I don't think I could stand that. I've got to get out of here, and the sooner the better.

I'm having coffee with Kelly, and I've told her everything about what happened with Dylan – pretty much every last detail. Well, what do I have to lose? As great as Luke has been at listening to me whinge, it feels like a huge weight has been lifted by telling Kelly. I may get on better with boys, but some conversations were made to have with girls.

'So, what are your options?' Kelly asks, sipping her coffee. I can't quite remember what kind it was, but it took her about five minutes to order it, probably because she insisted on having all the fun (calories) sucked out of it. I keep glancing down at my full-fat gingerbread latte guiltily, maybe I should be on the low-fat, low-calorie, low-fun stuff now that I'm a superstar, darling.

'Well I can go back to Leeds, try to find a job; my flat is still there waiting for me. I could stay here, keep doing the crappy interviews and try to find a place to live. Although it would be a long time before I could afford anywhere here, to be honest, and I can't stay with Luke forever.'

'I'm sure. If he's anything like his sleazy friend, you need to escape while he's too weak to hold you down.'

I laugh, but jump to their defence. 'Luke's been great with me and Eddie is lovely really. He was probably just trying to look cool in front of you. I do need to get out of there though.'

I neglect to tell her that I'd go crazy with jealousy the second I saw Luke with another girl. One of the only things I didn't tell Kelly about was my history with Luke. I'm not ready to tackle that one yet.

'My only other option is to be with my family. Throughout this whole thing my mum has told me over and over again that I can go live with them in France if I want to. I spoke to her this morning, and she said I could be there by tonight if I wanted to.'

'And do you want to?' she asks.

'I suppose I do.'

Kelly seems almost as surprised to hear me say this as I was when I realised it was true. I just want to get out of this situation.

'But, Nicky, you're turning into a little star here, you don't want to give up. You've got a platform, you can do anything. Not many people get this opportunity you know.'

'I know.' I hate being called Nicky, but it's Kelly Parker, she can call me what the hell she likes.

I pause to think about what she's saying, but I'm fast reminded of the harsh reality of my situation.

'Let's be honest, everyone hates me. I'm OK for the gossip pages while the whole Dylan thing is still raw, but pretty soon everyone will stop caring, Dylan will carry on playing happy families and I'll go back to being nobody with zero credibility. I've got to get out of here, Kelly.'

'Won't you stay for Christmas? You can celebrate it with me.'

Yet another thing that, a few months ago, would have been music to my ears, but not now.

'I'm not feeling very Christmassy.'

'But you did your Christmas shopping.' She nods towards my bags.

'Yeah, but if my life were a film I'd be carrying them down the street, through a blizzard, all alone, tears freezing on my cheeks, to the tune of "Have Yourself A Merry Little Christmas".'

She laughs. 'Oh, I can tell you're a writer. I hear you though.' She places an arm around me and rubs my shoulder. 'Well, I'll miss you, Nicole Wilde. We could have been great friends. You'll keep in touch, won't you?'

I had read interviews with Kelly in the past – I'd even written news articles about her – and I'd jumped to the conclusion that she was probably stuck-up. I couldn't have been more wrong, and I absolutely will keep in touch with her. I'd love nothing more than to stick around, playing with my famous friends and getting paid for talking about Dylan, but how long would it last? I can't force people to believe me and they're going to lose interest if I don't bang another celebrity soon. I don't have much choice, I have to go to France and the sooner the better.

Chapter 66

Arriving back at the flat, I can hear lots of noise before I even put my key in the door. Finally managing to get it open with all my bags in my hands, I stumble through and come face to face with the last thing I need right now ... happy people. Luke, Eddie, Mark, Ben, Carla – a few other people I recognise, and then a whole bunch of people I don't know.

'Nicole Wilde!' Eddie calls out enthusiastically, he's clearly wasted. 'We're having a jam, come and join us.'

Whenever you party with bands – even when you're not on tour – you can guarantee that someone will break out a musical instrument at some point.

'I'll pass,' I say, a little blunter than I had intended.

'Aww, Nicole, come on. Join in.' He counts Ben in and they launch into a beautiful rendition of 'Have Yourself a Merry Little Christmas', the last song I needed to hear right now. Maybe it's just the way I'm feeling, but it annoys me that Eddie can be so smashed and still sing this song so beautifully. These guys really do deserve all the success they're getting, and things are only going to get bigger and better for them. I couldn't feel more tragic and out of place if I tried.

'Hey,' Luke greets me with a kiss on the cheek and glass of

something.

'I didn't know you were having a party.' I take the drink anyway.

'It was a last-minute thing, I thought I'd surprise you.' He gives me that grin I've always been a sucker for, but all it does is remind me of how things were.

'I'm not really in the partying mood. I actually need some air, I'll be on the balcony if you need me.' I don't give him chance to say anything, I just push my way through the happy people and once I'm outside I close the door behind me. It isn't long before Luke joins me.

'What's the matter? Has something happened? You'll freeze out here, Nic. Can we go inside and talk?'

'I don't want to go back in there,' I sob, turning to face away from him so that he can't see me crying, although it's probably a bit late for that.

'Hey, don't cry.' Standing behind me, he wraps his arms around me to keep me warm. 'Tell me what's wrong.'

'I'm beat.'

'You're tired? I can clear this lot out in no time, you can go to bed. Things won't seem so bad in the morning.'

'No, Luke, I'm well and truly beat. I give up. I appreciate you letting me stay here for as long as I have.' I wipe my eyes and turn to face him.

'You're leaving? Don't go. I've got used to having you around. Don't go back to Leeds.'

'I'm not going back to Leeds, I'm going to France to live with my parents for a while.'

'What? Why?'

Of all the things I could have told him, I think that was the last thing he was expecting me to say.

'I need a fresh start, somewhere where I don't have such a bad reputation. And, to be honest, you're better off not associating with me. You guys are still quite new, you don't want my bad rep rubbing off on you. You're harbouring a home-wrecker.' I laugh through my tears.

'Nicole, I don't care about that. You can't go, you're winning people over, more and more people every day, don't give up now,' he pleads.

'I was, until this new story. I can't beat them and I've run out of energy to keep trying. My mind is made up, I'm going to France.'

'When?' he asks, unable to hide his disappointment.

'Tomorrow, if I can get a flight. My mum is going to try to sort me one out. If not tomorrow, then the day after that.'

'Your mind is made up?' Luke asks me. I've only just realised that he isn't drunk or high like most of the people at the party. Maybe his accident did knock some sense into him after all.

'My mind is made up.' I don't want to go, but I really have no choice now.

'I'll be absolutely devastated if you go, Nicole.' He squeezes me tightly, so tightly it must cause him pain in his ribs. As soon as he is alone in his flat again, he'll be glad to have a bit of privacy back, I'm sure of it.

'Will you sleep on it before you arrange anything final?' he asks.

'OK, I'll sleep on it,' I lie, but I'm out of here as soon as possible.

Chapter 67

I woke up in Luke's spare room, freezing cold. He is almost as useless at playing house as I am. Right on cue he barges through the door (without knocking, although it is his flat and he has seen it all before) with a parcel in one hand and a coffee in the other.

'Before you complain, the heating is on now. I have a coffee for you, to speed up the process, and a package arrived this morning.' He drops the big, brown envelope down on the bed. It must be from Jake, he told me he was going to send me my post from the past few weeks. I rip it open and begin sorting through it all, separating it into two piles: 'I don't care' and 'I really don't care'. As I near the end of the pile, a handwritten, padded envelope catches my eye. Curiosity gets the better of me and I rip it open. It didn't occur to me until after I opened it that it might have been something horrible, like a dead rat or something even more disgusting from a disgruntled Dylan fan. Luckily it's nothing grizzly, just a letter and a USB memory stick.

'So, have you thought any more about staying?' Luke asks, but I'm too caught up to pay any attention. 'Oi, Nicole,' he says loudly, and I snap out of my trance.

'Sorry, it's this letter. It's from Scott Hale.'

'Who's that?' Luke asks, confused.

'Scott Hale. He's that horrible blogger, the one that put up a story about me and you guys on tour, remember?'

'Oh yeah, the bloke with the fantastic imagination. Well, what does he want?'

'I can't read it.' I set the letter down on the bed and stare at it like I would have done if it really were a dead rat.

'I'll read it,' Luke says, snatching it up and reading it out loud.

'Dear Nicole, just like you, I have been played by Vicky Mason.'

We stare at each other for a second. 'Keep reading,' I rush him.

'It was your so-called friend Vicky who gave me the story about you and Two For The Road. She told me that she got the info from your best friend and I don't know how much she exaggerated, but I certainly put my own spin on the story to make it juicer. I had promised her that I would buy her stories if she got me one big scoop, and she did. Plastic Rap, the cheaters. Information she also got from your best friend. You might want to investigate this leak of information. It is my understanding that she also leaked this story to the *Daily Scoop*, who put it up before me, taking all of the credit. Anyway, that story was great, so I started paying her for more. She promised me something huge, something to do with Dylan King, but we couldn't get anything. You didn't come back with any stories from his wedding, and he seemed to really clean up his act. Then he turned up at your door, and so Vicky came to me. She told me where he was staying and I had one of my spies at The Châtaigne plant a camera in his room.'

Luke pauses again, and stares at me in disbelief. I laugh, almost hysterically.

'You mean he taped us? He has a tape of me and Dylan in his hotel room? The hotel room where nothing happened!' I say excitedly. 'Keep reading, keep reading!'

Luke continues reading as instructed, although now he has a huge smile plastered across his face. 'We'd hoped to catch him drinking or doing drugs – anything to get him in trouble with his wife. As you know, nothing remotely interesting happened that night, but Vicky got lucky with those photos of you outside. Very lucky. So lucky that she realised she could get much more money for them if she went to a tabloid, and so she stabbed me in the back. Just like she did with you. After that email you sent me, I didn't see why I should help you, but then I saw you on TV and I felt sorry for you. You have done nothing but tell the truth, and have remained classy when story after story came out about you. I am not being selfless, I want to bring Vicky down and discredit her as a journalist. I have included a memory stick, on there is the video of that night, dated. I ask you don't mention that you got it from me, but feel free to use it to clear your name and dirty Vicky's in the process. Thanks, Scott.'

I grab my laptop and plug in the memory stick. You know what they say, a watched laptop never starts up – or maybe that's just my laptop because there's so much rubbish on it.

'Do you want me to leave you to watch this alone?' Luke asks.

'Nothing happened!' I protest, hopefully for the final time. 'Stay. Share in my moment of victory.'

Scott was telling the truth, I recognise that beautiful room. The video is in black and white, and the date on the screen matches up with the night it all kicked off. He must have edited the video for me (or, most likely, to preserve the anonymity of the person who planted it) because almost straight away I see Dylan throw himself onto the bed. Then there's me, stumbling towards the mini-bar, emptying it and dumping the contents on the bed. I wasn't expecting to be embarrassed, but I can feel my cheeks flushing. Sitting down on the bed next to Dylan, I try to work the remote for the TV as he breaks open a packet of biscuits.

'Can we make this go a bit faster?' I ask Luke, and he obliges.

The rest of the video shows me and Dylan eating almost everything from the mini-bar before starting on the little bottles of booze. We eat, we drink, we laugh at the TV, but we don't lay a finger on each other. Eventually Dylan rolls off the bed and onto the floor, and I lie back and pull the covers over myself. Neither of us moves until the morning, when I get up, go to the bathroom, say goodbye and leave.

'Nicole, this is amazing. It proves that nothing happened, and if nothing happened then people will start to question the rest of it. You owe this Scott guy.'

'He was such an arsehole to me.'

'From that letter, it sounds like he still is an arsehole. But an arsehole that needs you to get revenge on Vicky.'

I can't believe Scott has decided to help me – whatever his reasons are. It's true what they say: the enemy of my enemy is my friend.

'Get Frank on the phone, and get him over here,' I tell Luke as I jump out of bed. 'I'm off to get myself dolled up, and then we're off to clear my name.'

'So you're staying?' Luke asks.

'It looks like I am.'

Chapter 68

'I always believed you,' Frank assures me as we sit in the reception at the *Daily Scoop*.

'Sure you did,' I say, fairly sure that he didn't believe me, but I don't think he cared either way. Guilty or innocent, he would have represented me anyway.

I feel like a child waiting to see the dentist – actually, I'm still scared of the dentist, so really I just feel like I'm waiting for a filling. Sure, you're seeing the dentist for your own good, but that doesn't mean it's going to be pleasant.

There's plenty of reading material laid out, but only copies of the *Daily Scoop*, or the supplements you get with it. It's strange seeing my face on a few of the covers; they've sure got their money's worth out of me.

I am so relieved, although I feel even sicker than I did when I thought I was screwed. Just imagine if Scott Hale hadn't decided to help me, I'd be packing my bags for France right now. It would have been nice to see my family for Christmas, but I've got to clear this mess up while I still can.

'Mr Boyes will see you now,' a pretty young blonde with an iPad in her hand informs us.

'Here we go.' I take a deep breath and follow the iPad lady.

This is it.

As I step into Mr Boyes' office, I am immediately overwhelmed by the view from the huge windows. It certainly puts my little office to shame. The second thing that catches my attention is just how gorgeous Mr Boyes himself actually is. He's probably in his late-forties, but very fanciable for someone double my age. I don't entertain the thought for more than ten seconds though, because this is the bastard who has been making my life miserable.

'Miss Wilde,' he shakes my hand. 'And Frank, long time, no see. Take a seat please.'

I sit down. I probably shouldn't feel this uncomfortable in what I'd imagine is a really expensive chair. I can feel my hands getting sweaty as I clutch my envelope of evidence even tighter, just in case he grabs it off me and throws it out of the window or something.

'What can I do for you, Miss Wilde?' Mr Boyes asks with a huge grin on his face.

'Mr Boyes—'

'Johnny. Call me Johnny,' he insists. Whatever.

'Johnny. You've been running quite a few stories about me, some of which I know you have entirely made up.' I can't resist slipping that in. There might have been a few incriminating-looking photos, but an awful lot of what they printed was pure fiction.

'Now, now, Miss Wilde. We're very careful about what we print. If we printed lies it wouldn't be the news, would it? We are a newspaper, after all.' If it's even possible, his smile grows even bigger.

I look at Frank for help, who gives me the nod to go ahead.

'Let's start at the top,' I say calmly, fidgeting with my envelope to try to find the USB stick. 'Nothing happened between me and Dylan.'

'Well I have it on pretty good authority that it did,' he says, still smiling, but in a way that seems far less friendly.

'Erm, I have it on pretty good authority that it didn't, what with me being there and all.'

'I'm a very busy man.' Boyes stands up. 'So if you're only here to waste my time—'

'I have a video that proves nothing happened,' I cut him off. 'Your employee, Vicky Mason, has been trying to sabotage me for weeks, and whatever line she spun you with that first photo she sold to you – it's bullshit.'

For the first time since we entered the room, Johnny Boyes isn't smiling or talking.

'And you're willing to show me this video?' he eventually asks.

'Yes. Can I use your computer?' I waggle my USB stick at him. I made sure that I backed the video up on my laptop before we left, just in case.

'Go ahead.'

'You'll find the correct date and time in the file info,' Frank tells him while I'm loading up the video.

'You can't fake these things you know,' Johnny warns us. As if we'd try to pull a fast one and land ourselves in even bigger shit.

'Well you're welcome to run the relevant tests, whatever you need to do to be confident it's legit,' Frank assures him.

'Here we go.' I hit play on the video. 'Feel free to skip through it,' I tell Johnny, and then take a step back.

Johnny remains silent as he watches. I glance at Frank nervously, and he gives me a confident wink.

'Take a seat, Nicole,' Johnny orders. 'Right, what's the deal?'

'Right.' Frank snaps into action, rubbing his hands. 'No one will see the video. It won't be going on the website, and screen grabs won't be going in the paper. You have seen it, that's all you need to run a story on it.'

'Right. OK.' Johnny sounds almost defeated. 'I'll have the video checked and show it to our reporters—'

'One of your reporters,' Frank corrects him.

'One of our reporters,' Johnny says back to him. 'We'll do that while you're here, you can take the video back with you. I'll have the story written up and I'll email you a draft to approve, Frank.'

'I want to write it myself,' I say, interrupting the grown-ups talking.

'You do?' Frank asks me.

'I do. I've had enough of other people writing about me, I want to do this one myself. I *am* a writer you know.'

Johnny thinks about it for a moment. 'OK, you can write it. I'll set you up on a desk downstairs, you can do it while you're here.'

'Then we have a deal,' Frank claps his hands. 'And we'll reconsider taking legal action – perhaps it won't be necessary now.'

'I'm sure there's no need for that.' Johnny starts grinning again.

'Karen,' he says to his phone and iPad lady enters the room seconds later.

'Can you take Miss Wilde to Jasper and tell him to set her up on a computer. She'll be writing a story for us.'

Chapter 69

The newsroom reminds me of the local paper where I did my work experience – only on a huge scale, and with less people getting excited about vandalised bus shelters. I'll say one thing for local news though, as boring as it is, at least it's honest.

Karen shows me into a side office and introduces me to Jasper, who looks exactly like a journalist is supposed to look. Only one name springs to mind: Clark Kent. Thick dark hair, a strong, manly jaw and even the thick-rimmed, black-framed glasses: check, check, check. He's wearing a suit and tie, slightly loosened, and I find myself unsubtly peeping down his shirt to check for signs of blue spandex.

The pair leave me in the private office and stand just outside the door in the busy newsroom. I can see them talking about me through the big glass window, but I can't hear what they're saying. Karen is obviously explaining the situation and I see Jasper raise his eyebrows in response to something.

'Yes, I'm familiar with Miss Wilde,' he says, loud enough for me to hear as he walks back into the room. Karen gives him a knowing nod and wanders off.

'Right then,' Jasper runs a hand through his Clark Kent hair. 'Let's get you set up so you can tell your story.'

Standing behind my chair, he leans over the desk with one arm on either side of me, trapping me in place.

'So you click here to get started,' he starts explaining the software to me. We just input the content straight into the website at *Starstruck*, but they have some fancy program here, for sending the article to production. I'm trying to pay attention, but with Jasper standing so close to me, I'm feeling kind of distracted. It's impossible not to notice how amazing his aftershave smells. I take a subtle but sharp sniff, wondering what it is that he is wearing.

'Bleu de Chanel,' he tells me.

'Excuse me?' I ask. Can he read my mind? *Is* he Superman?

'My aftershave, it's Bleu de Chanel. You sniffed me,' he laughs.

'I didn't sniff you.' I try to laugh it off. Not quite as subtle as you think, are you, Nicole?

'So, what do you do here?' I ask, changing the subject from me sniffing him.

'Showbiz,' he replies. I turn to face him, an accusing look on my face. 'And no, I didn't write any of the stories about you,' he insists.

I pull a face. I'll be checking that for myself later.

'You don't look the showbiz type,' I tell him.

'Right, this is where you type the body of your article. When you're done, I'll help you format it,' he says, back on topic.

'Mr Boyes says he wants it ready to go today – can you believe *he's* bossing *me* around?'

'Boyes will be Boyes,' he quips.

'Are you sure you didn't have a hand in the articles about me?' I tease after hearing that brilliant pun.

'Maybe just the headlines. So, if I don't look the showbiz type, what do I look like?' he asks, his face inches from mine and his arms still either side of me.

'I don't know, serious stuff. I had you down as a bit of a Clark Kent,' I confess. 'Exposing bad guys, corrupt politicians, that sort of thing.'

'You think I'm Superman.' His smile beams.

'What happens if I take those glasses off?' I ask, tilting my head and twirling a piece of my hair in my fingers for comedic effect. A sniff of Chanel, and I'm anyone's.

'If you take these glasses off,' he pauses for effect, 'I won't be able to see.'

I laugh briefly, and we stare at each other for a few seconds. I am snapped out of the trance this blatant superhero has me in by a tap on the glass. The desk on the other side of the glass I am sitting next to belongs to none other than Vicky Mason, and there she is, sandwich in hand, waving at me with a smug look on her face. She obviously doesn't know why I am here – yet. I don't think Johnny Boyes is going to let her bad behaviour slide. In fact, I think they're going to make her the fall girl.

I escape Jasper's clutches and put my face to the glass, breathing hard to steam it up. Before it can clear again, I use my finger to write 'fuck you' on the glass – backwards, obviously – so that Vicky can read it. She doesn't even have time to react before Mr Boyes and a security guard are at her desk, and again I cannot hear what is being said, but I imagine it's a polite version of what I just wrote on the window. Vicky gives me evil eyes as she collects her personal possessions from her desk, before being ushered towards the exit.

'Aww, what a shame,' I say to Jasper, without an ounce of sincerity in my voice.

'Remind me not to mess with you,' Jasper says, sounding almost impressed. He gets straight back to showing me how to use the computer – possibly because he's too scared to flirt with me now – and before I know it, he's back at his desk and I'm writing my story. It's a weird feeling, writing about myself. I'll start small, and try to think of an appropriate headline.

'Nicole's not so Wilde,' I say to myself quietly. I giggle, safe in the knowledge my headline will be a hit with these guys. With the article itself, it's hard to know where to begin. I don't want to sound smug, but at the same time I want to yell an extra loud 'I told you so' at all the people who didn't believe me.

I start typing, and hope that the right words will find their way to my fingers.

'My name is Nicole Wilde,' I type, 'and this is *my* story.'

Chapter 70

Not even my hangover can get me down this morning. I've only been awake for a few minutes, but there's that familiar headache, trying to bang its way out of my skull.

Last night was crazy – but in the best possible way. I finished up my story at the *Scoop* and had Jasper check it over for me. He was impressed. Not only did Mr Boyes agree to print it the following day (today!) if I could have it ready, but he also said it was going on the front page. By the time I left the office, it was me who was feeling bad because Boyes couldn't apologise enough for what had happened. Frank wants to sue them, but I could see the pound signs in his eyes as he suggested this. As far as I'm concerned, Boyes and his team have made amends for everything they did by simply letting me tell the truth.

The best part of the day was afterwards, when we all went out to celebrate. I invited Jasper to party with us, seeing as though he helped. He went to speak to his boss and came back to tell us he had go us into one of the hottest clubs in London, and that the *Daily Scoop* would be paying for all of our drinks. Do you see what I mean about them making amends? Consider me truly placated. Frank didn't want to celebrate with us 'young 'uns' as he so wonderfully put it in his fantastic accent, but I invited the

Two For The Road boys, as well as my new BFF Kelly Parker. I must have consumed a lot of alcohol because my memory fails me – but that's the sign of a good night, isn't it? At least I am in my own bed and alone.

Glancing at my phone, I realise it is 1 p.m., and that I have lots of messages and missed calls. I didn't even wake up early to buy a copy of the newspaper with my story on the front page. We got in so late last night, I probably could have picked up a copy on my way home if I had been thinking straight, although I doubt I was even walking straight.

It's a battle, but I pull myself upright and eventually climb out of bed, throwing on my dressing gown for now. A quick glance in the mirror confirms my worst fears, I look terrible. My circa '86 Bon Jovi hair has made a comeback, and I clearly didn't waste any time taking my make-up off before bed, because I have black smudges all over my face.

As I walk towards the door, I can't help but laugh at how much things have changed. Just a few short months ago there was no way I'd let Luke see me looking like this, but look at me now, strolling around in my dressing gown in front of him, looking like Alice Cooper and smelling like a brewery.

'Morning,' I sing brightly, surprised to see Luke out of bed before me. 'You're up first – again – I'm in shock.'

From behind the breakfast counter he brings out a huge bunch of roses and hands them to me.

'Oh, Luke, you shouldn't have—'

'They're not from me,' he interrupts me bluntly. 'Frank brought them over, they arrived at his office for you.'

Setting them down on the coffee table, I take the card and read it to myself.

'I'm sorry. Call me if you'll give me the chance to explain.
Charles x'

'They're from Charles,' I tell Luke, to which he rolls his eyes. 'He wants me to call him, so he can explain.'

'And you're going to?' he asks, giving me a seriously unimpressed look.

I think for a second. Am I interested in what he has to say? I reach into my dressing gown pocket for my phone.

'I'll go for a shower, give you some privacy,' Luke says, leaving the room.

Before I have chance to think about what I'm doing, I dial his number.

'Charles Pace,' he answers almost straight away, in his usual business-like manner.

'It's Nicole.'

'Nicole. I didn't think you'd call. How are things?'

I laugh. 'What do you want, Charles?'

'Did you like the roses?'

'They stink of guilt. But thank you,' I add, my manners kicking in.

He ignores my comment. 'Meet me. I want to explain, and I want to apologise.'

I think for a second. 'As it happens, I've got to pop out to pick up a newspaper.'

'Message me where you are, we'll meet for coffee.'

'Fine.' I soften slightly and give in. Hearing his voice only reminds me of how good things were between us before all this happened, and I can't help but miss him a little.

I dash to my bedroom to doll myself up. You know, in case I get papped.

Chapter 71

By the time I was out of the bathroom, Luke had already left. He didn't even tell me he was going out, which was weird. But as long as he isn't seeing his dealer, he can do what he likes.

I decided that Starbucks would be a good place to meet Charles – how can I get angry when I have a festive latte in my hand? Also, I'll be less likely to throw it at him because I won't want to waste it.

I don't have to wait long before he arrives. I don't get up from where I'm sitting, and he gestures that he's going to get a drink before he sits down. If I had any manners, I would have bought him one ready for him arriving, but then again I'm a, and I quote, 'kiss-and-tell tart' – we have terrible manners, you know. Poor Charles, he's going to have such a hard time getting my forgiveness.

He places his cup on the table, and then leans over for a kiss. I don't offer him my cheek, I don't even flinch.

'I've been an idiot,' he says, sitting down opposite me without so much as a handshake.

It's on the tip of my tongue to say 'duh'.

'I've been made a fool of by a woman before,' he tells me. 'I thought I'd never trust another woman again, so I threw myself into my work and I just didn't bother with women for a little while. But then I met you,' he smiles and I feel myself thawing out slightly. 'When Dylan used to talk about you, I used to think there is no way this girl can be as perfect as he makes her sound, but then meeting you that morning, you made one hell of a first impression.'

I cast my mind back to that morning. It was mortifying, but I can see the funny side now and can't help but smile.

'I just knew I wanted to be with you.'

I can almost understand him thinking the worst. If he's been cheated on before, he's bound to think all women are the same.

He glances at my newspaper, which I haven't actually read yet.

'That was all just a big misunderstanding.' He nods towards it. 'And for that I'm very sorry. Can we try again? Start from the beginning?'

I have to admit, I am not entirely against the idea.

'I don't know, how can we go back? Neither of us will forget this.'

'Well it's not like it's going to happen again, is it?' he insists. 'I was a jealous fool.'

'But what if you get jealous again?'

'We'll both have to make changes. I won't get jealous if you make sure there are no photos of you all over other men. I mean, this could have all been avoided if the pictures didn't exist. I know you were set up, of course, but if the pictures didn't exist in the first place – you and Luke, you and Dylan – we could have avoided all this.'

'Right.'

'If you act like a tart, people might think you are one, Nicole. Now you've made a name for yourself, you have to be even more careful. I'm only thinking of you.'

'One moment,' I tell him, going over to the counter. 'Do you do fruit smoothies?' I ask the barista, having never ordered anything that didn't involve coffee from Starbucks before.

'We do,' he tells me. 'What kind would you like?'

'Surprise me, but ideally it would involve purple fruits,

blueberries, raspberries – anything that might stain.'

While I wait for my drink, I go back over to Charles and start putting my coat on.

'Where are you going?' he asks with a confused look on his face. Clearly he doesn't think he said a thing wrong.

I go back over to collect my smoothie and pop the lid off as I walk back.

'Today is a great day, and I'm not going to waste it with someone who thinks that I behave like a tart.'

'That's not what I meant—'

'I know what you meant,' I interrupt him. 'I know exactly what you meant.'

And with that, I tip my (actually pretty delicious-smelling) smoothie all over his head, shirt and trousers.

'Here.' I toss my newspaper at him, happy to pick up another one on the way home. 'You can dry yourself with that.'

Grabbing my handbag, I leave to a round of applause and cheers from the others in the room, who clearly have no idea what he's done wrong, but enjoyed the floorshow nonetheless.

Chapter 72

Charles doesn't follow me, which is fine by me. I know that I didn't do anything wrong before, and he should have believed me. Even after proving my innocence, he still doesn't trust me and I don't think he ever will. I think Charles would have these feelings towards any girl, whether he's provoked or not.

My phone rings. It's Frank asking me to meet him at the office. I tell him that I'll walk because I'm not that far. I don't even have chance to put my phone back in my handbag before it rings again – he probably thinks I need directions.

'I'm not going to get lost, Frank,' I say, answering immediately without looking at my phone to see who is calling.

'It's not Frank,' a very familiar-sounding voice tells me. 'It's—'

'I know who it is,' I interrupt him.

'I'm sorry,' he tells me. 'I'm sorry for not telling the truth, I'm sorry for not backing you up. I panicked, I fucked up, I'm sorry.'

'You're sorry, Dylan. I get it,' I laugh. 'Are you allowed to talk to me now?'

'Yes, I've put my foot down. Now the truth is out there, Crystal has no reason to stop me seeing you.'

That's hardly putting his foot down, but I don't say that to him. I'm just grateful he has permission to be my friend again.

'Look, we've both handled this terribly,' I start, 'but in my defence this is my first time being on the receiving end of this shit. You should be used to it by now though.'

'You would think so,' he laughs. 'Seriously though, I'm sorry for saying that we had an affair when we didn't, that wasn't fair on you.'

'I get why you did it though,' I tell him. 'And I'm sorry for getting photographed outside your house, I don't know what I was thinking. In my rage it didn't really cross my mind that you were just doing what you needed to do to see your kids.'

This might be the most serious conversation Dylan and I have ever had.

'We are still friends, then?' he asks, sounding slightly worried.

I could be mad at him, refuse to speak to him again, but what will that achieve? I've lost enough friends recently and, deep down, I know that Dylan did what he thought was best. I love him and I know he loves me. We'll always figure things out.

'Of course we are. You're the second most famous person I know, I'm hardly going to cut off contact,' I tease.

'Ha!' he laughs. 'Wait, second most famous?'

'Yeah. Kelly Parker is my new bestie. She's way more famous than you.'

'I'd say we were equal, and *I'm* your bestie. Don't forget that, Nic. Anyway, you're quite famous yourself now, aren't you?' he teases.

'Yeah, thanks for that,' I say sarcastically.

'Is it everything you'd hoped for?' he asks, well aware of my love of the lifestyle.

'Not quite, but thanks for the leg up.'

I love that we're instantly back to normal, joking around and winding each other up. Not being friends was horrible and I never want to be in that situation again. Crystal being around is something I'll just have to learn to live it. Who knows, one day we might even be friends.

'So how's married life?' I ask him.

'Married life is, well, married life. I'll get used to it,' he says unconvincingly, 'but the babies are awesome.'

That part I believe. He probably has more in common with the girls that he does with Crystal, and they're only weeks old.

'Are you going home for Christmas?' he asks. 'You could come and meet them if not.'

'Maybe. I'm not sure what I'm doing yet.'

'Well it's only a couple of days away,' he informs me.

I hadn't actually realised what the date was, Christmas really *is* only days away.

'Shit! I hadn't realised Christmas was so close.'

'What will you do now? Generally, I mean,' he asks me.

'Generally, I'll probably go back to Leeds, see if I can get the magazine back online. I'm hoping my Z-list fame can help me pull in some big names, get some support. Hopefully they'll have me back at ByteBanter, although I'll need to find some new staff.'

'Not going to stick around and ride the fame train, then?' he asks.

'I think I've outstayed my welcome here.'

'You've been living with that guy from that band,' he tells me, like I might not be aware of it. 'I was reading one of Crystal's magazines the other day – you were named a couple to keep an eye on in the New Year.'

'Really?' I laugh. 'Luke and I are not a couple, just helping each other through a tough time.'

'I read about the drugs. Didn't sound like you; I can't even get you to hold my cigarette while I take a piss.'

'That's mainly because I don't want to smell like you do, Dill.'

'God, I've missed you,' he admits.

'I've missed you too, but listen, I have a meeting with my agent. I'd better go.'

'Ooh, get you with your agent. Well let me know when you're going home, we'll go for a drink, say goodbye.'

I agree and hang up the phone. Things almost seem back to normal.

Chapter 73

When I arrived at Frank's office, there was a caramel macchiato waiting for me – I could get used to this, although Kelly has been telling me how I need to take it easy on the sweet drinks. I called her quickly while I was on my way up in the lift to see if she wanted to go shopping with me this afternoon. I told her that Dylan and I were back on good terms, and that I wanted to pick up a couple of presents for his babies. 'I've got meetings all day,' she told me, adding that she hates shops that sell baby clothes because she only moans about how she wishes she could fit into them. I hope she was joking. We're in the first flush of our 'womance' and I'm loving it.

I plonk myself in the seat in front of Frank's desk and sip my free coffee – of course in my experience buttering someone up is usually a sign of bad news, so he's probably going to drop me now that the scandal had died down. Now the truth is out, no one is going to want to talk to me about what happened anymore, but that is fine by me – I can't imagine I'll need him when I'm back in Leeds. When I'm done here, I'm going to sort out my train ticket. I have been mentally planning how I'm going to spend Christmas ever since I realised it was so close. I'm going to go back to my flat, invite Jake over, we'll get drunk and I'll sleep through the parts where I'm alone. Joy to the world.

'I'll get straight to the point,' Frank tells me, sitting back in his big chair. Luke told me that Frank is the only person allowed to sit in that chair, and that the one time he joked about sitting in it, Frank gave him a proper bollocking. My butt *will* touch that chair before I leave.

'What are your plans for the future?' he asks.

'Going back to Leeds, restarting the magazine, getting my life back on track,' I tell him confidently.

'Scrap that. Well not the last part, we'll get your life back on track.'

I give him a confused look.

'The *Daily Scoop* loved your article, they want to hire you. They want you to bring the *Starstruck* magazine format with you and print it and sell it with the paper. They want to give you a job, Nicole.'

I can do nothing but blink at him. My ears must be deceiving me.

'They'll pay you a decent wage and I'll help you find somewhere to live.'

'They want to print my magazine?' I ask, still stunned.

'Yes,' he says excitedly, 'and if we go over there now, we can sign the contract.'

'Let's go!' I tell him without a moment's hesitation or a doubt in my mind. And let's go quickly, before they change their minds.

Chapter 74

We arrive at *Scoop* HQ and are instantly shown to Mr Boyes' office. Inside, waiting, are Jasper and Mr Boyes himself, and on the table is a huge bottle of Champagne.

'Wow, you look great,' Jasper tells me. 'After the night we had, I expected something far uglier.'

'Thanks, I think. If it's any consolation, I feel how you look,' I tease back.

'Feisty. We like it,' Mr Boyes says, interrupting our minor flirt-fest. 'Now, Frank explained the deal to you? You're happy with it?'

'I'm more than happy, I'm just surprised,' I confess.

'Don't be surprised, that piece you wrote was fantastic. And the headline!'

I knew he'd like that.

'Brilliant. After reading that, I had a proper look at your magazine online, it's good stuff. We don't want to change a thing about it, not even the name, and you can help pick your own team.'

'Sounds perfect.'

'I will be assigning Jasper to work with you, as this is his area, and he'll help you settle in, show you the ropes and what not.'

That sounds perfect too, but I don't say that. I just nod.

'I've saved you a desk next to mine,' Jasper tells me, with a wink. I think I'm going to like working here.

Chapter 75

I called Luke to tell him the good news as soon as we left *Scoop* HQ. He was out when I called him, but he promised me he would be home before me, and that we could celebrate later. I invited Jasper, and I've called Kelly – I might even give Dylan a ring, but I doubt he'll be allowed to join us.

As we're driving back to Luke's flat, a million thoughts are vying for my attention.

'We'll get Christmas out of the way, and then we'll find you a place to live. You're OK with Luke until then?' Frank asks.

'I'm sure it will be fine.'

'On the wage they'll be paying you, we'll be able to find somewhere nice,' he assures me.

When I was living from job to job, doing an interview here and a magazine article there, I knew that it could all come to an end at any moment. There was no stability, no security. This job at the *Scoop* means that I can pay my own way, I won't need to rely on Luke or my parents any more. I had never really given it much thought before, but there's something very freeing about knowing that I can take care of myself financially.

I need to call my parents and tell them the good news. Jake too. In fact, I'll call him now.

'Hello, stranger,' he answers. 'I was just reading about you.'

'Oh really? All good, I hope.'

'It's all good, but that writer is clearly in love with you. She even has the same name as you.'

I laugh, and tell him the full story. How I proved my innocence, my new celebrity circle of friends and my amazing job offer.

'The only thing is, I'll have to live here,' I say.

'Well I'll miss you, but you have to go for it. I can come and stay, right? Put in a good word with Kelly Parker for me.'

'Naturally.'

'I saw Emily today,' he tells me, the tone of his voice changing to a more serious one.

'Yeah?' I sound like I don't give a damn, although I probably do. We were such close friends for years, I can't just forget that no matter how betrayed I feel.

'She feels terrible about what she did; she didn't mean to ruin your life. I think the day it all came out, she was just acting defensively.'

'I know.' But that doesn't mean it wasn't a stupid thing to do, does it?

'Do you think you can ever forgive her?' he asks.

'Maybe one day.' I sigh. 'Look, let's not talk about this now. Happy times,' I remind him.

'Happy times,' he repeats back to me. 'Go enjoy your moment.'

'I will. Have a drink for me later. And one more thing.'

'Yes?' he asks ever so slowly, like he's bracing himself.

'Thank you – for everything. I wouldn't have got through this without you. My behind-the-scenes man.'

'She's a minor celebrity, and suddenly she thinks she's an actress too.'

We laugh together for a moment.

'I'll pop you an autograph in the post,' I jokingly assure him.

'Please do,' he replies. 'Just make sure it's Kelly's.'

Chapter 76

Frank drops me off outside Luke's, but he doesn't come up.

Tonight we are celebrating, so I have no choice but to spend the next four hours getting ready. I'm going to spend at least one of those hours in the bath because, for the first time in weeks, I feel like I am capable of actually relaxing. The truth is out, I have a fantastic job and I'm working things out with my friends – I don't think things could get much better.

'Honey, I'm home,' I call out as I walk through the door. Luke comes running out of his room to greet me, and listens patiently as I tell him the full details of my day and how I plan to relocate here.

'You've been great letting me stay here, but I won't be cramping your style for much longer,' I promise.

'You never cramped my style.'

'Well, maybe there's a place in this building,' I joke.

'Sit down,' Luke insists, suddenly quite serious.

As instructed, I take a seat on the sofa and Luke sits next to me, taking me by the hand.

'I'm glad you're staying,' he says, squeezing my hand.

'I'm glad I'm staying too.' I smile, unsure what he is going to say next.

'You were the only one who looked after me when I had my …' he pauses, wracking his brain for the appropriate word. 'Accident.'

'You helped me as much as I helped you, Luke.'

'I love you, Nicole,' he blurts out. 'I mean, I'm in love with you.'

'Have you bumped your head again?' I ask. A joke always serves me well in awkward situations.

He laughs. 'I've told you before and I'm telling you again. I want to be with you – properly. Is there any chance you might want to be with me?'

Of course I would, he's the big crush, the one I've lusted after for years. But he's also not the kind of guy who settles down. Then again, neither was Dylan, and look at him now, married with kids – I never thought I'd see the day.

'Don't go silent on me.' He laughs awkwardly. 'Is there any chance you might want to be with me, Nicole?'

'I'd be willing to give it a go,' I tell him slowly. If Dylan can change, then so can Luke. He's really been there for me these past few weeks, and he stood by me when most people didn't even want to know me.

He leans toward me and kisses me gently. My heart flutters. It's not the mad, passion-fuelled kisses we've shared before, but it's just as wonderful.

'Let me give you your Christmas present,' he says excitedly, jumping over the sofa and heading towards his bedroom.

'Oh! Is it something saucy?' I call after him.

'Wait and see,' he calls back. 'Now shut your eyes, and hold out your hands. Both hands.'

'Is it a big one?' I ask.

'Yes. But you'll need both hands for the present,' he warns me cheekily.

I laugh and do as I am told.

'OK, take this very carefully,' he tells me, gently placing something in my hands. It feels so soft and warm and it's wriggling. If I wasn't so curious about what it might be, I'd probably make a filthy joke.

'Open your eyes,' he says softly.

'Oh, Luke!' My heart melts as I look down and see two big brown eyes gazing up at me.

'This little chap is all that is missing from your weird celebrity checklist,' he teases.

'I can't believe you remembered that!'

I bring the tiny blonde Chihuahua puppy to my chest and cuddle him gently. We always had dogs growing up, and I miss our golden retriever, Harley, just as much as I miss my parents and my brother. I know I make jokes about wanting a 'handbag dog', but I will raise this puppy as though I had given birth to him myself.

'What are you going to call him?' he asks.

'Buddy.' The name instantly springs to mind. 'As in Buddy Holly. His dark little eyes remind me of Buddy's glasses.'

'It's perfect for him,' Luke laughs. He's probably just relieved I don't want to call him Tinkerbell or Bambi or some other Disney name he wouldn't want to call out in the park.

'I'm in love with him already,' I gush. 'Well, now I'm going to have to find a Chihuahua-friendly place to live, aren't I?' I say to the dog in the weird voice I use exclusively for talking to cute animals.

'You can live with me. Both of you can.' He tickles Buddy's ears.

'Seriously?' I ask.

'Of course. Nicole, I want to be with you. And, to be honest, I've got used to having you around, you can't leave me now.'

I bite my lip and think hard. 'Are you sure?'

'I wouldn't ask if I wasn't sure.'

'In that case, we'd better get tidied up. We'll have to celebrate here tonight, I'm not leaving little Buddy here all on his own.' I hold my baby up to my face and kiss his nose.

'Barking orders like a proper little wife,' he jokes. 'I'll get on the phone to the guys.'

Sitting on the sofa, I cradle Buddy in my arms and tickle his tummy. I can't believe how tiny he is. Before, I might have been worried that I couldn't take care of a dog, because I couldn't even take care of myself, but this just feels right. I feel like a different person, the kind who lives with a member of the opposite sex and takes care of people (and dogs).

In no time at all, Buddy is fast asleep, snoring so quietly I can only just about hear it.

'I think we're going to be all right here,' I whisper to him.

'Oh, Nicole,' I hear Luke call out from the bedroom. 'Our guests will be here at eight, time for me to show you that big one you were asking about.'

'Shh!' I call back. 'You'll wake up the baby.'

Luke walks back into the room with a faux frown plastered across his face.

'Oh crap,' he laughs, plonking himself down on the sofa next to us and placing his arm around me. 'I know that having a baby means you have sex less, I didn't realise the rule extended to puppies too.'

'Well it does,' I laugh. 'You sure you still want us?'

'More than I've ever wanted anything,' he replies sincerely. 'Go on then, I could do with a nap.'

I rest my head on Luke's chest, and in a matter of minutes both my boys are fast asleep. Before moving to London, the thought of one demanding bloke to take care of would have been enough to make me throw myself under a tour bus, but I feel good about looking after these two. I just wonder which one is going to be the hardest work.

Truth or Date

It's all fun and games, until someone falls in love …
Ruby Wood is perfectly happy playing the dating game – until she has a red-hot dream about her *very* attractive flatmate, Nick. He might spend every day saving lives as a junior doctor, but he's absolutely the last man on earth that fun-loving Ruby would ever date!

The solution? Focus on all of Nick's bad points. And if that fails, up her dating antics and find herself a man. So what if she manages to make disapproving, goody two-shoes Nick jealous in the process …

Only, after a series of nightmare first dates, there's still just one man on Ruby's mind. Maybe it's time to admit the truth and dare to ask Nick to be her next date?

Don't miss this utterly uplifting and laugh-out-loud romcom from bestseller Portia MacIntosh, perfect for fans of Beth O'Leary and Mhairi McFarlane!

Here Comes the Ex

Luca is used to being 'the single one' – which is partly why she is dreading going to the wedding of an old university friend. Surrounded by faces she hasn't seen in 10 years, Luca can feel herself being sucked back into the immature, decade-old gossip that no one seems to have forgotten.

But when Tom walks in, Luca's heart stops. He was her crush, her 'almost boyfriend' – but then he broke her heart at a party ten years ago. And now here he is, hotter than ever, and standing next to the girl he broke Luca's heart with.

As the day unfolds and the champagne continues to flow, it's clear that Tom can't take his eyes off her. Are some people best left in the past, or is Luca's luck in love finally about to change?

Don't miss this laugh-out-loud, second chance rom-com from bestselling author Portia MacIntosh

Drive Me Crazy

It was supposed to be the trip of a lifetime ...
In reality it was a business trip, prettied up as a romantic mini break, but the man behind the wheel was meant to be Candice Hart's boss and (married but separated, I swear!) lover. Not Danny the new guy!

Not only is Candice faced with a new driver, but the office's far too handsome hipster expects her to share the cramped space inside his "fully" restored VW Beetle, aka The Love Bug, and put up with his constant opinions about her life ...

Before long she is tired of playing the 'good girl' and, with Danny's help, is determined to finally show the world the real Candice Hart!

Don't miss this laugh-out-loud romantic comedy.

Acknowledgements

Massive thanks to the lovely HQ Digital UK team – especially Lucy, Victoria and Jo.

Thank you to all my music industry friends – if you guys didn't do half the hilarious/terrible/unbelievable things that you do, I wouldn't have anywhere near as much material to work with.

A big thank you to my Gosling Girls – Megan, Kirsty, Victoria and Laura – and to all the wonderful people who read and reviewed *One Way or Another*.

And finally, the biggest thank you of all to my family and my band boy. You put up with an awful lot and without you none of this would have been possible.

Dear Reader,

We hope you enjoyed reading this book. If you did, we'd be so appreciative if you left a review. It really helps us and the author to bring more books like this to you.

Here at HQ Digital we are dedicated to publishing fiction that will keep you turning the pages into the early hours. Don't want to miss a thing? To find out more about our books, promotions, discover exclusive content and enter competitions you can keep in touch in the following ways:

JOIN OUR COMMUNITY:

Sign up to our new email newsletter: http://smarturl.it/SignUpHQ

Read our new blog www.hqstories.co.uk

𝕏 https://twitter.com/HQStories

f www.facebook.com/HQStories

BUDDING WRITER?

We're also looking for authors to join the HQ Digital family!
Find out more here:

https://www.hqstories.co.uk/want-to-write-for-us/

Thanks for reading, from the HQ Digital team

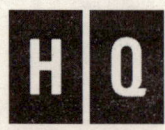